COPYRIGHT

The Dogs of War is a work of fiction. Any references to names, characters, brands, media, incidents, historical events, real people, or real places are the product of the author's imagination or are used fictitiously. Any resemblance to actual events or places or persons, living or dead, business establishments, events, or locales is entirely coincidental. The publication or use of trademarked products referenced in this work of fiction is not authorized, associated with, or sponsored by the trademark owners.

ISBN: 978-0-9986117-0-9 PRINT VERSION
ISBN: 978-0-9986117-9-0 DIGITAL VERSION
Published by the Falbey Group, LLC
Cover Design: Tatiana Villa at Villa Design

DEDICATION

To "Annie", who continues to show me every day what unconditional love and patience truly are. Sweetheart, you are the prettiest, calmest, most well-adjusted person I've ever known. You really don't know how special you are. And that makes you even more special.

TABLE OF CONTENTS

PART TWO
THE HUNTER-KILLERS

PAART THREE
DAYS OF RECKONING

FOR THOSE WHO CAME LATE

For Those Who Came Late...

The Dogs of War is the fourth novel in the Sleeping Dogs series of political/espionage thrillers.

The following is a brief summary of the action in the first three books in the series: *Sleeping Dogs—The Awakening; Endangered Species;* and *The Year of the Dog.*

Sleeping Dogs—The Awakening

In this first book in the Sleeping Dogs series, the president of the United States has been targeted for assassination—by his *own* handlers. The killing must look like the president's political opposition is responsible. Desperate to prevent the crime and the overwhelming outpouring of sympathy that will only further empower the real killers, the opposition turns to the only force that can stop it this late in the game—a mysterious hunter-killer team known only as the Sleeping Dogs. This darkest of black ops units was formed to carry out America's wettest, most politically incorrect missions abroad. Eventually, a U.S. president, fearing discovery of the unit's existence would spark an international crisis, ordered its members terminated with extreme prejudice. They escaped by faking their deaths in a plane crash, and went underground. Now, 20 years later, they are asked to leave the safety of their anonymity and risk their lives for their country one more time.

A seemingly unconnected car crash rapidly escalates into a series of plot twists and a rising body count involving Russian agents, crooked politicians, Ukrainian gangsters, a billionaire international arbitrageur, a secret society of patriots in the military and intelligence communities, the CIA, a doggedly determined FBI agent, and the six deadliest men on earth—the surviving Sleeping Dogs. The body count begins to soar from the first chapter, as Brendan Whelan and the other Dogs relentlessly pursue the would-be assassins and their handlers. As they do, they begin to uncover, layer by layer, a plot to bring America to her knees and impose a one-world government on the planet. The enemy is powerful, with access to unlimited funds and the ability to manipulate the rogue nations of the world. The problem? They've awakened the Sleeping Dogs.

Endangered Species

The world is descending into chaos. America is like a rudderless ship—its elected government gridlocked and ineffective. Rogue governments spit on Old Glory and defy a weakened America to stop them. Religious fanatics are dedicated to butchering all the world's citizens who don't convert to their beliefs. And the worst is yet to come. From Russian aggression to worldwide jihadism, from China's designs on Southeast Asia to a morally and financially bankrupt European Union, from violent and expanding drug cartels to Iranian nuclear designs, the members of the Alliance for Global Unity are close to achieving their goal—a single world government with them ruling it.

But appearances can be deceiving. In America, a shadow government of old fashioned patriots is working to change the course of events. Armed with deep financial resources and critical positions in the military and intelligence communities, it just might succeed. The key to success is the world's deadliest hunter-killer special ops unit—the Sleeping Dogs. But keeping the six Sleeping Dogs alive is challenging. An outstanding Presidential Decision Directive ordered the men to be terminated with extreme prejudice. An angry FBI agent, believing his wife had an affair with the unit's leader Brendan Whelan, is pursuing him with homicide on his mind. A rogue Russian agent seeks revenge for thwarting his mission to assassinate the president of the United States. And, most chillingly, a huge and mysterious brute named Maksym is systematically hunting the Dogs down individually. The fate of the free world hangs in the balance. There will be blood. Lots of blood.

The Year of the Dog

Thousands of Islamic terrorists have set up cells in America, stockpiling weapons, assembling explosives, and identifying soft targets, as well as police and first responder stations, military installations, and the nation's electrical and communications grids. The Chinese are solidifying their dominion throughout Asia, and setting their sights on the rest of the planet. The Russian president is intensifying his threat against the free peoples of Europe and beyond. Cyberwarfare is ramping up from Beijing and Moscow to Pyongyang, Tehran, Havana and elsewhere.

It's the eve of a presidential election, but the outgoing administration spent the past eight years, like a modern Nero, fiddling away the country's treasure, seemingly too oblivious or incompetent to recognize the threat. Time is running out, and a shadow government has learned of a pending threat to the U.S. homeland that will render the nation defenseless. It asks Brendan Whelan to reunite the members of the world's deadliest hunter-killer black ops team—the Sleeping Dogs—and try to stop it.

The question is, can Whelan get the Sleeping Dogs back together in time?

CAST OF CHARACTERS

THE DOGS OF WAR: A SLEEPING DOGS THRILLER

This novel is one of a series. Several characters recur throughout the series. Others from earlier books in the series may be referred to in subsequent books.

Brendan Whelan (WHEY-luhn) – by appearances, an innkeeper in Dingle, Ireland, but also the reluctant leader of the deadly hunter-killer black ops unit known as the Sleeping Dogs

The Sleeping Dogs – together with Brendan Whelan, the most lethal black ops unit in history; genetically evolved—Mother Nature's beta models for humans in future generations:

Sven Larsen – the "Man With No Neck," he is the most physically powerful of the Dogs and closest to Whelan

Marc Kirkland – the "Zen Warrior," he is completely dedicated to mastering every style of martial arts fighting and weapons techniques

Nick Stensen – the "Serial Killer," a loner and certifiably insane; his singular is hunting down and killing criminals who have escaped the punishment of the law

Quentin Thomas – the "Philosopher King," is the best pure athlete of the Dogs and a professor of Eastern philosophies

Rafe Almeida (RAIF al-MAY-duh)– the "Runt Of The Litter," is genetically gifted like the other Dogs, but an inveterate substance abuser and skirt-chaser

Liam (LEE-um) *Stone* – "Lime Stone," is an Aussie who also is genetically gifted like the other Dogs, but is a recent member recruited to the unit

Caitlin (KATE-lin) *Whelan* – Brendan's wife, partner, and mother of Sean and Declan, two young lads who appear to be chips off the old block

Cliff Levell (Luh-VELL) – former Recon Marine officer and CIA operative, now leader of the Society of Adam Smith. The SAS is a shadow government attempting to counter the elected government's destruction of American values and freedoms. Although confined to a wheelchair because of injuries incurred in an automobile accident, he is tougher than most able-bodied individuals

Mitch Christie – an agent of the FBI who originally pursued Whelan and the other Dogs. He experienced an epiphany and joined the SAS

Maksym (Mack-SEEM) *Kozak* – a ruthless killer and, like his brother Brendan Whelan and the other Sleeping Dogs, genetically advanced. He works for the highest bidder

Harland Fairchilde IV – fourth generation scion of an über wealthy family. Leader of the Alliance for Global Unity (AGU), a global organization of financiers and government finance officials seeking to impose a one-world governing structure on mankind for their own financial benefit

Kirill (Keer-REAL) *Federov* – a former Spetsnaz (Russian special ops) colonel serving in the SVR, Russia's external intelligence agency (*believed to be deceased*)

Andrei Ulyanin (An-DRAY Uhl-YAN-in) – former Spetsnaz colleague of Federov's, now pursuing his killers

Tom Murphy – Caitlin Whelan's father and a former member of the UK's SBS; currently *An Garda Síochána* (the Irish National Police force) District Superintendent for County Kerry, Ireland

Padraig (Paddy) Murphy – Caitlin's brother and the Sergeant in Charge of the *An Garda Síochána* station in Dingle, Ireland

Maureen Delaney - chief executive of one of the largest and most successful technology companies on the planet, and Levell's love interest

Luiz Fernando (Nando) Correia (Kor-RAY-ah) – Levell's personal assistant, driver, and bodyguard; a master, or specialist, in *Capoeira Regional* and Brazilian Jiu-Jitsu

The Mueller (MULE-er) *Brothers* (Alfred, Hermann, and Tomas) – billionaire industrialists and patriots who fund SAS operations and provided leading edge technological support

Camila Ramirez (Ra-MEER-ez)– a sheriff's deputy in Albuquerque, New Mexico and Mitch Christie's lady friend

Nadir (Nah-DEER) *Shah* – leader of the Holy Army of the Caliphate, a radical group establishing an Islamic state in the Middle East

Zheng Bao Xun (Zhing Bah-oh Zhun) - the minister of finance for the People's Republic of China

Turan (Ter-RAHN) *Salam* (SuH-LAHM)— a Pakistani Waziri teenager recruited to jihad by Bazir Haqqani, trained in the mountains of North Waziristan for an attack on the U.S. homeland

Carolina (Cah-row-LEEN-ah) *Avila* (Ah-VEE-la)—a teenage neighbor of Turan Salam's in Santa Fe. He's been smitten by her beauty, but she begins to suspect he may be something other than he seems

Bazir (Bah-ZEER) Haqqani (Hah-KAHN-ee)— a Waziri and

former Taliban fighter who has pledged his allegiance to Nadir Shah and the Islamic Caliphate. He recruited Turan Salam

Fermin "Frank" Cuellar (KWAY-lar)—a major in the New Mexico State Police and commander of its Special Operations Bureau

David Hidalgo (Hee-DAHL-go) — U.S. Customs and Border Protection agent stationed at the Antelope Wells Border Patrol port of entry and forward operating base (FOB)

HAC—the Holy Army of the Caliphate, the largest and most successful terrorist organization yet. It has declared a caliphate across a large swath of the Middle East and Africa with inroads into Europe, Asia, and the New World.

Prince Bandar bin Nayif al Saud - head of Saudi general intelligence and a close friend of Levell's

Characters from Previous Books Referred to in This Book

General Roscoe "Buster" McCoy – Marine Corps 2-Star General and head of Marine Corps Forces Special Operations Command, or MARSOC

Harold Case – retired CIA employee (*now deceased*) who uncovered the supposedly destroyed Agency file on the Sleeping Dogs while in the employ of Sen. Howard Morris

Chaim Laski – international arbitrageur and financial manager for an organization (AGU) seeking to destroy the USA from within (*now deceased*)

Senator Howard Morris – a formerly powerful senator from New York and darling of far-left causes. He had presidential aspirations (*now institutionalized with severe mental trauma caused by witnessing the execution of Laski by the Dogs*)

THE DOGS OF WAR

A SLEEPING DOGS THRILLER

By:
John Wayne Falbey

Cry 'Havoc!' and let slip the dogs of war.

—William Shakespeare, Act 3, Scene 1, *Julius Caesar*

PART ONE

A GATHERING OF WOLVES

For the strength of the Pack is the Wolf, and the strength of the Wolf is the Pack.

—Rudyard Kipling

CHAPTER 1

THE LODGE, TIDEWATER VIRGINIA

BECAUSE OF HIS DNA, Brendan Whelan was one of the most dangerous men on Earth, and one of the most wanted. For almost twenty years, he and his surviving colleagues had been living under the burden of a Presidential Decision Directive calling for their execution on sight. Yet here he was, in the place where it all began, the U.S.A.

Cliff Levell actually had begged him, not merely asked him, to remain involved in his organization's efforts to defend America. Though he owed much to his old mentor, Whelan could make a compelling argument that all debts had long ago been paid. But there was another consideration. If and when America fell, Ireland, and the rest of the free world would come plunging down right behind it. And Ireland was home. It's where his wife, Caitlin, and sons were, along with friends and relatives he truly cared about. Whelan struggled with the dilemma, but eventually agreed to stay. But only until he could determine if the efforts of Levell and his organization, the Society of Adam Smith or SAS, were making a meaningful difference. The problem was...now he had to break the news to Caitlin.

Although she tried to conceal it during their phone conversation, he could tell by her voice that she didn't agree with his decision. "Have you forgotten about Maksym? And his threats to murder our whole family? He's a monster, even if he is your brother."

Whelan closed his eyes and took a deep breath. "Cait, you know I haven't forgotten. I've taken precautions to protect you and the boys."

"And what are they? If it's Paddy and the townsfolk, I can't say I'm comforted, even though Paddy is my brother."

"It's much more than that. Sven Larsen is on his way back to Dingle in hopes Maksym does show up."

There was a moment of silence before Caitlin said, "Sven does have your genetic gifts, but he isn't you."

"Sven may be the most dangerous sonofabitch on the planet. Your level of protection couldn't be higher."

"I disagree. And at the risk of casting aspersions on your late mum, anyone who knows you believes that *you're* the most dangerous SOB on the planet. I...*we* all feel safest when you're here, Bren."

Whelan felt a heart pang. Caitlin was more than his wife. She was his best friend, business partner, playmate, and co-conspirator in adventure. Their love story had a fairytale quality to it. Except for Maksym. Whelan never wanted to disappoint Caitlin or cause her concern in any way. Yet as Levell often reminded him, individual liberties as well as Western culture were on the brink of extinction. He hadn't asked for it, but the capriciousness of genetics had gifted him and a handful of others with extraordinary skills, abilities that set them above and apart from the rest of humanity in terms of strength, speed, ferocity, and perception. Together they formed the deadliest, most frighteningly capable hunter-killer group on the planet. So far, there had been only one bad one in the bunch. Whelan's brother, Maksym.

Whelan said, "Cait, I promise you I'll be home just as soon as I'm convinced that Cliff, the SAS, and the other Dogs can hold things together without me. We're having that discussion this afternoon. If I think they can get by without me, I'll be on a plane to Ireland tonight."

"But why does it always have to be you? There are five others like you, including Sven. Why can't they handle this without you?"

"Because, according to Cliff, three of them currently are in various prisons around the world, another has taken to drowning his sorrows in a whiskey bottle, and Sven is obsessed with revenge for the murders of his wife and sons."

"So, you're in this...whatever it is...alone?"

He could hear the alarm in her voice, and more than a trace of anger. "For the moment. But Cliff and I are working on a plan to change that."

LATER, Levell asked Whelan to join him in his office. It was a sunny, well-appointed room just off the huge atrium that served as the Lodge's reception and social area. When Whelan arrived, Levell was sitting on a leather-covered triple sofa, staring pensively at the thickly wooded area beyond the oversized window. Whelan wasn't used to seeing his old boss seated in anything other than the ubiquitous wheelchair. Although Levell's bodyguard/driver/personal assistant Nando wasn't in the room, Whelan knew he would be close by.

"You look like you're lost in thought, Cliff," Whelan said as he entered the office.

Levell turned slowly, almost absentmindedly, and motioned to an overstuffed chair that matched the sofa. Whelan sat in it.

Levell continued to stare out the window. He sighed and then said, "I think there's an old saying…something to the effect that the clearer a situation seems to be, the more confusing it becomes."

After several moments of silence, Whelan prompted him. "I'm listening."

Still gazing out the window, Levell said. "I've asked someone to join us, someone you'll remember well, but perhaps not with pleasure. The fact is he's become a very important asset for us." Levell picked up the smartphone from the seat beside him and tapped a single button.

A moment later the door opened, and Nando ushered in a man whose face Whelan would never forget. Mitch Christie.

Christie glanced at Whelan. Both men nodded at each other.

Once Christie had taken a seat on the sofa next to Levell, the old man spoke. "You two have a history together. I hope there are no lingering resentments."

"Resentments?" Whelan said. "A couple of years ago, this guy had a global APB out on me. Later, he came to Ireland and nearly succeeded in killing me. What's to resent?"

Christie shifted nervously. "I was just doing my job at the Bureau. You were the prime suspect in the Harold Case murders, and I was the agent in charge. It was my job to bring you in."

Levell interrupted. "He has a point, Brendan. After all, you *did* kill Case and his hired muscle."

The expression on Whelan's face was cold and humorless. "And the attempt to kill me in Ireland?"

Christie examined his well-polished shoes. "That, ah, happened because I wasn't thinking clearly at the time." He paused for a moment or two. "When you kidnapped my wife and kids, she developed, ah, a kind of an infatuation for you. When she left me, I thought it was because of you."

Whelan grinned. "Relax, Mitch, I'm just messing with you. After your failed attempt to kill me, you met Caitlin. How could anyone who's met her think I would become interested in another woman?" He paused and then said, "But no, I'm not harboring any resentments."

Christie's head bobbed up and down eagerly. "Nor am I. In a way, I owe you. I was devastated when Debbie left, but I've since met someone new, someone wonderful. I think I understand your relationship with Caitlin. I hope mine can be as good."

Levell now was fully in the moment. "If you two have finished your lovefest," he said dryly, "there is a slightly more important subject to discuss—namely saving what's left of the world's sorry ass." He motioned to Christie with his left hand. "Mitch, bring the Irishman up to speed on the crisis du jour."

Now what? Whelan crossed his left ankle onto his right knee and slowly settled back into the overstuffed chair, gazing at Christie.

The FBI agent cleared his throat and shot a quick glance at Levell. "You may not be aware of it, but the Bureau recently transferred me from International Operations to the National Security Branch, specifically CTD, the Counterterrorism Division."

"Was that move your idea?" Whelan said.

"Ah...not at the time." Christie shot another quick glance at Levell.

"I arranged it," Levell said. "It was necessitated by evidence brought to the attention of the SAS by one of our members, a senior fellow in a think tank that caters to a single client—DHS. She shared information about alarming discoveries made during a joint exercise in the Southwest involving the Mexican army and U.S. law enforcement, in particular, CBP—the Customs and Border Patrol." He looked at Christie and nodded for him to pick up the narrative.

"Among other things, the CBP found a book, *In Memory of Our Martyrs*. It's an homage to Islamic suicide bombers. They also found prayer rugs, Qur'ans, terrorist flags and logos of the Holy Army of the Caliphate, Iranian military uniforms, and documents written in Arabic and Pashto."

"These materials were found on *both* sides of the border," Levell said.

"So, the logical conclusion is that there are an unknown number of terrorists already in this country," Whelan said. "Got a ballpark on how many we're talking about?"

Christie shrugged. "This and other evidence indicates they number in the thousands, with more coming all the time."

"Shit," Whelan said. "You're talking about dozens, more likely hundreds, of cells established in big cities and small towns alike. Their members will be busy mapping out soft targets all over the country, stockpiling weapons and ammo, building explosive devices, and making plans for the moment the word to strike is given."

"There's proof of that too," Levell said. "Mexican and U.S. officials recently found detailed plans of Fort Bliss, the home of the Army's 1st Armored Division."

Whelan shook his head in disbelief. "How can this happen? Is your southern border that porous?"

"'Sieve' would be a euphemism," Levell said.

"I haven't heard about any of this; yet it's the kind of thing the media should have jumped on," Whelan said.

"The media reports what the administration tells it to report. I understand that a TV station in Phoenix had a short piece on it. But the FCC quickly threatened their license, and that shut them up."

"Now I understand why the SAS wanted Mitch to transfer to the CDT. You needed a reliable resource in the center of the action."

Levell looked at Christie. "Tell Whelan just how sophisticated the Holy Army of the Caliphate operation is."

"HAC is infiltrating the U.S. with the aid of transnational drug cartels, specifically the Salvadoran criminal gang MS-13. The gang already has a presence in more than a thousand of our cities and towns. Our sources tell us that HAC pays MS-13 upwards of fifty thousand dollars for each sleeper agent smuggled into the U.S. from Mexico. They provide them with false identification, usually bogus matricula consular ID cards. They're virtually indistinguishable from Mexico's official ID and are accepted in the U.S. to open bank accounts and obtain driver's licenses."

"And it's not just HAC," Levell said. "Al-Qaeda's ally Al-Shabaab has a presence in south of the border too. They're all Sunni radicals, but Hezbollah, a Shiite group, also has had an established presence in Mexico for the past fifteen to twenty years."

"So, you've got both the Sunni crazies with HAC and other terrorist organizations, plus Iran's Shia wackos to deal with," Whelan said.

"Of all of them, we consider Hezbollah to be the A-team of Muslim terrorist organizations," Christie said. "Their operators are far more skilled, at this point, than those of most other radical groups. They're the equals of the Russian or Chinese operators."

"What makes them more dangerous than HAC or the multitude of other Islamic terrorist groups?" Whelan said.

"They're more strategy oriented, more patient. They think more long-term. For example, they're working with the drug cartels to build smuggling tunnels under the U.S.-Mexico border. Satellite images show they're very similar to the maze of tunnels running under the border between the State of Palestine's Gaza Strip and Israel."

"So much for campaign promises to build a big wall all along the Mexican border," Whelan said.

"Bah," Levell said irritably. "That wall is a fucking pipe dream."

"Even if it got built," Christie said, "It would be too little, too late, I'm afraid. The damage has been done. The presence of Hezbollah's expert tunnel builders on the Mexican side of the border eliminates any benefits a wall might have provided."

There was a dark wood credenza on the other side of the room. Whelan rose smoothly and gracefully from the embrace of the over-stuffed chair and walked over to it. A carafe of coffee sat amid an assortment of clean mugs. He picked one up, filled it half full, and returned to his seat.

Sitting down, he said, "Based on what you've told me, the jihadis are planning a major coordinated offensive throughout the United States. They'll knock out power, communications, and first-responder and military facilities. The resulting casualties will be in the hundreds of thousands, probably millions when you count those who will perish in the aftermath without the comforts and lifestyle of the twenty-first century. Yet the administration and Congress do nothing about it."

Whelan paused and took a sip of coffee. It was strong and hot. He had a feeling he would need the caffeine as the day wore on. "So, what are *you* planning to do about it?"

Christie sat back on the couch and looked at Levell, clearly deferring to him.

It was a long time before Levell spoke. It felt interminably long to Whelan. Among his genetic gifts was the ability to process thoughts and act in nanoseconds. But patience was foreign to him. Yet there was nothing he could do. The Old Man would speak only when he had gathered and vetted his thoughts.

At last, Levell said, "Unfortunately, at this point there's no silver bullet. As Christie said, the damage has been done." He looked at Whelan. "Your previous strategy proposal—assassinate the relatively small handful of international bad guys—would be optimal, if we had time. But there is no time. The threat to the homeland is immediate and dire. The best we can hope for at this point is to slow them down, confuse them, buy more time until we can figure out how to better contain the damage."

"Do you have a plan for that?" Whelan said.

"That depends largely on your willingness and ability to reunite your unit."

"Have you forgotten how things ended in Geneva? There is no Sleeping Dogs unit anymore."

"Just round them up. I'll take responsibility for getting them to play team ball."

"I assume you know where each of them is," Whelan said.

"Of course."

"Then why don't you round them up yourself? I'm the only one with a family. Unless there's some compelling reason why someone else can't round them up, I'm going back to Dingle."

"Don't you think I know your situation!" Levell said snappishly. "If there was any other way to do it, I would. But there isn't." He paused for a moment, trying to contain his frustration and anger. "I've told you that three of your colleagues are in various brigs around the globe, and a fourth, Thomas, seems to have been imprisoned by demons of his own making."

Whelan said nothing.

"It's going to take all six of you, maybe more, if we're going to slow down the terrorists."

"What does 'maybe more' mean? I thought the six of us were the only ones of our kind left, other than Maksym."

"There's a guy in Australia, name of Liam Stone, who supposedly has the same genetic gifts as you and the others. I want you to vet him, and if he works out, recruit him."

"In addition to springing three, or is it four, of the toughest bastards on the planet?"

"Yes."

Now, Whelan thought for a few moments before speaking. "Given our unique physical and intellectual assets along with our training and experience, why can't they free themselves?"

"One is in a maximum security federal prison. Another is being held as an enemy of the state under the tightest security in an ultra-modern facility in the Middle East. The third...well, it's Almeida. He's only in a local lockup in Tennessee. While he's like the rest of you genetically, he's not really as...let's say, competent."

"I know Rafe; I get it. What about Thomas? You said something about personal demons."

"According to my intel, Quentin developed a problem with alcohol. He seems to have it under control for the time being."

Whelan digested the information Levell had given him. "You're asking the impossible. Do I get any assistance?"

Levell shook his head. "Intel, weaponry, logistical assistance, yes. But, human-wise, there is no one else."

Whelan glanced at Christie. "What about Mitch?"

"No, I need him right where he is. He's a major source of intel on what's happening behind the administration's 'Great Wall' of bullshit and obfuscation." He paused momentarily. "Ordinarily, I'd suggest Sven Larsen, but I'm sure you want him in Ireland watching over your family."

Whelan nodded.

"Depending on how things go with the Aussie, he might prove useful."

Whelan took a deep breath and let it out slowly. "All right, get me all the available intel and logistics on where these men are. The sooner we start, the more effective we'll be." As an afterthought, he said, "Are there any other surprises, or is that it?"

Levell stared at his hands before he said, "Yes, there is one more matter, but I'm not sure of its relevance. Our old nemesis Kirill Federov is alive."

"What! I saw him sprawled in the hallway at your Georgetown home. Bleeding out from a big-ass gunshot wound in his chest. You told me he'd died."

Levell stared at his hands again. "Yes, well, I wasn't completely truthful. Thanks to some very good medical talent, he survived the gunshot wound. We detained him as an asset, a source of information about many subjects…including Nadir Shah and the Holy Army of the Caliphate, as well as Federov's former Russian masters, and not least, his most recent employer, the Alliance for Global Unity."

"So, you've got him squirreled away somewhere, hopefully waterboarding him or worse." Whelan remembered the visit Federov had paid to him and his colleagues when they were imprisoned in Dubai. Not only had the big Russian helped to betray them but he had taunted them viciously.

"Ah,…that's where the problem arises."

Whelan knew from Levell's hesitation that the news wasn't going to be good.

"Federov is a clever and capable bastard, I'll give him that. Somehow, he managed to escape," Levell said.

Whelan said, "And you have no idea where he is?"

"Not at the moment."

CHAPTER 2

BRIGHTON BEACH

EVEN HUNCHED OVER, it was clear that the man was taller than average. He moved slowly down the steps from the elevated platform of the BMT Brighton Line station on Brighton Beach Avenue. He didn't look like an old man, but he moved like one, as if he had an injury or illness. People, speaking mostly in Russian, pushed on by him. Occasionally, Ukrainian could be heard. The man was dressed poorly, like a homeless person. Although the day wasn't particularly chilly, he clutched his tattered trench coat tightly at the waist as if he feared someone might rip it off. He hadn't shaved in some time, and long, dirty blonde hair hung limply from beneath a watch cap pulled low on his forehead.

From the bottom of the steps, he trudged the short distance to the corner of Brighton Beach Avenue and Sixth Street. He turned right on Sixth and walked down to the third door on the right. It was in an ancient two-story red brick building with shops at ground level and mostly flats above. The door was made of heavy wood that had been painted red countless times, evidenced by areas where some of the more recent coats had peeled off or been chipped away.

Above the door, a small sign in Cyrillic script identified the place as Таверна Магазин. The man knew it meant Little Bear Tavern, and his humorless laugh sounded like an angry snort. He thought momentarily of the Russian president, a man he once had served. Although short in stature, the president was famous for his efforts to establish his machismo at every opportunity. The man in the trench coat had dubbed him "The Little Bear" in derision.

Inside, the tavern was long and narrow with a scarred wooden bar on the right and a row of battered and mismatched tables and chairs on the left. A narrow space ran between them to the restrooms at the far end of the room. Russian was the language spoken, and vodka was the universal choice of beverage. The barroom reeked of cigarette smoke, stale sweat, and the acrid aroma of Eastern European dishes. The tabletops were sticky from a long-standing accumulation of spilled foods and beverages. The floor was worse. The soles of shoes stuck to it, more so in some spots than others.

Despite city ordinances to the contrary, the place was dense with smoke. Inspectors were either on the take or too frightened to drop in, and the cops didn't care. The place was crowded and noisy. Mostly men. The few women there were dressed provocatively and wore far too much makeup and cheap jewelry. It did little to disguise their physical shortcomings, though each displayed impressive cleavage. It was easily their best feature. But it wasn't the aging hookers that interested the newcomer. It was the men. Most of them were large and heavily tattooed. They all had the sneering arrogance of thugs grown used to having their way. Many of them noticed the stranger when he entered, but they quickly lost interest. It was clear from his appearance that he didn't have anything of value to offer. Just some worthless fool hoping to find a drink.

Russian was the language spoken, and vodka was the universal choice of beverage. As the man in the trench coat stepped through the doorway, a large man in an ill-fitting suit rose from a stool near the door and stepped in front of him, blocking his way. The bouncer's head was shaved, and most of the observable flesh on his hands and neck was covered with gang tattoos. The kind found in Russian prisons.

"I haven't seen you here before. Are you lost?" The voice was deep and low, like rolling thunder.

The newcomer said nothing. Instead, he slowly straightened his slouched posture. Though lean, he was as tall as the bouncer. He had broad shoulders and a square jaw like a curbstone. But it was his eyes that gave the bouncer reason for pause. They were a deep blue, and they were cold. They radiated a message that suggested the things the stranger was capable of doing. After a few moments, the bouncer broke off the stare-down and returned to his stool by the door.

There were two old men seated at the end of the bar, sipping vodka and watching a hockey game on an old, boxy CRT television affixed high on the wall behind the bar. The stranger slid in between them. Anywhere else along the bar, he would have risked annoying one or more of the younger thugs. The two old men, friends for decades in the old country, also were not pleased to have someone crowd between them, and they let the stranger know it.

"I only wish to buy each of you a drink, grandfathers," he said to them in Russian.

That made a difference. The two men wriggled to create a bit more room between their bar stools. The stranger caught the eye of one of the bartenders, a heavyset man with a gruesome scar that ran the length of the left side of his face. He pointed at one of the old men's glasses and held up three fingers. Scarface nodded.

While he was waiting for the drinks to be served, the stranger scanned the faces of the other men in the room. At the far end, sitting at a table with two men, was the person he'd hoped to find.

When Scarface brought the round of vodka, the stranger handed him an extra twenty and asked him to send a drink to the man at the table. "Tell him his *Старый друг* is at the bar," the stranger said, using the Russian term for "old friend."

A few minutes later, the stranger watched Scarface deliver the drink to the man at the table. He saw the barman lean over and say something as he served it, nodding his head toward the stranger. When Scarface walked away, the man at the table stared hard toward the far end of the bar. His eyes came to rest on the stranger in the trench coat. His brow wrinkled as he squinted into the dark, smoky atmosphere. His expression was one of puzzlement, as if he saw something familiar in the stranger but couldn't quite place it.

The stranger raised his glass in salute and smiled. The man at the table said something to his two companions and then rose and walked down the bar. Stopping in front of the stranger, his eyes opened wide in astonishment.

"My God, it *is* you, Kirill!"

Kirill Federov, the man in the trench coat, nodded. "What's the matter, Andrei? You look as if you've seen a ghost."

Andrei Ulyanin reached out and touched Federov's arm, as if to convince himself he wasn't speaking with an apparition. "You are a ghost. You were shot dead a year ago, at least that is the official version."

"Official?"

"Yes. But through connections from the old days in Moscow, I had the DNA of your so-called remains tested. It was not you."

Federov grinned. "So it seems."

"I have suspected that you survived, and indeed you have. How did you manage that?"

Federov looked at the two old men. They were staring intently at him and Ulyanin. And hanging on every word. "Come," Federov said and placed a hand on Ulyanin's arm. "Let's go somewhere private. We have much to discuss."

"I know just the place. There is another, more private room upstairs. We must pay to enter it, but," and he grinned, "I have been making very good money lately."

Ulyanin led Federov to the back of the bar. Another large, bored-looking man was sitting on a stool beside a door that was as stained and battered as the rest of the tavern. This man was even larger than the one at the front door. Ulyanin handed him a one-hundred-dollar bill, and the man opened the door. A flight of worn wooden stairs led upward. The air in the stairwell was musty and stank of stale tobacco. Ulyanin pushed open another door at the top of the stairs. The room was roughly half the size of the one on the ground floor. It was sectioned off into high-back booths that afforded greater privacy than was available downstairs. Most of the booths were occupied by rough-looking, heavily tattooed men. But there were also a few better-groomed men among them. Federov knew that these were *kriminal'nyye avtoritety*—criminal bosses of the Russian gangs.

"They call this place 'Little Las Vegas,'" Ulyanin said. "What is overheard here, stays here."

The two men slid into one of the few empty booths. Almost immediately, a waiter appeared. He set a bottle of Ruskova vodka and two heavy shot glasses on the table and left. Federov could tell from the black label that it was the 100-proof version.

Ulyanin poured each glass to the brim, picked up his, and raised it in a toast. "*За нашу дружбу*! To old comrades!"

Both men tossed back a shot, and Ulyanin refilled the glasses. "So, Kirill, tell me how it is that you are alive and how you managed to find me."

Federov took a long sip. "I was indeed shot. Nearly died."

"Yes, I can see that you are much thinner than the old Kirill. And perhaps not completely healed?"

"I am fine, getting stronger every day." He took another sip. "I was shot in the thorax by a man I was supposed to kill."

"Does this man have a name?"

"Yes. Levell."

"Levell!" Ulyanin said with obvious surprise.

"Does that name mean something to you?"

"My employer wanted me to arrange to have this Levell's bodyguard killed as a message to him."

"Were you successful?"

Ulyanin hesitated for a few moments. "No. My employer didn't want me personally involved in the killing so I hired two acquaintances from the old days in Perovo. Unfortunately, they were not up to the task. They ended up dead in a car that was left in front of my employer's home on Long Island." He paused and looked at Federov. "The police said your fingerprints and hair fibers were found in the car."

Federov wagged his head slowly back and forth. A grin crept across his features. "I'm not surprised. Levell is a very clever adversary."

The two men each took another gulp of the vodka, and Ulyanin immediately filled the glasses again. "Why did Levell shoot you, Kirill?"

Federov studied the rim of his glass for a few moments. "I was careless. I was sent to kill him at his home in Georgetown. I let my personal anger and hatred of the man cloud my instincts for caution." He took another sip.

Ulyanin said nothing.

"A rogue FBI agent had just shot up the place, and Levell had a .45 pistol in his hand. He saw me and fired first. I got a shot off and winged him. But my wound was far worse than his. I almost bled out on his damn carpet."

"But you survived. How?"

Federov slid his glass toward Ulyanin for a refill. "Levell, as you may know, is a man with very good connections. He had me taken to a private hospital. I was later told that I had been in surgery for more than seven hours." He took a sip. There was a slight tremor in his hand. "America may be decadent and weak, but it does have the world's best surgeons."

Ulyanin nodded. "So, then what happened?"

"Throughout my recovery and rehabilitation, I was kept in a secure facility."

"You were a prisoner?"

"Yes."

"For what purpose?"

Federov shrugged. "Levell thought I had intel he could use."

"Did you?"

"Of course. Not that I shared any of it with him and his inquisitors. As you will remember, our VSR training was very thorough on the subject of interrogation by the enemy. I fed them half-truths mixed with nonsense that held the possibility of being valid."

"Somehow I cannot imagine that Levell tired of the game and simply let you go. So how is it that you ended up here?"

"I befriended a male nurse, a homosexual, who was attracted to me. I convinced him that if he helped me get out of the facility, we would go away together."

A cold grin spread across Ulyanin's features. "He's dead, isn't he? The nurse?"

Federov nodded. "Of course."

Ulyanin laughed. "Same old Kirill. Never leave a witness behind—real or potential."

Ulyanin topped off the shot glasses. "And how is it that you found me, Kirill?"

It was Federov's turn to grin. "This bar is known as a place where ex-Spetsnaz and SRV operatives congregate to tell war stories and look for work—wet and otherwise. Where else would you be?"

"But how did you know I was in this country?"

"Easy. After our adventures in the Middle East, there was no going back there. And Russia, where we are considered traitors, would have been even less hospitable. America *is* the land of opportunity. It is where the money is, lots of it. You are as much a mercenary as I am. I knew you would come to this country."

They drank in silence before Federov said, "Andrei, you mentioned your employer was someone who wanted to send Levell a message."

The other man nodded. "What of it?"

"That sounds suspiciously like the man I was working for when I was shot, the one who sent me to kill Levell. Is your employer Harland Fairchilde?" Federov studied the other man's face.

Ulyanin smiled easily and said, "I was wondering when you'd ask me that. Your name came up on the night he hired me. And again, when the police told him your thumbprint and hair were found in the car with the two dead men in it in front of his house." He paused, still smiling, before saying, "Are you thinking about asking for your old job back?"

"Why? You don't think there's room for the two of us on his payroll?"

Ulyanin shrugged. "That's his decision."

"Well, I have a better idea. Fairchilde is a useless prick but an extremely wealthy one." A sly look appeared on Federov's face. "I'm through working for others. Why don't you and I find a way to…, how do the Americans say it, redistribute the wealth?"

CHAPTER 3
PUEBLO, COLORADO

THE PUEBLO COUNTY DETENTION CENTER was a sturdy-looking, multistory buff-colored building constructed in an X-pattern. With its institutional public-use architecture and rows of long, narrow, barred windows, it looked like a lot of jails around the country. An inscription on a stone marker in front of the entrance identified it as the Pueblo Justice Plaza. Behind it, atop a tall flagpole, the U.S. and Colorado flags whipped and snapped in the thin air that was over six thousand feet above sea level. Inside, the sheriff, Frank Tuccio, was drinking his third cup of coffee in his glass-enclosed office on the building's top floor. He looked up when the head of the detention center, Captain Alonzo Parnell, tapped on one of the glass panels. Tuccio waved him in.

"Got a minute, Sheriff?" Parnell said.

"Sure." Tuccio pointed to a chair. "What's on your mind?"

"It's about the John Doe in solitary, the one we call Prisoner X."

"The guy that did society a favor and killed that fucking deserter Kevin Johnson."

"Yeah, him, the one with the crazy-ass eyes."

"I hope you've come to tell me that you've finally been able to identify him."

Parnell shook his head. "Nothing so far."

"And you've checked every database there is? FBI. Interpol. All of them?"

"Yeah, all of them. It's crazy. It's like the guy just arrived from outer space. There's no history of any kind. No police record, no military, no SS number. There were no labels in his clothes. No nothin'. We even ran the DNA from his eating utensils. Again, nothin'. I've never seen anything like this."

"Nothing on social media?"

"Nope. Drew a blank there too. The guy looks and speaks like an American. He's probably in his late thirties, give or take. How in hell does someone spend nearly four decades on planet Earth and leave no trace?"

Tuccio shrugged. "Doesn't make any sense. You still haven't been able to get him to say anything during interrogations?"

"Not a word. He just smiles that nasty cold smile. And those fucking eyes…," Parnell's voice trailed off. "He's unnerved everybody who's come into contact with him. I'm at a loss to know where to go from here."

"Well, we've got eyewitnesses to the killing, so a confession isn't necessary to convict him. But it would help to know who he is and whether anyone else was involved."

"More like an assassination. Eyewitness testimony makes it clear he was stalking the victim."

The phone on the sheriff's desk buzzed, interrupting the conversation. Tuccio leaned forward and picked up the receiver. "Yeah?" He listened for a few moments and then said, "The Bureau? Shit. All right, bring him up."

He replaced the receiver and looked at Parnell who raised his eyebrows quizzically.

"There's an FBI agent here. Says he wants to speak to our Prisoner X," Tuccio said with a sigh of frustration.

"What the hell does the Bureau want with this guy?'

Tuccio shrugged resignedly. "Seems clear the perp killed Johnson because of his military record. I guess, somewhere under the mountain of government regs, there's grounds for the Feds to get involved."

A UNIFORMED FEMALE deputy showed the federal agent into Tuccio's office and closed the door behind her as she left.

The agent looked around. *New, modern facility,* he thought, *but all jails, new and old, have the same look and feel—cold, sterile.*

The sheriff nodded at him and offered his hand. "I'm Frank Tuccio, and this is Captain Parnell." He pointed to a vacant chair. "Have a seat, Special Agent...?"

"Christie," the newcomer said and showed his credentials to the two men. He sat down facing them.

"So, Special Agent Christie, what's the nature of the Bureau's interest in our prisoner?"

"I'm with CTD, the Bureau's Counterterrorism Division. We suspect he may have been involved in other acts of terrorism. I'd like to talk with him. Also, while it may seem like a tenuous connection, because Johnson was on probation for United States military crimes, he remained under federal jurisdiction."

The two members of the sheriff's department exchanged glances. Parnell snickered.

"Well, I suppose I don't have any reason to refuse the Bureau's request, but you're wasting the government's time. The prisoner hasn't uttered a peep since we apprehended him. And it hasn't been from lack of effort on our part."

Christie smiled. "Maybe I won't get anywhere with him either but trying is part of my job. I'm sure you understand."

Tuccio nodded.

"There are some questions I want to ask him. His responses may help shed some light on matters I'm investigating."

"In the event you get anything outta this guy, you *are* gonna share intel with us, right?" Parnell said.

Christie smiled again. "Absolutely. I'm a big believer in interagency cooperation."

"Then you won't have a problem with one of our people sitting in on your session?" Tuccio said.

"Actually, there is a problem with that. The matters I'm dealing with here are of a highly-classified nature. For that reason, there can be no surveillance—electronic or otherwise. Sorry. But I assure you, I'll share any information that's relevant to your investigation."

Tuccio and Parnell looked at each other for a long moment. Christie could tell by the expression on Parnell's face that the jailer was angry about the arrangement.

Finally, Tuccio turned to Christie and shrugged. "Sure. What the hell. We haven't gotten anywhere with this bird. Maybe you can. Besides, my department is always happy to help the Bureau." His tone of voice said otherwise.

"One question...Special Agent...we haven't found a shred of evidence to identify this guy. He's like a ghost. You got any idea who he might be?"

Christie shook his head a couple of times and smiled again. "No idea. We just want to eliminate the possibility that he's involved in other...highly classified matters."

Christie thanked Tuccio for his time, and followed Parnell out of the office. The deputy escorted Christie into the bowels of the cellblock where Prisoner X was being held in solitary confinement. Before passing through the cellblock's outer door, Christie surrendered his weapon and was subjected to a wand search for other prohibited devices. His cellphone was not one of them. As a federal agent, he was required to have it with him at all times. The sheriff's office was aware of the regulation.

When they reached Prisoner X's cell, Parnell triggered a switch, and the heavy metal door slid open almost soundlessly. Parnell nodded for Christie to enter. "You got thirty minutes." There was a surly edge to his voice.

The door slid closed, and Christie heard the bolts click into place. He turned and looked at the occupant of the cell. The man was stretched out on the metal bunk, hands behind his head, eyes closed. Even lying down, he looked powerful. His facial features were angular. They reminded Christie of a hawk. The FBI agent pulled out his cellphone from a pocket and triggered a special application. It was designed to detect any electronic surveillance. It showed none. *The sheriff may not be happy with my being here, but at least he seems to be a man of his word.*

Christie couldn't tell whether the prisoner was asleep. "I'm Special Agent Christie with the Federal Bureau of Investigation."

The man showed no response.

For the sake of caution, Christie said, "I'm going to approach you. I have something you'll want to hear."

No response.

Knowing who the man was, Christie approached him with a fair amount of apprehension. Speaking softly, he said, "You're Nick Stensen. I have a message for you from Cliff Levell."

The man slowly opened his right eye and rolled his head to the right until the eye was fixed on Christie. There was a bright red dot in the center. He gave a barely perceptible nod and closed the eye.

"Levell needs you. He's sending Brendan Whelan to free you."

Christie was a little surprised when the man showed no response. *But*, he thought, *this guy's a Sleeping Dog, something*

that often seems more than human. Maybe nothing rattles their
cages.

"Because of the nature of the crime and who the victim was," Christie said, "the federal government is taking jurisdiction of your case. You're going to be transferred to a U.S. prison, ADX Florence. It's about forty miles west of here. U.S. Marshals will escort you by ground transport, using the back way, State Roads 96 and 67."

Christie paused for some response from Stensen. There was none.

"About thirty miles out, in a little settlement named Wetmore," he continued, "the marshals will turn onto 67 from 96. Somewhere between there and the ADX, Whelan will make his move. Be ready."

Christie wasn't sure, but he thought he saw Stensen nod his head again. "For what it's worth, if you actually do get to ADX Florence, you're fucked; nothing can be done once that happens. It's a supermax facility. It's where we're keeping Zacarias Moussaoui, Richard Reid, Ted Kaczynski, and a number of other bad actors.

"You'll never get out, not even to go to court. They'll put you in a prison 'studio' and beam all pretrial matters to a federal courtroom in Colorado Springs. The actual trial will also be beamed to a federal district courtroom. There will be no opportunities to escape. If Whelan doesn't succeed, you'll never set foot out of that prison. Ever."

THREE DAYS LATER, four deputy U.S. marshals presented the necessary paperwork to Sheriff Tuccio and took custody of Prisoner X. As they were waiting for Parnell and other deputies to bring the prisoner to them, Tuccio took the Supervisory Deputy Marshal aside.

"You know much about this prisoner?"

The other man shook his head. "There isn't much information on him. Why?"

Tuccio looked the marshal directly in the eye. "He's dangerous as hell. Never seen anything like him. I recommend you keep him shackled at all times. Don't take your eyes off of him."

The marshal cocked his head to one side and raised an eyebrow. "This ain't our first rodeo, Sheriff."

"I didn't mean to imply that. I've been in law enforcement for thirty years. I've seen strong guys, I've seen mean guys, I've seen crazies, but I've never seen anything like this one."

"How so?" The marshal wore a patronizing smile.

"For one thing, his eyes. There are little red dots in the middle of them. The dots grow when…he smells blood."

"Hmm. Sounds interesting," the marshal said with obvious disinterest. "We've transported a lot of crazies with wild-looking eyes."

"Yeah, but there's more. A couple of days ago, we let him into the yard to exercise. A couple of the prisoners started to fuck with him because he was the new guy. He moved faster than anyone we'd ever seen. Grabbed each of them and picked them up like rag dolls…and they were a couple of two hundred pounders. He slammed them together, splitting open their heads. Then he slung them twenty feet into a brick wall. It happened so fast and was so unnatural that no one, not even the guards, could react. Everybody just stared.

"Then this guy sauntered over to the weightlifting area. All the prisoners using the weights scrambled out of his way as fast as they could. The guy slid four hundred pounds on the bar and began cranking out bench presses like he was lifting a bag of marsh-mallows."

The patronizing expression vanished from the marshal's face, replaced by a look of concern. "Interesting," he said slowly. "We'll definitely follow the manual on this one."

PRISONER X WAS BROUGHT to the loading dock. The marshals placed him in full shackles and squeezed him into the back of a black Chevrolet Suburban, bracketed by two beefy marshals. The other two rode up front. There were two routes that could take them from the Pueblo County Detention Center to ADX Florence. The shorter way was more direct. It involved taking the Interstate north to U.S. Highway 50, then west to Florence via State Roads 120 or 115. The other route was more circuitous and slightly longer but less traveled. The marshals opted for that one. In fact, their choice of route had been entered into the U.S. Marshal Service's computer database days earlier. And Levell's people had hacked it. Whelan knew exactly where the Chevrolet Suburban would be and when.

SHORTLY AFTER THE marshals departed the detention center, a de Havilland Canada DHC-2 Beaver took off from a grass strip on a ranch owned by a retired Marine colonel who had served with Levell. The men had remained close over the ensuing years. The colonel was a patriot as well as a member of SAS. The strip, approximately fifteen miles southwest of Pueblo, was private. It also was small, out of the way, and off the FAA's grid.

The de Havilland was the quintessential bush plane. Although commercial production of the plane stopped in 1967, the rugged-looking workhorse was still one of the most cherished rough-country aircraft on the planet. In addition to the pilot, there was a single passenger. Whelan was seated on a tube-frame, web-fabric seat in the plane's spartan interior. The pilot was a veteran of the U.S. Air Force's 1st Special Operations Wing. One of its chief roles was agile combat support, including infiltration and exfiltration, for U.S. Special Operations Force operational elements. In civilian life, the pilot was a loyal and trusted employee of one of the Mueller brothers' global enterprises.

The plane, a STOL aircraft, designed for short takeoffs and landings—features that made it a good choice for this operation—flew almost due west, paralleling Colorado Route 96. The pilot kept it at a low altitude to avoid detection and tracking. When its course intersected Route 67, the pilot swung its nose to the north and followed the road. About six kilometers north of the wide spot in the road, known as Wetmore, the road began a slight curve to the west. Another four hundred or so meters farther there was a deep arroyo spanned by a bridge. Whelan signaled to the pilot to put the plane down.

The pilot located a twisting gravel farm road nearby, scoped it out for the presence of power poles, and finding none, prepared for a STOL landing. The pilot set the aircraft down with amazing ease, despite the bumpy surface of the road and the short distance between curves. He left the prop turning over as Whelan scrambled out of the cabin and opened the cargo door. Whelan was wearing a U.S. Army Desert Battle Dress Uniform, or DBDU, and matching balaclava, in case any unexpected witnesses showed up. He removed a duffle bag from the plane and began jogging with it toward the nearest point of intersection with the arroyo.

The pilot spun the plane around and taxied along the road to where he originally had touched down. He turned the plane again, revved the prop and, with the benefit of its STOL characteristics, took off. In a matter of seconds, he was airborne and began circling the area about one thousand feet above the bridge.

Whelan reached the edge of the arroyo and slid down its steep bank to the bottom. The dry creek bed was flat and sandy with a scattering of boulders and gravel. He navigated it with an easy lope until he reached the bridge. There, he slipped on surgical gloves and climbed up the bank beneath the span. Moving quickly but carefully, he removed a small brick of Semtex 1 from the duffle and, using his hands, fashioned it into a long strand. The gloves prevented any DNA material, like sweat or body oil, from getting on the explosive. He knew the government would reconstruct the scene and run tests on anything it could find that might be related to the crime. It was amazing what could be gleaned from the residue of an explosion.

Whelan stuffed the reworked Semtex into the crevice that was formed where the foot of the bridge extended out from the arroyo's bank. Semtex, a high-order explosive, would create a blast wave in the form of an intense over-pressurization impulse. Whelan arranged the explosive so that the wave would travel upward rather than horizontally. He took into consideration the blast wind and forced superheated airflow. Both effects were capable of inflicting traumatic injuries, even death. To the extent possible, Whelan wanted to mitigate potential damages to the marshals and especially to their prisoner. The goal was to render the marshals temporarily inoperative, not slaughter them. Or Stensen. Finally, he inserted the detonating cap, which was attached to the guts of a cell phone. The explosive material would be triggered by a signal from another cell phone in Whelan's pocket. *IED, Yankee-style.*

When he was finished, Whelan slid down the bank, peeled off the gloves, and slipped them into a pocket in his DBDU. He trotted back along the bottom of the twisting arroyo. When he was about a quarter mile from the bridge, he climbed the steep bank and hunkered down behind a Bebb willow tree, its growth stunted by the arid climate. He pulled out the cellphone and waited for the black Suburban to approach. He knew there would be injuries, perhaps critical ones, as a result of the explosion. Even with body armor, the marshals would not fare as well as Stensen. They lacked his genetic benefits. He remembered one of Levell's favorite sayings: *Some collateral damage is almost inevitable.* He just hoped Stensen survived the incident in sufficient physical condition to participate in the exfiltration. If not, Whelan was prepared to sling him over a shoulder and carry him out.

About twenty minutes later, the pilot's voice crackled in the earbud of Whelan's comm gear. "Black Suburban approaching from the south at sixty-five mph. ETA the bridge in approximately one minute."

In the distance to the south, Whelan saw the vehicle approaching. Timing, he knew, was everything. He punched in the speed-dial number, placed his thumb above the call icon, and waited. The seconds seemed to drag by. And then the Suburban was only a few car lengths from the bridge abutment. Whelan pressed the call icon.

Immediately, the south end of the bridge erupted in a large fireball. Even a quarter of a mile away, the sound of the explosion hammered Whelan's ears.

He had purposely used a measured amount of explosive and carefully arranged it so that it would blow away a portion of the bridge. If all went well, the vehicle would plunge into the resulting gap in the paved surface. The combination of the effects of the high-order explosive's power and the resulting crash should achieve the desired results. Overkill was to be avoided.

Whelan sprinted toward the billowing cloud of smoke, and quickly reached the shattered bridge. The badly damaged Suburban was nose down at the bottom of the arroyo, its rear wheels still spinning. From where he stood at the top of the arroyo, the five occupants all appeared to be motionless. Whelan, pulling the gloves back on, slid down the embankment and took a quick look inside. Stensen was in the center seat in the second row. He was hunched forward, not moving. The four marshals also were bent forward, held in place by their seat belts. There was blood oozing from all five men. Whelan pulled a thick rag from the duffle. Using it, he grabbed the right rear door and yanked. Even with his remarkable strength, it wouldn't budge. The effects of the blast and the crash had torqued the vehicle's frame and jammed the door. *Shit! I should have anticipated this.*

He looked around quickly and spotted a piece of concrete that had been part of the bridge. It weighed close to two hundred pounds. He picked it up and smashed it against the window. The laminated safety glass didn't shatter but did break into a crazed pattern. He used the piece of concrete to push the remnants inward and out of his way.

Whalen leaned in the opening and looked around the interior of the badly damaged vehicle. He immediately smelled the acrid odor of the explosive that had released the airbags. There also were other smells—blood, fear, and the talcum powder used by the airbag manufacturers to keep the bags pliable and lubricated while in storage. The powder residue was strewn around the Suburban's interior, but the bags appeared to have done their jobs in preventing more serious injuries.

The occupant closest to Whelan was a beefy marshal. The man was unconscious and bleeding from a number of superficial wounds. But Whelan didn't see signs of traumatic injury. Reaching through the opening where the glass had been, he undid the man's seat belt and dragged him out of the cabin. He laid him on his back on the ground with his head slightly elevated. Whelan frisked him quickly and found what he was looking for—keys to the shackles binding the prisoner.

Stensen was bleeding steadily from a gash in his scalp, and his nose was bloodied. Whelan leaned in and undid Stensen's seat belt, then unlocked the shackles that bound him. As carefully as possible under the circumstances, he pulled his unconscious friend out of the vehicle and stretched him out next to the marshal. Whelan quickly checked Stensen for injuries. Aside from the scalp wound and bloody nose, the man didn't seem to have any. Stensen's breathing was steady. Whelan pulled a vial of smelling salts from a pocket of his DBDU. He broke the cap off and held the vial under Stensen's nose. After a few moments, the unconscious man grimaced, coughed, and opened his eyes slowly. They were badly bloodshot from the concussive effects of the explosion. He struggled to focus on Whelan. For the moment, there was no red glow in their centers.

"Welcome back, Sleeping Beauty," Whelan said wryly.

Stensen stared at Whelan's lips and reached up with his hands to touch his own ears.

"It's temporary," Whelan said slowly and with exaggerated mouth movements so that Stensen, hopefully, could read his lips. In planning the mission, Levell's people had told Whelan that temporary deafness would be a given for the occupants of the Suburban.

Whelan knew that time was essential. When the marshals failed to report in, the state and federal authorities would quickly begin searching for them. He pulled Stensen to his feet. Standing directly in front of the man, he mouthed the words, "Can you run?"

Stensen nodded slowly.

Whelan scooped up the duffle bag and, grabbing the sleeve of Stensen's orange prison jumpsuit, pulled him along the creek bed. When he came to where the arroyo's bank was less steep, he helped his friend scramble up it. At the top, Whelan looked out toward the gravel farm road the de Havilland had used as a landing strip. The pilot had already landed and was taxiing toward the two men as they jogged in his direction. Whelan threw the duffle bag in the cargo compartment and helped Stensen, who was still groggy, get belted in. Then Whelan climbed aboard next to the pilot. In a matter of seconds, the plane was roaring upwind across the bumpy surface. Another few moments, and, the STOL craft was airborne. It banked to the east, putting distance between itself and the wrecked Suburban as fast as the pilot could get the old airplane to go.

SHERIFF FRANK TUCCIO was studying a sheriff's office budget report when he looked through the interior glass wall of his office. One of his deputies was striding briskly toward him. He followed the deputy with his eyes and thought, *Now what?*

The deputy saw the sheriff watching him, but started to knock on the glass door anyway. Tuccio sighed with an air of resignation and laid the report on his desk He waved the deputy in.

"You look like your pants are on fire, Roscoe." He pointed at the report on his desk and said, "I'm busy. Is what you've got important enough that I need to know about it right now?"

Roscoe's head nodded up and down vigorously. "Yessir, it is."

"That's what I was afraid of." The sheriff sighed again and leaned back in his chair, motioning for Roscoe to continue.

"It's that Prisoner X guy, Sheriff. One of the deputies over in Fremont County found the truck those marshals were using to transport him to ADX Florence."

The sheriff sat bolt upright. "Found it? Found it where?"

"In an arroyo about five miles south of the prison."

Tuccio jumped to his feet. "A fucking arroyo! How did it get there? Where are the marshals? Hell, where is the prisoner?"

Roscoe gulped, his Adam's apple bobbed visibly. "Somebody blew up the damn bridge over the arroyo. The marshals are alive but pretty badly banged up."

"Yeah, yeah, yeah," Tuccio said, his voice rising. "But what about the prisoner?"

"Gone. No trace of him. Dogs tracked him for a ways, but then he seems to have disappeared into thin fuckin' air."

"Sonofabitch!" Tuccio slammed his palm against the top of his desk. "He must have been picked up by someone in a vehicle. Hell, maybe even a plane or chopper."

"The U.S. Marshals Service and the Bureau of Prisons are organizing search parties," Roscoe said. "They tried to put out an APB too. He can't have gotten too far, what with being banged up in the wreck and all."

Tuccio waved his arms and yelled, "Jesus H. Christ, that's the one sonofabitch that should never have seen the light of day. He's the scariest bastard I've ever run across." He paused and looked at Roscoe. "Wait a minute. What did you say...tried to put out an APB?"

Roscoe looked down at his feet. "Well...there's sort of a problem."

"Problem?" Tuccio screamed. Beyond the glass walls of his office, all activity had stopped. His employees were staring at him.

"What the hell kind of problem?"

"Uh...it seems that neither the Bureau of Prisons nor the Marshals Service can find any of the information we gave them."

"Did those dumb-ass bureaucrats try looking in their computer databases?"

"Yessir. There's nothing there. They asked us to resend it."

"And you've sent it?"

"Uh...sir, that's the problem. There's nothing in our databases either. It's like they've been wiped clean. Like the guy never existed." The words spilled out of Roscoe's mouth in a torrent.

Tuccio stared at the deputy, his mouth moving but no words coming out. Finally, he was able to say, "But how can that be? I *know* we had a record on this guy, if only for the time we had him in custody. Fingerprints, DNA. How the hell does that kind of data disappear? Do we have a traitor in our midst?"

"Doubtful, sir. The FBI says someone outside did it. A hacker."

Tuccio shook his head in wonderment. "Good God, who is this Prisoner X? What the hell are we up against?"

CHAPTER 4

ZURICH

MAKSYM WAS RARELY in a good mood. Almost everything pissed him off. Cooling his heels waiting for someone was one of the worst sources of irritation. Even the elegance of his current surroundings didn't ease the growing anger. He was seated in the lobby of the Dolder Grand Hotel and Resort, a luxurious castle-like complex, originally built more than one hundred years earlier. Its one-hundred-seventy-six rooms and suites were nestled in a four thousand square-meter park-like setting. But, despite its ornate pedigree and old-world exterior, the hotel's vast lobby seemed modern and sterile.

Maksym had found a large leather club chair that would accommodate his muscular mass. He purposely chose one at the far end of the lobby, away from the main entrance and the registration area. The front wall of the lobby consisted of several panels of wood-and-glass French doors that faced southeast across the motor court and a golf course. The panels were expansive with no muntins to interfere with the view. Maksym assumed that most of the French doors were locked to encourage foot traffic to use the ones directly in front of the registration area. He didn't care. If he needed to leave quickly, locked doors wouldn't pose a problem for him.

He looked at his watch and felt his impatience rising. The man who was keeping him waiting was coming directly to the hotel from the airport. Maksym had flown in earlier that day and knew it was only fifteen kilometers or so from the airport to the Dolder Grand. His cab had made the trip in about twenty-five minutes. Zheng Bao Xun, the minister of finance for the People's Republic of China, had landed more than an hour earlier. He had called Maksym on his cellphone as he was clearing customs. *So why isn't he here yet?*

The minister was coming to Zurich for an informal meeting with financial functionaries of the European Union. It also gave Zheng an opportunity to meet with Maksym, a man he liked to think of as his "employee." But Maksym had made it clear that he considered their arrangement a "partnership."

Finally, a limo rolled to a stop in the hotel's motor court, and Zheng emerged with two "assistants." Maksym knew the two were Zheng's security. *Fresh meat?* He smiled a mean smile as he thought about how many members of Zheng's so-called "security team" he had killed in the recent past. Death was such a convincing way to drive home a point.

As the minister entered the hotel's lobby, he glanced around and spotted Maksym. He said something to the two young men on his security staff. There was some hesitation on their parts, but reluctantly they moved away toward the registration desk. Zheng strolled the length of the long, narrow lobby and took a seat facing Maksym. The Chinese man was not large to begin with, but sitting next to Maksym, he looked elfin.

"How nice to see you again, Maksym. I trust your flight from New York was pleasant."

Maksym stared icily into Zheng's odd golden brown eyes. "Cut the shit, Zheng, you pint-sized fucking Uyghur. I didn't fly all this way to exchange pleasantries."

"It's what civilized people do, Maksym. But perhaps that description doesn't include you." Zheng made no effort to hide the sarcasm.

"If you want your pencil neck snapped, Zheng, try one more insult."

The smile vanished from Zheng's face. "You are right. Chitchat is for social occasions. This is business."

Maksym nodded approvingly. "Speaking of which, it appears that circumstances in China are working in your favor."

"Yes. The Chinese Paradox—bellicose words and actions based on a crumbling economy." He laughed. "Didn't I tell you my efforts would prove successful? There is much going on behind the scenes."

"Really?" Doubt was clearly evident in Maksym's voice. "Your president is an extremely powerful man. It's said that he's China's most powerful president since Mao."

"That appearance is based on the fact that he holds all three of my country's primary offices—president, party general secretary, and chair of the Central Military Commission. He uses the latter position to shuffle the top military commanders by promoting the ones most loyal to him."

"That sounds like a definition of power to me."

Zheng smiled easily. "Fortunately, he is his own worst enemy. He's an inveterate micromanager. His incessant interventions in economic policy are poorly conceived and badly implemented. He attempts to mask his ineptitude with his self-proclaimed war on corruption. That, too, is only an excuse to purge bureaucrats and party officials that he suspects of disloyalty.

"But he is sowing the seeds of his own downfall. A growing mountain of regulation that has slowed growth to its weakest rate in more than two decades. Manufacturing has begun moving to other parts of Southeast Asia, and property prices are in decline. Most telling of all, the flight of capital has begun. At record levels. A crisis of confidence in the stock and currency markets could affect the overall economy, which actually is quite fragile."

"All of which plays into your hands as the savior of the Chinese economy, yes?"

Zheng nodded. "Indeed. Behind the scenes, I have influenced the central bank to devalue the yuan. The effect I desire has been achieved—adding further panic to the equity markets. Needless to say, there is now a large measure of distrust between the central bank and the securities industry and regulators."

"So," Maksym said, "when the economy is in the tank and the bureaucrats are at each other's throats, you will do...what?"

"I have been assiduously courting the second generation of the urban middle class. These are the ones who will play the essential role in China's future. Whoever they believe in will become their...leader."

"What's so special about them?"

"They're different than their more trusting, more obsequious parents and grandparents. They are far more questioning. They have known only steady growth and an appreciating quality of life. They are faced with the unintended consequences of the foolish one-child policy. It is a demographic time bomb that many nations in the West are also facing. The birth rate has plunged, yet more and more people are living longer. This is the inheritance for this second generation of the urban middle class."

Maksym thought for a few moments about what Zheng had said. "Given your president's paranoia and micromanagement, how have you managed to, as you phrase it, 'court' this undoubtedly large and widely scattered demographic?"

Zheng smiled triumphantly and tapped the side of his head with an index finger. "Social media. It provides channels of communication on both the Surface Web and the Deep Web. They accommodate conversations too numerous for sensors to track. And they are outside the range of official government channels and its attempts at monitoring communications."

"And what's the situation with your Uyghur homies?"

"As you know, Uyghurs are followers of Islam. It's always been a bone of contention with the ethnic Chinese—one of the reasons we so despise them. In fact, I have attained the highest rank ever for any of my people."

"Part of that," Maksym said grudgingly, "is because you *are* a wizard of international finance. And part also is Beijing's attempt to pacify a large and restless Uyghur population."

The finance minister nodded. "True on both counts, and I am held in high esteem among my people as a result. And this is my ultimate weapon in the Alliance for Global Unity's efforts to use Muslim extremists to destroy the United States and other nations. For the most part these extremists are members of diverse groups and sects. There is very little cohesiveness beyond their mutual hatred for the West. On the other hand, my people—the Uyghurs —are a huge group united in the desire to control the dictates from Beijing. What better way to do it than with me as China's president? And when the West falls and the world is in chaos, I will use the might of an unscathed China to assume global control."

"That's when I will kill Fairchilde and the AGU hierarchy," Maksym said.

Zheng nodded.

Maksym studied the minister's face. "You are a clever little bastard, Zheng. Maybe that's why I like you. Partner."

The smile of self-satisfaction quivered on Zheng's face and almost disappeared, but he caught it in time to maintain it. "Thank you, Maksym. Now, we both have important matters to attend to; let us get to the business at hand."

The minister slid forward in his chair to draw closer to the other man. Maksym, likewise, leaned toward Zheng.

"I have received information that your figurehead employer, Harland Fairchilde, has encountered a bit of trouble."

Maksym raised an eyebrow.

"It seems he attempted to eliminate someone who was close to your 'old friend' Levell. He foolishly believed that with the elimination of that someone, Levell would be frightened into working with the AGU. It backfired. The result is that Fairchilde has gotten himself unnecessarily involved in a police investigation. Additionally, he has developed a healthy fear of Levell and that group of his, the Society of Adam Smith. As a result, he may no longer be as effectively focused on his one-world objectives."

"You want me to kill him now? My killing him was always the plan."

"Not yet. If he can carry through on his scheme to promote global chaos, it will greatly benefit my own plan to gain control of China and then the rest of the planet."

"Then what *is* it you want me to do?"

"Fairchilde employs you because of his enormous respect for your…rather deadly skills and intelligence. He's been using you as his representative with the Mexican gangs and drug cartels that are smuggling Islamic terrorists into America. Stay close to him. Observe him. If he seems to have lost some of his abilities to lead AGU successfully, let me know. But don't kill him until we can arrange for succession. Otherwise, we risk the loss of all AGU has accomplished over the past century."

Zheng started to rise, but paused. "Oh, and one other thing. As you probably know, Fairchilde hired a Russian ex-SVR operative as a combination security and glorified errand boy. You knew him, a

Colonel Federov. He seems to have gotten himself killed in an attempt to assassinate Levell." Zheng paused for introspection. "That old man really is a tough one. In any event, Fairchilde replaced Federov with another SVR operative, a man named Ulyanin. Just so you know."

"I hate the fucking Russians," Maksym said. It came out in a deep growl.

"I'm not fond of them either. Kill as many of them as you like," Zheng said with a cheerful smile.

CHAPTER 5

THE LODGE

STENSEN STILL HAD a small bandage on his forehead. It covered the twelve stitches in the fast-healing wound he'd suffered in the wreck of the Suburban. The white bandage contrasted with the bright red dots in the middle of his deep-set, ice blue eyes. He picked up the bottle of beer he'd been drinking and took a long pull. It was the only painkiller he ever used. He was sitting with Whelan and Levell in the Old Man's spacious, airy office in the Lodge.

Levell snorted impatiently. "There's so much to do and so little time to do it. I honestly don't know whether we can make much of a difference at this point."

"I know you well enough, Cliff, to know you're going to try your damnedest to make it work," Whelan said. "Let's stick with the plan."

Levell looked out the expansive windows at thickly forested surroundings that had been heavily sown with seismic and infrared sensors. For a few moments, conversation stopped. Then Levell turned back to Whelan and Stensen. "All right, we go operational. You two know what's expected of you."

Whelan nodded. "We're going to need all of the Dogs for this one. So, Nick is going to Tennessee to spring Rafe's sorry ass from the slammer. Cliff, you're personally going to visit Quentin in Chicago to see if he's fit for this mission. I'm..."

"And you," Levell interrupted, "are going to Australia to check out the report that this Liam Stone guy has your genetic gifts too. If it's true, recruit him."

"Check that. I'll *try* to recruit him. He may have other ideas."

"Bullshit. You're an Irishman. Use that gift of blarney your people are famous for."

"And if we can't get Almeida, Thomas, or this Aussie dude to sign up?"

"Dammit, that's not an option," Levell said irritably. "Our biggest initial challenge is getting Kirkland back. He's in a fucking maximum-security facility in Qatar. Getting him out of there will take nothing short of a miracle."

Stensen finished his beer and placed the empty bottle on a side table next to his chair. "Same old, same old. The improbable we do immediately, the impossible takes a bit longer." He smiled at his use of the old bromide.

"Yeah," Whelan said. "On the surface, busting Marc out of Qatar does seem impossible. But I'm sure we'll come up with something."

Stensen shifted his weight in the chair. "What's the plan for me springing Almeida? This isn't Monopoly; I don't have any get-out-of-jail cards."

"You're an enterprising thinker," Levell said. "You'll figure something out. The good news is he's in a county lockup in Tennessee. That should be the easiest of the three exfil efforts. Just try to keep the collateral damage to a minimum."

"And that still leaves Sven. What's the plan there?" Stensen said.

"The only leverage we have over him is Maksym. We'll have to commit all of our resources to finding Maksym and killing him *after* this mission is complete."

CHAPTER 6

TENNANT CREEK, NORTHERN TERRITORY, AUSTRALIA

WHELAN STUDIED the brown desert landscape passing beneath the southbound Cessna 402. *Deserts are aptly named. So inhospitable that most forms of life gladly* desert *them.* He was on the next to the last leg of his journey. Once the four-passenger plane landed at Tennant Creek, he would pick up his rental car and drive back north. Backtracking irritated him. It felt like a special brand of failure, having to retrace his steps instead of moving relentlessly forward. To compound his frustration, he'd had to fly all the way across the Australian continent from Sydney in the south to Darwin on the north coast. Now he was flying back south, only to have to turn around and drive ninety miles north from Tennant Creek. *I'm beginning to feel like a fucking yo-yo.*

So far, he had spent more than thirty hours getting from Reagan National to Darwin in Australia's Northern Territory. It had combined more than twenty-six hours in various airplanes with seemingly interminable layovers in L.A. and Sydney. And that didn't count the previous night he'd spent at Rydges Airport Hotel next to the Darwin International Airport. He'd left Washington,

D.C. on a Friday and, because of the effect of the International Date Line, he'd arrived in Darwin on a Sunday. The flights to Tennant Creek were scheduled only on Mondays and Wednesdays. He'd spent the night in a plain-Jane hotel room, listening to the occasional red-eye flight coming or going.

At least he'd enjoyed his dinner, barramundi prepared in a spicy salt. The server told him that barramundi was based on a loanword from an Aboriginal language. Being an IPA man, Whelan had washed the fish down with a couple of pints of Modus Operandi Former Tenant. He took an instant liking to it. *If this is typical of the Australian brewers' art, this trip won't be a complete loss, no matter how things work out.* The ruby red India pale ale had a complex blend of citrusy hops and savory caramel malt flavor, followed by a slightly sweet finish, and aromas of passion fruit and mango. The server had told him that, in botanical terms, the mosaic and galaxy dry hops generously used in the ale were closely related to marijuana. Whelan had to admit that the inside of the glass smelled like a college dorm room on a Friday night.

At last, the small aircraft touched down at the Tennant Creek Airport following a two-and-a-half-hour flight from Darwin, more than six hundred miles to the north. Whelan checked his watch. It was going on eleven in the morning, local time. He was the sole passenger on the flight, so it didn't take the copilot long to remove Whelan's bag from the plane's cargo bay and hand it to him. Whelan strode across the runway to the small, tired-looking passenger terminal. Originally, the airstrip had been used for military purposes during the Second World War. Later it had been improved for commercial use. But that had been decades ago, and it looked it.

He quickly picked up his rental vehicle, a Mitsubishi Outlander, checked it over to familiarize himself with the locations of the wipers and headlights switches. And the horn. He threw his bag in the back. As he drove away from the airport, he thought about the differences in U.S. and Australian English. Trunks were "boots." Gas was "petrol." The windshield was a "windscreen." And the steering wheel was on the right. Cars were driven on the left. *Just like Ireland. No problemo.* Irvine Street, the road that led from the airport to the main drag, was two lanes and paved. The land surrounding it was reddish-brown dirt with small, rocky hillocks. The few improvements were mostly metal buildings plus a solitary junkyard.

Tennant Creek straddled the Stuart Highway, known locally as Paterson Street. It was a major highway that formed the principal north-south route through the central interior of mainland Australia. Locals often referred to it as "The Track." It was shown on Whelan's map as National Highway 87. Originally, there had been no speed limits imposed on travelers; now there was a limit of 130 kilometers per hour, or 80 miles per hour. During the briefing, Levell's people had advised Whelan that police rarely patrolled this stretch of 87.

The town itself was dusty and old. It reminded Whelan of some of the struggling outposts in the American desert Southwest. The buildings were almost all single-story and tired. The majority of businesses seemed to be food or booze services, with a smattering of small motels, laundromats, and gas stations. Whelan's own research showed that the town's population had been slowly dwindling over the past few years. Half the population was Aboriginal. He wondered which half of the citizenry was shrinking fastest. The town's main drag was divided by a sparsely landscaped median that ended less than half a mile north of Irvine Street.

Tennant Creek was in the middle of Australia's huge, sparsely populated Northern Territory and had been the site of the country's last gold rush. It sat in the center of the western half of the sprawling Barkly Tableland, vast, elevated grassland plains that rose to more than one thousand feet. Most of its one hundred ten thousand square miles consisted of rich black soil and very few people. The dominant flora in the semiarid climate was golden Mitchell grass, a hardy grass that encouraged the presence of huge cattle ranches called "stations." Stations provided the main source of income in the area. One of those stations, Helen Springs, was Whelan's destination.

As he drove the four-wheel drive Outlander north on Highway 87 beyond the edge of Tennant Creek, it was nearly midday and the temperature already was close to ninety degrees. The extremely low humidity made the superheated air less uncomfortable. Still, Whelan cranked up the air conditioning. Five klicks outside of Tennant Creek, he passed Mary Ann Dam Road that ran out to Lake Mary Ann, a local recreational area. Twenty klicks later he passed through Three Ways, a small compound with a roadhouse and Shell station where Highway 66 from Barkly Homestead and Mt. Isa in Queensland T-boned 87. He wondered if he should stop for lunch or chance finding another place farther up the road. He opted to keep going.

Narrow and two-lane, 87 was mostly straight and well paved, or "sealed" as the Aussies said. The shoulders varied in width and consisted mostly of rust-colored crushed rock. This section of the highway skirted along the eastern edge of the Tanami Desert with only the occasional thorny acacia tree dotting the hot, dry plain.

The area was mostly devoid of signs of habitation. Other than an occasional empty cattle truck hurtling by in the opposite direction, Whelan encountered very little traffic as he rolled along at 130 kilometers per hour. In less than forty minutes, he had passed the cutoff to Churchill's Head. As he crossed the seasonally dry Morphett Creek, two and a half klicks farther, his hunger pangs sharpened. It had been several hours since breakfast in Darwin.

A little more than twelve klicks up the highway, he saw a sign for Banka Banka Station and slowed down. The name reminded him of something his father had said many years earlier, when the family had first immigrated to the United States from Ireland. Looking at a map of their new homeland, his father saw the town of Walla Walla, Washington. "Must have liked the town so much, they decided to name it twice," he'd said. It was a few years before Whelan was old enough to realize his dad had been kidding. He smiled at the memory.

He turned left into the small, developed area, passing between two ancient rusted automobile hulks that bracketed the red gravel entrance like outsized sentries. Levell's briefers had told him that the station had been the first operational pastoral lease in the region. It consisted of several scattered buildings in addition to an adjoining campground. One of the buildings, the original mud brick homestead, was a single-story, three-room rectangular building with a pitched, corrugated metal roof and concrete floors. A veranda surrounded it. One of the rooms was a bar offering food service. And cold beer. Whelan headed for it.

The interior was dark and dank and had a musty smell, as though fresh air was forbidden. The temperature in the bar was warm but not uncomfortable. The thick mud brick walls had an insulating effect against the hellish temperatures outside.

There were only a few other people in the bar. They looked to Whelan like they were just passing through. There was a young couple sitting at a table. The girl wore a faded baggy shift and tattered sandals. The guy was short and thin with a sallow complexion, ragged cutoffs, and a T-shirt that was at least a size too large. Whelan figured them for college kids, experimenting with roughing it. Two suntanned young guys were at the bar. He pegged them for surfers, drifting from one coast to the other, seeking the perfect wave. Whelan took a seat at a table, the mud brick wall at his back and an open view of the rest of the room before him. *Dog instinct.*

An older man with a bad leg limped over to his table and took his order. A minute or two later he returned with a Modus Operandi Former Tenant, Whelan's pleasant discovery from the previous evening. Whelan took a long, deep pull and was grateful the Aussies liked their beer cold, unlike their cousins the Brits. He was about to take another swig when he was distracted.

"Hey, babe," one of the surfers at the bar said to the girl. She was skinny and plain looking with pasty skin and unkempt reddish blonde hair. To Whelan, she looked like she was barely eighteen.

"What's a hot chick like you doin' in this fucking wilderness with that dweeb?" The surfer jutted his chin at the young man she was with. "How'd you like to spend some time with a real man?"

The man at the bar had an American accent. He was the taller of the two. Otherwise, they had the same look—lean, tanned bodies, and tousled, sun-bleached hair.

The girl tried to ignore them, but she and her boyfriend wore deer-in-the-headlights expressions. They started eating their sandwiches faster. Whelan glanced at the bartender who was passively observing the unfolding scene, clearly unwilling to get involved. Whelan assumed it was because of his age and infirmity.

The mouthy guy at the bar got off his stool and swaggered over to the couple. He placed one hand on the tabletop and the other on the girl's shoulder, angling his back toward her boyfriend. "Me and my buddy," he motioned with his head toward the other man at the bar, "haven't seen too many chicks in this fucking campground wilderness. We'd like to show you a really good time." He glanced at the boyfriend. "Something this little runt wouldn't know how to do."

"Hey, watch it!" the boyfriend said without much conviction. He also had an American accent. His voice sounded high-pitched and frightened. Whelan assumed he was. He had a nerdish look— thin, bony features, a receding hairline, and thick glasses. He reminded Whelan of one of the characters on *The Big Bang Theory*. *Probably smart, but hardly physical.*

The surfer turned to the boyfriend and grabbed the front of his T-shirt, yanking him out of his chair. "Yeah? Watch it or what?"

The smaller man stuttered. "Look, I...we don't want any trouble. We were just leaving anyway." He gave the girl a pleading look.

She stood up and said, "Let him go! Why don't you pick on someone your own size!" She, too, had an American accent.

"Ain't anyone in here *my* size," the surfer said with a sneer and grabbed his crotch for emphasis. He glanced quickly at Whelan as if to caution him against getting involved. Satisfied, he shoved the boyfriend, sending him stumbling backward. The smaller man fell awkwardly onto the hard concrete floor and made no effort to get up. Then the surfer pulled the girl in against his body. "You feel that, babe? Why don't you and me and Jason here," he again nodded toward the other man at the bar, "go back to our tent and party?"

The girl struggled to get away, banging her small fists against his chest.

The man laughed. "If you fuck like you fight, this could be one to remember."

Whelan didn't want to jeopardize his mission, but he had seen more than enough. He glanced at the bartender. The old man was frozen in place. Whelan slowly stood up. When he did, the other surfer at the bar slid off his stool and started walking toward his friend and the girl.

The troublemaker saw Whelan coming toward him and said, "Do you really want an ass-kickin' that bad?" He released the girl, threw a quick glance at his buddy, and stepped toward the advancing Irishman. To the girl, he said, "Don't go anywhere. Kickin' this guy's ass is just gonna warm me up for you, babe."

The bully was as tall as Whelan and had a lean, rangy build. Whelan estimated the man's body weight at around one eighty-five. Whelan was two hundred forty pounds with zero percent body fat. And the two surfers were Norms. He wasn't.

"You look like you spent some time in the gym," the bully conceded. "But there's two of us and only one of you."

"Stop whining about being outnumbered," Whelan said. The words came out in a low growl, like a wolf just before it attacks its prey.

The bully had stopped and was facing Whelan from about three feet away. His buddy moved in a circular pattern, trying to get behind Whelan. The Irishman knew where the other man was by watching the bully's eyes and body language. When the man's eyes focused fully on Whelan and a ripple of motion began in his lower torso, Whelan knew a kick or punch was about to be launched. In his years of training in hand-to-hand combat, he had learned early on that all motion begins near the navel. Once the opponent's arm or leg begins to move, it can be too late to defend yourself.

Whelan's right hand moved so fast it had the bully's throat locked in an unbreakable grip before the man could react. The Irishman tightened his grip, and the bully's mouth twisted into a grotesque shape. His eyes appeared ready to burst from their sockets. Whelan spun around and slung him at the other man, sending them both sprawling like ten-pins. *A perfect strike.* He did it with such quickness that those watching weren't sure how he'd done it.

The bully was sprawled on the concrete, both hands around his throat, struggling to breathe. The other surfer shook his head to clear it and awkwardly scrambled to his feet. He started backpedaling in an effort to keep distance between himself and Whelan. With the exception of a half dozen or so individuals on the planet, there was no way anyone would be able to do that. Whelan was on him like a cheetah on an eland, grabbing the man's shirt in one fist and backhanding him with the other. He dropped the now-unconscious surfer on the floor next to his gasping friend.

Whelan shot a glance at the bartender. The old man stood stock-still, his eyes at their widest. His mouth too. The Irishman looked at the girl. Her expression said her brain was working overtime, trying to process what had happened. Whelan walked over to her boyfriend who was still sitting on the floor. He gently lifted him to his feet. "You okay?"

The young man nodded, not sure what to say.

"I'm sorry for your inconvenience," Whelan said to the couple. "Sit back down and finish your meals. No one's going to bother you."

Simultaneously, the two shook their heads, grabbing each other's hand, and took off for the entrance. They never looked back.

Whelan walked over to the bar. "What do I owe you for the beer?"

The old man stared at him before stammering, "No...nothin' mate. Nothin'."

Whelan laid twenty dollars Australian on the bar and turned to leave. He grabbed both of the troublemakers by the collars of their shirts and began dragging them toward the door. "I'll haul out the trash on my way."

As he approached the door, the bartender said, "Wait."

Whelan turned around.

"The way you move, mate, what you just done. I only seen one other bloke who was like that. An Aussie." He pronounced it "Oz-zee."

Whelan's interest piqued. "Was he from around here?"

"I can't say, mate. But I heard he works on a station north of here. Helen Springs. Stay on the Track; it will take you close."

"Would his name be Liam Stone?"

"Yeah, mate. That's him. Liam Stone."

CHAPTER 7

HELEN SPRINGS, NORTHERN TERRITORY, AUSTRALIA

It was another forty-five klicks from Banka Banka Station to the turn-off from Highway 87 that led to the headquarters for Helen Springs Station. The landscape bored Whelan. It was mostly flat, with reddish-brown soil covered by patches of tough-looking grasses and the sporadic stunted acacia tree. Occasionally, he saw a dirt road branching off into the trackless Outback. Few of them were graded. From the highway, he saw no signs of human habitation as the roads disappeared into the arid, broiling landscape. From time to time, the highway bridged gullies. Whelan noticed that most were drying up, now that the rainy season had ended. Along the gullies, the ubiquitous acacias gave way to River Red gum trees, a type of eucalyptus native to Australia.

Though the barren wasteland made it seem longer, the drive from Banka Banka Station took only twenty minutes. Whelan crested a small rise. On the gentle descent, through the heat shimmers rising off the pavement, he saw a dirt road running east off of 87. A small sign announced Helen Springs Station. Whelan turned right. The Outlander's tires began making a crunching sound as the car left the paved highway and hit the road made of reddish-brown gravel. Unlike most of the side roads he'd passed earlier, this one was graded.

The road wound in an easterly, and then a northerly direction. After about four klicks, Whelan drove up to the station's homestead, the center of operations on a cattle station where the manager or property owner usually lived. Helen Springs was a compact cluster of sturdy-looking buildings with blindingly white roofs. Its landscaping gave it the appearance of an oasis in the middle of an otherwise inhospitable world. A scattering of cottages provided quarters for the employees. There were other structures, too, including storage sheds, a mechanic's workshop, school facilities, and a small general store. The improvements were clustered along the southerly side of a gully that, in places, still had water in it.

On instinct, Whelan turned to the left and followed a road that skirted the complex of buildings. It passed a large industrial building and crossed both forks of the gully, ultimately terminating at an area with huge cattle pens.

Helen Springs was a breeding property that ran on average fifty thousand Brahman and Charbray cattle, a crossbreed of Charolais and Brahman that were better able to withstand the heat, humidity, and cattle ticks in Australia's Top End. The Helen Springs station covered over 5 thousand square kilometers, about 1.25 million acres. Its substation, Brunchilly, was even larger. The properties were part of Kidman Holdings, the eighth largest landowner in the world and the largest private landholder in Australia with about 24 million acres of land.

The cattle pens were empty, but eight or nine stockmen—"cowboys" in America—and jackaroos—their apprentices—were repairing the cattle pens in preparation for the thousands of head of cattle the drovers would bring in once the mustering season began in a few weeks. The workers seemed oblivious to the blistering heat and the swirling clouds of red dust that caked their sweaty bodies like mud. Most of them were shirtless, wearing only denim cutoffs, boots, and wide-brim straw cowboy hats.

All of the men were lean and wiry. Except for one. The man who had to be Liam Stone stood out from the others. He was bigger. A lot bigger. His sweat-soaked, mud-caked body looked like it belonged to an all-pro middle linebacker/gym rat. For Whelan, it was almost like looking into a mirror and watching his own body toiling away in the rugged Outback conditions. He parked the truck in the shade of a metal building and got out.

One of the jackaroos took off his hat and swiped it at the ever-present flies. The gesture was known as the Aussie salute. Looking up, he saw Whelan approaching and said, "We got a blow in."

The others paused and stared at Whelan as he walked over to the big man. Like Whelan and the other Dogs, Stone's eyes were the color of Arctic blue ice. Whelan said, "Liam Stone?"

"Who's askin', mate?" Stone appeared to be completely relaxed, as if the concept of threat was inconceivable.

Stone and Whelan were almost identical in size and build. They were each a shade over six feet two. Each was a thick-muscled two hundred and forty-something pounds. "My name's Whelan."

"You're a Yank."

"Irish."

"Yeah? Where's the bloody brogue? You sound like a Yank."

Whelan smiled and slid easily into the Irish-accented English he spoke at home in Dingle. "Raised in America because of circumstances, but Irish by the grace of God."

A faint smile broke across Stone's rugged features. "My oldies were born in Ireland," he said in reference to his parents. Then the smile faded, and he said, "What brings you to the Back of Beyond, mate?"

"I came to talk to you about a job."

"We got all the men we need."

"No, I'm here to talk about a different job *for you*."

Stone shrugged. "I'm makin' a quid here, mate."

"I don't know what you're being paid, but, if what I'm offering works out, you'll earn more money than you ever dreamed of."

One of the other men spoke up. "The whacker sounds like a big talkin' seppo, Liam. Kick his arse, and send him back to where he come from."

"Do you know what a 'seppo' is?" Stone said. He gave Whelan a challenging stare.

"No."

"It's short for septic tank. It's what some Aussies call Yanks."

Whelan studied the crew of Aussies. He hadn't come all this way to get suckered into a fight. "Instead of us trying to kick each other's ass—that probably wouldn't end well for either of us—let's have a test of physical skills. I think the outcome might surprise you."

Stone looked at him suspiciously. "Physical skills? Wha'dya have in mind, mate?"

"Running, jumping, lifting something heavy, arm wrestling. Think of it as a qualifications test for the job I mentioned."

Stone smiled. "Would you be willing to put a few quid on the outcome?"

Now it was Whelan who smiled. "Why not." He took a hundred dollars Australian from a pocket and held it up.

Stone took it and matched it with a hundred of his own. He handed the money to a jackeroo standing next to him.

"All right then, let's give it a burl."

The other men had gathered around Whelan and Stone and began to verbally encourage their mate.

"Kick his bloody arse, Stoney!"

"His Green Phantom will be payin' for the piss and plonk while we rage on all night!" The comment was a reference to the portrait of Dame Nellie Melba on the one-hundred-dollar note.

Whelan pointed to a stack of fence posts about one hundred meters away. "Have one of your mates give the signal, and we'll race to that pile over there."

Stone nodded at the man holding the money and said, "Banjo, you give a shout when we're both ready." He looked over at Whelan who was wearing cargo shorts, a polo shirt, and a pair of Brooks Glycerin running shoes.

The man called Banjo drew a ragged line in the reddish dirt with the toe of his boot and said, "Line up here, blokes."

Stone looked over at Whelan. "Kiss your quid g'bye, mate. No one's ever run as fast as me. No one."

Whelan smiled and nodded. He crouched slightly while Stone remained erect and at ease.

"All right, mates. When I give the signal, you run your bloody arses off." Banjo looked at the two runners and shouted, "Go!"

Both men were in full stride within two steps. They were shoulder to shoulder for the first sixty meters. Whelan, though, had some advantages. One of them was the element of surprise. Stone had no idea that anyone shared his genetic construct. Whelan's other edge was his disciplined daily training routine. Stone got a rugged workout on the cattle station almost every day, but it wasn't the same. Ultimately, Whelan was ahead by a stride when he passed the pile of fence posts. He slowed to a walk and went over to where Stone was standing. Both men were breathing heavily.

"Crikey, mate, I never met a bloke faster than me. Who the fuck *are* you?"

"The one who wasn't running in boots. But we'll talk about that later over a beer. Or as you and your mates might say, 'a pint of piss.'"

"You won the first round. What's next?"

Whelan pointed to a metal shed. Its flat roof was about six feet above the ground. "We'll see who can jump onto the roof of that shed."

The two men walked over to the small outbuilding, followed by the other men who were silent, apparently stunned that the unthinkable had happened. Someone had beaten the fastest man they'd ever seen.

Whelan took three quick steps and leaped. He landed on the edge of the roof, turned, and easily jumped back to the ground.

"I've got you now, Irishman. I can do that with only two steps." And he did, but caught the heel of his left boot on the edge of the corrugated metal roof and nearly tripped. He steadied himself and looked down at the others below. "We're even now, one and one. What's next?"

Whelan motioned toward the large industrial building he'd passed on the way in. It housed a mechanic's workshop. He led the others over to the building and looked around inside. Spotting a sturdy-looking wooden bench, he carried it outside. Over the years, a lot of debris—truck and auto parts, obsolete machinery, and other unidentifiable junk had accumulated in and around the building. Whelan set the bench next to a rusting axle of some type. From the size of it, he judged it to be from some long-gone truck. It still had the old tires on each end. He squatted, grabbed one end of it, and stood up, getting a feel for its weight. He set it back down and said, "That feels like about 135 kilos, give or take. Three hundred pounds American."

Stone eyed the axle and the bench. "You thinking about a weightlifting contest?"

"Yeah. Each of us does it once. The point isn't to see who can do the most reps, just to see if we each can bench it once. Given the weight and the challenge of balancing it, I'm guessing none of these other guys can do it." Whelan slid onto the bench on his back. "Have some of your guys hand it up to me."

Stone pointed at two men. "Jarrah, Ned, get the other end." He bent down and grabbed one end himself. Together they positioned the axle over Whelan.

The Irishman spread his hands out just beyond shoulder width and firmly gripped the awkward object. "I've got it."

Stone moved around behind Whelan to spot him, in case he had trouble handling the heavy axle. He watched Whelan slowly lower it to his chest and hold it there for a three count before easily pushing it back to full extension. The men watching began murmuring among themselves. How was it possible that there was *another* person as strong and fast as Liam Stone?

When Stone, with Jarrah and Ned, had control of the weight, Whelan slid off the bench, came around, and took the end Stone had been holding. Stone, in turn, stretched out on the bench reached up for the axle. When he nodded, the others released it. He repeated the motion exactly as Whelan had. When finished, he stood up and said, "So where are we in this contest of yours, mate?"

"I won one, you won one, and the third ended in a draw, so we're even."

Stone scowled. "A bloody draw. I hate draws."

"I know what you mean," Whelan said. "A famous American football coach named Vince Lombardi once said, 'A tie is like kissing your sister.'"

Stone thought about that for a moment or two then agreed. "That's fair dinkum. So how do we settle this?"

"I saw a table in the building where we found the bench. It looks like what the Yanks call 'a picnic table.' I assume you guys eat lunch there."

They walked back inside the workshop building. It was just a corrugated metal roof and open on all sides, but it was marginally cooler under it. Whelan sat down at the table and motioned for Stone to sit opposite him. He put his elbow on the table, forearm up, hand open—the universal invitation to arm wrestle. Stone did the same and the two men locked grips.

Banjo yelled, "Start!"

Whelan, again, had Stone at a disadvantage. Undoubtedly, the Aussie had never been challenged by anyone of his kind. He probably had dealt with Norms all his life, some of them strong men, but none like him. Whelan, on the other hand, had trained for years with the other Dogs. He had beaten Almeida, Kirkland, and Stensen without fail. He and Thomas were about equally matched. He had never beaten Larsen. No one had. Because of these experiences, he knew what to expect. For several minutes, the men's locked hands wobbled back and forth; neither of them seemed able to seize the advantage.

Whelan looked at Stone. He saw the shocked expression on the Aussie's face. This must have been the first time the man had ever been seriously challenged. Stone threw everything he had into trying to move Whelan's arm. His face slowly turned beet red. Rivulets of sweat flowed down it, forming a small puddle on the tabletop. Nothing he did seemed to work. And then Whelan began to prevail. Slowly, inexorably, he forced the Aussie's arm downward. Stone's mates were screaming at him to win. It took a while, but eventually, Whelan forced the man's knuckles to touch the scarred tabletop. It was over. The Aussies were speechless.

Stone rubbed his shoulder and grimaced. "Fuck, mate, like I said, who the hell *are* you?"

Whelan said, "Over a beer, remember?"

Stone looked at the others. "Is it quittin' time yet?"

There was a chorus of yeses.

He looked at Whelan. "You got a first name, mate?"

"Brendan."

"All right, Brendan. Me and the lads will get cleaned up, and then we'll make a run up the Track to Renner. You and me have some talking to do, so I'll ride with you. The others can take one of the *ferals*." The reference was *Strine,* Australian slang for a dirty, beat-up ute or utility vehicle. The large cattle stations usually had a number of them.

CHAPTER 8

RENNER SPRINGS, NORTHERN TERRITORY, AUSTRALIA

RENNER SPRINGS WAS LITTLE MORE than a wide spot in Highway 87, about eighteen klicks north of the entrance to Helen Springs Station. The drive took about fifteen minutes and gave Whelan an opportunity to learn more about his passenger. He wasn't surprised to learn that Stone's life had been similar to his own and those of the other Dogs. He had possessed their same preternatural gifts since birth. And it had affected him the same way it had all of them.

As a youngster, he'd been delighted to discover that he was stronger, faster, and smarter than any of his contemporaries. But he soon learned that the gift was really a curse. Humans fear what they don't understand, and he quickly became a pariah. Eventually, he made the same behavioral adjustments Whelan and the others had. He became something of a loner and learned to perform, physically and intellectually, at a level that put him in the top-tier in sports and at school but not above it. It was an immensely frustrating experience, but a necessary adjustment if he didn't want to be treated like a sideshow freak.

He'd had opportunities to play soccer and Australian Rules football professionally but viewed them as proverbial catch-22 situations—with superstar status, he'd be exposed as a mutant, an aberration, or he'd continue to chafe at the irritation of suppressing his abilities.

Instead, he joined the military, known as the Australian Defense Force or ADF. For a while, he believed he'd found a home. He quickly caught the attention of his superiors and was recruited by the Special Air Service Regiment, or SASR, an elite special operations force of the Australian Army. Eventually, he'd been persuaded to apply for admission to the Tactical Assault Group, the cream of Aussie Special Forces. The selection process was considered the most demanding of any in the Australian Army. Stone sailed through the rigorous qualifications tests with scores never before seen. He ended up a member of TAG West, Australia's version of the Navy SEALs. Its primary areas of responsibility included offshore recovery operations, such as ship-boarding, as well as international or overseas incidents.

But signing up for TAG West had been a mistake on Stone's part. His colleagues were the very best fighters in the ADF, but he was light years better than any of them. The result was a repeat of his earlier experiences. He was regarded with fear and labeled a freak. Few wanted to associate with him. When his tour was up, he left the military and returned to civilian life an angry man. He spent the first year or so boozing and brawling, with a few short stretches in jail for assault and disorderly conduct. Eventually, he decided to lose himself in the vast, lonely Outback, which he referred to as the Back of Beyond. The hard-living stockmen and jackaroos accepted him without judgment. This time he had finally found a home.

REFERRED TO AS A "ROADHOUSE," Renner Springs was a combination truck stop, motel, campground, general store, and restaurant and bar. A small sign out front announced it as "The Renner Springs Desert Hotel/Motel." There were gas pumps in front and a pond out back with a windmill to pump water from the deep bore, or artesian well. It was used to fill what was billed as a "lagoon," complete with geese swimming in it. Here the acacia trees were profuse and healthier looking.

A half-dozen Aborigines squatted in the shade under a roof overhang near the general store. Next door to it was a small wood-paneled restaurant with a handful of four-tops. Adjoining it was a larger room that housed the bar. Besides the ubiquitous TV and pool table, there was a profusion of ball caps dangling from the ceiling. To the right, a colorful jukebox was wedged between the back wall and a narrow hallway that led to the restrooms. The shelves behind the bar were lined with bottles of liquor and bracketed a large commercial cooler crammed with cold beer.

The place wasn't crowded at that early hour on a Tuesday night, but Stone assured Whelan it soon would be. And that things could get rough. Stone's mates from the station—Ned, Banjo, Clancy, Jarrah, Lawson, Darwin, Murray, and Archie were already there. Jarrah waved the two newcomers over to the bar. They sat down on a couple of backless stools.

"Thank God Aussies don't drink that warm bat piss like the Brits," Whelan said.

"We don't do much of anything like them pommy bastards," Jarrah said with obvious contempt.

Stone signaled a young woman behind the bar and ordered two pints of Abbotsford Invalid Stout.

It was inky black with a foamy head. Whelan tasted it. Even though he was an IPA man, it was passing good for a stout. But not as good as Guinness. He was, after all, an Irishman. He motioned to

Stone to follow him to a table in a corner of the barroom. Time to get down to the business at hand.

Once seated, he read Stone into the SAS and the Dogs: their history, their upcoming operation, and other pertinent data. Stone's interest was obvious to Whelan. The thing that seemed to interest him most was the existence of others like him. Whelan couldn't tell for sure, but he sensed a strong feeling of relief on the Aussie's part. By the end of their third round, Stone had agreed to consider coming to America to check out the opportunity Whelan was offering. But the Irishman made it clear that it wasn't a guarantee. Stone would have to prove a good fit first. But from what Whelan had seen and heard so far, he was confident it was just a matter of time.

They wrapped up the conversation and walked back to the bar, now crowded two deep. Ned and Banjo each were occupying stools, so Stone and Whelan wedged in behind them and ordered another round.

"I'd like to have a naughty with the sheila," Banjo said, nodding in the direction of the girl who was tending bar.

"You been crackin' on her for months, mate. You ain't got a Buckley's with her," Ned said.

"What about you, mate? You got someone back home in Ireland?" Stone said to Whelan.

"Yeah," Whelan said, still speaking with an Irish brogue. "I have a wife and two sons."

Someone behind Whelan pushed him. Hard. He turned around and saw a short, thickly built man in leathers scowling at him. The man was surrounded by an assortment of similarly dressed men.

"Bikies," Stone said, using the Australian term for members of motorcycle gangs.

"I don't want no blue with you, mate," the man said to Stone. The fear in his eyes said he knew who Stone was. He turned back to Whelan. "It's this spud nigger. I hate the fuckin' Irish."

"It's worse than that," Stone said, and winked at Whelan. "The bloke's a bloody Yank as well."

"A seppo? I knew I smelled shit when I come in." He turned and smirked at the men behind him.

"Let's give the bastard a good floggin', Andy," one of the men said. It was followed by a chorus of yeahs, "Kick 'is bloody mickey arse," and "give 'em a bunch of fives."

The people around Whelan scurried to get away from him. Except Stone.

Andy eyed him nervously. "This bloke with you, Stoney?"

"Never saw him before today. No worries, mate, just think of me as an interested spectator."

That seemed to stoke Andy's aggressiveness. He grabbed the front of Whelan's polo shirt with both hands. With speed that only Stone could have matched, Whelan reached under Andy's arms and grabbed the sleeves of his leather jacket near the armpits. He bent slightly at the waist as he yanked the man forward. The bikie's face slammed into the top of Whelan's forehead. The blow destroyed Andy's less than handsome features and snapped his neck backward with such force that he blacked out. Whelan dropped the inert mass to the floor, blood flowing from what was left of Andy's face.

The other nine men with Andy charged Whelan en masse. Stone stepped forward with Whelan. In less than sixty seconds, all the bikies were unconscious, some closer to death than others. Whelan and Stone dragged the unconscious men outside and, for good measure, kicked over their bikes. Then they tossed the bodies on top of their machines and returned to the bar.

"Now that's a right nice pie, mate. Hot metal for a crust and a bunch of fuckin' near cactus dills for the toppin'."

"I thought you were gonna sit this one out," Whelan said.

"I don't always tell the truth," Stone said with a grin. "Besides, those blokes had you bailed up."

"Bailed up?"

"Cornered. You're my new cobber, but I couldn't let you have all the fun with those clackers."

Banjo met Whelan and Stone at the entrance to the bar and handed each a fresh beer. He laughed and said, "Those whackas come a gutser."

"Fuckin' bushrangers, the lot of 'em," Jarrah said.

Clancy said, "A bunch of fuckin' hoons."

Whelan shook his head. "And some people think the Irish are hard to understand. I'm not sure I caught half of what you lads said."

"Stick around, mate. We'll have you speakin' Strine like a native," Stone said.

Whelan glanced at his watch. "Like to, but I need to get going; I've got an early morning flight out of Tennant Creek." He tossed back the beer and shook hands with the crew from Helen Springs.

Stone walked him out to the Mitsubishi. "I was stuffed, mate, to learn there's another bloke like me."

"More than one. And I suspect you'll fit right in."

"I dunno. I make a good quid here, and I'm not treated like a bloody piker, a fuckin' freak of nature." Stone was silent before adding, "But I admit, I'm intrigued. It's not London to a brick, but I'll give it a dinkum consideration."

Whelan grinned. "I think you just said you'd think it over."

With a nod, Stone said, "I will. Give me a week. Either way, I'll text you."

The two men shook hands, and Whelan climbed into the Outlander. He pulled back onto 87 heading south toward Tennant Creek. Off to his right the sunset was magnificent. *An omen of a bright tomorrow?*

CHAPTER 9

THE LODGE

ON A COUPLE OF PREVIOUS OCCASIONS, Mitch Christie had been in the wine cellar, which was hidden beneath the library. The entire setup at the Lodge impressed him, but this so-called "War Room" topped everything. Its state-of-the-art security against every form of eavesdropping, electronic and otherwise, was amazing. Perfect acoustics, no intrusion of sounds from beyond its walls. No musty smell, just clean, fresh seventy-two-degree air circulating throughout. No one other than the Mueller brothers could have created it or the Lodge, or the entire SAS operation for that matter. Their almost unfathomable wealth, coupled with their control of many of the top technology, electronics, and weapons research and development companies on the planet, put them in a unique position to fund and sponsor a shadow government—the Society of Adam Smith. Christie was struck by the irony. The biggest customer for the Muellers' products and R&D efforts was the U.S. government. The very entity that the SAS was working to reform. The big question was whether it was still possible, at this stage, to reverse the government's destructive behavior.

Christie glanced around at the others gathered in the War Room. In addition to Levell, seated as usual at the midpoint of the conference table, there was Cabot Mather, the Assistant Under-Secretary of State for Near Eastern Affairs. On his left, at one of the power positions at the end of the table was Lieutenant General Ricardo Martinez, Deputy Commander of United States Special Operations Command (USSOCOM). To his left was Clyde Seaton, Deputy Director of the CIA's Directorate of Operations, formerly known as the National Clandestine Service. Harriman Floyd, head of the NSA's Directorate Q, which was responsible for security and counterintelligence, was seated next to him, across from Levell. Also in attendance was long-time SAS member General Martin van Vliet, Vice Chair of the Joint Chiefs. As always, one of the Mueller brothers was present. Tonight, it was the middle brother, Hermann. Earlier in the evening, Christie had heard that Alfred, the oldest of the Muellers at eighty-five, was in poor health. He wondered what the fate of SAS would be once the Muellers had passed from the scene. *All the more reason to move as expeditiously as possible.*

Christie's thoughts were interrupted as Levell cleared his throat and, in his Eastwood-like rasp, said, "Let's get to work. First up, the Middle East." He looked at the man from State and said, "Mather, any progress in getting the Gulf Arabs to coalesce into an effective force?"

All eyes turned to Cabot Mather. He stared at some papers in his hand, shuffled them, and stared some more.

"Dammit, Mather, speak up or I'll do it for you," the CIA's Seaton said. "And you and your cronies at State won't like the way I tell it."

"Gentlemen," Hermann Mueller said, "this nation is adrift in a sea of turmoil. It won't help matters if we're at each other's throats."

"Do you have anything or not?" Levell said.

"Well…yes, but it isn't very promising."

"When is it ever?" Seaton said.

Levell motioned impatiently for Mather to continue.

"The Sunnis in the Gulf States are talking a good game. They know the extremist movements in their countries are dedicated to overthrowing the existing regimes, but—"

Van Vliet finished the sentence for Mather. "They're trying to look formidable to the Holy Army of the Caliphate and the other terrorist groups. But they don't have the support of their own people necessary to take effective military action."

Levell looked at the man from State and said, "So what you're saying is after years of cajoling, begging, bribing…hell, threatening the Saudis, Emiratis, Jordanians, Egyptians, and Qataris, you haven't got shit to show for it."

Mather stared at his sheaf of papers and continued to shuffle them nervously.

"Let's not get on Cabot's ass too hard," Martinez said. "We all know State isn't calling the shots. Those directives come straight from the Oval Office."

Levell gave an angry snort. "I know where the problems originate. This sonofabitching administration has been soft on Marxism and radical Islam since Day One. But, hopefully, the election next month will change that." He looked at Martinez. "Since you brought it up, tell us what the status is of our Special Ops efforts to train, equip, and marshal an effective fighting force among the Sunnis. Is *any* progress being made?"

Martinez suppressed a bitter laugh and shook his head. "Again, it's the White House. It won't allow us to commit a sufficient force to accomplish anything. It's all show and no go. Making the public think the administration is working in their best interests."

"And our efforts to supply and equip one of our top allies in the Middle East, the Kurds?"

"Same old shit. Everything the Peshmerga needs has to go through Baghdad. Damn little ever reaches the Kurds. The fucking Iraqis are selling most of it out the backdoor to the highest bidders."

Levell turned to Mather. "I'm sure the administration is making no effort to get the Turks off the Kurds' asses."

Mather's jowly face quivered like Jell-O as he wagged his head back and forth vigorously.

"Hell," Levell said, "we've got two decent indigenous fighting forces in the theater, the Israelis and the Peshmerga, and the administration has thrown both of them under the bus. Meanwhile, HAC grows their fucking caliphate ever stronger."

Hermann Mueller said, "And grows its forces in the United States, as well."

The room was quiet for a few moments. Then the NSA's Harriman Floyd said, "What about your personal efforts, Cliff, to forge a coalition of forces in the Middle East?"

"I've met with key insiders from the Sunni states, as well as Egypt and Turkey, and I trust my contacts...to an extent, though ultimately they answer to higher-ups."

"So, no progress," Floyd said.

Levell nodded. "Not so far."

Van Vliet said, "Cliff, what about this legendary band of hunter-killers you've used in the past?"

"The Sleeping Dogs. What about them?"

"From everything I've heard, they're everyone's worst nightmare. Could they be inserted into the caliphate to take out its leaders?"

"That's a suicide mission. They deserve better than that." Levell motioned to Christie. "Tell them the real reason why we can't spare the Dogs at this time."

"Defense of the Homeland."

Van Vliet shook his head. "Knocking out HAC *is* an act in defense of the Homeland."

"It's too late to defend against radical Islam on foreign soil."

The room was quiet for a couple of beats. The silence was broken when several people spoke at once. Christie raised his hand until everyone quieted down. "The evidence is indisputable. There's going to be a major strike on our soil, something far bigger than 9/11."

"When?" Floyd and Seaton said simultaneously.

"We don't know the exact date and time yet, but very soon."

"Why doesn't the Agency have that information?" Seaton said.

"Or us?" NSA's Floyd said, and turned to stare at Christie. "What the hell have you Bureau weenies been holding out on us? We're all supposed to be on the same team."

"All right, girls, calm down," Levell rasped. "We all know how things work in this current administration. Would you really want them to know what we know?" He paused for effect. "Of course not. None of your agencies, and that includes the military, could sit on this or act unilaterally. Once the White House knew you knew, it might well alert the enemy, and the plans would change. We might not be onto these towelhead bastards next time. And if word of this got out, can you imagine the extent of the panic it would cause? The country would freeze up."

"So, what *is* being done?" van Vliet said.

"That's where those hunter-killers you mentioned come into play. We're preparing to use them to throw a monkey wrench into the jihadists' plans. At least until after the election and a new president is sworn in."

Hermann Mueller said, "Even that might not help."

CHAPTER 10

CLEVELAND, TENNESSEE

LIEUTENANT BARNEY BIGGS of the Bradley County Sheriff's Office laid aside the reports he'd been reading from the previous night's patrol activities and stretched. He reached over, grabbed a soft pack of Camel regulars and shook one out on his desk. Lighting it, he took a deep drag and slowly exhaled the smoke toward the ceiling in a long stream. He scratched lazily at the large belly that hung over his well-polished leather belt. It reminded him that his wife had been nagging him to lose some weight. *Easy for her to say. She's still got the God-awful gorgeous body of a teenager. And why not? She's more than fifteen years younger than me. And she goes to her damn gym every day while I work to bring home the bacon. Hell, a man shouldn't be expected to keep the same body he had as a high school jock. And a grown man needs food—lots of it—to carry him through the day.* He took another long pull on the Camel.

Biggs had started with the SO right after the military and, over the past twenty-plus years, had worked his way up the ladder from patrolman to assistant director of administrative services. With the members of the command staff close to retirement, he had no reason to doubt that he would make captain before he reached retirement age. But he had an uneasy feeling about his wife, Janeen. She was still hot to trot while he was tired most of the time and liked spending most nights drinking beer and watching TV. Was Janeen thinking about straying? Or maybe she already had. There were those young hard-bodies hanging around the gym. He'd seen the way they looked at Janeen in her painted-on leotards. *Well, those ol' boys better keep their distance. I find out there's something going on, I'll visit them late one night with a blanket and a length of lead pipe.*

His intercom buzzed, interrupting his thoughts. He leaned over, pressed the button, and said, "Biggs."

"Hey, Barney." It was the sheriff. "I got some guy on the phone, says he's with the fuckin' Bureau. Wants to know about one of those guys we busted for robbin' the Ocoee Valley Community Bank."

"Yeah? What's he wanna know?"

"I don't fuckin' *know*. I don't have time to talk to him. I want you to see to whatever it is he wants." The sheriff's voice sounded impatient.

"Yeah, sure. I'll take care of it."

"And try not to be too fuckin' helpful. Those Bureau assholes never are."

Biggs stubbed out his cigarette in an ashtray that overflowed with stale butts. He buzzed the main switchboard and said, "You got some FBI guy on hold?"

"Yessir."

"Put 'em through to me." A moment later his phone rang, and he picked up the receiver. "This is Lieutenant Biggs."

"Lieutenant, I'm Special Agent Dunleavy with the Federal Bureau of Investigation. We're looking into some criminal activity that may involve one of your prisoners. I wonder if you could spare me a couple of minutes?"

"Yeah, maybe. But no more'n a couple. I got a pile of work on my desk." He hoped he sounded brusque, disinterested, maybe even rude. *Fuckin' Bureau. Always take, take, take. Never much give.*

"I understand. I'll be brief."

"So, which prisoner is it?"

"His name is Rafael J. Almeida. I believe he's being held on multiple counts, including accessory to crime, specifically bank robbery."

"Yeah, caught him dead to rights. What about him?"

"I'd like to speak with him. He may be able to provide some helpful information."

"When?"

"I'm in the area. I could be at the jail in a few minutes."

"Don't bother. He ain't here."

There was silence at the other end of the line as if the agent was processing information he hadn't expected. Finally, he said, "I don't understand. I thought he was being held for trial."

"He is," Biggs said dryly. "But perps don't get a free ride in Bradley County. He's earnin' his keep."

"What exactly does that mean?"

"He's on a road gang, cleanin' up the shit tourists and that ilk toss on our highways."

"Will he be doing that much longer?"

"Yeah, 'til he gets convicted and sent up."

"I mean much longer today."

"It's gonna be a while. We work 'em until sundown."

There was a pause at the agent's end and then, "I've got business in Atlanta later today. It would be easier for me if I could talk with him on site. Where's the road gang working?"

"Out Route 60, near Georgetown."

RAFE ALMEIDA SWATTED at the cloud of gnats swarming around his sweat-drenched face. He was hot, he was hungry, and he was pissed. The rip currents whipped up by the tractor-trailers zooming by on the highway buffeted him but didn't seem to faze the gnats. And then there were the kids in the family sedans and soccer-mom minivans. The young ones made faces at him and the other prisoners on the road gang. But it was the older kids, the teenagers driving their own cars, that really angered him. They yelled curses and insults, gave him the finger, and threw all kinds of shit at him. All he could do was trudge along, just off the paved area, swatting gnats, picking up debris, and sweating his ass off in the heavy, bright orange jumpsuit.

It wasn't fair. Bill, the asshole who'd actually robbed the bank, was back in the air-conditioned cellblock. His brother, a well-heeled stockbroker, had hired a decent lawyer for him. The guy had produced evidence of some kind that Bill was disabled because of some childhood accident. That was enough to keep him off the road gang. *Why couldn't I have had a rich relative who'd set me up in a life of luxury? My brothers are all losers, just like me. Shit, they're probably in jail somewhere too.*

He bent over and picked up a crushed beer can. There was a used, shriveled condom lying next to it. *Well, at least some sonofabitch had a good time.* He straightened up and dropped the can into the sack he was carrying. He left the condom where it was. Glancing furtively in both directions, he saw that each of the guards was bored and strolling idly with a shotgun in the crook of an arm. Periodically, each would look around to make sure all of the prisoners were present. Almeida was sure that, like him, the guards had someplace they'd rather be.

He wondered if he could find a way to escape. After all, he had those genetic gifts. He was fast. He was strong. He thought about it for a few moments. But the two guards each had a shotgun. *Hard to outrun that.* If he could find a way to overpower them, then catch a ride, that might work. *Catch a ride with a smoking hot chick. Better yet, a car full of smoking hot chicks. Stop at the nearest motel and repay their kindness with a group session they'd never forget.* He scuffed his foot at a stone. No, that wouldn't work. The cops would be on him in a flash. He'd never even get the first chick off, let alone the rest of them. *Shit, maybe I could find a tall cliff and throw myself off of it. Not much of this sorry life worth living.*

He heard the deep rumble of a powerful motorcycle and looked up. A BMW R 1200 GS was cruising slowly along the westbound lane toward Georgetown, a village three miles to the west. The driver was stocky. His face was hidden behind the dark full-face shield on his helmet. Still, there was something strangely familiar about him. The biker brought the BMW to a stop between the two guards who were about twenty yards apart. It sounded like he said something to them, but, with the face shield, it was hard to tell.

The guards looked at each other, and one of them nodded. The other guard removed his shotgun from the crook of his arm and let it hang, muzzle down, with his right hand wrapped around the stock, just behind the trigger guard. He strolled over toward the motorcyclist. When he was about six feet away, the biker's right hand darted inside his bomber jacket, whipped out a firearm and shot the guard. Before the other guard could react, the rider shot him too. For a moment, there was only silence and no motion. Then, except for Almeida, the group of prisoners exploded into action, running hell-bent for leather toward a forested area behind them.

Almeida had seen the kind of hand speed the rider had demonstrated in a very limited number of people—only the other members of the Sleeping Dogs. The rider stuffed the weapon in the waistband of his jeans and motioned to Almeida to climb on the back of the bike. As he did, the biker handed him a helmet with a full-face shield. Almeida had barely settled onto the seat when the rider gunned the throttle, and the bike spun a tight one-eighty and shot off back toward the direction from which it had come.

The driver weaving around the sparse traffic, covered a little over two miles at speeds approaching one hundred miles per hour. Almeida hung on for dear life. The bike suddenly slowed, and the driver made a right onto Rabbit Valley Road. It was a narrow, mostly flat two-lane farm road that wound through wooded areas mixed with small homesteads. About four miles later, the rider blew through the stop sign at the intersection with Bigsby Creek Road. A few hundred yards farther he slowed the bike and turned into an open field. A small helicopter was sitting in the middle, rotors slowly turning.

The biker motioned Almeida toward the chopper. After dumping the bike in a ditch, he ran to the bird and climbed in behind Almeida, signaling the pilot to take it up. Quickly aloft, the chopper flew southeasterly, heading across the Tennessee-Georgia state line. About ten miles into Georgia, the pilot descended to a small farm airstrip. He put the bird down next to a Cessna 172. As soon as the two passengers were out, the chopper lifted back off and angled away toward the west.

The cyclist, still wearing the full helmet with face shield, shoved Almeida toward the Cessna. There was a pilot inside, and the prop was slowly turning over. The two men had barely climbed aboard when the pilot shoved the throttle in, and the plane began bouncing across the field. In moments, they were airborne again. This time they were heading northeast. With a mild tailwind, the plane cruised at one hundred twenty-five miles per hour. They were aloft for a little more than five hours, crossing over North Carolina and into Virginia. It was a long, silent trip for Almeida. On the few occasions, he did try to strike up a conversation with the pilot and his rescuer, they ignored him.

At last the plane landed on a small strip not far from the

Potomac River in Tidewater Virginia. The biker pulled Almeida from the Cessna and hustled him to another small chopper. In less than five miles, it touched down on a helipad at their final destination. The Lodge. Once the chopper had departed, the biker removed his helmet and smiled mirthlessly at Almeida. The malevolence was accentuated by the man's eyes or, rather, the glowing red dots in their centers.

"Jesus, Stensen. I should have known. Who else could it have been."

"Nice to see you again, too, Rafe."

"Tell me, did you really have to kill the fucking guards?"

"Collateral damage." The red dots suddenly expanded like solar flares.

Almeida involuntarily took a step backward.

Stensen laughed. It sounded almost demonic to Almeida. "Come on, Rafe. It's not good to keep Levell waiting."

A FEW HOURS LATER, Almeida finished the first decent meal he'd had since before his incarceration and washed it down with several cold beers. He belched loudly and pushed himself away from the table in the Lodge's kitchen.

Levell, who had been sitting quietly across from him, said, "We really can't let you out of our sight, can we? We do and, sure as hell, you go and do something really stupid and get your ass in a world of trouble. What the fuck's the matter with you?"

Almeida's face assumed a pout. "What's the matter with me? What about that fucking psychopath Stensen? Did you know he shot two cops to death today?"

Levell laughed coldly. "Things aren't always what they seem, Almeida. Nick was using a weapon developed by one of the

Mueller brothers' munitions works. It looks and sounds like the real thing but is far more humanitarian. It fires a low-power projectile that injects a very fast-acting substance directly into the nervous system. It renders the victim unconscious almost instantly. But it doesn't kill them."

Almeida stared at Levell, trying to decide if the old man was putting him on. Finally, he said, "Whatever. He's still a fucking psychopath."

CHAPTER 11

ON THE BORDER IN NEW MEXICO

RAUL OJEDA WAS in the cab of his Border Patrol vehicle just inside the U.S. border, roughly seventeen kilometers—about ten and a half miles—west of Antelope Wells. It was in the shadow of the six-thousand-foot Whitewater Mountains; harsh empty country—stark and broiling during the day, frigid and sinister at night.

He put some drops in each eye, hoping to alleviate the stinging. Several hours of staring at the less-than-state-of-the-art monitor was taking its toll. And it wasn't just his eyes. The sheer boredom was almost palpable. His shift often lasted ten hours or more—ten hours of operating the sophisticated Forward Looking Infrared night-vision equipment, or FLIR.

Ojeda was using the PTZ-35x140 MS that was designed especially for Border Patrol applications. A powerful, multisensor, midrange, thermal imaging system, it featured two cameras. One had a wide-angle field-of-view. The other had a narrow field-of-view designed for midrange target recognition. It also had a daylight/low-light camera. By registering the difference between the temperature of the ground and the temperature of a human, the

PTZ-35x140 MS could detect objects the size of a person more than two kilometers distant. Its functionality was unaffected by total darkness, smoke, light fog, and the most adverse weather conditions. It worked particularly well in the desert, which cooled significantly at night. Human heat signatures showed up better as a result of the contrast. The system had been integrated with radar in what was called a "slew-to-cue" configuration. If an object were spotted by radar, the thermal imaging camera would automatically pan in that direction to reveal the nature of the blip on the screen. It was a major plus that the system had a low false alarm rate.

The significant drawback, however, was that the vehicle had to have its engine running in order to provide electrical power to run the system. As a result, the heat that built up in the cab was stifling. Ojeda took several gulps of water from the plastic gallon jug in the cab. He shook his head at the thought of the disconnect between the sophisticated FLIR and the rest of the equipment involved in the process. There was the monitor, of course. But there also was the truck, a plain vanilla, run-of-the-mill Ford F350. A simple crane-like device was mounted on its flatbed. The FLIR camera was attached to the top of the crane that could be raised to a height of twenty feet and panned and tilted to scan the border for smugglers, and worse.

It frustrated its operators that the camera's scope was limited to a strip about five hundred feet in width. The operator had to constantly pan and tilt the camera while, at the same time, he was listening to various frequencies on his radio in case other Customs and Border Patrol agents needed assistance elsewhere. *So here I sit*, he thought, *in the middle of a dark night, in the middle of a dark desert, probably surrounded by bogeys.*

He reached down on the seat beside him and felt the reassuring comfort of the H&K P2000, a Customs and Border Patrol issued .40-caliber pistol. In his position, CBP agents usually worked alone.

It was dangerous. The bad guys sometimes attacked agents out in the lonely desert wastelands. Some agents had even had their vehicles attacked with Molotov cocktails. As bad as getting killed was, there was something worse. The smugglers were mostly members of the worst Latino criminal gangs, particularly MS-13. Life was absolutely meaningless to them. If they captured a CBP agent, they would torture him or her until every last bit of information was disclosed, such as shift changes, radio frequencies, and the positions of some of the 13,000 or so seismic sensors buried along the border with Mexico.

Ojeda's thoughts were interrupted by a ping sound from the radar equipment.

He studied the blip on the radar screen while the thermal imaging camera automatically homed in on what was causing it. In moments, Ojeda saw the thermal images of more than a dozen humans. The complementary GPS system flashed the coordinates on his monitor. They were about a mile south of his position. As he panned the area, he saw the images of several more individuals. They were moving in his direction. And moving quickly.

Using his comm gear, Ojeda swiftly made contact with a CBP patrol, led that night by David Hidalgo. There were three other CBP agents with Hidalgo in a green and white Suburban, about halfway between Ojeda's position and the CBP station at Antelope Wells.

"Hidalgo here. Whatcha' got?"

"Looks like at least twenty, maybe more, AMMs." Adult Male Mexicans. Ojeda gave Hidalgo the GPS coordinates for the presumed illegals.

"I assume they're headed for the border."

"Yeah, right at me, as a matter of fact. Should I relocate?"

Hidalgo detected a trace of apprehension in Ojeda's voice. "No, we're on our way. ETA ten minutes."

"How many guys you got with you?"

"All told, there are four of us, plus a couple of county Mounties are coming in from the Hidalgo County SO.

"These guys are on foot, but they're moving pretty quickly." Now there was more than a trace of apprehension in Ojeda's voice.

"Can you tell if they're armed?"

"They're definitely carrying something, looks like backpacks and that kind of shit."

"Probably hauling drugs. Should be a nice bust."

"Could be a fucking shootout too."

"Hang tight. The cavalry's on the way." He clicked off and turned to the CBP agent sitting next to him in the passenger seat. "Raul sounds like he's scared shitless."

IN HIS BARELY SEVENTEEN YEARS, Turan Salam had never ventured more than fifty kilometers from his home in Wana, the summer headquarters of the South Waziristan Agency in Pakistan's Federally Administered Tribal Areas—FATA. Fully recovered from his wound suffered in the aborted attack at Tora Tiža, he now found himself half a world away. The journey had taken three months with all the stops, detours, and training sessions along the way.

First, he had traveled to the South American Tri-Border Area—TBA—also known as the Triple Frontier. Surrounded by dense jungle, it straddled the borders of Brazil, Argentina, and Paraguay where the Iguazú and Paraná rivers converge. His mentor, Bazir Haqqani, had told him that the unique combination of geography, rampant political corruption, impotent antiterrorism laws, weak judicial systems, and large Muslim populations combined to foster a veritable Eden for Islamic terrorists of all flavors—Hezbollah, Hamas, Al-Gama'a al-Islamiyya, Al-Jihad, Al-Qaeda, and Al-Muqawamah, among others. Recently, the current five-hundred-pound gorilla of jihadism, HAC, had developed a presence in the TBA by muscling, and in some cases, bribing disaffected Al-Qaeda members.

There was a long-established route from the Middle East to the TBA. It wound from Greece and Turkey into Europe and then South America. Once in the TBA, the jihadis would polish their Spanish before moving on to Mexico via Venezuela where they obtained fraudulent passports and visas. In Mexico, they would blend in with illegally emigrating Latinos and be smuggled into the heart of the Great Satan. After that, the killing would begin when Nadir Shah, the leader of the Holy Army of the Caliphate, gave the signal. Turan, along with many of his fellow travelers, had been training for that event almost from the day Bazir Haqqani had recruited him from the rubble of his madrassa, destroyed by one of the Infidels' Hellfire missiles. Soon he would have the opportunity to repay the Great Satan for that transgression and countless others. But this time, instead of the members of its military, it would be its women and children, its old and infirm who would suffer the wrath of Allah, the Vengeful One. Turan could barely wait for that day to come.

And now, here they were—within ten to twelve kilometers of their goal: the United States' southern border. The high, rugged terrain surrounding the little village of San Luis—in the northern-most reaches of the Sierra Madre Occidental Mountains—had been their final staging area. Bazir Haqqani had driven them relentlessly, day and night. He had woken them at odd hours and forced them to practice defending against surprise raids. They had been trained in the use of asymmetrical military tactics, including ambushes, sabo-tage, raids, petty warfare, hit-and-run tactics, and mobility, which was needed when fighting a larger and less-mobile traditional military.

Their training included explosives skills and bombing strategies, how to use a baited ambush to lure enemy forces into established kill zones, sniper skills, and techniques for destroying communication and power grids. They had been taught that during firefights, they were to stay close to the enemy units to avoid indirect fire and discourage close air support. They had trained ceaselessly in hand-to-hand combat, marksmanship, and weaponry. In addition, they had been taught techniques for recruiting U.S. Muslims to use for cover and for gathering intel, as well as for additional manpower. Turan and the others also had studied English some part of every day.

He stood in the middle of the tiny village of San Luis and looked up and down its single street, rough and unpaved. There was a general store that mostly sold farm and mining tools and supplies. Next to it was a cantina where infidel Mexican peasants drank alcohol, smoked, and gambled. Across from it was a small, pitiful-looking church where the locals worshipped the false prophet. Several mud brick houses, little more than huts, finished out the town's improvements. The village clung to a small plateau high up the flank of a mountain. Above it, near the mountaintop, was the HAC training camp.

After months of travel, including weeks in the rain forest of the Tri-Border Area, Turan was relieved to be in territory that reminded him of his mountainous home near Wana. Except for the music and the aromas of the food the Mexicans ate. Although he and his companions had been in an immersion Spanish language program near Ciudad del Este in the TBA, he was comforted by the presence of fellow countrymen at the HAC encampment. Arabic was the native language of many of the warriors in the camp, reflecting the influence of Islamic terrorism's major financiers, the Saudis and other Gulf States. Although Bazir forbade Turan and the others to speak any languages other than Spanish and English, when he wasn't around, Turan would sometimes converse in Pashto with others from Pakistan. That and the fact that these mountains reminded him of home brought Turan a sense of comfort for the first time in a long while.

Bazir Haqqani had told him and the others to be ready to leave that night. When asked where they were going, Bazir only smiled and said, "To do Allah's work." Turan hoped it meant they would be crossing over into the land of the Great Satan. That's where the real work of Allah needed to be done. The Infidels needed to be slaughtered, nonstop, until America no longer was a threat to Islam. Or anything else.

Turan took one last look around the tiny village. He wondered if he would ever be back this way again. If he survived the war against the Great Satan but wasn't able to return to his homeland, the area around San Luis would be an acceptable option.

Haqqani oversaw the loading of the men and their equipment into several large four-wheel drive pickup trucks. The vehicles slowly descended along rough, rudimentary roads to the valley floor below. The caravan slogged north until it reached Mexican Federal Highway 2 at a small town called Rancho El Valle. The highway was mostly a two-lane paved road that paralleled the border in two long segments across the far north of Mexico. Using a major commercial highway so close to the border made it much more difficult for the U.S. Border Patrol to detect their approach. The full stretch of Highway 2 that Turan's group was using ran seven hundred miles from Tijuana to just outside Ciudad Juarez, Mexico's poor cousin to El Paso, Texas. They weren't going that far tonight, just sixteen kilometers or so east from Rancho El Valle to a point less than two kilometers from the border with New Mexico.

Bazir Haqqani never said so, but Turan knew he was Bazir's favorite. Since Haqqani had recruited him in the hospital ward in Wana, Pakistan, and put him through the intensely rigorous HAC training regimen, Turan had grown three inches and packed on twenty-five pounds, mostly muscle. He had the quickest mind in his group, grasping concepts and details faster than any of the others. And he was the most committed to the holy war against the Western devils. It came as no surprise when Bazir took him aside before they left the encampment above San Luis. He was to be entrusted with carrying the most important piece of equipment, the central reason for this particular mission.

Bazir hadn't told him what the object was, but it was heavy, at least fifty kilograms—about one hundred ten pounds. All Bazir had told Turan was that the object would cause the most fearsome and frightening attack ever on American soil. It was enclosed in a large eighty-liter rucksack, the kind used for serious trekking.

The convoy of trucks pulled off Route 2 at a point just east of the end of the foothills that ran south, swelling into the rugged mountain fastness Turan's group had just left. The shoulder of the road had once been graded into a wide area, presumably as a resting point for the countless long-haul truckers who traveled the lonely highway. The area now was pocked with potholes and stained by the drippings from the undercarriages of the vehicles that had stopped there over the years. The ruins of a small building added to the neglected, forlorn aura of the place. Perhaps, Turan thought, it had been a filling station or a cantina, maybe both. On the north side of the highway, there was a matching rest area with even larger potholes. At its western end, there was a white sign with black lettering: *Conserva. Limpia la carretera.* Turan's growing proficiency in Spanish enabled him to translate it—Preserve. Clean the road. He looked at the trash littering the area and smiled to himself. *Perhaps it's intended as a joke.*

He looked north beyond the rest area. There was a low fence with a single strand of barbed wire. Beyond it lay a hike to the border, a little more than two kilometers—about a mile and a quarter. With some assistance from Bazir, he hoisted the heavy rucksack onto his shoulders. His best friend in the group, Karwan, who was also from a small Pashto settlement near Wana, carried Turan's AK-47 and other gear. The group of twenty-five stepped over the fence and set out toward the U.S. border.

Because of its inland position and higher elevation than the Sonoran Desert to the west, the Chihuahuan Desert had a slightly milder climate and different flora. This part of the desert was mostly flat and covered with mosaics of grasses interspersed with stunted trees and shrubs, and a variety of cacti.

Among the things Turan had learned in the encampment above San Luis was that he and his colleagues wouldn't be the only predators roaming the desert at night. Gray wolves, ocelots, coyotes, bobcats, and the occasional mountain lion or jaguar prowled the darkness, hoping to dine on a stray coatimundi, javelina, or jackrabbit.

The group crossed the border in just under twenty minutes. It was a dark night with only a quarter moon to light their way. Bazir had hired a guide in San Luis. The man was a tough-looking hombre. Rumor had it that he was a member of MS-13 and supposedly knew the infiltration routes and placements of seismic sensors better than anyone else. Even so, Bazir had warned his men that the U.S. Border Patrol used equipment that could see in the dark, just as if the sun was out and brightly shining. But to counter the advantage, HAC was not without modern surveillance equipment of its own. Bazir had told Turan that an advance HAC scouting party had used a drone to locate this machine that could see in the night. They were going to target it purposely, as a means of sending a message to the Infidels that they no longer had any real technological advantage.

The guide signaled them to stop. He squatted and motioned Bazir to draw close. Whispering in Spanish, he said, "The *Norteamericanos* have a machine up ahead that will spot us very soon, if it hasn't already. As was agreed, this is the point where I leave you. You have maps and information on where you will be picked up." He looked around at Bazir's men, and then continued, whispering to the leader. "You know what is going to happen next. I trust your boys...." He paused and sneered. "Your 'men' will be able to contribute and not get themselves killed."

Bazir's expression was hard and cold. "They have been well trained and know what to expect. They will perform well."

The Mexican nodded. "Just continue to walk straight north." He pointed in the direction. "You don't have to worry; the Border Patrol will find you. After that, you're on your own." He stood up and swiftly disappeared into the brush, heading back toward the border.

To stay low, Bazir duck-walked over to Turan. "The package you are carrying is critical to our mission." He glanced around at the others and then leaned in close to Turan. "The others are expendable. Let them do the heavy lifting tonight. You stay back until I give you the signal to move forward. Protect your precious cargo, with your life if necessary."

Turan nodded solemnly. Despite the strain of carrying the heavy load, he was deeply honored to be the one chosen by Bazir Haqqani for this special task. He would much rather die than disappoint this great warrior.

Bazir turned to the other men and said, "Check your weapons one more time, and then sling them behind your backs as you have been taught. I don't want the Infidels to know we are armed until we are upon them." When the others had complied, he stood up and motioned for them to begin walking again. They proceeded in single file, following Bazir. As instructed, Turan hung back, following well behind the last man in the line.

HIDALGO ROLLED the white and green Border Patrol Suburban to a stop behind Ojeda's modified Ford F350 flatbed. He and three other agents climbed out and walked toward the truck. Ojeda emerged from the cab and met them in the middle.

"What's the situation?" Hidalgo said.

"Same, only closer now."

"How many?" one of the other men, Mike, who arrived with Hidalgo, said.

"Looks like about two dozen," Ojeda said.

"AMMs?"

Ojeda shrugged. "That would fit the profile."

"Drug smugglers?" Mike said.

Ojeda shrugged again. "Whatever. They're all illegals."

"Do they look like they're armed?" Hidalgo said.

"They might be packing. I couldn't really tell."

Another car pulled up behind Hidalgo's vehicle. It was a sheriff's unit. Two uniformed deputies got out and joined the Border Patrol agents.

Hidalgo filled them in on what information he had. He motioned for Ojeda to get back into the truck's cab. "When the FLIR shows them within a hundred yards, flip on the big spotlight bar on the roof of your cab."

He turned to the other five men. "We'll split off three to a side, about twenty yards apart. When the lights go on, I'll give them the drill." He held up a battery-powered bullhorn. "Once they're on their knees, hands behind their heads, you two," he nodded at Mike and another agent named Ramon, "will put the flex-cuffs on 'em as usual. The rest of us will cover you." He looked around, making sure every man was carrying a shotgun.

The six men spread out and waited. A few minutes later the powerful flood lights atop Ojeda's truck suddenly lit up the night.

The line of men led by Bazir froze, blinking at the intensity of the lights.

Hidalgo clicked the switch, activating the bullhorn. Speaking in Spanish, he said, "This is the Border Patrol of the United States of America. You are all under arrest. Stop where you are. Drop whatever you are carrying, and get on your knees, hands behind your heads."

Mike and Ramon cautiously started moving toward the illegals. The night suddenly exploded in gunfire. As the slugs began to rip through the bodies of the Border Patrol agents and sheriff's deputies, they realized the shots were coming from behind them, not from the men they were attempting to interdict. Their assailants already had been in-country. That knowledge came too late to be of any use to them. All six men were down in a matter of a few seconds; the gunfire continued for several more.

When the gunfire erupted, the cab's windows shattered, cutting Ojeda in a number of places, mostly on his head and neck. Panicked, he dove into the foot well and curled into the fetal position. When the firing stopped, he grabbed his cellphone from the passenger seat and began desperately trying to reach the Border Patrol station at Antelope Wells. His fingers shook badly, making the task almost impossible. With an overwhelming sense of morbid curiosity, he found himself rising slowly to see what was going on around him. He quickly spotted the bodies of the other agents and the deputies. All were motionless. Through the shattered windshield, he saw a line of men advancing slowly toward him. They were the ones his FLIR equipment had picked up. And they definitely were armed.

He turned and looked through the space where the rear window had been. Already nearly frozen in fear, what he saw completely paralyzed him. Less than thirty feet behind the truck, there was a group of heavily armed men—the shooters. What topped off

Ojeda's terror was their clothing. He had seen it before, on television newscasts from the Middle East. They were clad in the black uniforms of the fighters with the Holy Army of the Caliphate. As he stared in horrid fascination, one of the men in black held something up. It looked like a bottle. With a rag stuffed in its top. Casually, the man thumbed a lighter and the rag caught fire. A moment later, he hurled it at the truck. It shattered against the bottom edge of the blown-out rear window. Instantly the cab became an inferno. Ojeda died with his scream still on his lips.

Bazir and his crew gave the burning truck a wide berth and joined the men in the black uniforms. As Haqqani and their leader embraced, Turan arrived, still carrying the heavy backpack.

"Abdallah, my brother, tonight we have drawn the blood of the Infidels in their homeland. The war has now begun," Bazir said.

"It has indeed, Bazir. Gather your men quickly. We need to leave this place before other Infidels arrive. There will be more of them, and better armed."

Bazir nodded. "First, I want to make sure there are no survivors." He turned to Turan and three others. "If any of these devils are still alive, finish them off."

A young man, still in his teens, standing next to Turan said, "How do we know if one of them is alive, Bazir?"

Bazir snarled. "Kick him. Hard. If he cries out, shoot him in the head!"

Turan and the others turned and hurried to carry out the directive. The other three trotted to where the bodies of the outermost of the Americans lay. Turan, by default, went to the body closest to the truck. He stared down at the man. He was dark-skinned, like the people who lived in San Luis. The man clearly had been shot in several places. His Border Patrol uniform was soaked in blood. Something caught Turan's eye. Partially exposed in the man's back pocket was a leather object. Turan knelt and pulled it free. It was a wallet. The blood on it made it slippery, and he dropped it. When it hit the ground, it flipped open. Turan picked it up again. Inside was a photograph of an attractive dark-haired, dark-skinned woman and two young boys. All were smiling.

The man's family, Turan thought. Suddenly, the long-awaited war against the Infidels took on a distinctly human aspect. *We have killed a father and a husband. Someone these people love, just as I loved my family. Now they won't be smiling. They will be sad, heart-broken. There will be a hole in their lives, a hole that will never be filled again.* He dropped the wallet as if it had seared his flesh. Several yards away he heard a thud-like sound. He knew that one of his companions had kicked one of the fallen men. The sound of the kick was followed immediately by a groan and then a gunshot.

Turan backed away from the body of the wallet owner.

Bazir saw him and called out, "Is he dead?"

"Yes."

"And you are sure?"

"Yes…I…I kicked him and he didn't move or cry out."

"Good. You are learning, Turan. One day soon you will be a mighty warrior for Islam. Now pick up your precious cargo, and let's follow our brothers out of here."

"Where are we going?" Turan said.

"Our brothers parked their vehicles a short distance away. We will split up and go with various of them to our ultimate destinations." He smiled mischievously. "You, Turan, are coming with me to Santa Fe."

CHAPTER 12
CHICAGO

THE MUSCULAR BLACK man approached McGillicuddy's Pub, a neighborhood corner bar on West Irving Park Road in Chicago's North Center community. Still a block from the pub, he noticed the Lincoln Town Car limousine idling at the curb near the pub's front door. Its darkened windows made it impossible to see who was inside the car or how many of them there might be. As a man of unusual perception and training, he sensed the potential for danger and slowed his pace as he continued to stare at the car. *Was it picking up an affluent patron who'd had too much to drink? Not likely, it was early in the afternoon, plus the pub didn't attract the wealthy class. A cab maybe, but not a limo. Was it a new driver who was lost and asking for directions? Also an unlikely scenario.* Then a frightening thought crossed the man's mind, and he slowed his pace even more. *Was it Maksym or one of his minion's intent on finishing the previously bungled assassination attempt?*

The man stopped walking and stared at the car. If it was another attempt on his life, would his unique reactions be sufficient to out-quick the shooter's aim? He glanced around. The pub occupied the west half of a two-story red brick building that had a 1930s look. The east half was vacant with large plate-glass windows across the front. He considered the possibility of leaping through one of the windows and quickly discarded the thought. The glass would do nothing to stop a hail of bullets from an automatic weapon. And he doubted he could clear the rear of the space before the shooter recovered his aim. Next to the vacant side of the building, about five feet to his left, was a narrow alleyway. A heavily padlocked wooden gate topped by a section of chain-link fence blocked it. All told, the gate was about six feet high. That was of no concern. The man could leap it with ease. But what was on the other side of the gate? A dead end?

After a few moments of the standoff, the rear window on the curb side of the limo began to descend. If the muzzle of a weapon peeked through the open window, the man would be over the gate in a heartbeat. A Norm wouldn't have the quickness and hand-eye coordination to move the gun fast enough to hit him. *But what if it wasn't a Norm? What if it was Maksym himself?*

But it wasn't a weapon that appeared. It was a face, a familiar face. And the raspy voice was equally as familiar—Cliff Levell.

"Indecisiveness will get you killed, Thomas. I thought I trained you better than that."

Quentin Thomas walked over to the limo, rested his hands on the roof, and leaned in. Levell looked unchanged, as if immune to the passage of time. And gunshot wounds. "I figured I was faster than any Norm. And if it was another Dog, he wouldn't be trying to kill me."

"Yeah, but what if it had been Maksym? The sonofabitch is still at large."

Thomas shrugged. "Then I would have been dead."

Levell turned to the driver. "Nando, I want to have a conversation with Mr. Thomas inside," he turned and read the sign above the door to the pub, "McGillicuddy's."

A stocky Hispanic man emerged from the driver's side, went to the trunk, and removed a wheelchair. He unfolded it and easily lifted Levell into it. The three men went inside. Thomas slid into a booth in the rear. Nando rolled the wheelchair up to the open end of the booth then stood against the rear wall where he had a sweeping overview of the room. Though the place was a little less than half full, Thomas knew it would fill up with regulars as the afternoon wore on. After a couple of minutes, the bartender came over. She had bright purple hair, multiple piercings, and graphic skin.

Thomas smiled. "Hi, Tasha, how've you been?"

"Quentin," she said with obvious delight, "it's been a while. In fact, the last time was when you had that come-to-Jesus moment with the skinheads. What was that…three, four months ago?"

"Something like that."

"I thought maybe you gave up drinking."

"I did."

"Yeah, you were hitting it kind of hard. Did you get some help, like AA?"

Thomas nodded. "Funny thing, though. I wasn't drinking because of an alcohol addiction."

"That's good. I think. What was it, if you don't mind me asking?"

Thomas turned toward Levell and grinned. "Actually, it had more to do with this guy, my former boss. The kinds of things he had me do were haunting me. Drinking was my way of trying to drown out the memories."

Levell frowned and shifted his weight in the wheelchair.

Tasha gave Thomas a puzzled look. "What kind of things?"

Shaking his head but smiling coldly, Levell said, "Sorry, that's classified. He could tell you, but then I'd have to kill you both."

"Yeah," Tasha said to Thomas. "You mentioned that you'd been a soldier of sorts. Is that what you mean?"

"What he means," Levell said, "is that it's time for you to take our drink order and give us a little space."

Thomas motioned at Levell with his head. "He's old. Thinks it gives him a license to be grouchy."

Tasha laughed. "My grandmother's the same way. What would you like?" she said to Levell.

"Scotch. Neat."

She looked at Thomas. "Coffee?"

"Beer, really cold."

Tasha hesitated for a moment. "Are you sure that's smart?"

"Like I said, it's not an addiction. The truth is I was trying to run from something I loved. Thought I could immunize myself with booze."

"And now you're not running?" Tasha said.

Thomas shook his head back and forth. "No. I've made peace with myself. Acknowledged that my old way of life actually was what I was born to do. There were some tough moments in it, but whose life doesn't have a few?" He paused and looked up at Tasha. "Hell, I'm not cut out to be a schoolteacher. In fact, I'm about as far removed from that as anyone could be."

"But you *are* teaching school. At St. Dom's."

"Not for long. I suspect this man," he nodded at Levell again, "is gonna make me an offer I can't refuse."

"Well, if so, I'll miss you," Tasha said wistfully and left to get their drinks.

"It sounds like you're going to make this easier than I thought it would be," Levell said.

Thomas grinned. "So, you *are* here to recruit me."

Levell pointed at one of the large flat-screen TVs on a wall. Fox Business News was on. The host was discussing the effect that the previous evening's slaughter near the border in New Mexico was having on the market. "You paying attention to what happened in New Mexico last night?"

"Yeah, that thing on the border?"

"It was an ambush. Five CBP agents, two sheriff's deputies."

"The news shows are saying it was drug related. Like cartels or gangs. You know, the Zetas, Sinaloa, maybe MS-13."

"That's bullshit. Gangs may have had a collateral role, but it was terrorism, plain and simple."

"The reports say there were no survivors. A terrible thing."

"The media was misinformed on purpose. There was one survivor. Barely. He's fighting for his life in a hospital in El Paso. With any luck, he'll pull through and give us vital intel about the attack. That's strictly off the record. We don't want the bastards who did this to come back and try to finish off the witness."

"Does SAS have someone on the inside?"

"Yeah, the FBI agent in charge of the Bureau's side of the investigation. A guy named Mitch Christie."

"Christie!" Thomas sat up straight. "Isn't he the one that was pursuing Whelan and, by extension, the rest of us for the Harold Case murders?"

"The same."

Thomas shook his head. "And now he's one of your guys."

"*Our* guys. I'm putting the unit back together."

"And you want me to join up."

"Face it, Quentin, you're no different than the rest of the Dogs. For whatever reason, Mother Nature created a special breed of animal...to hunt down and kill this country's enemies like no one else in history ever has. It's what you are. It's what you were born to do. Buster McCoy and I and the others just polished all of you up a bit."

Thomas's face drew into a pensive expression. "Last time we all were together—in Geneva—the wheels came off the bus. Everyone quit, went their separate ways. Are you telling me that the others are back on board?"

Levell fidgeted and looked away for a moment. "I had to promise Larsen we'd go after Maksym full bore. Whelan clearly gets what's at stake. If the U.S. goes down, so will Ireland and the rest of the free world. Stensen is always up for wet work. Almeida doesn't have any other options. He's fucking incompetent on his own. In fact, Nick had to break him out of a county lockup for trying to rob a bank. Almeida couldn't even do that right."

"That leaves Kirkland. He in?"

"Ah…that's a bit of a problem."

"This ought to be good. Let's hear it."

Levell sighed. "Marc is in a fucking maximum security prison in Qatar."

"Qatar? How did that happen?" Thomas grinned. "The sheikh catch him in the harem?"

"That would be more Almeida's style," Levell said dryly. "The fact is he killed the five bastards the president swapped for that deserter Kevin Johnson."

"I remember reading about that. And about someone killing Johnson. Was that Marc too?"

Levell shook his head. "No, but you're on the right track."

Thomas stared at Levell for a moment. "Stensen!"

Levell nodded.

"But it was Marc that offed the Qatari Five?"

"Yes. And the first thing you and the others are going to do is get him out."

"That ought to be interesting. And then what?"

"Then you go after those sons of bitches that were responsible for last night's massacre in New Mexico. They're part of a much larger threat, and we have to stop it. If it's not too late."

"Do we know who's behind it?"

"HAC. The Holy Army of the Caliphate."

CHAPTER 13

NEW MEXICO

FOLLOWING the lead of the men in the black HAC uniforms, Turan, Bazir, and the others who had participated in the attack on the Border Patrol agents and deputies trudged northward across the darkened landscape. The desert didn't hold heat after the sun went down. Temperatures dropped quickly, but adrenaline kept the men warm. In addition, Turan was lugging a heavy, awkwardly large burden. About one and a quarter kilometers from the scene of the attack, they came upon a rutted dirt road. It ran along the edge of a small but steeply banked pond. Bazir said that such ponds were called tanks in this area.

Two large black SUVs were parked on the edge of the road. Behind them was an old, battered bus. Bazir told Turan and his two-dozen companions to load into the bus. The black-clad men changed into nondescript civilian garb and all but one of them climbed into the SUVs. The sole exception slid into the driver's seat on the bus and fired up the engine. The bus began moving and was soon rattling, bouncing, and rocking from side to side as it followed the SUVs.

The caravan moved along the rough, bumpy dirt road for about three kilometers until it intersected with another wider road. It too was unpaved but had been graded recently. That smoothed out the ride noticeably. The road ran mostly due east for about eight kilometers and then made a wide, lazy swing to the left. It ran north for another four kilometers until it intersected a paved road, New Mexico Highway 81. It was a narrow, although well-maintained road that cut across the endless New Mexican desert from the CBP station on the border at Antelope Wells to the town of Hachita forty miles to the north. Hachita was small, about a dozen city blocks divided by mostly unpaved streets. There 81 formed a T-intersection with State Road 9. The caravan turned left at the intersection.

As Turan gazed out the dirty window of the bus, it was clear to him that Hachita was a dying town. Other than the ubiquitous old stone church, St. Catherine's, the homes and places of business were in states of decay that ranged from dilapidated to gutted. The bus turned into a wide parking lot on the west side of an abandoned building with the word "Saloon" painted on the front of it in faded letters.

Across the parking lot to the west was another abandoned building. A battered sign in front identified it as a café. The rusting hulk of the town's original water tank loomed on the other side of Highway 9. The place reminded Turan of many of the towns and villages in his native Waziristan. Their declines were attributable to the endless wars and tribal feuds that had ravaged the land for centuries. He doubted that was the cause of Hachita's demise. America hadn't known war on its homeland for more than 150 years, and it had no warring tribes, only imaginary social and political grievances that its citizens seemed to whine about incessantly

The memory of the photo in the Border Patrol agent's wallet edged into his mind. He saw the pretty wife, the two children, the dead agent lying at his feet. Turan was suddenly angry with himself. *What is the matter with me? These people mean nothing to me. In fact, it is my sacred mission to kill as many of them as I can.* But the anger passed as he thought about a family whose members' lives were now empty, filled with sorrow. He felt a strange tightness in his chest and a sense of guilt, even though he hadn't actually pulled the trigger and killed the agent.

He was shaken from his thoughts as Bazir put a hand on his shoulder and shook him forcibly.

"Are you dreaming about the virgins awaiting you in Paradise, Turan?"

He looked up and saw a big grin on Bazir's face. "No...I...was just thinking about the mission. That's all."

Bazir laughed. "You are a young man, Turan. You should be dreaming about the virgins. Let's hope you don't keep them waiting too long." He pointed to the large, heavy bundle Turan had been carrying. "We've arrived at the point where our group will split up. Pick up your burden and follow me."

There was a variety of ordinary-looking vehicles in the parking lot. Bazir and the HAC fighters directed small groups of two or three people from Turan's group to the specific vehicles that would take them to their respective destinations. Bazir escorted Turan and his package to a ten-year-old Crown Victoria. The heavy rucksack went into the trunk. Bazir and Turan sat in the back seat. Two of the HAC warriors sat in front. The driver started the car, and they pulled out of the parking lot heading west on Highway 9. Two hundred meters later, the driver swung the car to the right and headed north on Route 146. Thirty, mostly silent, kilometers later— about nineteen miles—the route intersected Interstate 10. The one break in the silence happened when Turan, speaking Pashto, asked Bazir about the destinations of the others who had accompanied him and Bazir from San Luis.

"They are not your concern," Bazir said. "Focus on your mission. Yours is the most important of all."

"But I saw them get into vehicles and head in various directions. Are they not part of the mission too?"

Bazir turned in his seat and faced Turan. "Part of *the* mission, yes, but not part our assignment. Each has his own task to fulfill."

"Why are they not working with us? We trained together."

"Not that you need to know, but since you ask, they will be taken to other parts of the United States. They will join cells already set up and waiting for the signal from Nadir Shah. When it is given, we each have assignments to fulfill. Together, these assignments will cripple the Great Satan." He paused and looked sternly at Turan. "Your task is one of the most important. That is why I specifically chose you."

The HAC man in the front passenger seat turned and began yelling angrily at Turan and Bazir in a language that Turan didn't understand.

Bazir, speaking Arabic, with which Turan had a basic grasp, said, "Turn around and mind your own business, you Uzbek dog! I don't give a shit if you can't understand the language we speak. You fucking Uzbeks barely have a language as it is. What my comrade and I discuss with each other is none of your business."

The man glared at Bazir, his face contorted in anger. Finally, he turned around and stared through the windshield at the road ahead.

The driver entered an eastbound lane of the Interstate and the silence settled in again. Eventually, they exited the freeway at Deming about thirty miles down the road, pulled into a McDonald's, and parked. The four men got out and headed for the restaurant. It felt good to Turan to stretch his legs. They ordered food, ate it in silence, and took turns using the men's room.

Turan went last. When he returned, he saw two uniformed members of the New Mexico State police sitting three tables away from his group. One of the cops, a chubby white man with a florid complexion, was staring at him. Turan's stomach knotted up, and he felt himself beginning to sweat. When he sat down, Bazir smiled pleasantly at Turan and leaned over, whispering, "If they speak to you, reply in Spanish. If they ask for ID, use your matricula consular ID card. Remember, the cards are indistinguishable from Mexico's official ID. You remember your cover story, don't you?"

Turan nodded and kept his head down, staring at his Egg McMuffin. From the corners of his eyes, he could see that the two HAC fighters each had a hand resting in their laps, close to the open zippers on their windbreakers—inches away from the butts of the weapons shoved into their waistbands. Bazir was chatting amiably in Spanish with Turan. The McDonald's was fairly crowded. Most of the patrons were dark-skinned and looked like the people Turan had seen in San Luis. Spanish seemed overwhelmingly to be the language of choice.

Turan sensed another presence at the table and quickly glanced up. The chubby cop was standing next to Bazir. The name badge on his uniform said "Sergeant Reynolds." His partner, a wiry Hispanic man, remained at his table but was staring at Turan's group.

"Me and Officer Esparza there," the cop nodded in the direction of his partner, "don't recollect seeing you boys before. You from around here?"

Bazir smiled pleasantly. "No, officer, just passing through." He spoke English with a slight accent that purposely was hard to identify.

"From where to where?"

"Animas to Las Cruces, officer."

"If you don't mind my askin', what's your purpose in goin' to Las Cruces?"

Bazir looked around the table at the other men and said, "We're hoping to find work there. My cousin Miguel told me there are many more farms and ranches in that area than in Animas."

The cop slowly eyed the four men, one by one. His gaze lingered on Turan. "Looks like this young fella isn't old enough to grow a decent set of whiskers. He old enough to work? You know, we got laws in New Mexico against forcin' kids to do labor." He put emphasis on the word "New."

"He's my little brother. Believe me, I can vouch for every one of his eighteen years."

The cop studied Turan for a few more moments and then said, "All right, boys, you drive safely now." He turned and walked back to his table and sat.

It was only a few more minutes before Turan's party got up and left the restaurant, though it seemed like an eternity to Turan.

Back on the Interstate, the driver pushed the car along at seventy-five miles per hour. Once they turned onto U.S. Highway 70, they had to reduce speed as they navigated through the Las Cruces traffic. The highway made a hard left and circled north and east, connecting with Interstate 25 outside of town. They stopped once more for gas just before entering I-25. From there, the Interstate paralleled the twisting, silt-laden Rio Grande River, contorting its way ever southward toward the big bend at the border with Mexico. Two hundred miles later, they were cutting through downtown Albuquerque and stopped again for fuel and to relieve their bladders. Eighty-six miles later, they reached the historic state capital of Santa Fe. Before entering the more developed area of the city, the driver exited onto Cerrillos Road. His companion pulled out a sheet of paper with instructions and a crude map on it and spoke to the driver in Uzbek.

"In Arabic, dammit," Bazir said with a growl.

The man switched to heavily accented Arabic and continued giving directions to the driver. The man took a series of lefts and rights through a residential area. After several turns, he pulled into a driveway. They had reached their new home.

Turan climbed out of the back seat and looked around. Compared to the cities and towns in his native Pakistan, the neighborhood was a study in luxuriousness. To most Americans, however, it would have been considered only a couple of steps up from a barrio. The houses were small, most of them badly maintained, and all looked the same—traditional Spanish pueblo architecture with soft rounded corners, irregular parapets, vigas, latillas, nichos, and bancos. All painted in bland earth tones. A long time ago. Many of the yards were overgrown with weeds. The vehicles that were parked on the street or in driveways definitely weren't luxury models.

After they had lugged Turan's rucksack into the house, they checked to make sure the place had been stocked with food and fresh clothing. It had. Turan began to wonder just how large and organized HAC was. He knew it had hundreds, maybe thousands, of cells around the country. And all of them probably were as well stocked as this one. But what made this house special was its location—twenty-five miles, as the crow flies, from the Los Alamos National Laboratory, America's top-secret nuclear facility.

CHAPTER 14

THE LODGE

A HUMID BREEZE drifted in from the Potomac, less than a mile away, bringing with it the unmistakable aromas of the river. It rustled the leaves near the lofty tops of the old-growth red maples, hickory, beech, and scarlet oak. But it didn't have much effect at a lower level where the dense profusion of red chokeberry, witch hazel, spice bush, and Virginia's state tree, flowering dogwood, struggled to crowd each other out. At ground level, the heat and humidity presaged an early summer. In the middle of this forested refuge was an oasis of calm, barely forty miles from the 24/7 turmoil inside the Beltway. The Lodge, looking like a huge, log ski-chalet, occupied a large cleared area.

Mitch Christie had arrived a few minutes early for a meeting that Levell had insisted he attend. Christie was reluctant to visit the Lodge too often. Every security agency in the federal government was aware that it attracted important figures from the political and military communities, as well as titans of industry. That was partly explainable by the fact that the multibillionaire Mueller brothers often entertained there. What raised suspicions, however, was its invulnerability to all snooping devices. It also was a consulate for a foreign nation, one in which the Muellers had made very generous investments. As much as the current administration wanted the various agencies to raid the property, they couldn't. Pursuant to Article 31 of the Vienna Convention on Consular Relations, the host nation was prohibited from entering consular premises. Over the years, the agencies had tried to place moles in the ranks of members and employees, but none had managed to survive the Lodge's intense vetting process.

Christie tossed the keys to his blue-gray Hyundai Santa Fe to a valet and was escorted into the main structure. Christie's escort was well dressed, stocky, and very fit looking. His appearance spoke volumes about the man's background. Like all of the Lodge's security personnel, he was former Special Ops.

INSIDE THE LODGE'S mammoth main building, the others already had begun to gather for the meeting. It was being held, as usual, in the large underground wine cellar/boardroom beneath the library. Levell was seated in his customary position at the middle of the table. Nando stood a few feet behind him, only an inch of two away from a wine rack. The rack held bottles—some of them priceless—at a slight incline so the wines could work on their respective corks. A thin layer of dust stylishly coated each bottle.

Rafe Almeida walked slowly along the racks, inspecting the wines. Once in a while, he would pick up a bottle and examine its label. He stole occasional glances around the room. It wasn't lost on any of the others who were present.

"Leave the fucking wines alone, Almeida," Levell said without having to turn around to see what the other man was doing. "There'll be plenty of time for you to booze it up after the meeting."

"And it won't involve that pricey stuff you're fondling," Nick Stensen said.

"Yeah," Quentin Thomas said. "Rafe can get by just as well with a bottle of rubbing alcohol. Those high-priced vintages would wreck his stomach."

Sven Larsen said, "I heard he likes to strain Vitalis through rye bread and drink that."

"And then he makes a sandwich with the bread," Stensen said.

Almeida turned toward the others in the room and said, "Keep it up, assholes, and I'll lay waste to this whole fuckin' dungeon. No one will survive." He eyed Nando who was staring at him with a stone-faced expression.

"Except for Cliff, that is," Almeida quickly added.

Seated across the table from Levell, Whelan grinned. It was getting to be like old times again. With the exception of Marc Kirkland, the Sleeping Dogs were back together. And, just like old times, the others were mercilessly ragging on Rafe Almeida. He always had been the group's omega wolf, the lowest one on the totem pole. Whelan understood why. Although Almeida had the same rare genetic gifts the other Dogs had, he was a natural-born fuck-up. Time and again, when the right choice was an easy one to make, Almeida invariably went the other direction. To Whelan, Almeida's penchant for making poor decisions also seemed almost genetic. Still, despite their unrelenting harassment, the other Dogs liked Almeida and covered his six. It was difficult for rough men not to like him. He was a product of his hardscrabble upbringing: a brawling, hard-drinking, blue-collar tough with a huge chip on his shoulder. In their dangerous world, he provided much needed entertainment in the form of unintentional comic relief. He could drink all of them under the table, and his adventures as a skirt chaser were legendary.

There was a heavy stone slab at the top of the steps that led to the library above. Mitch Christie appeared in the opening and trotted quickly down the steps. He took the vacant chair on Levell's right. Christie nodded at Whelan and sat down.

"All right, the whole gang's here. Sit your ass down, Almeida, and let's get this show on the road," Levell said in his familiar rasp.

There were a few moments of silence, broken by the scraping of chairs on the rough stone floor as those present pulled closer to the table.

"Men, the future of this country is at greater risk than it ever has been," Levell said. "Despite the efforts of SAS, diplomacy isn't working. The fucking administration is destroying the country faster than we can counter them. The same is true of our efforts to establish useful military alliances. As a result, your unique talents are needed more than ever before."

The red dots in Stensen's eyes flared in striking contrast to the darkened atmosphere of the wine cellar. "Sounds like you have a kill list for us. When do we start?"

Levell shook his head. "That comes later when we have the luxury of time. Right now, we have a disaster happening here in the homeland. It's too late to stop it completely, but we have to root out and destroy what we can as quickly as possible. Once that's done, we can focus on killing the bad actors in other parts of the world, including that sonofabitch who leads the caliphate and those bearded rug merchants running Iran."

Thomas leaned forward. "What's this disaster you mentioned?"

Levell looked slowly around the room, purposely making eye contact with everyone. At last, he said, "I assume all of you have seen the latest news."

"You mean Comedy Central, aka the ongoing presidential campaign?" Larsen said with what, for him, passed as a grin.

Levell scowled. "Very funny, wiseass. No, I was referring to the incident on the border in New Mexico."

There were nods around the table.

"I'm going to let Agent Christie, here, explain what's going on. But, before he begins, there's someone else who wants to join us." Levell motioned to Nando.

The Brazilian pulled a cellphone from a pocket and spoke softly into it. "Send him down."

The stone slab covering the entrance to the steps that led from the library silently slid open. For a moment, the opening was backlit by light from the library. Then, a large figure filled the space. All heads turned to watch as the man descended the stone steps. He was a big man, about Whelan's size. He had longish blond hair and the deep tan of a man who spent much of his time outdoors. But his most striking feature was his eyes. Like the other Dogs, they were a bright glacial blue.

The room fell silent as everyone stared at the newcomer. He stopped on the bottom step and looked at each of the other men. "G'day, mates," he said.

Whelan, a big grin on his face, stood up and walked over to the man, extending his hand to him. "Looks like my selling job worked on you, Liam."

"You did make it sound interesting, mate. Working on a cattle station can get a bit boring after a while, so I thought I'd check you out." Stone looked around the room again. "These blokes the ones you told me about? Freaks, like you and me?"

"Except for Cliff Levell." Whelan nodded at the man in the wheelchair. "And the man on his right, Mitch Christie. The man standing behind Cliff is Nando. He doesn't say much, but he's cool." He turned to face the others at the table. "Men, this is Liam Stone. He's an Aussie." Whelan pronounced it "Oz-zie."

"Lime Stone? What the hell kind of name is that?" Almeida said with a shit-eating grin.

"That's Rafe Almeida," Whelan said. "He's our version of a class clown."

"More like ass clown," Stensen said.

"Ignore Rafe, he's the runt of the litter," Larsen said.

"Yeah, we keep him around for entertainment," Thomas said.

"More likely target practice," Stensen said.

Almeida half rose from his chair. "Keep it up, motherfuckers. I'll rip the asses off of every fuckin' one of you."

"He also suffers from delusions of grandeur," Larsen said with a slight grin. It was his good grin, meaning no one was about to die.

"All right, for the last time, get off Rafe's ass," Whelan said. "At least for the remainder of this meeting. After that, you can all go back to playing grab-ass."

Whelan waved Stone to a vacant chair. He gave the others in the room the elevator speech about the Aussie's background, particularly his service with TAG West, Australia's version of the Navy SEALs. He closed by stating the obvious: "For better or for worse, Liam has the same genetic construct we all have. At Cliff's suggestion, I asked him to check us out. We'll all reciprocate, although I vetted him when we met in Australia. If he likes what we do, and he checks out okay by our standards, we just might have a new dog in the pound."

There was a welcoming chorus from the men at the table.

Stone smiled and said, "My mates call me 'Stoney.'"

"Cool name," Almeida said. "Maybe we can get 'stoned' sometime."

Levell slammed the edge of his fist against the top of the table. "Dammit, let's get back to business." He turned toward Christie. "Finish telling us about that raid in New Mexico."

"As usual, the news reports are just the tip of the iceberg. The official report is that a group of CBP agents and Hidalgo County sheriff's deputies stumbled upon drug smugglers armed with automatic weapons. The agents and deputies all died in the ensuing firefight."

"Yeah," Larsen said, nodding his head slowly. "That's what Headline News is saying.

"Fox News too," Stensen said.

"To repeat, that's the official version," Christie said.

"And the real story is?" Whelan said.

"The real story is that the agents didn't stumble upon anyone. They were intercepting a group of illegals that had been picked up on FLIR—Forward Looking Infrared. Forensics has determined they were gunned down from behind. In other words, there was another group that sneaked up behind them." Christie paused. "And there's an eyewitness. Although some of the victims were killed execution-style with a gunshot to the head at close range, one survived. That information is not to leave this room."

"You're saying the ambushers came at them from the U.S. side?" Thomas said.

"Yes."

"If it was drug smugglers," Whelan said, "was it MS-13. They've become entrenched on this side of the border."

"MS-13 likely played some part," Christie said. "And smuggling definitely was involved, but it wasn't drugs. It was human smuggling."

"Same old, same old," Larsen said. "Just people hoping to find a better life for themselves and their families. And, most of the time, they're willing to work at jobs Americans won't touch."

Almeida said, "Shit, Larsen, I hope we don't drown in the outpouring of your bleeding heart."

"What else did the official version distort or omit?" Whelan said.

"These weren't poor *campesinos*. Far worse than that."

"If it wasn't about drugs or illegal workers, what was it?" Stensen said.

Christie looked around the table. There was a grim expression on his face. "Jihadis. Specifically, members of the Holy Army of the Caliphate."

"HAC? Christ!" Almeida said, shaking his head.

"No shit?" said Thomas.

"Just between us," Christie said, "there already are thousands of them here in the United States. They're spread out in cells throughout the land in villages, towns, and cities. They're heavily armed with automatic weapons, RPGs, sophisticated explosives, the whole nine yards. And they've carefully mapped out strategic sites, including military and first-responder facilities, communications and power grids, and innumerable soft targets like malls, schools, and other public facilities."

"And they're just waiting for the signal," Whelan said.

"Yes. There is absolutely no reason to doubt that a massive, nationwide strike is coming, and soon."

"I assume there's a tie-in with the attack on the border guards?" Whelan said.

"Yes. We think it served two purposes. One was to make a statement that HAC is in control, not us."

"And the second?" said Thomas.

"We have intel that suggested the smugglers brought something unusual with them."

"Like what?" Stensen said.

"We're not positive, but we're reviewing satellite coverage of the incursion. It appears that traces of radioactivity were present."

PART TWO

THE HUNTER-KILLERS

Fate whispers to the wolf; 'you cannot withstand the storm' and the wolf whispers back, 'I am the storm' — Anonymous

CHAPTER 15
THE LODGE

OPERATIONS AT THE LODGE ran on a twenty-four-hour schedule and required a large staff to fill its wide variety of positions. One of the employees, a striking young blonde woman named Ashlee Erickson, worked the day shift as an assistant manager in Food and Beverage. She had a perfect body, and she knew it. Her clothes were tailored to accentuate her physical charms.

Her attractiveness wasn't lost on any of the males who worked at, or visited, The Lodge, including the Dogs, especially Rafe Almeida. Today, she was wearing a perfectly fitted navy blue suit. The skirt's hemline stopped at mid-thigh, showcasing her long, beautiful legs.

Almeida, Stensen, and Thomas were sitting in the large atrium area just inside the Lodge's main entrance, waiting for Levell and the other Dogs to arrive for an information session. Almeida had just mixed his third rum and coke when he heard the sound of high heels clicking on the stone floor. As if guided by radar, his head swiveled around to follow the sound.

"Shit, I'm in love," he said, as his eyes followed Ashlee's long, rhythmic strides across the atrium.

"Love? Nah, man, you're just in a perpetual state of lust. Every time you see anything female," Thomas said, shaking his head slowly in mock disapproval.

"You're old enough to be her father," Stensen said.

"But you look more like her grandfather," Thomas said.

"Great-grandfather," Stensen said.

Ashlee glanced over at the three men and smiled. It was like looking at an orthodontist's retirement plan.

"See! She wants me!" Almeida said. He tossed back his drink, stood, and started to follow the young woman.

"Rafe, leave the help alone," Thomas said.

"Maybe after I'm finished with her," Almeida said with a lascivious grin. He rubbed his crotch for emphasis.

"Okay," Stensen said. "In that case, we'll set our watches for two minutes. That ought to be more than enough time."

"Eat your hearts out, you fucking losers." Almeida turned to go after Ashlee, but she had crossed the atrium and entered an office on the far side of the room. He had taken a couple of steps toward the office when he heard a familiar raspy voice.

Levell, being wheeled by Nando, entered the room with Whelan, Larsen, and Liam Stone. They were returning from a round of target practice on The Lodge's private underground range.

Levell seemed to size up the situation in an instant. "Almeida, what the hell do you think you're doing?"

Rafe shrugged sheepishly and said, "I was just gonna go for a walk."

"Walk, my ass. Do I need to instruct the kitchen staff to feed you a steady diet of saltpeter?"

"That's an urban legend and a waste of time," Stensen said. "Just castrate the little bastard."

Everyone laughed except Almeida.

"Okay," Levell said, "fun and games are over. Time for business. Everybody in my office. Now."

A few minutes later all of the men were gathered in Levell's office. He had Nando purposely position his wheelchair so that the others had their backs to the wide glass wall that showcased the thickly wooded area outside. He didn't want anyone to be distracted from the business at hand. The men had moved some of the furniture so it formed a rough horseshoe facing Levell. When everyone was seated, Nando slipped quietly out of the room. Surrounded by the most lethal group of men on the planet, Levell could afford to give the Brazilian capoeira expert some down time.

Levell cleared his throat and said, "Before we get into the nitty-gritty, I want the rest of you to know that our newest member impressed the hell out of me on the shooting range today." He glanced at Stone. "Best natural shooter I've ever seen, bar none. That's saying something, considering who's in this room."

Larsen, seated next to Stone on a leather sofa, nudged the Aussie with an elbow. It was his way of paying a compliment.

"Way to go, Stoney," Thomas said.

"All right, enough with the accolades. We've got a colleague to exfiltrate from a hellhole."

"Why doesn't the government get him back? He's a fuckin' American," Almeida said. "They traded those rug merchants Kirkland killed for the deserter that Stensen offed."

Whelan expected Levell to go postal at both the interruption and the idiocy of the question, but the Old Man's rugged countenance was expression-free.

Levell sighed. "Because no one knows he's an American. There's no data on any of you anywhere. We've gone to great lengths to see to that, broken countless laws. If the U.S. government requests extradition, it gives the farm away. We'd never be able to scrub all of the databases scattered around the world once they had that information." He paused momentarily before adding, "Then there's the fact that our government doesn't know who or what he is and has no reason to want him returned."

"Even if they did," Stensen said, "the current administration wouldn't do it unless it thought there was political value in it for them, which there isn't. Like Rafe just said, it was Marc who sliced and diced the five jihadis this administration traded for the deserter, Kevin Johnson. They thought there was political capital in that move. How do you think they'd feel about Marc taking their dumbass moves off the table for the future?"

But Almeida wasn't through. "Yeah? Well, there's a race for president goin' on. The new guy could try to get him back."

"Are you shitting us?" Whelan said. "Are you paying any attention to the caliber of candidates left in the race?"

Levell raised his hand to refocus everyone's attention. "Brendan is right. The American electorate has just what it asked for…incompetents who were smart enough or lucky enough to tap into the various threads of anger and frustration that have clouded the perspectives of our fellow citizens. It's just further evidence of the average American's comic-book mentality."

Almeida had a puzzled look on his face. He wasn't the only one in the room who did. "What do you mean 'comic-book mentality?'"

Levell cocked his head to one side—a telltale idiosyncrasy that indicated he was going to discuss something that troubled him personally—and looked around the room. "The sad truth is that for far too many Americans, their deepest level of reading and understanding literally comes from reading comic books. Their intellectual level is based on a fetish with superheroes. They flock to those movies and collect a shitload of crappy merchandise based on them."

"So, what does this have to do with the election?" Larsen said.

Whelan answered for Levell. "It explains why the electorate in general, the majority of which formerly was right-of-center individualists, conservative types, is now enthralled with the blowhard, sociopathic egomaniacs currently running for president. They buy into the rhetoric and regard them as superhero types who will save the day."

"Got the same bullshit in Oz, too, mates," Stone said, shaking his head.

"Well, hell, we're all superheroes. Look at the fucking genetic gifts we have," Almeida said. "We should run for president. Everybody would vote for us."

Whelan laughed. "There are damn few people outside this room who even know we exist. Hard to get elected as a complete unknown."

"Shit, then we just need to come out of the closet, so to speak, and let 'em know who we are," Almeida said.

Levell shook his head emphatically. "That ship passed with your first mission. You are the planet's apex predators. Given the things you've done, even if they were in defense of this country, no one can ever know who you are. The majority of the population couldn't handle it, not to mention that such disclosure would destroy a good bit of your effectiveness for the future."

Thomas said, "I don't get the feeling you brought us together to lament the decline of American exceptionalism, Cliff."

"Moving right along," Stensen said with a deadpan expression.

"Quentin's right," Levell said. "At the moment, the most important task is to get Kirkland out of that Qatari prison and back here."

"Hell, why don't we do it the old-fashioned way: break into the prison, kill everyone in sight, burn it to the fuckin' ground, and bring him home?" Almeida said.

"Must be a blessing to be so fucking simpleminded," Stensen said.

Levell impatiently waved off Almeida's response. "If it were that damned easy, we would already have sent a team of ex-Special Ops people to do it. The reality is that the prison is almost a super-max. Trying to shoot your way in would be a suicide mission."

"If Mohammad can't come to the mountain, perhaps the mountain should come to Mohammad," Whelan said.

"What the fuck does that mean?" Almeida said. "Why are you talking about some Arab guy?"

"It means, why even try to get into the prison?" Whelan said. "Why not make the Qataris bring Marc to us?"

No one said anything for several moments. Finally, Almeida said, "That's nuts. Ain't that like making the Mexicans pay for a fuckin' wall they don't want? Why'n hell would they do that?"

"Put a cork in it, Rafe, and let him finish," Thomas said.

"The little bloke there," Stone nodded at Almeida, "doesn't seem to know Christmas from Bourke Street. But one thing I noticed about Brendan, he's always got a full quid. Let 'em speak."

Almeida stared at Stone. "What the fuck language is that? It sure ain't English."

"It's Strine," Whelan said. "Better get used to it."

"Strine? What the hell's that?"

"Australian the way Ozzies speak it."

"Finish what you were saying about making the Qatar people bring Marc to us," Larsen said to Whelan. He gave Almeida a look that would have killed Dracula faster than a stake through the heart.

"It's not all that complicated," Whelan said. "Why did the Taliban return Kevin Johnson?"

"Because our candy-ass president offered them five of their top lieutenants back," Levell said.

"Exactly," Whelan said.

"So, what are we supposed to offer the Qataris that they'd really want?" Thomas said.

Whelan smiled a hard, mean smile and looked around the room. "What do you know about Qatar?"

"Bunch of fuckin' towelheads," Almeida said.

Stensen said, "For once the little shit got something right. But to elaborate, it's an oil-rich emirate on the Persian Gulf. The ruling family pretends to cozy up to the West, but they're among the staunchest political and financial supporters of jihadism, including the Holy Army of the Caliphate. For example, Qatar is the home of the Al Jazeera Media Network, which is partly funded by the Qatari royals. Like most of the ruling families in that part of the world, they're a bunch of thugs sitting atop billions in oil and pretending it gives them a patina of legitimacy."

"What's a patina?" Almeida said. Everyone ignored him.

"If you've got all the luxuries petrodollars can buy and plenty of wealth to replenish them, what's the one thing that would get your attention?" Whelan said.

The room was silent for several moments. Finally, Levell spoke. "I see where you're going with this. You can replace cars, jewels, yachts, homes, and jets many times over. You can even replace some human beings—but not all of them."

He paused for effect and looked around the room. "You're proposing to kidnap one or more members of the royal family and ransom them back for Kirkland."

Whelan nodded. "The emir, or sheikh, or whatever he calls himself has three wives and several children. His favorite wife, Sheikha Aisha, is the mother of his son, Crown Prince Ali. I doubt there is anything he wouldn't do to get them back."

Thomas let out a low whistle. "So, you want to snatch both of them."

Whelan nodded again.

"That's good oil, mate," Stone said with a broad smile.

Almeida wagged his head back and forth. "I don't get it. Why would a guy with a bunch of wives and kids give a rat's ass about losing a few of them?"

"Like I told you earlier, you've never been in love or had kids. I doubt you could understand," Thomas said.

CHAPTER 16

THE PRINCIPALITY OF MONACO

A SMALL SIGN on the entrance to the office identified the business as Sècuritè Personnelle S.A. It was located in an aging building of corrugated steel at the intersection of Route de la Turbie and Route Moyenne Corniche, about two kilometers west of the border separating France from the Principality of Monaco.

The building clung to the steep, rocky flank of Tête de Chien (Dog's Head), a 450-meter tall rock promontory, the highest point on the Grande Corniche road. The site overlooked the azure waters of the Mediterranean Sea, but the building lacked windows. Even if it had them, an ugly brick wall with cracks and peeling paint would have blocked the view. In the United States, the building would have been labeled flex-space, an industrial warehouse with room for an office in front.

Inside the office, a thin, swarthy man sat behind a cheap metal desk. He had a bushy mustache and longish, hair that had a well-oiled look. When Whelan entered the office, he glanced up from his newspaper. There was a distinct aroma of food. Whelan thought it smelled like couscous and stew. An empty bowl sat on the desk in front of the man. He just stared at Whelan for several moments with an expression that was a cross between annoyed and bored. Finally, he said, "What is your business?" He spoke French with a heavy accent. Whelan suspected it was influenced by a North African version of Arabic. Three of the top four largest groups of immigrants to this part of France had come from Tunisia, Morocco, and Algeria.

"I work for a wealthy American businessman. I'm here to arrange for local security during his stay in Cap d'Antibes. The Hôtel du Cap-Eden Roc," Whelan said in French.

The man dropped the newspaper on the desk and slouched back in the chair. "Do I look like a fucking receptionist to you?"

"You look like someone with no customer service training."

"I'm a chauffeur. I drive people around. I'm just sitting at this desk because the boss told me to."

"Where's the receptionist?"

He shrugged his thin shoulders. "Sick. She says."

"Who besides you is here?"

He made a motion behind him with his head. "Four muscle-heads in the back. They're the next shift on a job we're doing in Monaco. I drive them down there and bring the old crew back here."

"That's it? You don't have any management, clerical help, other drivers, or mechanics around?"

The man shook his head. "This is just a pickup and drop-off point for the crews we have working in the area. The receptionist, when she's here," the sarcasm was heavy, "schedules the crews, usually by phone. You call back tomorrow, she'll probably be in."

Whelan slipped a Glock 23 out of his waistband and aimed it at the man's head. "Are you positive there's no one else here, other than the four guys in back?"

The man stared in terror at the cold, expressionless maw of the

Glock. The words spilled out of him. "No. That's it. Nobody else. Are you going to rob us? We don't have shit." He seemed to rethink that last statement. "…Other than the motor coach we use to shuttle the crews. It's out back." He jerked his head toward the wall that separated the office from the garage area. "Take it. Here, you can have the keys." He picked a key fob off the desktop and held it out to Whelan. It rattled as his hand shook.

Whelan, wearing a tactical communications device with throat microphone and earbud, said, "Four bogies out back. Take your positions, but wait for my signal. And send Rafe in here through the front door."

He heard Larsen's voice. "Roger that."

A moment later Almeida came through the door. He was carrying a SIG MPX-K with a suppressed four-and-a-half-inch barrel and a magazine with thirty 9mm rounds. He saw the man cowering in the chair and said, "Want me to shoot him?" He waved the SIG menacingly.

"No, I want you to secure him. If he does something stupid, then you can shoot him."

"He speak English?"

"Doubtful. He barely speaks French." Whelan turned to the man and explained to him in French what was expected of him, and the penalty for varying from it.

With Whelan continuing to cover the man, Almeida shouldered the SIG and pulled some flex ties from a pocket of his cargo shorts. He bound the prisoner's ankles and wrists with his arms behind the man's back. As a finishing touch, he stuffed a thick bandana in the man's mouth and secured it with a wide strip of packing tape. He effortlessly dragged the man into a corner then traded weapons with Whelan. Almeida sat down in the desk chair formerly occupied by his prisoner and trained the Glock on the man's center mass.

Whelan moved swiftly to the interior door opposite the entrance and used the comm device again. "Situation?"

Larsen responded, "Everyone's in place."

"Remember, these guys are all ex-military, mostly French and German Special Ops with a few Brits too. They're trained to react, so you'll probably have to kill them."

"Affirmative."

"All right, on my signal. Three. Two. One. Go, go, go!" Whelan threw the door open and leapt inside in a low crouch. There were four thickly built men in the warehouse space. Three were sitting at a battered card table, smoking. The fourth sat on a soiled, sagging couch reading a British tabloid. Just as Whelan had predicted, all reacted quickly to the sudden noise as he burst through the door from the office. Without hesitation, they went for their weapons. And just as quickly all four of them were dead. Larsen, Thomas, Stensen, and Stone had flowed like wraiths through the wide space where the large overhead garage door was. It had been left open in hopes of catching a whiff of breeze for the unairconditioned industrial space. On a sunny day in May, with a pleasant breeze wafting in from the Mediterranean, there had been no reason to anticipate a hit on a legitimate business in a quiet neighborhood.

"Nice work," Whelan said to the others who were gathering the spent shell casings.

"Crikey, mates, it feels good to be back in action," Stone said as he checked the bodies to make sure they were dead.

"Nick, bring the van around and let's get these guys loaded up," Whelan said. "Stoney, get Rafe out here with the prisoner."

"Prisoner?" Stensen said. "We never take prisoners. What gives?"

"I want to have a conversation with this guy."

"And then?"

Whelan shrugged. "And then whatever."

A few minutes later, Stensen, wearing a hairnet and thin rubber gloves, backed a nondescript late model Citroën Jumper, a large cargo van, through the open garage door. The men quickly wrapped the four dead bodies in canvas tarps from the van and piled them into its cargo area. Next, they changed into uniforms identical to the ones worn by the dead men—gray trousers, white dress shirts, navy blue blazers with the Sècuritè Personnelle S.A. logo on the breast pocket, and pale blue neckties. Thanks to SAS documents experts, Whelan and the others not only had the proper clothing, but also creds identifying them as employees of Sècuritè Personnelle.

When Almeida brought the prisoner into the garage area, Whelan grabbed the man by an arm and pulled him over to the rear of the van so he could see the blood-soaked tarps that held the remains of his former fellow employees. The prisoner immediately began trembling and making a high-pitched whimpering sound. Whelan dragged the man over to the ancient and now bloody sofa and shoved him onto it.

He pulled the tape covering the man's mouth aside, yanked the bandana out, and said, "I'm going to ask you some questions. I'll know when you're lying." He nodded toward the van. "And when you do, I'll kill you. Understand?"

The terrified man's head bobbed up and down vigorously.

Whelan spent several minutes listening to the prisoner detail the route he would have driven to deliver the hired security men to the Hôtel de Paris Monte-Carlo, the timing of the shift change, a description of the men who would be coming off duty at the hotel, and how many others would be guarding the target. Because of the intel Levell had shared with him, Whelan knew the answers to some of the questions and asked them only for the purpose of testing the prisoner's truthfulness. The man was too terrified to lie.

When he was satisfied the man had shared all he could, Whelan replaced the gag and tossed him into the back of the van with the corpses. The prisoner continued to quiver and make squealing noises behind the thick wad of bandana that filled his mouth.

Whelan closed the rear doors of the van and turned to Almeida. "Put on the gloves and hairnet. Do not leave spit, snot, urine or any other body fluids in the van. Don't smoke or chew gum or pick your nose in the van. Don't leave a fucking thing in the van that can be traced back to you. Understand?"

"What, you think I'm some kind of slob?"

"I think you have a habit of doing some dumb-ass things." Whelan paused briefly for effect. "You remember what to do with the van and the bodies in it, right?"

"Yeah, I ain't fucking retarded."

Stensen snorted.

Almeida turned and glared at him then said to Whelan, "What about the prisoner?"

"He's a Muslim," Whelan said.

"I figured he was a towelhead."

"You know any Muslims who are actively and openly fighting Islamic terrorism?"

"No."

"Ever heard of any?"

Almeida paused to think about that one. "No."

"There are one and a half billion Muslims on this planet," Stensen said. "And every damn one of them seems to hate the West, especially the United States."

"Can't leave any fucking wog bastards behind," Stone said.

"They're all enemies in my book," Larsen said.

"They can't *all* be our enemies," Thomas said.

"Put a cork in it, Quentin," Larsen said with a snarl. The Man-With-No-Neck rarely spoke, but when he did, everyone listened, even the other Dogs.

"What's our policy regarding captured enemies, Rafe?" Stensen said.

"That's easy. We kill 'em, every fuckin' one of 'em."

"Congratulations," Stensen said, "you finally got one right. Somebody call the Guinness Book of Records."

CHAPTER 17

HÔTEL DE PARIS MONTE-CARLO

WHELAN, Larsen, Stone, and Stensen gathered up the identical backpacks that had belonged to the men they'd just killed. All bore the name and logo of Sècuritè Personnelle. The men emptied them and replaced the contents with their own materials.

"Quentin, you drive the coach," Whelan said. He pointed at the Fiat Ducato passenger van tossed Thomas the keys the prisoner had given him.

"It's a Black thing, isn't it?" Thomas said with a scowl.

"What are you talking about?"

"I'm talking about there being four of you white guys, not counting Rafe, but you want me to drive the van. That's a racial stereotype."

"Why? Rafe's driving the cleanup van. Would you rather do that?"

"No, Rafe's doing that because he's a fuckup and can't be trusted with much of anything else."

Whelan shook his head. "We went through this earlier. Think

about where we are. What we're trying to pull off. Who we're supposed to be."

"Yeah?"

"Our cover story is we're a group of mercs—ex-Special Ops employed by a private security company in Nice. It hires mostly French, German, and an occasional Aussie or Brit ex-Special Ops. You're probably better than anyone they have on their payroll, but it's doubtful they'd hire a black man even if he was from a former French colony. We show up with you in the mix and right away a red flag goes up."

"That's racist."

"I'm not arguing the point, Quentin. It's just the way this is playing out. We don't need any unwanted attention. Besides, you don't deal as well with the collateral damage."

"Collateral damage? Why not call it what it is? Needless bloodletting."

"Just drive the damn van, Thomas. You know the drill."

Thomas nodded sullenly. "Yeah, I know the fucking drill. Drop the rest of you at the hotel and go babysit this coach in a parking lot until 'da massa' calls for his house boy."

THOMAS WHEELED the Fiat coach to a stop in front of the entrance to the Hôtel de Paris Monte-Carlo, a grande dame of La Belle Époque. Four large and very muscular men climbed out, shouldered identical backpacks, and marched in a phalanx up the steps and into the hotel's lobby. They were dressed alike and stared straight ahead. People scurried to get out of their way. The doorman, recognizing their uniformity of clothing, powerful builds, and humorless expressions, hurriedly opened the door.

"Good afternoon, messieurs," he said nervously in impeccable

French. "As always, the changing of the guard precisely at one o'clock."

The four men, Whelan, Larsen, Stensen, and Stone, ignored him and strode briskly through the hotel's luxurious lobby. It featured an atrium with stained-glass dome, marble pillars, crystal chandeliers, groupings of red velvet Louis XVI chairs, and sumptuous carpets. Iconic luxury shops opened directly off the lobby— Prada, Hermès, Valentino, Gucci, Bulgari, Piaget, Christian Dior. It was filled with a pleasant aroma that legend had it was created especially for the hotel.

They crossed the lobby and went straight to a small, private area and entered the elevator dedicated exclusively to accessing the eighth floor. Their intel had identified it as being occupied by the Qatari royals. Liam Stone pressed the button and the four men rode to the top. On the way up, they each clipped the fake creds Levell had provided to the lapel of their blazers.

When the elevator door opened, two men dressed similarly to Whelan and the others were standing there. They were wearing comm gear and each man was pointing an H&K MP7 at them. One of them stepped forward and examined each set of creds then stepped back and nodded at the other man.

It was the second man who spoke. His French had a heavy German accent. "You are not the people who relieved us yesterday." He was frowning.

"They were reassigned," Stone said, looking directly into the German's eyes. "Something about a big rock star coming to Nice and death threats. The company thought those other guys were the appropriate ones to send."

"Why have we never seen you guys before?" the German said. "And what kind of accent is that? You are not a Brit."

"No, I'm Australian, former SASR. TAG West to be specific."

"And these other guys?" The German motioned at Whelan and the other Dogs with the muzzle of the MP7.

Still locking eyes with the German, Stone said, "Same as you and me—former military. We were all hired to do the same jobs as you."

The German studied the four men for a few moments then glanced at his partner and nodded. They lowered the muzzles of their weapons and stepped back to make room for the four men to exit the elevator. With the German in front and his partner bringing up the rear, the six men began walking down the hotel corridor toward the far end. The walls were covered in red velvet. Rare items of furniture were discreetly placed along the way, along with prints of paintings by Winston Churchill, a former guest.

Stone said, "Where are the assets?"

Without turning around, the German said, "Shopping. It's what they came here to do."

They reached a double set of large ornate doors at the end of the corridor. There was an elegant and tasteful bronze plaque on the wall to the left of the doors. In baroque script, it read Diamond Suite Winston Churchill. The German paused in front of the doors and spoke into the boom mic of his comm gear. A moment later he opened the door on the right and walked in. The other man and the four Dogs followed him. Beyond a small antechamber, the room opened into an enormous living room with marble and brass finishings. To the left, another set of double doors opened to a large master bedroom suite. A single door at the opposite end of the living room led to a slightly smaller bedroom suite. Windows in the far wall offered a panoramic view of the harbor and the famous Rock of Monaco.

There were two other men in the living room, both seated on a sofa that looked like it cost more than the average home in America. They stood up when the others entered. One of them, speaking flawless French said, "This is officially your shift now." He and the other men prepared to leave.

"So, none of the assets are here?" Whelan said in French, affecting an English accent.

"I told you they're shopping," the German said.

"All three of them? Kids too?"

The German nodded. "Yes."

"And what about members of the household staff—nannies, servants, and such?"

The German shrugged. "Unless their services are required, they are to stay in their own rooms." He grinned sardonically. "Cheaper rooms. Lower down, no views."

"If all four of you are here, who's providing security for the assets while they shop?"

The Frenchman who had been sitting on the sofa furrowed his brow and said, "Why are you asking these questions? Weren't you briefed?"

"Barely," Stone said. "We were called in so quickly, we weren't given the full scenario. That's why we're asking you."

The Frenchman thought about that. "You are aware that the assets brought their own security detail with them from the royal palace, aren't you?"

"Well, yeah," said Whelan, "but we weren't given any specifics, like how many of them there are or what our responsibilities are in relation to theirs. What the hell's the protocol here?"

The man who had been with the German at the elevator shook his head. "I told you this fucking company is getting very lax," he said looking at his colleagues. He, too, was French. "Sending a shift out without proper preparation is a bad sign."

"I don't disagree," Whelan said, "but, like it or not this is our assignment. How about filling us in on the basics, like what we're dealing with as far as the assets are concerned. We know there's

Sheikha Aisha, her son Crown Prince Ali, and daughter Princess Fatima. What's the situation with the homegrown bodyguards?"

The German sneered. "Typical arrogant sandmonkeys. We get paid to take one for members of the royal family, but not those little bastards."

"How many of them are there?" Stone said.

"Six," the Brit said. "They work eight-hour shifts like we do. Two of them shadow the family at all times. The others sleep or get pressed into double duty if the Sheikha demands it."

"How many are with her now?" Whelan said.

"Four."

"Yeah," the German said. "The bitch thinks she and her precious children are safer with their own poorly trained, inexperienced camel jockeys than with us."

"Good to know," Whelan said. "When are they due to return?"

"When the bitch feels she's spent enough of her old man's petrodollars," the Brit said with a shrug. "But they've been gone all morning, so the kids will be acting up. Should be back any time now."

Whelan looked at the other Dogs and nodded. Instantly, each of them whipped out a knife of choice. For Whelan, it was a SOG SEAL 2000, while Stensen used a full-size black KA-BAR. Larsen and Stone both preferred the Gerber LHR Fixed Blade Combat Knife. The other men were well-trained former military operatives, and very quick. But they also were Norms. It took barely more than a second for the Dogs to plunge their respective weapons into the hearts of their victims.

Larsen grabbed two of the bodies by their shirt collars. Whelan did the same with the other two. They dragged the dead men into the master bathroom and piled them in the oversized marble tub to finish bleeding out. Stensen and Stone used huge, thick Egyptian cotton towels from the other bathroom to wipe up the blood. They had just finished when the alarm went off alerting them that the private elevator was in use. Larsen and Stone took two of the H&K MP7s and went down the hall to meet its occupants.

They returned a few minutes later with an attractive young Middle Eastern woman and two children, a boy of about eight and a girl who was a few years older. They were accompanied by four large swarthy, bearded Arab-looking men dressed in designer suits. None of the Dogs doubted they had been tailored specifically to conceal weapons in shoulder holsters. Three of the Arabs, laden with shopping bags bearing the logos of many of the world's most exclusive shops, stood in front of the royals. The fourth man approached Whelan and Stensen and examined their creds. Satisfied with their authenticity, he said in French, "You are new. Why is that?"

Whelan gave him the same explanation they'd used before, about a rock star and death threats.

The Arab said, "Your accent is British?"

"Yes."

"What about these others?" He glanced around at the other Dogs.

"One's an Aussie, another's French, and the big fellow is Norwegian."

The Arab's eyes came to rest on Larsen. He'd seen many large powerful men before, but never one whose muscularity was so pronounced that he had no neck. "Norwegian? Does he speak French?"

Whelan nodded. "Passably. Now, since we're here to help protect them, perhaps it would be appropriate for you to introduce us to the members of the royal family."

The Arab shook his head. "They don't need to know your names. They'll point at you when they want something. Otherwise, you communicate with them through one of us." He motioned toward the other three Arab bodyguards.

"Understood," Whelan said.

The Arab turned to his colleagues and, in Arabic, said, "Youssef and Hadi, you are not needed now. Get some rest. Report for the five o'clock shift in the morning. Ghalib and I will handle things now."

Youssef and Hadi placed the shopping bags they were carrying on the sofa and turned to leave. As they did, the royals began to walk toward their respective bedrooms.

"Now," said Whelan and reached inside his blazer.

In a nanosecond, all four of the Dogs had whipped out SIG P239 Tactical pistols—9mm automatics with eight rounds in the mag and one in the chamber. The weapons all had SRD9 silencers screwed into their threaded barrels. The sounds of the suppressed firings erupted almost simultaneously, and pinkish mists and brain matter exploded from the heads of the four Arab bodyguards. They collapsed instantly, blood and cerebrospinal fluid oozing onto the highly-polished marble floor and staining the priceless area rug in the center of the room.

The three royals stared in horror at the scene, then the little boy began screaming "Mama" in Arabic. A second or two later, his older sister joined in. The Dogs holstered their weapons and swiftly surrounded them.

"Are you going to kill us?" the young sheikha said, eyes wide in terror as she gathered the two children to her protectively.

Whelan was impressed with her reasonably calm demeanor, given the circumstances. "That depends on two things. One is that you do exactly what we tell you and don't vary from it. The other is your husband's response."

Larsen yanked the children away from their mother's side and slung one across each of his massive shoulders. His sheer bulk and absence of a neck further terrified the kids. He carried them into the master bedroom and dropped them on the extra-large king-size. They began screaming again as Whelan escorted the sheikha into the room by the arm. He wasn't concerned that their noise would be heard elsewhere in the hotel; it had recently undergone a multimil-lion-dollar renovation. The Churchill Suite had been among the first units to be renovated; its already formidable soundproofing had been further enhanced. *At €12,500 per night, it should be quieter than a tomb.*

He produced the SOG SEAL 2000 and said to the children in Arabic, "Stop screaming or I'll kill your mother right now." He had no intention of harming any of the royals, but he'd learned at an early age that there were only two factors that could control human behavior—greed and fear. Of the two, fear was far more reliable and effective. The screaming stopped, replaced by sniffling sounds and stifled sobs.

Stensen opened the backpack he'd brought with him and removed a small case. Whelan nodded and Stensen removed three syringes and an alcohol swab. He wiped a spot on one of the sheikha's arms, pulled the plastic shield off the tip of one of the syringes, and jabbed it into her arm. She gasped and stared at him, wide-eyed.

"It's just a sedative. It'll wear off with no side effects," he said with a pleasant smile. The red centers in his eyes were just tiny dots.

Stensen put a small bandage on the site of the injection and moved on to the children. He quickly sedated them. In a few minutes, all three of the royals were unconscious.

Whelan pulled a satphone from his backpack. It was encrypted with an algorithm proprietary to the Mueller brothers' operations and worked off commercial satellites built and serviced by one of their companies. One of the unique aspects of the communication system was its ability to encode conversations into music formats transmitted from the satellites.

When he heard Thomas at the other end, he said, "We're good to go," and disconnected the call.

Moving swiftly, he and the other Dogs emptied a large trunk and two large suitcases. They placed the sheikha in the trunk and a child in each of the suitcases. Larsen lifted the trunk onto one of his thick shoulders. Stone picked up the suitcases. Armed with one of the MP7s, Stensen took the point while Whelan, similarly armed, covered the rear. He closed the door behind them and hung a fancy sign on one of the handles. It said *Ne pas déranger*—Do Not Disturb.

The four men took the elevator to its small private lobby on the ground level. Stensen took its separate exit to the sidewalk as Thomas pulled up to the curb. He went back inside and signaled the others, who brought the luggage out and loaded it into the rear of the Fiat Ducato motor coach.

Within moments, Thomas had navigated the twisting Moné-gasque streets and had them heading east on the coastal highway. They changed into casual sports attire in the van before passing through Menton, the last town of consequence in France. They ditched the Fiat in favor of a Mercedes-Benz motor coach that Levell's people had arranged for them. To be sure their captives didn't suffocate, the men had punched a few holes in the luggage they were in.

A short while later they crossed the border between France and Italy about seven kilometers west of Ventimiglia. They were all carrying fake Schengen visas and creds that identified them as members of a Belgian weightlifting team on their way to a competi-tion in Genoa. Because Belgium and Italy were signatories to the Schengen Agreement, there were no routine immigration checks at the border crossing, and they passed smoothly through.

Two kilometers beyond Ventimiglia, Thomas turned north and drove seven additional kilometers up the Strada Provinciale that ran through the Nervia Valley along the mostly dry Torrente Nervia. They passed through Camporosso and, just before reaching the ancient mountain village of Dolceacqua, turned off the main road and began climbing the narrow unpaved switchbacks. Two kilometers above Dolceacqua they reached their destination, a quaint stone manor house perched on the top of a ridgeline overlooking the Nervia and Dolceacqua. All told, the trip from Monte Carlo to their destination had taken less than an hour.

The manor house was called Casa di Alta Montagna—the House of the High Mountains. It had been rented over the Internet for a week by someone who paid the full rate via PayPal. The instructions had been clear. The occupants wanted complete privacy —no servants, no agents. No one was to interrupt them during their stay. To assuage the concerns of the property owner's agents, they also had put down a security deposit equal to double the full week's rental.

The four men carried the trunk and suitcases into the house, removed the still unconscious royals, and bound them comfortably with plastic ties. About an hour after they had arrived, the sheikha began to revive.

Once she was fully awake, she said to Whelan, "Why are you doing this? What do you hope to gain? Are you political enemies of my husband, the emir?"

He stared at her for a moment and shook his head. "Your country has something we want. If they give it to us, you and the children will be returned to Qatar unharmed."

"And if they refuse...?"

"Both 'returned' and 'unharmed' become problematic."

CHAPTER 18
BRIGHTON BEACH

HARLAND FAIRCHILDE IV purposely kept Federov and Ulyanin cooling their heels in his study. He was angry that they had come to his Brookville Long Island estate uninvited and unannounced. After he'd gotten over the shock of Federov being alive, he recalled something else that disturbed him greatly. The car with two dead men inside that had been abandoned outside his large, rambling, expensive estate had had Federov's hair fibers on the upholstery and Federov's thumbprint on the steering wheel.

And he hadn't forgotten what his contact in the local police force had reported to him—the detectives assigned to the murders were keeping an occasional eye on his house in the event the murderer might return. In fact, the suspected murderer, Kirill Federov, was sitting downstairs in his study. *What if the police were to "drop by for a chat?"* And what the hell was that damn Ulyanin thinking, bringing Federov here? Why hadn't he at least called first? Perhaps Ulyanin knew he would have been refused.

Fairchilde didn't want Federov anywhere around him. The police couldn't help but implicate him in the murders if they knew he'd had an employment relationship with Federov, their prime suspect.

Shit! It wasn't as if he didn't have enough stress in his life managing one of the oldest and wealthiest firms on Wall Street, while simultaneously guiding the Alliance for Global Unity on the inevitable path to a one world government and global financial dominion. *On the subject of which, there are at least three current members of AGU's governing board that have become disturbingly dissident. I arranged their appointments to the board and now they have the audacity to question my actions? There are ways to deal with their ilk. I would prefer to have Maksym handle them, but he has begun spending entirely too much time traveling abroad. He claims it's for the purpose of finding opportunities to invest the funds AGU is paying him. Perhaps, he's being paid too much.*

Fairchilde's thoughts returned to the two men waiting in his study. Maybe this was a situation where they could be particularly useful.

TWO MEN SETTLED into a scarred and dirty booth in a bar in Brighton Beach. It was twenty-six miles as the crow flies, thirty-five by car, from Fairchilde's Long Island estate in Brookville. The barroom reeked of cigarette smoke, stale sweat, and the acrid aroma of Eastern European dishes. The booth's tabletop was sticky from an accumulation of spilled foods and beverages. The floor was worse. The soles of the men's shoes stuck to it, more so in some spots than others. The place was crowded and noisy, and the only language spoken was Russian.

A thickly built bartender approached the two men. Every visible inch of his skin was heavily tattooed. A rubber band bound his long, greasy hair in a ponytail. He had rolled the sleeves of his white shirt up to his elbows displaying massive forearms and badly scared knuckles. Another ugly scar ran right to left across his nose to a point just below the corner of his mouth. He made no effort to smile. Without having been asked, he thumped a bottle of Russian vodka and two heavy glasses on the table, then turned and walked away.

"Pleasant fellow," Andrei Ulyanin said dryly.

"*Krest'yanin*," Federov said, spitting out the Russian word for peasant. He filled the two glasses and shoved one toward Ulyanin. Some of the liquid slopped out, adding to the rich medley already coating the tabletop.

Each man tossed back a full shot and Federov refilled the glasses.

"I thought the conversation with Fairchilde went well," Ulyanin said. The men had ridden mostly in silence from Brookville to the bar.

Federov glared at the tabletop and shook his head. "The fucking pansy didn't seem happy that I survived. He disrespected me."

"I wouldn't say that. He hired you back."

"Yeah, to kill three rich old farts because they dare to question his leadership. The arrogant, thin-skinned prick."

"It's a job and it pays well, Kirill. Is America a great country or what? Where else could we each make fifty thousand per killing? And three useless old men at that."

"We could make a helluva lot more helping ourselves to Fairchilde's own money like we discussed."

Ulyanin nodded and reached for the bottle, pouring another round in each glass. "How do you suggest we go about doing that? He has staff around him at all times, as well as a house full of electronic equipment designed to alert that staff and the local police. I doubt he leaves substantial money lying around his home."

"I'm sure he has a safe somewhere in that big-ass mansion of his. And the members of his staff are domestics, not professional security people."

"So, you're saying we get him to open his safe for us? And then what? At his first opportunity, he'll call the cops. And with his influence and connections probably the feds as well."

A malicious grin spread over Federov's face. "Dead men don't call for help."

"But what if there's no cash in that safe? What if it's bonds or jewelry? That stuff is easily traceable and would be difficult for us to dispose of without getting caught."

"Then perhaps we execute what the Americans call 'Plan B.'"

"Which is?"

"He is one of the wealthiest men on Wall Street. His family has been moving hundreds of billions of dollars for generations. First, we clean out the cash in his safe, then make him call his office and order the sale of millions of dollars of his equities. The proceeds are to be transferred to an account we set up and control."

"The first problem I see with that is that the Feds can trace the transaction."

Federov grinned again. "You are not thinking…how do they say, out of the box, Andrei."

Ulyanin shrugged. "Enlighten me."

"The funds are converted into cryptocurrency such as Bitcoin or Moneta then transferred by way of one of the Dark Net markets like Silk Road 3 or whatever its current iteration is. Technology is a wonderful thing, Andrei."

For a few moments Ulyanin thought about what Federov had said. "I don't really understand this Bitcoin, Dark Net business. Do you know how to use it?"

Federov leaned forward conspiratorially and said, "That's part of the beauty of it. We don't have to know how to do it. Mother Russia continues to produce some of the best computer criminals in the world." He sat up and glanced around the bar then leaned back in. "I am certain that some are sitting here in this bar right now."

Now it was Ulyanin who leaned back in his seat and nodded his head up and down. "I like it, Kirill. When do we do this?"

"Ah," Federov said, wagging his finger. "There is more."

Ulyanin raised his eyebrows questioningly. "More?"

"Taking Fairchilde's money and killing him is only the first step. His death will create a crisis for the Alliance for Global Unity. I want to take command of it."

Confusion clouded Ulyanin's expression. "Why? What is to be gained?"

"Think about it, Andrei. The world is being consumed by a rising crescendo of chaos and violence. This is all happening as AGU draws closer to creating a single global state. We would have riches, yes, but we would be adrift in all this chaos. On the other hand, if we control AGU, we control our destiny."

"In other words, it is we who would run this one-world entity?"

"Exactly."

"But how do we gain control of it following Fairchilde's death?"

"By being the most ruthless of them all. First, we terrify the other members at a meeting we will have Fairchilde set up before we kill him. Then, at the meeting, we do something similar to a scene I saw in an old American movie, *The Godfather*."

"Which is?"

"With our people securing the room so that no one can leave, we open the meeting by pulling Fairchilde's severed head from a bag and tossing it into the middle of the table. Then we reassure those in attendance that the thing that most interests them, their participation in global financial domination, remains unchanged."

Ulyanin frowned. "I don't know, Kirill. It seems there should be more to it than that."

"Of course, there always is. While I was a 'guest' of Levell and the SAS, I learned that China's current minister of finance intends to usurp the role of the AGU following the collapse of world order by having its leaders killed."

"So, we would also be offering the leaders of AGU an opportunity to survive the perfidy of the Chinese."

"Yes, but there is a certain preliminary step that we must take."

"Preliminary to killing Fairchilde?"

"Yes. According to Levell's intel, this Chinese minister has a man working for him who Fairchilde believes is his employee, a man named Maksym." Federov spit the name out like it had a bitter taste. "I know this man. He is very formidable. I want him out of the way from the beginning."

"Where do we find this Maksym?"

"He is purposely mysterious. I am not the only one who wants to kill him. Fairchilde obviously has a way to contact him. I want you to find out what it is, then get word to him that not only am I still alive, but planning to kill his supposed employer. You will mislead him and we will kill him."

CHAPTER 19

CASA DI ALTA MONTAGNA, LIGURIA, ITALY

THE AROMA of fresh pasta sauce wafted through the sprawling two-hundred-year-old Casa di Alto Montagna. Planted firmly on the peak of the area's highest ridgeline, it overlooked the sunny Nervia valley and the ancient Ligurian village of Dolceacqua. The town's tall stone houses, accessible via narrow twisting alleys, clustered their way up the steep sides of the valley, sleeping peacefully under the protective gaze of the twelfth century Castle Doria.

The pasta sauce hadn't been prepared by a local. The only people allowed near the Casa were Whelan, his colleagues, and their captives, the Qatari royals. Oddly, the best cook among the Dogs was the vigilante and serial killer Nick Stensen. Whelan once again pondered that enigma. *How is it that someone who had appointed himself to the task of cleaning up society's trash is also a talented chef? Go figure.*

Whelan turned to his left as Larsen, seated next to him at the large wooden dinner table, passed a big terra-cotta bowl of strozzapreti noodles mixed with Stensen's sauce. Another bowl filled with huge succulent meatballs followed closely behind it. The

Irishman filled his plate and passed the food to the man on his right, Quentin Thomas. Looking around the table, he saw that most of the Dogs were present, including the newest one, Liam Stone. The only one missing was Marc Kirkland, and their first order of business was to secure his release. That was the purpose for the presence of their prisoners, secured in the basement beneath the Casa.

"Nick," Whelan said, "did you make enough for the sheikha and the kids?"

"Yeah, I figured I'd send Rafe down with the leftovers."

"No!" Whelan said. "Rafe is not to go anywhere near the sheikha. Understand?" He looked around the table, making eye contact with each man.

"Shit, why you singling me out?" Almeida said.

"Because you think every woman on the planet is dying to bang you. She's the emir's favorite wife. We're not sending damaged goods back to him. Got it?"

"But she's smokin' hot. What if *she* wants me?"

"She'll just have to suffer through it on her own." Whelan said.

"Not to change the subject, mates," Stone said, "but when do we let the husband know we have his family and demand Kirkland in exchange?"

Whelan glanced at his watch, a combat timepiece specifically designed for Special Ops combatants. The digital numbers read four thirty in the afternoon, Central European Summer Time. "They're on Arabia Standard Time in Doha, which puts them an hour ahead of us. I figure we finish dinner then make the phone call."

"By now the whole world is aware that the royals are missing, and there are a lot of dead bodies in and around Monaco with ties to them," Stensen said.

"I'll bet all of Qatar is swarming like a nest of disturbed hornets," Larsen said.

"Mind sharing with us what you plan to say to them?" Thomas said to Whelan.

Whelan shrugged. "It's pretty simple, really. They've got Marc. We've got Crown Prince Ali, his sister Fatima, and their mother, Sheikha Aisha. They release Marc unharmed per our directions, or else."

Thomas squinted. "Or else what?"

"Or else we start sending pieces of the little prince to Doha."

"Shit! No way," Thomas said. "I'm not going to be a part of killing little kids. Count me out!"

"Aw, don't get the shits, mate," Stone said. "Brendan's not gonna harm the little bugger. He's the only one of us that's got kids of his own."

Thomas turned toward Whelan. "That true? You're not really going to hurt the kid?"

Stone's remark brought thoughts of his own wife and sons rushing into Whelan's mind, juxtapositioning them with the task at hand. The parallel was uncomfortable. He smiled enigmatically and shrugged. "Depends on how reasonable his old man is."

AN HOUR LATER, all of the Dogs except Whelan were still sitting around the dinner table. Larsen sipped a diet cola while the others drank beer.

"This Italian piss is not worth a zack," Stone said with a grimace as he examined the bottle in his hand.

"Who the fuck is Zack?" Almeida said.

"It means sixpence in slang, mate. That's a bloody nickel, US."

Larsen sat forward in his chair. "If you don't like it, why drink it?"

Stone frowned. "It's all the hell we've got. For now."

All heads turned as Whelan entered the room and took a seat at the table.

Stensen passed him a bottle of beer. "So, tell us about the phone call. Did you get through to the emir?"

"Didn't try. I spoke to his brother…one of his twelve brothers. He's the chief of the Qatar Armed Forces and head of the emir's personal security. It was his men we killed in Monte-Carlo."

"Twelve brothers?" Almeida said. "His old man must have been pretty busy in the sack."

"He's got twenty-seven sisters too."

"No shit?"

"What you don't seem to grasp, Almeida," Stensen said, "is that his father had multiple wives. It's an Islamic country, remember?"

Almeida closed his eyes, smiled, and rubbed his crotch. "Multiple wives. What a hell of a life."

Stensen said, "Don't get your hopes up, you couldn't keep the one wife you had."

"Why didn't you call the emir himself?" Thomas said to Whelan.

"The brother's running the search for the missing royals. Besides, according to Levell's intel, the emir is in seclusion trying to deal with what happened to his wife and kids."

"You just dialed the guy up?" Larsen said.

"Not exactly. Levell's people provided the general's personal number."

"Shit," Almeida said. "Can't they trace that call back to this place?"

"No, numbnuts," Stensen said, "Brendan used a burner phone specially modified by the SAS's best techies. The call bounced all over the planet—and a few satellites as well. No one could trace that call. Not even all the Chinese gnomes staffing that apocryphal forty-two-story building in Shanghai."

Opening his eyes and reaching for another beer, Almeida said, "How in hell did Cliff get the big guy's phone number? If it was private and all, that must have been tough."

"It was obtained by an American operative, a female."

"No shit? She actually screwed some fucking flea-infested towelhead?" There was an expression of disgust on Almeida's face.

Stensen snorted. "This from a guy who'd fuck a garter snake if someone would hold it still for him."

"I doubt he could even satisfy the snake," Larsen said with his good smile. There were snickers all around the table.

"Fuck you, motherfuckers! If I wanted to, I could kick the shit out of all of you."

"You know what they say—no time like the present," Stensen said.

Almeida scowled. "I'll do it in my own time, Stensen. But it's coming."

"If we don't all die of old age first," Stensen said.

"You're a troglodyte, Stensen. A pusillanimous troglodyte," Almeida said, flipping Stensen off.

"Wow," said Thomas, "I'm impressed. Keep that up Rafe and you might actually speak rudimentary English someday."

"Nah," Larsen said. "He's just been watching too much TV."

"All right, girls!" Whelan said. "We have more important things on our plate than tossing barbs at Rafe,"

"Speaking of Barbs, I've screwed a few of them too," Almeida said.

Larsen shook his head. "See that? He's always thinking with the little head, never the big one."

"Tell me something, Rafe," Thomas said. "With all the slugs and shrapnel that have filled the air around us over the years, how have you managed to survive?"

"It just proves I'm better than you," Almeida said smugly.

Stensen said, "No, it's because he's a dwarf. Too small to provide much of a target."

Almeida rubbed his crotch again and said, "It's just penis envy. All of you. 'Cause there's one part of me that sure as hell ain't a dwarf." He raised his arms. "See, I got big hands. You know what that means."

"In your case, size would have been better used on your IQ," Thomas said.

Whelan shook his head in frustration and said in a low growl, "One more pissant comment out of any of you, and there *will* be some ass-kicking. We need to stay focused." He shook his head in frustration. *Herding cats would be a helluva lot easier than this.*

There were several moments of silence while the other Dogs stared at the labels on their beer bottles, or the vaulted ceiling, or out the large muntin windows. Anywhere but at Whelan.

Finally, Thomas cleared his throat and said, "What did this Qatari general have to say? Are they going to release Marc?" That refocused everyone's attention on Whelan.

"He tried to get cute, of course. Wanted to know who we were. Thought he could negotiate."

"What did you tell him?" Stensen said.

"That if Marc wasn't delivered safely to the negotiator and out of their airspace in one hour, I'd send him the little prince's hands and feet."

Thomas shuddered involuntarily.

"And if they harmed Marc in any way, I'd send the heads of all three royals."

Thomas looked like he was going to be ill.

"And I'd let the emir know that his family died as a result of the actions of his stupid fucking brother."

Larsen put his diet soda on the table. "What's your sense of this?"

"That we're getting Marc back in one piece. And soon."

"God, I hope so," Thomas said. "I don't want to be a party to harming civilians, especially women and kids."

"None of us does," Whelan said. "But it's the emir's call at this point."

CHAPTER 20

SANTA FE, NEW MEXICO

It was a pleasant midmorning in Santa Fe, and the air was dry and cool. Turan Salam was bored. He had grown up roaming the hills and mountains near his home in Waziristan; being cooped up in the little house with Bazir Haqqani and the two sullen Uzbeks was difficult. They had been here for three weeks, preparing over and over again for the mission they would carry out when the order to strike came from Nadir Shah.

Occasionally, Turan would take a walk by himself around the neighborhood. At first Bazir was opposed to the idea, but relented when he saw how agitated being cooped up made Turan. But Bazir had laid down strict rules: do not leave the immediate neighborhood; do not behave in a fashion that might draw attention or arouse suspicions; and speak to no one unless it was unavoidable then speak only Spanish or English. The Uzbeks had demanded that one of them accompany Turan at all times, but Bazir knew that Turan despised the Uzbeks. They were a principal reason he wanted to get out of the house.

This particular morning was garbage pickup day in the neighborhood. Although the trash containers were supposed to be put in the street against the curb, most residents placed them on the narrow sidewalk. It forced Turan to make frequent detours into the cracked and uneven street filled with potholes.

His Bazir-prescribed route was roughly circular and about a kilometer, or little more than a half mile in distance. When he exited the small home he and Bazir shared with the abominable Uzbeks, he always turned right on Santa Inéz Road. It wound around to the east and intersected Montéz Road in front of an elementary school. He would walk south along Montéz to its T-intersection with Santa Rosario Road then westerly along it until it made a sharp curve to the right and became Santa Inéz Road again.

Most of the small pueblo-style houses along the way were not well maintained. The yards were mostly bare hardscrabble dirt or paved over to create additional parking space for an assortment of older model vehicles. They appeared to be as poorly maintained as the homes. More than a few of the yards were filled with rocks and overgrown with weeds. While some were fenced, there didn't seem to be any restrictions on materials used—chain-link, adobe brick, concrete block, poured concrete, wooden slats, latillas, and, rarely, an attractively maintained hedge. There wasn't much shade along the streets because the trees were few and mostly bare.

But not all homes in the neighborhood were rundown; a scattered few were being well maintained. The best maintained home was also the largest and sat on a huge corner lot with a large sweeping front lawn encircled by a decorative wrought-iron fence that had been freshly painted. A rustic pine bench with marble accents running along the top of the backrest was positioned under the roof overhang just to the left of the front door. Several large trees in the carefully maintained yard shaded the bench throughout the day.

Turan always made it a point to walk slowly past this particular house. On his first stroll around the neighborhood, he had seen a girl getting out of a car in the long driveway. She appeared to be about his age. The fact that she drove meant that she had to be at least sixteen and a half. He was seventeen. He had been struck by her dark beauty. On one other occasion, he had seen her in the yard with her parents. He assumed she was a Latina. And she was the most beautiful girl he had ever seen.

Today she was sitting on the bench near the front door, speaking in perfect English to someone on a cell phone. He slowed his pace even more.

The girl looked up and saw Turan staring. She waved at him then said something to the person on the other end of the phone and ended the call. Putting the phone on the bench, she stood and walked across the yard toward the fence. She had a smile on her face and moved like a young woman, not a girl.

Turan was momentarily transfixed. Then he realized she was intent on speaking to him. He felt a warm flush spreading rapidly across his cheeks and started to leave.

"Hey, wait a minute," she said.

Turan glanced nervously up the street toward his house. Part of his brain screamed, "run," but the other part wouldn't let him—that part won. He stood there, embarrassed that he was embarrassed, and on the verge of trembling. In his religion, men and women who weren't related were not allowed to speak to each other unless a relative of the girl was present. *Maybe the West was more enlightened.*

As she reached the fence, her smile deepened prettily. "You're cute. I've seen you in the neighborhood before. What's your name?"

"Tomás," he stammered. She was even prettier up close. He could smell the soft delicate scent of her perfume. He was almost hypnotized by the highlights dancing in her cascade of long, thick dark hair. It framed the smooth, flawless skin of her face with its warm, dark eyes and long lashes.

She stuck her hand out toward him. "I'm Carolina." She pronounced it 'Kah-roh-LEE-nah.' As he reached shyly for her hand and shook it, she said, "It's the middle of a weekday and you're not in school and you're not at work. Why?"

His mind spun, trying to come up with a cover story. "Uh…I applied to Santa Fe Community College and hope to enter in the spring." He was beginning to sweat despite the cool, dry weather.

"SFCC! That's where I go!" she said. "I'm taking a couple of mandatory general courses this term, but don't really get into it full time until the spring. What are you going to study?"

"Uh…business management. What about you?"

"Biology."

"Biology?" But…you're a …."

Carolina gave him a flirty smile. "I'm a what? A girl? What's wrong with being a girl?"

"Uh…nothing." Turan glanced automatically at the curve of her breasts then reddened even darker.

She saw his embarrassment and smiled coyly. "Biology is a good pre-med degree. You *have* heard of female physicians, haven't you?"

"Well…um…maybe, I guess."

"You guess? You have a funny accent. You're not Mexican. Where are you from?"

Turan was sweating freely now. "Uh…Argentina."

Carolina cocked her head to one side and wrinkled her nose as if puzzled. "Argentina is a Spanish-speaking country, but you don't sound like any Latino I've ever heard."

Glancing nervously up the street, Turan saw Bazir standing on the sidewalk in front of their house. He was motioning impatiently for Turan to come home. Relieved, he turned to Carolina and said,

"My brother's calling me. I have to go see what he wants." He started to walk away.

"Hey," Carolina said, "It was really nice to meet you, Tomás. Don't be a stranger; after all, we're going to be classmates." She giggled girlishly and walked back toward the bench.

As SOON AS Bazir had closed the front door behind them, he grabbed Turan's shoulder and said in Arabic, "Who were you just speaking with?"

The younger man shrugged and looked at the floor. "Just some girl."

"What did you say to her?"

"Nothing. I was just being polite," Turan said defensively.

"Nothing, huh? I will be the judge of that. Start at the beginning. Tell me everything you said and she said."

When Turan had finished describing the conversation with Carolina, Bazir just stared at him for several moments with narrowed eyes.

Turan felt angry that Bazir didn't trust him to have the good sense not to say anything to the girl that might jeopardize their mission. He had proved his loyalty to Bazir and HAC. He resented being doubted, and he felt frustrated at having to feel so defensive.

After a while, a smile spread slowly across Bazir's face. "She is pretty, yes?"

Turan continued to stare at the floor. He felt the color rising up his neck again, spreading out through his cheeks. He nodded. "Yes, she's pretty."

"And you want to fuck her, yes?" Bazir continued to smile good-naturedly.

Turan's head snapped up, his eyes ablaze with anger. "No! I

didn't think about that. I just thought she was…is pretty. And nice. And my age. I just wanted to talk with her."

Bazir laughed and reached out and tousled Turan's hair. "Ah, my wayward young warrior, those seventy-two virgins will have their hands full when you get to Paradise." He paused and laughed again. "The question is whether you will be a virgin by the time you get there."

Turan blushed again and returned to staring at the floor.

Bazir's tone became more serious. "You, we, all of us must be very careful how we interact with these accursed infidels, no matter how charming or desirable they may be. We, along with thousands of our brothers, are part of a sacred undertaking. Under no circumstances are we to jeopardize our chances for success."

"Are you saying that I should never speak with her again?"

Bazir threw an arm around Turan's shoulders. "That would be my preference, but I am not so old that I don't understand the needs of a young man your age. I am simply cautioning you to be very careful what you tell her. If she asks sensitive questions, change the subject or simply lie to her; but be careful not to get caught in your own lies. And never bring her to this house. Understand?"

"Yes, I understand," Turan said with a nod. He felt a bolt of excitement flash through him. He could talk with Carolina again!

CHAPTER 21

THE CABIN, TRANSYLVANIA, NORTH CAROLINA

PRINCE BANDAR BIN NAYIF AL SAUD, the head of Saudi general intelligence, was a longtime friend of Cliff Levell's. He also enjoyed the trust and good will of the Qatari royal family. Under those circumstances, he made an excellent neutral party to negotiate the exchange of Marc Kirkland for the kidnapped crown prince, his sister and his mother. His cover was that, because of his relationship with the Qatari royal family, he had been contacted anonymously by a representative of the kidnappers. He had been provided with their demands and a DVD to be viewed by the Qatari emir.

Initially, the Qataris had attempted to play hardball. At first, they weren't certain that the party demanding Kirkland's freedom actually had the kidnapped royals. They threatened to kill Kirkland on live TV on Al Jazeera, which was headquartered in Doha, Qatar and partially owned by the royal family. He was shown on his knees, bound hand and foot, with a hooded man behind him. The man was holding a long ugly, knife to Kirkland's throat.

Prince Bandar immediately provided the DVD showing the three Qatari royals in a similar pose. But instead of a single would-be executioner, behind each royal was a hooded and heavily muscled man stripped to the waist. In one hand, each had an unshakeable grip on a royal throat; in the other was a long, shiny knitting needle mere centimeters from a royal ear. For anyone watching, there was no doubt that each man possessed the strength to plunge the needle in one ear, through the skull and out the other ear. The audio portion of the recording was filled with the terrified screams of the three kidnapped victims begging the emir, their father and husband, to free his prisoner and save them.

It took the emir little more than an instant to order Kirkland delivered immediately whole and unharmed into Prince Bandar's custody. A few hours after Prince Bandar's plane had departed Qatari airspace the three kidnapped royals were found drugged and unconscious, but alive and well, in an old panel van parked along Italian Route SS1, the coastal highway, just east of Vallecrosia. It was less than twelve kilometers from Casa di Alta Montagna, but in the absence of any clues, it could have been twelve thousand.

THE DOGS, including the newest one, Liam Stone, stayed up much of the night celebrating Kirkland's return from captivity. Whelan conducted a booze-infused ceremony in which he presented Kirkland with his beloved sword, the katana he called *doragon no chi*—"Dragon's Blood." Levell, in his mysterious ways, had located it in a pawn shop in Doha and had an operative purchase it.

To no one's real surprise, Stone also was a master of *iaido*, the Japanese art of drawing the sword. His skill level was not quite on a par with Kirkland's, but it wasn't far behind. He and Kirkland formed an instant bond.

But the next day it was back to business, as Levell and a couple of SAS staffers arrived at the Camp to begin briefing the Dogs for their mission. Six of the seven men rolled out of their bunks at sunup and went for a 10-kilometer run before breakfast. The seventh, Rafe Almeida, tried to stay in bed rather than face his massive hangover. While the others had stuck with beer, he personally consumed a one-and-a-half-liter bottle of cheap tequila—along with countless beers.

The run had helped Whelan and the other Dogs sweat out the beer from the night before. They piled eggs, grits, sausage, and toast on their trays from a buffet line. Grabbing mugs of coffee, they sat at picnic tables arranged in a semicircular pattern around Levell and his aides. Levell had to send Larsen and Stensen to get Almeida out of bed and drag him to the meeting. Almeida leaned against a tree stump as far from the smell of food as he could get. He held an ice bag to the back of his neck and nursed a soda.

Kirkland said with a malicious grin, "What's wrong, Rafe? You look awful—all pasty and bloodshot."

"And old," Stensen said, drawing a laugh from everyone except Almeida. Even Levell chuckled.

Almeida sighed and shook his head slowly. "For Chrissakes, Kirkland, you just got back. Can't you at least wait a day or two before giving me shit?"

Levell cleared his throat as a signal the session was beginning. "You all had your fun last night. Now it's time to get serious." He paused and looked pointedly at Almeida. "That especially includes you, dickhead."

Almeida shrugged, his posture sagging a little more.

Levell switched his gaze to Kirkland and said, "Nice to have you back, Marc. Hope you enjoyed your vacation on the Persian Gulf. I understand it can be a little warm this time of year." There was a trace of a smirk on his face.

"It's nice to be back, Cliff. Nothing like a holiday by the sea to restore a man's vigor."

The smirk vanished from Levell's face. "I hope you appreciate the job these others did to get you back. You owe them big time."

Making eye contact with each of the other Dogs, Kirkland said, "If not for you guys, I would have been tortured and beheaded. You're an amazing bunch. Nobody else on this planet could have pulled it off."

"We always have each other's six, but let's cut to the chase," Whelan said. "We're all aware that SAS's main concern is the thousands of Islamic terrorists that have set up shop in this country. What's the plan, and how do we fit in?"

His real concern was: *How do I fit in the plan?* If the other six could handle the mission, he had a promise to keep with Caitlin. Her safety and that of the boys had never been far from his mind during the episode with the Qatari royals.

"You all are aware of the recent incident on the border between Mexico and New Mexico involving the deaths of several CBP agents and two sheriff's deputies," Levell said. "We now have confirmation that the traces of radioactivity picked up by satellite were real. The trail began on the Mexican side of the border near a small mountain village called San Luis."

"Why there?" Thomas said. "Besides being close to the border, is there anything special about San Luis?"

Levell nodded. "According to the always unreliable Mexican authorities, there may be a terrorist base camp above San Luis."

"May be?" Larsen said. "Why don't the Mexicans go there and check it out?"

"It's simple," Levell said. "For one thing, they're afraid of the terrorists—apparently, they're affiliated with HAC. And the situation is compounded by an alliance between the jihadis, the Mexican MS-13 gang, and the Zeta drug cartel. Another reason is that the relevant Mexican authorities are on the Zetas' payroll. Even if they had the balls to attack the encampment, they'd be killing the golden goose *and* putting a price on their own greedy little heads."

"So…what?" Thomas shrugged. "You want us," he motioned at the others sitting at the tables, "to neutralize the encampment?"

"Not precisely. What I want is for you to extract intel concerning the people who smuggled the nuclear device into the country. Where are they now, and what is their target?"

Stensen said, "If satellites picked up traces of radioactivity when these people came across the border, why didn't they follow up after that?"

Levell sighed and said, "Unfortunately the trail was lost just inside the U.S. It must have been loaded into a vehicle with some form of shielding. Anyway, we lost it, and your job is to find it and the people who plan to use it."

"Any idea what they may be planning to do?" Stone said.

After a short pause, Levell said, "The terrorists are massing in preparation for a major strike. And soon. It doesn't take a genius to figure out that the nuke is to be part of that. A dirty bomb is the most intimidating form of terror."

"Sounds like time is a critical factor in locating this thing," Thomas said. "Where do we start?"

"As you said, Quentin, time is working against us. We start with the people responsible for letting the terrorists set up shop near our border and smuggle the nuke into the U.S. That intel should put us on the track of those who have the nuclear device. As for what I want you to do, I want you to do what you do best. Hunt and kill."

"Why aren't we hunting the jihadi leadership in America instead?" Larsen said. "Killing their leaders might stop the bomb strike."

Whelan said, "This device, nuclear or whatever, is in the possession of someone highly important to the terrorists' plans. Find him and he could point us in the direction of their leaders in the U.S. Otherwise, it would just be a wild goose-chase."

"So, the plan is to start with the terrorist camp near San Luis, Mexico, and follow the trail across the border into New Mexico?" Stensen said to Levell.

"No. Like I said, that's step two. First you extract intel from the people who set this up. That way you'll know exactly what you're getting into at San Luis. Preparation is always the key to success."

"So, who are these blokes?" Stone said.

Levell turned and looked at him. "The Zetas."

"Shit! The nastiest bunch of bastards in Mexico," Almeida said. "Why don't you just ask us to take on a full PLA division and slap the balls off their commanding general until he gives up China's top-secret military plans?"

Levell smiled sardonically. "Maybe that's next."

"And when we ultimately find this nuke, you'll have the people that can dispose of it, Cliff?" Kirkland said.

Levell nodded. "If you find it in time."

CHAPTER 22

BEIJING ON THE HUDSON

FAIRCHILDE HAD SET up an office for Maksym in the same building that housed the billionaire's investment banking firm. The firm occupied the top two floors of the modern Wall Street tower while Maksym's office was on a floor that was much closer to ground level. It was a place where Fairchilde could keep Maksym close at hand without him hanging around the investment offices where his mere appearance would terrify most of the firm's employees and clients. Just this afternoon, as he left the meeting with Fairchilde, an executive had started to enter the elevator with Maksym. One look at the sullen, scar-faced giant was all it took. The man had almost fallen backward in his haste to avoid riding alone with him in the car.

Because Maksym didn't need any employees of his own, his office consisted of a single, sparsely furnished space. It was fifteen by eighteen feet with a desk, computer, lamp, two chairs, a credenza and no windows, but there was a large map of the world on the wall behind the desk. A small metal plaque on the wall beside the door said "Alliance for Global Unity—Security."

Maksym had just returned from a meeting in Fairchilde's penthouse suite. The AGU leader had blathered on and on about his displeasure with three members of the organization's board. Maksym had assumed the ultimate purpose of the meeting was to assign him the task of removing the irritants, but surprisingly, Fairchilde had said he'd made "other arrangements." That annoyed and confused Maksym; if he wasn't the AGU boss's fixer, then what was his role? And whom did Fairchilde intend to use to solve this particular problem? He'd asked that question, and been surprised by the answer—Federov and Ulyanin.

Maksym had believed for some time that Federov had died of the gunshot wound he'd suffered at Levell's home in Georgetown. But he'd learned very recently in a phone call from Ulyanin that the Russian had survived. Not only that, but Ulyanin had told Maksym that Federov was planning to kill Fairchilde. That had puzzled him. Why would Ulyanin sell out his friend and countryman? Was he trying to manipulate Maksym into killing Federov for real? Very puzzling.

Maksym purposely hadn't mentioned this bit of information to Fairchilde in their meeting earlier. He didn't really care what happened to that effete product of serious inbreeding among elites. Fairchilde had been clear that he'd assigned the two Russians to the task. But, not surprisingly, he wanted Maksym to be prepared to finish the job in the event things went south.

In addition to feeling uneasy from his meeting with Fairchilde, Maksym also was bored. Although he kept the office locked when he wasn't in it, there were never any guarantees that it's security hadn't been breached. He removed a small device from his pocket and used it to sweep the small room for bugs. Satisfied the room was clean, he sat down behind his desk and picked up the latest copy of Stratfor's quarterly forecast. After a few minutes, he tossed it back on the desktop and picked up the day's edition of *The Wall*

Street Journal, but spent even less time with it. Ultimately, he fired up his computer, fed in the thirty-digit passcode, and began examining his sparse collection of email. There were a half dozen items of spam and a message from Françoise Gauthier.

That one caught his attention. Mlle. Gauthier was the code name Zheng had chosen for his confidential communications with Maksym. The text of the message read, "Having a delightful journey, but wish I could hear your voice. I'll be so happy to be back in New York three weeks from today. Do you miss me?" That meant that Zheng would call Maksym today at three o'clock New York time. The big man glanced at his watch. It was ten minutes to three. The part about "Do you miss me?" meant that if Maksym got the email in time for the call, he should respond. Otherwise, Zheng would send another message later to reschedule.

Maksym hit the Reply symbol, then typed "Yes" and hit Send. He pulled a device from his pocket that resembled a common brand of cellphone. Zheng had given it to him. It was a special phone made by the Chinese government's tech gnomes. The phone was similar to the highly-encrypted communications devices produced by a top-secret Mueller brothers' company and distributed to Levell, Whelan, and some of the other Dogs. Maksym activated it and placed it on the desktop. He rose and went to the office door, locking it, then returned to his seat and waited for Zheng's call.

The phone rang at exactly three o'clock. Maksym picked it up.

Zheng said, "This phone call, of course, is secure, but have you swept the room for surveillance devices that could pick up your end of the conversation?"

"Yes, five minutes ago." *This fool must think I'm an idiot.* Resentment began to rise.

"Excellent."

"What's the reason for this call?"

There was a trace of humor in Zheng's voice. "Always direct and to the point, aren't you, Maksym?"

Maksym said nothing.

"You are my eyes and ears at AGU. Although I am very busy with my duties as finance minister of the Peoples' Republic, I like to stay informed about developments involving Fairchilde and AGU. Do you have anything of significance to report?"

Is this little Chinaman prescient? Maksym wondered. "Something did come up. I've been told that a Russian named Federov, who works for Fairchilde, is planning to steal money from him and then kill him."

Zheng was silent as he thought about what Maksym had said. After several seconds, he said, "This is not good. Fairchilde is to be disposed of eventually, once I no longer have need of him. But now is not the time."

"Do you want me to get rid of Federov?" Maksym smiled at the thought. He had a history with the Russian and it hadn't been an enjoyable one.

"Not at the moment. As a member of AGU's board, I will speak with Fairchilde and warn him. In all likelihood, he will turn to you, as his security, and have you deal with Federov. That will further ingratiate the two of us with him."

Maksym said, "By appearances, I work for Fairchilde, but, in reality, you and I are *partners* in your scheme to take over AGU when the time is right." He put particular emphasis on the word "partners," because he knew it aggravated Zheng. He didn't doubt that, like Fairchilde, Zheng intended to eliminate Maksym when he believed he no longer had a use for him either. Maksym had other plans. "We're just letting Fairchilde do the heavy lifting for the time being, but ultimately you want me to kill him."

"Yes, that is so."

"Then why don't we let Federov kill Fairchilde now and take

the fall for it? You could easily assume leadership of AGU. Especially if I remove any serious competition from the scene."

"It's not quite that easy. China is using AGU for a specific purpose. It could be awkward if I tried to assume its leadership until the purpose of that relationship has been achieved. It would risk calling attention to China's behind-the-scenes activities."

Maksym snorted. He sounded like a huge bull pawing angrily at the ground.

Zheng was silent for a moment. "Why the skepticism, my friend?"

"Do you self-styled sages in Asia believe the world, other than the United States, doesn't know what you're up to?"

"Ah…what are you suggesting?"

"That you are fully engaged in both asymmetrical and unconventional warfare against the West. Moreover, that certain members of your PLA have written the bible on unrestricted warfare, or how China can defeat the West, a technologically superior opponent, without direct military confrontation. One of its principal strategies is the use of terrorism. Not that China wants to engage in it directly and risk further sullying its reputation, or face devastating unified attacks from the nuclear superiority of the West. No, you are supporting and using those insane ragheads in the Middle East as proxies for your war of terror on the West." Maksym paused briefly. "Not that I give a shit."

Zheng laughed softly. "As usual, you are very perceptive, Maksym. In the larger scheme of things, we do funnel support for HAC and other jihadist groups through AGU. Western military powers are so prehistoric; they still believe warfare is might against might, army against army, with the victory going to the most technological superiority. How ironic that the Americans have forgotten how they won their independence from the English crown, by terrorism and guerrilla warfare. That is exactly what the Islamists are using to defeat them.

"We let Fairchilde and the other fools in the AGU believe China is allied with their goal of creating a single world government in the wake of the chaos that will soon engulf the globe. Of course, we want AGU to succeed. Then we simply step in and take over. By then, there will be no powers in the West or elsewhere that can stop us."

CHAPTER 23

NUEVO LAREDO, MEXICO

ALL SEVEN OF the Dogs were sitting on benches or squatting on the bare and cracked concrete floor of a small, ancient hangar outside the South Texas village of Morales-Sanchez. The rarely used dirt strip was about eight miles due east of the Rio Grande River, which formed the border with Mexico.

It was almost midnight on a dark moonless evening, and the temperature was still in the high 80s. Because the Sierra Madre Oriental mountain range blocked the dryer air from the Pacific, the prevailing winds were heavy with humidity from the Gulf of Mexico. If there was a breeze, it wasn't stirring in the hangar. Sweat soaked the men's three-color desert battle dress uniforms—BDUs—and glistened on the camo paint that covered their faces, ears, necks, and hands. The presence of body armor made the situation worse. Each man had checked his weapons and gear countless times, and Kirkland was honing the blade of his katana. They were waiting for a stealth helicopter, compliments of a company owned by the Mueller brothers. It was to transport them approximately fourteen miles to their objective on the other side of the border.

For this operation, each Dog carried a SIG SG 553 Commando compact assault rifle that was chambered for NATO 5.56x45mm ammunition in 30-round magazines. The mags were clamped together for quicker reloading. The weapon had semi-auto and full-auto settings plus an additional trigger module for a three-round burst setting. Whelan had chosen the weapon because it combined the accuracy of an M16 with the reliability of an AK-47. The SG 553s also were reasonably good at long ranges and these were fitted with 4x magnification scopes and red dot sights.

Whelan glanced at his watch. "Rafe was right to be pissed at Levell for sending us to raid Los Zetas in their home turf," he said, with a nod in Almeida's direction.

"The Zetas are bad news, eh, mate?" Stone said.

"They're considered the most savage and violent of all the Mexican cartels. And the most technologically sophisticated, as well."

Stone shook his head slowly. "Now that's saying something, mate."

"They're former Mexican army Special Forces. Originally, they were hired to be the military or enforcement wing of the Gulf Cartel, but they got greedy and formed their own organization. They use a simple business model: violently gain control of territory, then extract protection money—which they call 'piso,'—from all others involved in illegal activities. This includes prostitution, running contraband, distributing drugs, extortion, the whole gamut."

"Ex-Special Forces? Interesting," Stone said.

"It's not so unusual," Whelan said. "I understand that over a certain period of time, sixty percent of the soldiers in the Mexican Army deserted and went into the drug industry."

"That's why Levell didn't get the Mexican military to do this job. Many of the ones who are left are probably on the Zetas' payroll," Stensen said.

"The Zetas also have a crew of techies who monitor all military communications," Whelan said.

Stone appeared to be pensive for a few moments. "What about the local cops? Are they all on the take too?"

"It was so bad that several years ago the Tamaulipas state authorities disbanded the police. By default, that left the army responsible for security, which has resulted in a completely lawless environment. The Zetas have taken butchery to new heights."

"As bad as those bloody HAC bastards?"

"Worse. Not only beheadings and mass killings, but they've also broadcast graphic slaughter on YouTube and other sites. And they've been known to toss body parts into crowded nightclubs. They're very effective in the use of terror."

"And these are the blokes Levell wants us to raid? And on their own turf at that?" Stone said. "Sounds like an exciting evening ahead." He smiled broadly.

"Now you see why I'm pissed at Levell," Almeida said. "It's a fucking suicide mission."

"It could have been worse," Whelan said. "At least we're not raiding the Zetas' HQ in downtown Nuevo Laredo. That place is a fucking fortress guarded by a small army with sophisticated weaponry. Narrow streets, countless sniper nests, a hostile local population; it's an urban death trap."

"Yeah, so instead we get to hit them at their boss's ranch in the middle of the fucking desert," Almeida said.

"What does Levell's intel say about the place?" Thomas said.

"It's on a narrow peninsula that extends northward into the Rio Salado where it begins to widen before flowing into the Rio Grande. The base of the peninsula is sealed off and the whole thing is protected twenty-four-seven by cameras with infrared sensors, motion detectors, and guards armed with FX-05 Xiuhcoatl assault rifles. They fire a 5.56 NATO round from a thirty-round mag."

"Zee—what?" Larsen said.

"It's pronounced zee-uh-co-wahtl and means fire snake in the indigenous Nahuatl."

"Show off," Stensen said with a grin.

"Well, what did you expect?" Thomas said. "The guy's got more degrees than a thermometer."

"We've been over the mission endlessly," Whelan said. "Any questions before we ship out?"

"Yeah, just one," Stone said. "Since I'm the newbie, are there any sort of rules of engagement I should know about?"

"Kill everything that moves. Quickly. Quietly. The only survivor should be the boss man, Z-50," Whelan said, using the Zeta code name for the cartel's current leader, Gustavo Reyes Chacón. "You've seen photos of him. Wing him if you have to, but don't off him."

AN HOUR later a substantially modified black Airbus Helicopter H155 rose slowly and quietly from the isolated airstrip. It carried two pilots and was powered by two Turbomeca Ariel 2C2 turboshaft engines. At cruising speed, it would reach the objective in about five minutes.

Additional main and tail rotor blades dampened the noise generated by the bird by cutting the speed of the rotor in half, particularly in forward flight below maximum speed. It greatly reduced the helicopter's classic whop-whop signature. The bird also had an elaborate system of exhaust ducts and fresh-air mixers in its tail boom. The tips of the main blades had been changed to a variation of Eurocopter's Blue-Edge rotor blades. It also had an engine exhaust muffler, lead-vinyl pads to deaden skin noise, and a baffle to block sounds slipping out the air intake. In addition, it had a modified tail boom and a noise-reducing covering on the rear rotors.

The airframe was made of advanced composite that enabled reductions in the aircraft's radar cross-section. Other enhancements reduced visual, radar, infrared and acoustic signatures. It also featured a digital camouflage system. The result was that, unlike typical choppers, this bird emitted very little noise, making it the perfect delivery vehicle for the mission at hand.

The passengers sat in jump seats behind the pilots, three on one side of the aircraft and four on the other. Their helmets, jump boots, and balaclavas matched their BDUs. All means of identifying the source of the clothing had been removed. None of the men carried any identification. Each wore enhanced night-vision goggles, or ENVGs, mounted on their helmets, which fused image intensification technology with thermal imagery for optimal night operations.

The mission called for an extremely low-level jump. Always tricky, it was made more challenging because of the darkness. Night jumps typically finish in the Dark Zone—the last one hundred feet. The closer the jumper gets to the ground, the darker the ground becomes. This makes it difficult, if not impossible, to judge the distance and anticipate impact. Below the hundred-foot mark it can be similar to landing in a black hole. The ENVG eliminated this problem.

Because they would have almost no time for free-fall and chute deployment, they were using chutes similar to those used by BASE —Buildings, Antennas, Spans, and Earth—jumpers. The canopies of their chutes were seven cells rather than nine for a quicker, more vertical descent, and had been specially folded for quick release. There were no sliders around the lines to control the opening, because that would reduce the rate at which the lines could spread, slowing the opening of the chute. It also meant the chutes would open with a much harsher deployment on the harness and the jumper wearing it. Their rigs incorporated an oversized pilot chute so it could immediately grab the air to pull open the main canopy. At this altitude, timing was crucial.

Low-altitude, low-opening jumps, or LALO, were especially hazardous. Jumping at night compounded the risks. Each Dog clipped a shorter than usual static line to the cable running above the chopper's doors. The other end of the line was attached to the jumper's deployment bag, which held his pilot chute, main canopy, suspension lines, and harness. The pilot approached the target at a high altitude. Once over Z-50's sprawling rancho he spiraled the nearly silent craft down to a point two hundred and fifty feet above the desert terrain below. He chose a spot about halfway along the mostly desolate peninsula and began to move the chopper in a small circle.

On the pilot's signal, each man jumped one after the other using the doors on either side of the craft. Whelan and Larsen led, followed in order by Stensen, Kirkland, Thomas, Stone, and Almeida. The motion of the aircraft and the weight of the men's bodies instantly pulled their static lines taut, yanking the D-Bag from the jumpers' packs and causing their chutes to open automatically.

Each man exited the aircraft facing downward to avoid tumbling as he entered the chopper's slipstream and possibly tangling the lines as his chute deployed behind him. They had to focus on avoiding collisions with other jumpers or maneuvering over top of them and stealing their air. They had minimal time to turn into the wind and prepare to land. With their long years of experience, as well as their abnormal reaction times and strength, each Dog executed a perfect landing. They swiftly gathered up their chutes and stuffed them under stunted shrubs that dotted the area then formed a circle around Whelan.

Whelan looked around at the other Dogs. "As planned, Marc

and Stoney will come with me. Sven, you take Nick, Quentin, and Rafe, and approach from the east. You've all studied photos of Chacón, aka Z-50. When the killing starts, the goal is to take him alive. Otherwise, this operation is a waste of time."

The peninsula was about a mile long and, on average, a half-mile wide. Z-50's massive home was at the northern tip overlooking the wide Salado arm of Falcon Lake, which was built to provide water to both Mexico and the United States. There were a few much more humble outbuildings about two hundred yards inland from it. This where the staff and security guards lived.

They separated into the two groups and moved off in opposite directions, each circling toward the buildings at the northern tip of the peninsula about a half-mile away. Larsen's group had the benefit of the dirt road that ran from the entrance post at the foot of the peninsula to the compound at its tip. Whelan and his men had to slog through a groundcover of thick, knee-high grass and weave between the clusters of shrubs and thorny honey mesquite trees native to the parched area.

It was a little after one o'clock in the morning, Central Standard Time, when the two groups approached the cluster of small buildings that housed staff and security personnel. Swiftly, silently, the Dogs killed the sleeping off-duty guards. To limit collateral damage, the domestics were injected with a drug that insured their continued unconsciousness. Then, they turned their attention to the sprawling main house.

It sat on an outcropping that jutted into the Salado arm of Falcon Lake directly across from the site of the ruins of Guerrero Viejo, an ancient village that had been relocated because of the rising waters of the Falcon Lake reservoir. Unfortunately, the lake's waters had eventually covered most of the village anyway.

A forty-six foot Mercedes-Benz SLS AMG Cigarette boat was conveniently docked in front of Z-50's mansion. It had a maximum speed of 135 miles per hour. Chacón could cover the eight miles between here and sanctuary in the United States in less than twenty minutes, should the need arise. The boat was to be part of the exfil plan Whelan and Levell had devised for the Dogs.

The home itself was a multilevel structure that made expansive use of glass. Whelan knew the glass was bullet proof. When you lived the life Chacón did, you became a target twenty-four hours a day, no matter where you were. This also explained the armed men posted on the roof of the building and the roving patrols.

Using intel gathered from SAS's resources, Whelan had estimated that there would be three men posted at elevated points on the house, and another six patrolling the grounds with dogs. Then there was the electronic surveillance. The flaw in the security system was that most of it was geared toward the water, the most likely direction of an attack. Additional security, about a mile from the house at the base of the peninsula, protected the flanks. The one thing Chacón didn't expect was an airdrop. His Zetas owned the Mexican military, so it wouldn't send airborne troops. The other cartels employed hordes of vicious, savage killers, but the Zetas were the only criminal organization that had former paratroopers. Further, the Zetas knew that, despite the longstanding war on drugs, the U.S. had a clearly established a policy of not invading the sovereign territory of Mexico.

Stensen and Kirkland each carried an SR-25, a semi-automatic long-range sniper rifle manufactured by Knight's Armament Company. The weapons were enhanced by SF3P-762-SR25 flash hiders and SureFire SOCOM Series 7.62mm/.308 caliber sound suppressors. To further dampen the sound of the rounds being fired, they were loaded with subsonic 175-grain Black Hills Ammo. The weapons were equipped with Schmidt & Bender PMII 5-25×56 DT scopes. From approximately two hundred yards away, Stensen and Kirkland quickly dropped all three of the guards who were in the elevated posts. There were minimal sounds and no muzzle flashes to reveal the shooters' presence.

Kirkland handed the weapon to Stone then pulled a small device slightly larger than a smartphone from his pack. He made some adjustments to activate it then placed it on the ground. All wireless communication other than the Dogs' own, which operated on a special frequency, was now being scrambled and rendered worthless. Taking the SR-25 back from Stone, he focused in on a telephone line running along the back wall of the house. A single suppressed shot eliminated all communications to and from the building.

But in the tradition of Murphy's Law—if something can go wrong, it will—the unexpected happened.

THE DOGS HAD BANKED on the lateness of the hour. Everyone except the security people on-duty should have been asleep. But one domestic must not have gotten the memo. When Kirkland took out a guard near the roof of the second level, the man's body twisted as he fell and slid over the railing. It hit the ground two floors down with a distinct thud. Almost immediately there was a loud, shrill scream. Whelan, Stone, and Kirkland whirled in unison, focusing on the spot where the scream had come from. Through the technological magic of their ENVGs, they saw a young woman frozen in horror. She was naked from the waist down. The guard's body had landed three feet from her. Standing beside her staring down at the body was one of the guards who was supposed to be on patrol. His pants were around his ankles.

"Shit! We've interrupted a lovers' tryst," Kirkland said, and shot the guard in the head. The woman screamed again. Kirkland put a 7.62mm round through her throat.

Bedlam erupted. Lights went on in a room in the front part of the house's third story. Dogs began barking in a frenzy. From their sound, they were very large dogs and moving quickly toward Whelan and his two colleagues. They heard men shouting in Spanish, and the sounds of their footsteps could be heard following the dogs.

In just a few seconds, three huge German Shepherds raced around a small hedge and sprinted toward Whelan, Kirkland, and Stone. Kirkland whipped his katana from its *saya*, a lacquered wood scabbard, and stepped forward to meet the attack. The animals had incredible speed and reflexes, but the only humans they had ever known were Norms. The lead dog launched itself at Kirkland, and, with a right *gedon* cut, his blade neatly severed its neck while it was in midair. The second part of the technique Kirkland was using was a *yoko giri*, or side cut, designed to flow easily from the end point of the *gedon* cut. But the second dog was too close and clamped its teeth around Kirkland's left wrist, dragging him to the ground.

The dog let go of the wrist and lunged for Kirkland's throat. There were two somewhat suppressed shots. The dog's body flew apart as the .45 caliber dum-dums from Stone's sidearm exploded through it. When the third dog leaped at Kirkland, Whelan tackled it in midair, falling on it with his two hundred and forty pounds of body weight plus the added weight of his gear and body armor. It barely phased the beast in its blood lust. As it tried to get free, it snapped at Whelan. Acting on instinct, the Irishman grabbed the animal's lower jaw with his right hand and its upper jaw with his left and ripped them apart, destroying muscle and tendon. *There are days,* he thought, *when it was good to be a genetic freak.* The dog's snarling and growling was replaced by a piteous whine. Whelan grabbed its rear feet, swung the animal's body over his head, and slammed it into the ground. It died instantly.

He shook his head. "I wish that could have been avoided. I like German Shepherds better than I like most people."

Kirkland scrambled to his feet and wiped the blade of the katana on his pant leg and resheathed it. "Thanks," he said to Stone with genuine gratitude.

Stone grinned as he holstered his H&K .45 Tactical. "I didn't trust those fucking NATO rounds to do the job"

Gunshots erupted and bullets began whizzing perilously close to the three men. One struck Stone in the chest as he dove to the ground. He landed awkwardly and grimaced, but gave Whelan the OK sign. "Bloody vest earned its quid!"

Through his ENVGs, Whelan could see six men running toward them while firing what looked and sounded like H&K MP5s. They clearly weren't suppressed. Whelan knew the noise would carry a long distance in the still desert night. That meant the security people manning the entrance to the long skinny peninsula would hear it. He was glad they'd killed the off-duty guards.

He assumed the men were firing 9mm ammo because of the effect it had had on Stone and his body armor. The .40 or .45 caliber models would have done greater damage. As it was, Stone would have a badly bruised sternum for the next few days.

Kirkland's left wrist was dripping blood, and the palms of Whelan's hands had been ripped open by the teeth of the dog he'd killed. The blood made it difficult to hold their weapon securely as they fired.

The six unfriendlies had hunkered down behind trees and a low wall that cut across the property from the house to the shore of the Salado. They were showering a steady hail of lead at Whelan and his two comrades who were prone on the open ground. About sixty yards separated them.

"Sven," Whelan shouted into the throat mic of his comm gear, "we've got a problem and could use some help. Fast."

"Roger that," Larsen said. "You've drawn all the guards. We've breached the house. Do you want us to proceed to the target or assist you?"

"We're pinned down in the open and can't hold out for long. Come around behind these guys and neutralize them ASAP."

"Roger. I've sent Thomas and Almeida to flank the unfriendlies. Stensen and I are heading to the second level now. We can pick them off from there."

Whelan, Stone, and Kirkland alternated firing in three-round bursts to allow each other time to reload. Slugs whizzed by scant inches away, some thudded into the ground close to them. One grazed Stone's left arm, gouging a furrow on his forearm.

Through his ENVGs, Whelan saw two more shooters appear on a balcony on the second level. He recognized Stensen and Larsen. A second later he saw the six unfriendlies begin firing behind their position. He knew that Thomas and Almeida were assaulting them from the opposite direction, creating a deadly crossfire. Simultaneously Larsen and Stensen began picking off the Zetas from their elevated position on the balcony. After a few seconds, it was suddenly quiet—until Thomas and Almeida worked their way past the fallen guards. Individual shots rang out as they put a bullet in each man's head.

Whelan and his two colleagues were up and running toward the house when a series of shots rang out from a balcony on the third level. The five Dogs at ground level sprayed the balcony with slugs from their SG 553s, and it stopped.

"That was our target, Chacón," Whelan shouted. "Sven, Nick, get up there. Don't let him get to a safe room."

Whelan and the other Dogs sprinted into the house. He motioned to Stone and Thomas. "Clear the house. Other than Chacón, no survivors."

The two men moved off, and Whelan led Kirkland and Almeida

up the stairs to the third level. They found Larsen and Stensen at the end of a wide hallway that led to the front of the house. It was blocked by a thick, ornately carved wooden door.

Larsen said, "It's locked."

"Shit, it's one delay after another," Whelan said, and glanced at his watch. "We're running short of time to grab this guy and exfil."

Kirkland was the top explosives expert in the group. Whelan looked at his torn wrist. It was dripping blood. "Can you blow this door, Marc?"

Kirkland shrugged. "It'll be challenging."

Stone said, "I done a bit of blasting with Tag West."

Without hesitation, Whelan said, "Use a very small amount of Semtex from Marc's kit. This particular batch is super powerful. I don't want to bring the fucking house down around our ears."

Stone nodded. "Got it, mate." He set to work rigging the explosive charge.

Whelan looked at Stensen and Thomas. "The racket the unfriendlies' weapons made will have drawn the attention of the crew manning the entrance, especially now that they can't communicate with the house. You two sprint up the road and intercept them. We'll grab Chacón."

The two men took off at a fast trot as Stone herded the others around the corner of an intersecting hallway. He looked at Whelan, who nodded, then he pressed the button on the remote. There was a loud blast followed immediately by a cloud of smoke and a hail of debris. Shots were fired from the room at the end of the hall. Whelan leaned around the corner and tossed a flash-bang grenade into the room. Each Dog screwed his eyes tightly shut, stuck his fingers in his ears, and turned away from the direction of the blast. It was at least as loud as the Semtex explosion.

Without further hesitation, the five men sprinted around the corner and into the targeted room. As the smoke cleared, they could see the wreckage of what had been a huge bedroom suite. There were three naked young women on a round bed that must have been twelve feet in diameter. They appeared unharmed, but stared, glassy-eyed and giggling, at the intruders. Whelan recognized the women were in a deeply drugged state.

"Shit, fringe benefits," Almeida said with a wide smile and began moving toward the bed.

"Keep it in your pants, Rafe. This is strictly business," Whelan said. He glanced around the room and saw a naked man on his hands and knees near the shattered glass door that opened to a balcony. The man's head was down, and he was vomiting. "That's Chacón," he said. "Grab him, Sven, and shackle his ass. We're getting out of here."

At that moment, Whelan's satphone buzzed. He yanked it free from the case attached to his belt. Knowing it was Thomas or Stensen, he said, "Situation?"

"Houston, we have a problem," Stensen said, paraphrasing the famous line attributed to Apollo 13. "We're half a klick up the road and pinned down by an unknown number of unfriendlies. And they've got a fucking M60 mounted on a jeep. Could really use some assistance."

"Continue to engage, but withdraw slowly and carefully. I'll send in the cavalry." Whelan clicked off, then punched in a symbol and two numbers on the satphone. A moment later he heard the voice of their chopper pilot, who had been flying wide, low altitude circles just across the Rio Grande.

"We've got a situation. Things have gone totally FUBAR. Two of our men are engaged in a firefight with a superior force about a third of a mile south of the main house. They need a hand."

"Roger that," the pilot said. "We're on the way."

Less than two minutes later, the chopper was over the scene. The bird's thermographic cameras easily picked out all of the participants in the firefight, highlighting them in bright red. The cameras also identified Stensen and Thomas by the large bright purple Xs that had been applied to the top of their balaclavas with a special chemical. The pilot swung the chopper around and activated the craft's computer-guided machine guns. Recognizing the symbols on the two Dogs' headgear, the computer adjusted the kill zone accordingly. After the pilot flipped the appropriate toggle switch, the guns began seeking out targets and chewing them up.

The gunner in the jeep saw the chopper and started to swing his M60 around. The copilot launched a computer-guided Hydra 70 rocket. The jeep, the M60, and the gunner disintegrated in a fiery explosion.

"Okay, our work here is done. Chalk another one up for our side, Finn," the pilot said to Whelan over the satphone, using the Irishman's call sign for the operation. Finn MacCoul was the English version of the legendary Irish hero Fionn mac Cumhaill, the last leader of the fierce warriors of Irish mythology known as the Fianna. "We're headed for home." The pilot turned the aircraft toward the east and increased the airspeed.

Larsen had Chacón on his feet with his hands bound behind him with Safariland double-cuff plastic restraints.

Z-50 was tall and rangy. He had short, thick, well-groomed black hair and a pencil mustache. "You fools don't know how much shit you're in," the Zeta leader said with a snarl; his English was nearly flawless. "You've signed your own death warrants. And I guarantee they'll be the worst deaths you could imagine."

Whelan stepped up and grabbed Chacón by the throat. He squeezed with enough force that the man's eyes began to bulge. Putting his face less than an inch from the Mexican's, Whelan growled in flawless Spanish, "Your men are all dead. No one's coming to rescue your miserable ass. I can start cutting you into little pieces right here, or you can shut the fuck up and take your

222 JOHN WAYNE FALBEY

chances with the people waiting for you on the other side of the Rio Bravo." He purposely used the Mexican name for the river known on the U.S. side as the Rio Grande. He literally threw the man to Larsen as if he were a rag doll.

Larsen wrapped a thick hand around the back of the Zeta's neck. "Start moving. You're going for a nice river cruise."

Struggling to speak after Whelan had nearly crushed his larynx, Z-50 said in a croaking voice, "But I am naked. At least allow me the dignity of getting dressed."

"Not gonna happen," Kirkland said. "Being naked makes you feel more vulnerable."

"Let's move, we're behind schedule," Whelan said.

Larsen shoved Chacón so hard the man stumbled and fell as he moved toward the door.

"Hey," Almeida said, "what about the babes?" He pointed at the three naked women on the bed. "Shouldn't we rescue them too?"

"Leave them. They're not part of the mission," Stone said.

"But what'll happen to them?"

"They're addicts, Rafe," Kirkland said. "They'll just cozy up to another drug lord until either he kills them during rough sex, they OD, or they start to get fat. Then he'll pass them off to his henchmen until one of them eventually kills them."

Almeida shook his head. "What a tragic waste of good tail."

As they exited the shattered bedroom, Stone leaned over toward Whelan and said, "At times that Rafe bloke seems bloody dill. Is it my imagination?"

"No. His excuse is that he's oversexed and under-loved. The reality is he's a fucking mess, but he has his uses at times."

"I take it no woman is safe around him?"

"Not unless she's armed to the teeth and quick on the trigger."

As the five Dogs and their prisoner were leaving the house, Stensen and Thomas came running up.

"Any injuries?" Whelan said.

Thomas said, "We've got some dings, but nothing serious."

"Nothing a little R&R wouldn't fix," Stensen said with a grin.

"That's back upstairs in the bedroom," Almeida said unhappily.

The group made its way down to the dock at a fast trot. Chacón complained that the rough ground hurt his bare feet, and that the desert's chilly night air was uncomfortable. Larsen ripped a strip of duct tape from a small roll and slapped it across the Zeta leader's mouth.

The eight men piled into the Cigarette boat. Whelan sent everyone except Larsen below with the prisoner, then fired up the craft's twin-turbocharged 552-cubic inch, 1,350 horsepower Mercury Racing engines. Larsen cast off the lines, and Whelan eased the powerful craft away from the dock. When he reached the channel, he gradually powered the beast up and pointed the bow eastward toward the Salado's intersection with the Rio Grande and the U.S. shoreline on the far side.

There were only two chairs topside—Whelan sat on the right, or starboard side, and Larsen rode shotgun on the port side. As they were powering up in the channel, two small speedboats packed with armed men emerged from the darkness near the ruins of Guerrero Viejo, an area that had been taken over by the Mexican drug cartels. They immediately gave chase, with the occupants firing wildly at the big Cigarette boat. Whelan yelled down into the hold for everyone to hang on and shoved the throttles all the way forward. The forty-six-foot boat leaped from the water like a billfish trying to shake the hook.

Even with the load the boat was carrying, it reached 120 miles per hour in what seemed like seconds. The other boats were left to bounce in its wake. Eighteen minutes later, Whelan eased the big craft into a small cove on the Texas side of the Rio Grande. There were three unmarked black Suburbans lined up nose-to-tail on Pump Road, facing back toward safe haven.

The two small speedboats were still barreling toward the Texas shoreline. Two men got out of the lead Suburban and walked to the water's edge. Each shouldered an RPG launcher. A few seconds later, the small speedboats and their occupants disintegrated in brilliantly hued balls of flame.

As Whelan nudged the bow of the Cigarette boat into the soft bank of the cove, Larsen said, "Uncle Cliff thinks of everything."

"One of his favorite expressions is 'expect nothing, prepare for everything,'" Whelan said.

The men in the lead Suburban placed Chacón's hands and feet in heavy-duty shackles, pulled a hood over his head, and shoved him to the floor behind the driver's seat. Two large men climbed into the second row of seats, where they could keep a close eye on the prisoner's every move. The vehicle pulled smoothly away, stirring up clouds of dust behind it.

The seven Dogs piled into the remaining Suburbans. They were taken first to a medical clinic in Zapata about four miles away. The clinic had received a generous donation from an SAS front organization. While there, Whelan received a call from Levell on the über-encrypted satphone.

"I was watching on a special satellite relay. A little sloppy, but you achieved the objective," Levell growled humorlessly.

Whelan frowned. Levell was a bitch of a taskmaster. "Yeah. Thanks, I guess. What's the deal with Z-50?"

"He's on his way to an interrogation center. Our people will extract the intel from him and I'll pass it along to you."

Whelan's frown morphed into a smile. He could imagine what that extraction process would be, and he had no doubt that Chacón would tell the interrogators everything Levell wanted to know. And sooner rather than later. "What do you want us to do in the meantime?"

"There are rooms reserved for you at Casino del Sol in Tucson."

"Is it decent?"

"Hell, yes. It's got a spa, casino, big-name entertainment."

Always suspicious of Levell's true motives, Whelan said, "Why there?"

"It's outside of town and only five miles from Ryan Field, a relief airport that we'll use to get you boys in and out of the area when we're ready to move you."

"Any idea when that will be?"

"Hell, no. Do you think I have a crystal fucking ball?" Levell hung up.

Same old Cliff, Whelan thought with a smile. *Good to know some things never change.*

After the men received medical attention, the Suburbans took them about nine miles northeast of Zapata to a small municipal airfield. They climbed aboard a waiting King Air 350i, a turboprop plane that could accommodate the seven men and the relatively short runway length. A jet, such as a Gulfstream G450 or Bombardier Global 5000, would have required more length for takeoff than the small field offered. The plane was provided through a series of companies ultimately controlled by the Mueller brothers. For the battle-weary Dogs, it was just fine. It took the fully loaded aircraft a little over two and a half hours to reach Ryan Airfield southwest of Tucson, Arizona. A motor coach met the plane and shuttled the seven men to the Casino del Sol, an enterprise of the Pascua Yaqui Tribe of Arizona, which explained the presence of the gaming operations.

After showering and running up a small fortune in food and beverage charges, six of the Dogs retired to a cocktail lounge and pushed two tables together. While waiting for a round of drinks,

Stone leaned over to Whelan on his right. "We're missing a mate. Where's Rafe?"

"Get used to him wandering off. We usually have to take turns baby-sitting him, but he's earned a night to party."

"Yeah? He strikes me as a wild little shit. What's he likely to get up to?"

"He'll start with gambling."

"He any good?"

"No, a born loser. At everything."

"Then what? A woman?"

"His usual MO is to find some drugs and booze, then he looks for women…plural."

Stone grinned. "Hell, mate, maybe I should have gone with him."

Whelan shook his head. "I partied with you in Oz and you're pretty hardy, but that little shit would leave you in his contrails. Believe me."

Stone thought about that for a few moments. "I don't get it. He's not in the same condition we are. He looks more like our oldies than one of us. And most of the time he acts like a drongo. Why do you blokes keep him around?"

"Simple," Whelan said. "In a hot zone, he *is* one of us, and more than once has saved the ass of everyone here. It's during the down times that we have to watch him like a hawk, 'cause sure as hell he'll get into some kind of trouble. It's like he's got a magnet."

The drinks arrived. Everyone had ordered beer except Larsen. He was drinking the usual diet soda.

"Hey, Brendan," Thomas said from across the table. "Other than being in the middle of nowhere, this place is pretty nice. How long we going to be here?"

Whelan shrugged. "Until Levell gets what he wants out of Chacón."

"Any idea where we're headed after that?" Larsen said. "I got a man named Maksym that needs killing."

"My gut tells me we're going back to Mexico," Whelan said. "This time it'll be to kill Islamic terrorists. It should make our recent soirée at 'El Rancho Chacón' look like a Cub Scout meeting."

CHAPTER 24

SANTA FE, NEW MEXICO

TURAN HAD GOTTEN to know Carolina Avila well enough that sometimes he was invited to stay for dinner. He liked her parents. They struck him as good people—open, friendly, nonjudgmental. But it did bother him that her mother, Marisol, was employed by the New Mexico State Police. Her boss was a major who ran the NMSP Special Operations Bureau. Turan wasn't sure exactly what that meant, but it definitely wasn't information he shared with Bazir Haqqani. In fact, he'd told Bazir that Mrs. Avila was a school traffic guard and that's why she wore a uniform.

Her father Al, short for Alejandro, was a claims adjuster with a regional automobile insurer. Turan enjoyed watching fútbol, or soccer, with Al. He'd even been invited to go with Al to a local match, but had begged off, knowing Bazir would never permit it. In fact, Turan felt exceptionally fortunate that his handler even let him spend time with Carolina. But he knew Al would ask him again, and he wasn't sure how he could get out of it next time.

Marisol, Carolina's mother, was a beautiful woman. It was clear to Turan how Carolina had come by her own beauty. Marisol was also an incredible cook. Tonight, they had just finished a meal of chicken in a mole poblano sauce with enchiladas. Mrs. Avila had made it a point to let Turan know that Carolina had done the heavy lifting when it came to making the sauce, a complicated, multi-step process.

Turan helped Carolina with the dishes and cleanup, and then they planned to take a walk around the neighborhood. First, to be polite, they joined her parents, who were watching the evening news in in the TV room.

As they sat down, Carolina held her new iPhone up and snapped a selfie of her curled up next to Turan.

Surprised, he said, "Why did you do that? Give me that picture."

Carolina smiled impishly. "I want to send a picture of you to my cousin Sarita in Albuquerque."

"Ah…I think that's a bad idea. We need to destroy it. Now." Turan was clearly agitated.

"Why? What's so wrong with a picture of a friend?"

"Yeah," Al said with a friendly grin. "You're not a drug dealer on the lam, are you?"

"No, no, of course not," the words spilled rapidly out of Turan. "I just…I don't know. I don't like it."

Just then a news alert interrupted the regular TV programming. A young blonde woman affiliated with the FOX station in El Paso, Texas, was standing in front of a pylon sign identifying the location as the William Beaumont Army Medical Center. A smaller brown metal sign on a fenced section to her right identified the gate as Alabama Street. The young woman was talking with ersatz excitement about a story that had just leaked from the medical center.

"KFOX14 has just learned from an unidentified source that there is a survivor of last Tuesday's ambush of five Customs and

Border Patrol agents and two sheriff's deputies. Originally, it was reported that there had been no survivors. No reason has been given for this mix-up, but it's been suggested that it was purposely done in order to protect this sole witness."

The screen switched to a photo of a young Hispanic man wearing a CBP uniform. He had his arm around an attractive Latina. Two cute little girls, with big grins on their faces, stood in front of them.

"He is Border Patrol Agent David Hidalgo, a two-year veteran of the agency and a married father of two. Apparently, he was airlifted here to this medical center because it was the closest facility equipped to treat his horrendous wounds."

Turan barely caught himself from jumping off the sofa. He was no longer listening to the blonde woman. He recognized the man in the photo. It was the same man he was supposed to have finished off the night he, Bazir, and the others had sneaked over from Mexico and ambushed the border patrol agents and deputies. And he recognized the woman and the two children. They were the same ones who had been in the photograph in the man's wallet. His thoughts tumbled through his head in a panicked olio of English, Spanish, and Pashto. *Shit! What if Bazir sees this? What if he knows I am responsible for the man not being killed?*

He stood up shakily and started toward the door. "I have to go."

"Wait, Tomás" Carolina said. "What about our walk?"

"Yes," Marisol said. "You just finished dinner, Tomás. Surely you don't have to leave yet."

"No, really. I just remembered that I promised my brother I'd help him with a project he's working on. I have to go."

"What kind of project?" Al said.

"Uh…I…he wants to do some sightseeing in the area and asked me to help him find good locations."

Carolina stood up. "I'll come with you. I've lived in Santa Fe all my life. I know where all the interesting stuff is."

"No! Uh, I mean the place is a mess. My brother's a poor house-keeper—a slob, really. I can't let you see the place looking like it does. Maybe another time." He walked out the door and away from the house as quickly as he could.

When he reached his own home down the street, the thing Turan feared most was happening. Bazir Haqqani was watching the news on TV. So were the two Uzbeks. He wished he had the superpower to make himself invisible and slip unnoticed into his room. But that wasn't going to happen.

Bazir looked up as Turan entered, a terrifying look of rage on his face. *Does he know it was me?*

"Can you believe this shit!' Bazir viciously kicked the coffee table and sent it crashing against the sagging bench that held the TV. "Do you realize this is the kind of incompetence that ruins even the best-laid plans? I will kill the fucking moron responsible for this!"

It was all Turan could do to maintain sphincter control. He backed up against the wall by the front door. "Do...do you know who...it is?" His voice was an octave or two higher than normal.

"Yes. I have a very good idea," Bazir said, his dark eyes were staring straight at Turan.

"I...I...I," Turan stammered.

"It had to be that fucking Sahim, the lazy bastard. He never did anything right. I am going to make him pay dearly for this."

"You...you're sure it was him...Sahim?"

Bazir's eyes were blazing. "Yes!" He saw how terrified Turan was and lowered his voice. "Why couldn't he have been more like you, Turan? You have always done everything I've asked." A snarl escaped his lips. "But not that incompetent fucking Sahim."

Haqqani pulled a smartphone from his shirt pocket and pressed a number on the speed dial. Speaking in Spanish, he told the party on the other end of the line to bring Sahim Yousafzai to him in Santa Fe immediately. He said the special project he was working on required an additional helper, and he specifically wanted Sahim for the task.

CHAPTER 25

LOWER MANHATTAN

HARLAND FAIRCHILDE IV had been born into wealth and power. He liked to say that if one looked up "old money" in a dictionary, they would find pictures of his family members. His investment banking firm was one of the oldest and most successful on Wall Street. His personal office occupied almost one quarter of the top floor of one of the city's most prestigious glass and steel office towers. From this exalted perch, he could see most of the five Burroughs and beyond. But he rarely looked out the windows. It was like moving from Kansas to the coast of Florida; after several weeks, the beach was no more enchanting than a cornfield. It was just there.

Fairchilde reveled in his power. It was more than mere wealth. Since childhood, he'd dreamed of being the most powerful man in the world. One of the elements of power that had always fascinated him was the apocryphal story of the Red Phone. According to the myth, during the Cold War era, a highly-encrypted line ran from the Oval Office to the Kremlin. The story had been debunked years earlier, but Fairchilde still found it fascinating. So much so that he carried a special red smartphone with him at all times. It had been given to him by Zheng Bao Xun, the minister of finance for the People's Republic of China. Zheng also had one. These phones, manufactured by the Chinese, of course, had a special app installed that encrypted all calls made between them to a degree that the conversations couldn't be deciphered by any currently known technology. It pleased Fairchilde to no end that of the more than seven billion people on the planet, he was one of only two who had this particular app. At least that was what Zheng had assured him.

He was preparing to buzz his executive assistant to bring him a cup of his special Jamaican Blue Mountain coffee, when the red phone vibrated in his pants pocket. Fairchilde fished it out and thumbed the answer icon.

As expected, it was Zheng. "Good morning, Mr. Minister," Fairchilde said. "Or perhaps I should say good evening, as you are twelve hours ahead of us."

"Indeed. Perhaps the first order of business once the planet is governed by a single entity will be to consolidate all time zones into a single one."

"Possibly so," Fairchilde said cheerily. He never could tell when the minister was kidding. *The damn Chinese truly are inscrutable.* "To what do I owe the pleasure of your call?"

"There are two matters. First, I want to congratulate you on the chaotic American presidential campaigns. You have wisely identified and capitalized on the anger, frustration, and fear of the American electorate."

Fairchilde basked in the praise. "Thank you, Minister Zheng; you're very kind. While I did have the AGU provide immense financial support to numerous leftwing causes and candidates over the decades, I also anticipated the problems the liberal/progressive agenda might generate with a basically center-right population."

"Yes, you have been very wise. Your covert sponsorship of that businessman from New York was a stroke of genius. He probably would have won his party's nomination anyway, but you made it more certain. It is doubtful, however, that he will win the election."

"That is certainly the expectation," Fairchilde said. "But one of the benefits of the two-party system, at least in this election, is that even if he did win, AGU's goals will be furthered by his inexperience and incompetence."

"Truly. And the other party's nominee, provided she hasn't been indicted, has no choice but to push the government further to the left, which guarantees its downfall."

"And her lifelong greed and corrupt nature have placed her in the pocket of every major global entity. Given that we control most of them, we essentially own her. What a beautiful thing."

"Again," Zheng said, "you have orchestrated things magnificently."

Fairchilde felt a warmness in his cheeks. *Could I actually be blushing?* "I believe you said you had two matters to discuss, Mr. Minister?"

"Yes, but before we address the second, what is the current situation regarding SAS? Your effort to scare or buy off Levell doesn't seem to have had much traction."

Fairchilde made a scoffing sound. "Levell and the SAS are short timing it. Their political members will be thrown out of office over the next few years as the electorate continues to express its dissatisfaction. The military members will protect their pensions and acquiesce to the directives from the White House, which we will continue to control. And the members from industry will be too busy struggling to survive in the cyclone of regulations being thrown at them along with the deteriorating economy, closing of free markets, and the howling mobs of protestors our leftist puppets will sic on them."

"So, you are telling me that SAS and, in particular, Levell's paramilitary unit are no threat to our plans?"

"Not in the slightest," Fairchilde said. "His so-called Sleeping

Dogs are, after all, mere mortals. I have a man working for me, Maksym, who is more than a match for them."

"Very good. Speaking of Maksym, let's move on to the second issue." Without waiting for a response from Fairchilde, Zheng said, "It has come to my attention through sources I'm not at liberty to disclose, that you may be in danger."

That got Fairchilde's attention. "Danger," he said. "What kind of danger?" There was a decidedly nervous edge to his voice.

"Apparently, you also have a man working for you named Federov."

"Yes. He's a former Russian Special Forces colonel. What about him?"

"I have it on good authority that he intends to kill you."

The statement shocked Fairchilde, and frightened him more than a little. "Why? When?"

"Why? It seems he doesn't like you, but he does like the thought of helping himself to a portion of your wealth. As to when, I don't know, but soon, I think."

Fairchilde, stunned by this information, said nothing.

"I've seen this Maksym fellow at recent AGU gatherings. He seems a most formidable character. If I were you, Harland," Zheng said, "I would have him take care of Colonel Federov as quickly as possible. After all, it wouldn't do to have the very capable chairman of AGU prematurely removed from the scene."

"Prematurely? What do you mean?"

Recognizing his Freudian slip, Zheng said, reassuringly, "Only that I wish you a long and active chairmanship, terminating only upon your demise from natural causes at a very advanced age."

CHAPTER 26

SANTA FE, NEW MEXICO

THE DAY after Bazir's angry phone call, Sahim Yousafzai arrived at the house Turan and Bazir shared with the two Uzbeks in Santa Fe. He was dropped off in front of the house on Santa Inéz Road by a man driving a six-year-old Ford sedan. The two Uzbeks had appeared to be working on a car in the driveway. As Sahim approached the house, they silently fell in behind him. When he reached the front door, it opened and Bazir Haqqani stood just inside. He grabbed the front of the newcomer's shirt and yanked him inside. The Uzbeks entered and pulled the door closed behind them.

Bazir, still grasping the front of Sahim's shirt, dragged him into one of the house's two small bathrooms. The two Uzbeks crowded in behind while Turan paused in the doorway. The bathroom was filthy in the way a house might be if it were occupied by several men who knew little about hygiene and cared even less. The walls, floor, and shower were tiled. Black mold thrived in the grout lines and the toilet bowl. The sink looked like it hadn't been cleaned since its current occupants had rented the house. The buildup of lime and calcium from the hard water had rendered the shower door almost opaque. Incongruously, there was a plastic chair in the tiny shower.

Sahim looked confused and more than a little frightened. "Why did you bring me in here? Is there something wrong?" He spoke in Pashto.

Bazir pointed to the chair. "Sit!"

He quickly sat down. "But I don't understand. I've done nothing wrong." Sahim's voice was shrill with fear and confusion.

"Nothing wrong? Do you know why Amir brought you to us?"

Sahim looked down at the floor. "It wasn't my fault."

"You grabbed a young woman's breasts in public and it wasn't your fault?"

"She…she was dressed provocatively. She looked like she wanted to be touched."

"Just like all those women in Germany wanted to be touched on New Year's Eve? You imbecile, do you take me for a fool? We and our brothers in Europe are on a sacred mission, and you fools call attention to yourselves by breaking laws and outraging the citizenry."

With his voice just a whisper, Sahim said, "Please forgive me. It won't happen again. I swear."

The two Uzbeks crowded into the shower stall. One bound Sahim's arms behind his back. The other bound his legs. Satisfied with their work, they squeezed out of the stall and closed the door.

Bazir moved around behind Sahim. "Ah, my wayward one, if only that were the end of it. But it's much worse than that. You have betrayed our mission, disobeyed orders, and placed all of us in danger."

"No! Please! It was just a stupid mistake," Sahim wailed.

"The girl? Yes. But I'm not talking about her. No, Sahim, when we ambushed the Border Patrol, you were told to make sure they all were dead. You told me you had done that. But one of them survived. I'm certain it was one you were responsible for."

"No!" Sahim screamed. "The ones I checked *were* dead. I even shot one in the head to be sure."

Bazir slipped a knife with a six-inch blade from a scabbard on his belt. He wrapped his left hand tightly in Sahim's long dark hair and placed the edge of the blade against his throat. "Paradise is not for those who lie." He drew the blade swiftly. Its sharpness bit deeply into and through the flesh, blood vessels, and trachea, all the way to the cervical vertebrae. Blood spurted all over the shower stall, Sahim, and Bazir. But Haqqani wasn't finished. In a wild, snarling rage, he kept carving with the knife while twisting Sahim's lifeless head to and fro. When it was completely severed, Bazir threw it against the tile floor. He turned the water on, stripped off his blood-soaked clothes, and rinsed the blood from his body.

When finished, he stepped out of the shower and wrapped a dirty towel around his waist. "Clean this up and dispose of him," he said to the Uzbeks.

Turan's knees were so weak he wasn't sure how he was still standing. Bile clogged his throat. He was quaking like an aspen. Now he understood why Bazir had engaged the Border Patrol, despite being on such an important mission with the dirty bomb. Bazir was more than a fierce Islamist. He was also a megalomaniac and narcissist who believed so strongly in his own "rightness" that he thought nothing could stop him. His nature compelled him to make that terrifying statement with the slaughter of the CBP agents.

"I am truly sorry you had to witness this," Bazir said, "but this is how a warrior of Allah deals with traitors and incompetents."

Two days later Bazir asked Turan to accompany him on a drive to Los Alamos. It had been a tough two days for Turan. Following the horrific killing of Sahim, he was consumed with a mixture of fear for his own well-being and guilt that Sahim had paid such a dear price for Turan's error. He had no appetite. He just went through the motions, trying to get through each day. He wanted to see Carolina, wanted the comfort of her calm, unthreatening presence, but he was afraid to leave the house. Bazir seemed increasingly less stable, and the two Uzbeks were even worse. They had never showed him anything but contempt. Since Sahim's murder, they eyed Turan like hungry cougars eying a grazing deer. It seemed as if the barbaric crime had inflamed their bloodlust. His shame over Sahim's death was compounded by the realization that he had unthinkingly joined a group of madmen.

When Bazir asked him to accompany him on the drive to Los Alamos, Turan quickly said yes, especially when it became clear that the Uzbeks were not to be included. Turan knew Bazir considered the Uzbeks to be an additional risk; they were crude and unwilling to try to blend in with the population. They wore their hatred for America and its peoples openly. As a result, Bazir refused to allow them to leave the house. That only made them more difficult to tolerate. Turan understood that Bazir needed them as security for the mission. He also was certain that Bazir intended to dispose of them the minute he deemed their presence no longer useful.

Before they left for Los Alamos, Bazir had the Uzbeks load the mysterious rucksack into the trunk of the car. Turan wondered if that meant the time for fulfilling their mission had arrived.

During the forty-five-minute drive to Los Alamos, Bazir shared information about the mission with Turan. He confirmed what Turan had suspected—the rucksack held a terrifying weapon. It was what was known as a weapon of mass destruction, or WMD. In this case, it was a small nuclear device often erroneously referred to in the news media as a "dirty bomb."

Bazir explained how it functioned. "It is a Russian-made device, one of dozens, maybe hundreds, that disappeared with the fall of the Soviet Union. They are called portable tactical weapons and were sold and delivered to numerous parties around the world, including the Chinese. Nadir Shah was able to acquire several of them. They are extremely small and can be made to fit in a large carrying case such as the rucksack we are using. Even so, they weigh around one hundred pounds, or forty-five kilograms."

Turan marveled at this. "So small! Does it have much power?"

"The maximum yield, which is the amount of energy released when the weapon is detonated, is in the ten-kiloton range."

"I don't know what that means," Turan said.

Bazir laughed good-naturedly. "A kiloton is equivalent to one thousand tons of TNT. A ten-kiloton yield is about fifty percent of the power of the bombs dropped on Japan. For our purposes, it is enough."

Turan inadvertently turned and looked at the rear of the car, as if he expected to see the small nuclear device concealed in the trunk. "It's heavy, but it's so small. How can it have so much power?"

"It's what is called a linear implosion device. The core is a solid elongated mass of plutonium 239 called the pit. Plutonium pits are the smallest in diameter. The pit is embedded inside a cylinder of high explosive with a detonator at each end. The explosion compresses the mass, resulting in detonation."

Turan shook his head in wonderment. "How do you know all of this?"

"I was specially trained for this mission," Bazir said with a shrug.

"Are we going to use it to destroy an important American facility?"

"Certainly. But Nadir Shah has more of these weapons. He has other True Believers targeting other important sites too."

"Will the others detonate their bombs at the same time we do?"

Bazir hesitated before answering. "No. We will be the first to do so. The Caliph wants to let the Infidels know what is coming. That's terrorism at its best."

ALMOST THE FIRST sign of habitation at the edge of Los Alamos was a restaurant called Nuke's. Bazir turned into its parking lot, nosed into an empty space, and shut off the engine. It was almost 3 p.m. and there were only a couple of cars in the lot. Inside, Nuke's was nearly empty. Only two tables were occupied. Bazir walked to the one where two men were sitting. They were swarthy, with stubbled beards and casual, nondescript clothing. They looked to Turan very much like people he had grown up around in his native Waziristan. The two men watched expressionlessly as Bazir approached them. He pulled up a chair and sat, motioning at Turan to do the same.

Bazir nodded at the two men. "This is Pedro and Juan."

Turan looked at them. *They don't look like a Pedro or a Juan; more like an Abdul and a Mahmoud.*

As soon as the lone waitress had taken their orders, Bazir and the two men began speaking in Spanish. The strangers weren't very good at it; they mixed in a lot of Arabic words. Turan assumed they all had a purpose by appearing to be Latinos. Even though the place was all but deserted at this time of day, Bazir and the two men leaned in and spoke quietly to each other.

"You have the device with you, yes?" said Pedro.

"It's in the trunk of the car," Bazir said. "We'll need to transfer it to your vehicle."

Pedro nodded. "Not here, it's too dangerous. Someone might see us and get suspicious."

"Where then?"

"We will show you," Juan said and placed a small map on the table. He pointed to a spot on the map. "We are here." He drew his finger across the map to the east along the road Turan and Bazir had come in on then indicated a hairpin turn that climbed into the forested foothills. Eventually, he pointed to a spot on a dirt road that didn't appear to lead to anything. "We will meet you there in thirty minutes."

AFTER TRANSFERRING the weapon from their car to the one driven by Pedro and Juan, Bazir headed his car back toward Santa Fe.

"What will those men do with the bomb now?"

The other man smiled without looking at Turan. "They will detonate it, explode it inside the Los Alamos National Laboratory."

"What is this National Laboratory? Why is it the target?"

"For three good reasons. First, it was the site of the Manhattan Project, which birthed the nuclear arms that gave the Great Satan its position of world domination. It's also where the Infidels conduct research and design new weapons. Finally, there is a stockpile of plutonium 239 there. It should add to the toxic effects that will spread following the explosion."

"Will Pedro and Juan detonate the bomb?"

"Yes."

There was a puzzled look on Turan's face. "But surely this National Laboratory is well protected. How will Pedro and Juan get the bomb inside?"

Bazir laughed loudly. It had a harsh, cold ring to it. "Because they *are* part of the security force."

"But they are Muslims, yes?"

"Of course. The Infidels are very foolish, so consumed with a desire for multiculturalism and political correctness that they stupidly hire the fox to guard the henhouse." He laughed again. "The stockpile of plutonium is in a facility on Pajarito Road. Since their 9/11 experience, the Infidels have restricted Pajarito Road to National Laboratory badge holders for security reasons."

"But surely there is tight security there. How will the bomb get positioned?"

"When one of them is working a shift at the security gate, he will clear the other one through. The weapon will be carried right through the gates. It will be detonated in the facility where production of plutonium pits occurs. Pit manufacturing requires constant production to maintain quality and increase efficiency. As a consequence, a large amount of plutonium is maintained at that site. Also, by interrupting the processing, we cause delays in production and increase the risks of introducing deviations into the manufacturing process."

"Many people will die, yes?"

"Indeed. The manufacture of a single pit requires nearly seven hundred employees. There are always multiple pits in production, so expected deaths should be in multiples of seven hundred. But it's even better than that. This time of year, the prevailing wind is from the south and is at its strongest. By early morning, a southerly flow will carry the radiation over the entire plateau, including the town. It will kill the workers, and also the townspeople. The irony of this target is a beautiful thing."

"Why do you say that?"

"Los Alamos has the highest millionaire concentration of any city in America. Twelve and a half percent of households have at least one million dollars in assets. Truly, we are striking the Infidel in one of its dearest places."

CAROLINA HADN'T SEEN Tomás in a couple of days, which was unusual. He generally came by every afternoon. She was bothered by the way he'd bolted out of her house after the televised newscast about the wounded Border Patrol agent. Yes, it was a terrible thing, but it didn't involve anyone they knew. Besides there was always something ugly happening along the border.

She felt strongly that something was very amiss and wanted to help Tomás if she could. After all, what were friends for? And she did like Tomás. A lot.

When her mother arrived home from work, Carolina said, "I haven't heard from Tomás since he left so strangely the other night. I'm going to walk down to his house and see if he's all right."

"Okay, but don't be gone long. Your father will be home soon and you know he likes to eat early when there's a big fútbol match on TV."

Carolina started to leave, then hesitated. "Mom, we've never met Tomás's brother. Can I invite him to dinner too?"

Marisol Avila smiled at her only child. "Whatever makes you happy, Cari. Just let me know how many to plan on for dinner."

The house Turan lived in with Bazir was eight houses up the street from Carolina's. As she approached it, she noticed how rundown it looked. The yard was a mess of weeds and bare patches. The trees and shrubs hadn't been trimmed in a long while and the place was badly in need of painting. The brother's car wasn't in its usual place in the driveway. *Maybe they're out? Shopping? Job-hunting? Doing the sightseeing Tomás had mentioned?*

She walked up the cracked and oil-stained concrete driveway and tapped on the front door. She could hear someone moving around inside the house. A curtain on a window near the front door was pulled aside briefly as someone glanced out. It wasn't Tomás.

She had only seen the brother from a distance, but it didn't look like him either. She knocked again.

After another few moments, the door opened about twelve inches. Two men, one behind the other, stared out at her. They were both short and somewhat Asian-looking with scraggly beards and dirty clothes. They smelled as if they hadn't bathed in a long time. Both of the men stared at her breasts. One of them grinned and reached down and started rubbing his penis through his trousers. Carolina glanced quickly down in shock. It was clear that he had an erection. She instinctively took a step backward.

"Is Tomás home?" she said. Her voice shook slightly. The two men just continued to stare. Suspecting they might not have an understanding of English, she switched to Spanish and asked the same question. The two men said nothing, as if they didn't under-stand Spanish either. They just stared at her body. The man who was rubbing himself licked his lips and took a step forward, mumbling something in a guttural language Carolina had never heard before.

Carolina took two quick steps backward and said in English, then repeating in Spanish, "Just tell Tomás that Carolina stopped by." With that she spun around and half-ran toward the street. When she reached the sidewalk, she broke into a full run and didn't look back until she reached the sanctuary of her own home.

CHAPTER 27

BRIGHTON BEACH

FEDEROV AND ULYANIN were in a booth in the semiprivate bar on the second floor of the Little Bear on Sixth Street. It was early afternoon and there were a few people drinking in the saloon downstairs, but the upstairs was empty except for a thickly built bartender lazily polishing glasses behind a small bar.

"Tell me again," Federov said. "What did you say to that fuck Maksym?"

The other Russian shrugged. "Like I told you the previous ten times, he was at Fairchilde's estate a couple of days ago. I was able to get a couple of minutes alone with him. I said you had told me you were going to kill Fairchilde and steal his money."

"And he said?"

"He asked why I was telling him that. He knew you and I are colleagues who served together in the SVR and with Nadir Shah in Iraq."

"And you told him?"

"I told him I liked working for Fairchilde. The money is good. I didn't want to see it go away."

"He doesn't suspect you're working with me on this?"

"He's Maksym. He probably suspects a lot of things. But he's given me no reason to think he wishes to harm me. It's you he's after."

"Just as we planned," Federov said with a mean little grin. "Killing that son of a bitch will be such a pleasure. He's been a pain in my ass ever since he fucked up the assassination attempt on the American president, and let those Sleeping Dog bastards execute Chaim Laski. Mother Russia spent years and billions of dollars to put him in place as the financier of destructive leftwing causes in America. Maksym's incompetence ruined my career in the SVR. And I was in line to replace Vasilyev as its head!" Federov slammed his fist down on the table top.

The bartender looked at the two men for a few moments then resumed polishing the glasses.

"Kirill, let's try to stay focused on the task at hand," Ulyanin said. "Maksym believes you are here celebrating your scheme to kill Fairchilde and steal his money. I assured him I would get you drunk so he could sneak up on you and kill you. He will be here shortly, so stay focused."

Federov turned to look at the bartender, but the man had finished with the glasses and disappeared. "What about the bartender?"

Again, Ulyanin shrugged. "What about him?"

The wicked grin creased Federov's Slavic features one more time. "No witnesses. I'll kill Maksym. You take care of the bartender."

Ulyanin nodded. "Sure." A moment later his cell phone buzzed and he answered it. It was one of the men sitting at the bar downstairs. Ulyanin had given him fifty dollars to alert him when Maksym arrived. Although the man had never seen Maksym, Ulyanin assured him he would know him when he saw him. There was no one in New York or elsewhere that resembled him. When a man with long dirty hair and a scarred face suddenly filled the doorway from Sixth Street so completely it all but blocked out the daylight behind him, the man at the bar knew exactly who it was. He called Ulyanin.

"He's here, coming up the stairs as planned," Ulyanin said.

Federov turned the bottle of vodka over on the table top and pulled a Browning 1911 model .45 from beneath his jacket. He thumbed back the hammer and slipped the weapon under the table. He leaned forward across the table as if he'd passed out and closed his eyes to a mere squint.

His plan was to deceive Maksym into believing Federov actually had passed out. Maksym wouldn't be able to resist walking right up to Federov and either killing him with his bare hands or by placing the barrel of his gun against the Russian's skull. But Federov wasn't going to let him get that close. When his target was about ten feet from the booth, Federov would begin firing and continue to do so until he'd emptied the .45. It held seven cartridges in the magazine and one in the chamber. Each was nearly half an inch in diameter. The bullets were jacketed hollow points. The purpose of the hollow points was to cause the slugs to expand on hitting the target. These were Remington 185 grain Golden Saber +P. They would expand; drilling eight holes three quarters of an inch in diameter through Maksym's body. In addition, Ulyanin would empty all sixteen .40 caliber Magtech 180 grain bonded slugs from his Glock 23. Even a man of Maksym's nearly superhuman bulk wouldn't be able to survive that. It wouldn't even be necessary to bury Maksym; just slice him thin and use him on deli sandwiches like Swiss cheese.

Ulyanin slid over into the corner of the booth and slouched down, his right hand clutching the grip of the Glock in a pocket of his windbreaker. He didn't want to be an easy target in the event Maksym started shooting as he approached the booth.

Both men heard the sound of heavy footsteps climbing the stairs from the tavern below. They heard the door being pushed open. Then it was silent for several moments before the footsteps began again, this time moving slowly away from the door and toward them.

Sweat began to bead on Ulyanin's brow despite the chilly temperature in the bar. He had to consciously restrain himself from leaning out to see where Maksym was. He knew the tension was affecting Federov too. He saw the other man's eyelids quivering with the effort to maintain the barest of squints.

Ulyanin's brain barely registered the tip of the Remington Express Tactical shotgun slipping over the back of the booth behind Federov. The sudden deafening blast more than startled him. He almost squeezed the trigger on the Glock. If he had, he would have shot himself in the leg. He stared in disbelief at Federov's body. The high-powered, twelve-gauge blast from such close range had opened a large hole in his back, severing his spine in the process. The big Russian collapsed sideways, sliding out of the booth onto the dirty floor. A sea of blood welled from his corpse.

The bartender loomed over the back of the seat Federov had occupied. He had the shotgun aimed at Ulyanin, whose heart was racing as he tried to comprehend what had gone wrong. His right hand squeezed the Glock's grip so tightly that his arm shook.

The huge figure of Maksym materialized in front of the booth. He stared down at Federov then stooped and picked up the Russian's .45 where he had dropped it. Stone-faced, Maksym fired a round from the gun into the dead man's skull.

Then he turned to Ulyanin. "It is always good to be certain, is it not Andrei?"

The Russian didn't move. He just turned to look at the bartender then back to Maksym.

"Want me to kill him too?" the bartender said.

Maksym stared balefully at Ulyanin for several moments. Then a trace of a grin played across his scarred features. "No. Our mutual employer may still have a use for him. He seems to think there may be occasions when I need an accomplice. Perhaps he feels generous toward him because he alerted me to the late Colonel Federov's plot." He paused briefly and locked Ulyanin in a squinty-eyed stare. "Or perhaps Major Ulyanin's actions were all part of the plot to lure me here and kill me."

Ulyanin shook his head back and forth. "No, I had no idea what Federov was planning. He invited me here today to drink and talk about old times in the SVR. I thought he was drunk. I didn't know he had a gun." He looked at the bartender, still not quite sure how it had unfolded this way.

"Vasily here," Maksym nodded at the bartender, "is a man who appreciates capitalism. Because I suspected Federov was setting a trap, I paid Vasily ten thousand dollars to make sure that didn't happen. Looks like he earned his money."

The barrel of Vasily's shotgun never wavered. It was pointed directly at Ulyanin's chest.

"Stand up," Maksym said. To emphasize his order, he leaned over and grabbed the front to Ulyanin's jacket, yanking him out of the booth. He held his huge hand out. "Give me your gun." He still held Federov's .45 in his other hand. In his huge paw, it looked like a child's toy pistol. And it also was aimed at Ulyanin's chest.

Ulyanin hesitated for a second or two, as if calculating the best course of action—to comply, or to try and shoot his way out of the situation. When Maksym looked at Vasily and his shotgun, Ulyanin made his decision. He slowly pulled the Glock from his jacket pocket, laid it on the table and nudged it gently over to Maksym. "I always hated Federov. At times, I thought about killing him myself," he lied.

An hour later a very apprehensive Andrei Ulyanin was sitting in a chair in front of a desk in the den of Harland Fairchilde's estate home on Long Island. On the one hand, he was happy and relieved to still be alive. On the other, he wasn't sure how long that status would continue.

Fairchilde was behind the huge, ornately carved desk. The mass of Maksym was sitting in the other chair on Ulyanin's side of the desk. Even at ease, he looked like an enormous jungle cat poised to spring at any instant.

"So, Major Ulyanin," Fairchilde said, "the question that confronts us is what to do with you."

Ulyanin said nothing.

"You did alert Maksym regarding Federov's plan to rob me and kill me. I certainly am grateful for that kindness." He paused and stared thoughtfully at Ulyanin for a few moments. "However, you were with Federov at the site where Maksym's ambush was planned, and you were armed. I'm sure you can understand our dilemma."

Ulyanin was trying hard not to sweat, but was on the verge of losing that struggle. "Yes, of course I can see how that might look. But there is a simple explanation."

"By all means, please enlighten us."

Ulyanin licked his lips, but maintained eye contact with Fairchilde. To do otherwise might be perceived as fear, or worse, lying. "I was at the Little Bear because Kirill...Colonel Federov had asked me to meet him for drinks and war stories. That didn't seem unusual. He and I have been friends for years and served together in the military. We often met at the bar. But I had no idea he planned to try to kill Maksym there. It was my understanding that you were his target, just as I shared with Maksym some days ago."

Fairchilde waggled his head slowly from side to side as if considering Ulyanin's words. "But the weapon? Maksym says you were armed. Were you planning to participate in killing Maksym?"

"No, not at all. The Little Bear is a very dangerous place. There are always fights, stabbings, sometimes shootings. Few people go there unarmed."

Fairchilde thought about what Ulyanin had said. After a few moments, he looked at Maksym. "Andrei has been useful to me in the past. What do you think?"

The big man looked bored and shrugged noncommittally. "He does have his uses, and I can always kill him later if he proves troublesome."

"Well, Andrei, it looks like this is your lucky day." Fairchilde made a dismissive gesture with his hand and began studying some documents on his desk.

As Maksym escorted Ulyanin toward the mansion's service entrance, he pulled him aside into a small alcove near the kitchen. He stared malevolently at Ulyanin for several moments before speaking. "My initial instinct is to kill you, but I went along with that fop Fairchilde for a reason. You now owe me your life."

Ulyanin was a big man at six two and two hundred pounds, but seemed dwarfed in the presence of Maksym who was standing only a few inches from him, purposely using his bulk to intimidate.

"I am very grateful, Maksym. How can I repay you?"

"A time is coming soon when I'll need a man with your experience and skills to assist me in a special matter. It involves a debt that needs to be settled. I used some other men a while back. But they were incompetent fools and got themselves killed. The debt remains unpaid, but you and I will see that it is settled."

CHAPTER 28

SAN LUIS, CHIHUAHUA, MEXICO

THE BELL 412EPI helicopter had been loaned to the Dogs for this mission by a wealthy rancher who'd served with Levell in the U.S. Marines Force Recon. Intended for civilian purposes, it had comfortable seating and other appointments not typically found in military equipment. The noise inside the cabin made conversation challenging, but not impossible.

Whelan examined the new enhanced night vision goggles (ENVG) Levell had provided. The ones they'd used in the raid on Chacón's estate had been impressive, but with these new ones, the operator could identify people and objects in almost all low-light and no-light situations. They had a FLIR—forward-looking infrared — component that enabled the operator to see through light fog, rain, and smoke. In an urban environment, streetlights and other sources of strong illumination could overwhelm night vision goggles and wash out the image, but not with these.

Whelan, leaning over and shouting to be heard above the noise of the chopper, said to Marc Kirkland, sitting next to him, "Did you check these out yet?"

"Yeah. Lucky us. These babies are still in the experimental stage at a Mueller company."

Whelan grinned and shook his head. "The things ol' Cliff has access to. Did you know they're digitized?"

"Yeah. The operator can send the images via a communication link to other guys in his unit, as well as back to a command post."

"And the software in these goggles enables the system to adjust the image and brightness automatically," Whelan said

"What impresses me most is the increase in the user's field of view to around ninety-five degrees. It's not like staring down a bowling alley anymore."

"These babies ought to be particularly useful tonight with the near-absence of ambient light and the anticipated gunfire and other explosions."

Kirkland bobbed his head and shouted back, "Didn't take Levell's people long to break Chacón. What? Less than two days?"

Whelan nodded.

"How do you suppose they did it?"

"Probably in a kinder, gentler fashion than we would have. Chemicals, maybe."

It was the intel provided by Chacón that had brought the Dogs to this place just above the tiny Mexican village of San Luis. The Zetas had helped HAC pick the location and set up the camp to be a staging area for jihadi warriors. From here they were led by Zeta guides across the border, barely eleven kilometers away. At upwards of fifty thousand dollars a head, it was a lucrative business for the Zetas and their MS-13 partners.

Unfortunately, Chacón hadn't known know anything about a nuclear device being smuggled into and out of the camp. He'd suggested that the only one who would have that information was the camp's commandante. The Dogs would have to get that intel the hard way—by force of arms.

The infiltration required Whelan and the other six Dogs to make another difficult night jump. The insertion point was in the arid lands west of the imposing mountains that sheltered San Luis. While the new ENVG helped, the rugged terrain and prevalent wind gusts made the jump that much dicier. In spite of the challenges, all seven men stuck their landings in a dry creek bed, or arroyo, roughly five klicks on a direct line from the jihadi encampment.

But it wasn't possible to approach it on a straight line. The craggy mountain chain, with its sheer-walled, jagged ridgelines, made the trek more than twelve klicks in distance. The cold, dry nighttime mountain air helped some, but it was still a physically challenging trek, even with the benefit of their rare genetics. In addition to wearing body armor, their backpacks weighed more than one hundred pounds apiece. They were crammed with medical supplies, food, and comm gear, but the bulk of the weight was water, ammunition, and explosives.

The jump had occurred just as the last bit of light faded at nine o'clock. It took the men four hours to cover the seven and a half miles to the Islamists' camp. The last several hundred yards were almost straight up, and there were sentries to neutralize.

When they finally reached an elevated position slightly above the camp, they first determined that nothing differed from what the previous satellite surveillance had shown. According to the surveillance intel, approximately fifty jihadis were currently in the camp. They trained and practiced maneuvers during the day and early evening. At night, they were housed in groups of six to eight men in small cabin-like structures elevated on low concrete pillars. There was a latrine on the edge of the camp.

Whelan looked at his watch. It was one o'clock. He had the men rest for two hours, hoping their prey would be in the deepest stage of sleep when the Dogs attacked. The men took turns grabbing catnaps, keeping three men on alert at all times. At 0300 hours,

Whelan sent three of the Dogs circling around to the right. Another three went left. When the six men were in position, Whelan spoke the signal into his throat mic.

Swiftly, silently, the seven men closed the circle on the ten little cabins in the camp. As the Dogs worked their way through the encampment, they placed charges of high explosives under the cabins. Satellite intel together with COMINT—communications intelligence—deciphered by cryptanalysts working for SAS, had located the commandant's cabin at the center of the camp. Whelan assigned himself the task of capturing him. He slipped quietly among the cabins toward the slightly larger one in the middle. Compared to the unexpected difficulties encountered during the operation at Chacón's ranch, things were progressing smoothly tonight. Or maybe not. Somewhere close by, Whelan heard someone belch. It was long and loud, and wouldn't have been made by any of the Dogs, not even Almeida.

He quickly stepped against the wall of the nearest cabin. Through his ENVG he saw a man about ten feet away, dressed only in his underwear. He was leaning against a cabin wall with one hand and holding his penis with the other while he urinated. *So much for using the latrine.*

As if by instinct, the man raised his head and stared in Whelan's direction. Although there was precious little ambient light and Whelan was dressed in an Army multicam black tactical response uniform with balaclava, the man must have thought he saw something. He squinted his eyes and continued to stare in Whelan's direction.

As part of his equipment, Whelan had a Smith &Wesson SWTK10CP throwing knife. But his body armor inhibited the throwing motion, and even if his throw was accurate, it didn't guarantee the man wouldn't cry out. Only in the movies did all of the pieces come together flawlessly. Instead, he reached for his holstered SIG Sauer P226. Even suppressed, it would make a clearly audible sound, but it would be far quieter and shorter than a wounded man's scream.

The man had stuffed his organ back in his pants and took a step toward the spot in the gloom where Whelan was hiding. It was his only step before the 9mm hollow point slug drilled through his forehead and blew out the back of his skull. Unfortunately, the slug continued on and buried itself with a thud in the wall of the commandant's cabin.

"What the hell was that?" Larsen's voice came through the comm gear. "Did someone shoot somebody?"

"Unavoidable," Whelan said into his throat mic. "Guy taking a leak was onto me. Everyone accelerate at your end. Go, go, go!"

Whelan ran to the commandant's cabin. As he reached the front door, it swung inward and the commandant himself stepped into the doorway. His eyes opened wide as he saw Whelan standing in front of him. Still holding the P226 in his right hand, Whelan grabbed the man by the collar of his shirt and yanked his chin into Whelan's forehead before he could even get his mouth open to scream. The blow shattered the man's lower jaw and instantly rendered him unconscious. Whelan slung him over his left shoulder and started to turn when he heard someone inside the cabin yell at him in Arabic. The English translation would have been something along the lines of "What the hell is going on?" Whelan responded by sending two 9mm slugs through the center of the man's thorax.

The camp was beginning to stir and lights came on in a couple of the cabins.

"Marc! Blow the fucking cabins starting with the ones on the opposite side of the camp," Whelan shouted into the throat mic.

Kirkland's voice came over his ear bud. "Roger that." There were two enormous explosions no more than a second apart.

Whelan sprinted past two cabins at the edge of the camp and

onto the higher ground where the other Dogs were waiting. Stone and Stensen squatted on either side of his path. They opened up with their SIG SG 553 Commando compact assault rifles. Originally chambered for NATO 5.56x45mm ammunition, SAS technicians had modified them to fire 9mm rounds from 30-round magazines. The weapons had semi-auto and full-auto settings plus an additional trigger module for a three-round burst setting. It was the three-round bursts they were firing. As Whelan reached the rendezvous point and hit the ground with his captive, Kirkland detonated the remaining explosives. It was deafening. *Probably visible to astronauts in the space station*, Whelan thought.

The team waited for a few minutes to make certain there had been no survivors, then began the arduous hike back to flatter country where a stealth chopper could exfiltrate them. It was barely a mile as the crow flies, but the rugged terrain turned it into almost three and a half miles. The Dogs took turns carrying the trussed-up commandant. He regained consciousness at about the halfway point and his captors took pleasure in making his journey unbearable.

A short flight back across the border took them to an isolated ranch less than a quarter of a mile over the border into New Mexico. Whelan spoke with Levell by way of the heavily encrypted Mueller brothers' satellite system. He confirmed what Levell had seen on satellite relay—the operation had been a success. When he disconnected the call, he turned back to his men. "Let the fun begin."

Thomas immediately left the small ranch house and took a long slow walk in the silent, chilly desert.

The red glow in Stensen's pupils flared.

Kirkland slowly drew a long, thin blade from a scabbard attached to his belt.

But it wasn't until Larsen smiled his bad smile that their prisoner lost complete sphincter control.

CHAPTER 29

SANTA FE, NEW MEXICO

CAROLINA AVILA AWOKE WITH A START. She lay there in her darkened room trying to remember what she'd been dreaming. As she stretched, she felt a slight tremor that lasted for several seconds. Loose objects rattled on her dresser and night stand. So did the panes in her window. *A sonic boom...or maybe an earth tremor?* She'd lived in Santa Fe her entire young life and knew the area experienced an occasional small tremor, but geologists didn't consider Santa Fe to be in an earthquake zone.

She glanced at the clock on her dresser. It was 6 a.m. Time to get up. Her first class started in two hours. She knew her mother would already be up, preparing for her workday at the New Mexico State Police HQ, which began at 7 a.m. Carolina swung her legs around to the side of the bed. That's when she heard it. It was an odd sound, unnerving, then as the fogginess of sleep passed, she identified it. Someone was softly sobbing. She listened for a moment, her concern rising.

Moving quickly, she grabbed her robe from the foot of her bed and struggled into it. The sound was coming from the living room.

As she dashed out the door and down the hall, the air was redolent with the acrid smell of coffee that had been left on the burner too long. Entering the living room, she heard the muted sounds of the TV. Her mother was on her knees in front of the television, her hands balled into fists and pressed against her face. Tears streamed freely from her eyes. Her body shook with gasping sobs. An empty coffee cup lay on its side on the carpet near her. Its contents had left a small puddle on the tile floor.

The sight momentarily froze Carolina, then she rushed to her mother's side. "What is it, Mom, what's wrong?" She knelt beside the older woman and put her arm tightly around her shoulders. Her mother was the rock of the family, a cop and a tough one at that. Carolina felt her own sense of panic rising.

It took her mother a few moments to respond. Finally, pointing to the TV, she was able to softly choke out, "Mi hermana...y su marido."

Carolina was confused. While she and her parents spoke fluent Spanish in honor of their ancestry, they always used English around the house. It was their way of showing pride in being Americans, of demonstrating that they were fully and willingly assimilated into American culture and society.

"I don't understand, Mom. Aunt Soledad? And Uncle Ernesto?" That was when Carolina realized her mother was still pointing at the TV.

She turned and stared at the large flat screen. It was filled with a scene straight from Hell—billowing clouds of smoke and dust with fires raging in the background. Ashes swirled in the air. A trailer at the bottom of the screen crawled slowly from right to left. It said something about a nuclear explosion at the Los Alamos National Laboratory followed by severe earthquakes in the area.

Carolina gasped. Now she knew why her mother was so emotional. Carolina's Aunt Soledad and Uncle Ernesto lived in Los

Alamos and worked at the facility. Soledad was in HR. Ernesto was in accounting. She reached forward to turn up the volume, simultaneously screaming "Dad!"

A moment later her father burst into the room in his underwear, face lathered in shaving cream and a Remington 870 Express Tactical Shotgun clasped in his hands. "What is it? What's wrong?"

Carolina pointed at the screen.

The camera was focused on a man holding a microphone. Fires raged in the distance behind him. Medical teams, uniformed police, and national guardsmen could be seen scurrying in the background. With a slight quaver in his voice, the newsman was saying, "The cause of the explosions at the Los Alamos National Laboratory," he turned and pointed, "is unknown at this time, but authorities haven't expressly ruled out terrorism." He partially turned again and looked over his shoulder, then said the obvious. "The scene is one of utter chaos." With a sudden panic-stricken look, the newsman dropped into a crouch. The camera that was focused on him wobbled back and forth. "There it is again," the reporter shouted into his microphone. "We're being told that these are aftershocks following a significant earthquake that came directly on the heels of the explosion."

The scene switched back to the studio where the news anchor introduced two men. One was seated at the news desk with the anchor; the other was being patched in by phone. The newsman introduced his studio guest as Dr. Philippe Heilmann, a noted nuclear physicist and a former Assistant Secretary of Energy for Nuclear Energy. "Dr. Heilmann," the anchor said in a smooth, polished voice, "there seems to be a great deal of uncertainty whether this disaster was the result of an accident or a terrorist attack. What is your theory, given your experience and background in the field?"

The physicist seemed nervous and uncertain, as if worried his answer might demean his former colleagues at the Los Alamos National Laboratory. After several moments, he said, "Given the destructiveness and the inevitable radiation effects, as well as the resulting earthquakes, it's probably going to be some time before we're able to determine the actual cause." He smiled weakly.

"Okay," the newsman said, clearly disappointed with the answer. "We also have retired general Harold Garvey on the line. General, you were, until your recent retirement, our military's top expert on nuclear energy and weaponry. What is your gut reaction to what happened at the national laboratory?"

Unlike Heilmann, Garvey didn't mince words. In a gravelly voice mostly devoid of warmth, he said, "I don't have a gut reaction without any information to base it on. The more immediate issues, the ones we should be focusing on, are how to limit further damage and render aid to the victims of this damn disaster. At this point, there's no arguing that this was a nuclear explosion—the preliminary radiation readings are telling us that. My concern is the extent of the nuclear fallout. That's largely a matter of the size of the explosion. The damn air is full of dust and other radioactive matter, and the wind is blowing it onto nearby inhabited areas."

"General, it was an open secret that the laboratory is the facility for the manufacture of America's nuclear devices. It also is the site where the nation's plutonium supplies are stored. How did, or might, this have factored into the cause or effects of the explosion?"

"What the hell do you think?" the general said as if he were speaking to an idiot. "There is—or was—as much plutonium stored at the lab as is contained in the combined nuclear weapons arsenals of Great Britain, China, France, India, Israel, and Pakistan. When you factor in the exposure of sixty-six hundred or more kilograms of plutonium as a result of the blast, you can compound the disaster geometrically. The whole damn area's going to be radioactive for a very long time."

Marisol's sobs grew louder as the full extent of the disaster began to dawn on her.

Her husband gently rubbed her shoulders. "Querida, why don't you try to call Soledad. Where she and Ernie live may not have been damaged that badly."

Marisol shook her head. "I did try to call. Three times. There was no answer." She choked back a sob then seemed to brighten. "But her phone rang. I heard it. She's never without her phone, so if it's okay, she must be okay too."

Al gently said, "I'm sorry, Marisol, but the caller hears a ring at her end even if the other person's phone has been destroyed."

Their focus was drawn back to the TV. The anchorman was saying, "We've just been advised by a spokesperson for the Department of Homeland Security that the explosion was in the ten-kiloton range. That's the equivalent of ten thousand tons of TNT. We're being told that the explosion detonated at ground level and created a crater about three hundred to three hundred fifty feet in diameter. Eyewitnesses who were miles away from the site report that they saw an intense, blinding flash of light followed by a fireball that rose into the mushroom-shaped cloud that's typically associated with nuclear explosions."

He glanced down at the monitor built into the desk in front of him. "Apparently, we have professor Gabrielle Morneau in the studio of our Los Angeles affiliate. She's a nuclear physicist on the faculty of the California Institute of Technology in Pasadena. Good morning Professor. Thanks for joining us."

The professor was thin. Her sharp features were accentuated by her round, rimless glasses. Her long, gray hair was swept up in a bun. She spoke English with a strong French accent. "Perhaps not such a good morning, yes? Especially for those who were living in the area of Los Alamos."

"Let's talk about that, Professor. With a nuclear explosion in the ten-kiloton range, what kind of damage can be expected?"

"The explosion would vaporize everything in the immediate vicinity. The blast would create an enormously powerful wave that would flatten even steel reinforced concrete buildings within a radius of approximately half a mile, and brick and wooden buildings out to a mile and a half. Major damage would extend beyond three miles. Immediately after the blast wave passes, tornedo-force winds would sweep out from the blast site then back inwards to fill the vacuum created. The velocity of these winds can reach almost four hundred miles per hour. It's a nightmare situation."

"That truly is a terrifying scenario, Professor Morneau. But what about loss of life? What do the statistics tell us is the likely outcome of this tragedy?"

"Certainly, we can expect the total loss of life within a radius of a mile and a half. Roughly half of the survivors from a mile and a half to three miles out, perhaps farther, will be seriously injured. Compounding these problems is the damage to local medical facilities and the loss of electrical and water services. The roads may be impassable, making much of the affected area inaccessible. Rescuing and properly treating the victims is going to be very challenging at best."

"But what about these tremors, Professor?"

"That is another very serious concern. Apparently, the plutonium processing facility and the nuclear materials storage facility were built directly on top of several active intersecting fault lines, as well as in the middle of a volcanic field. All these factors will lead to additional casualties. In fact, scientists are very concerned that the earthquake activity triggered by the blast could result in volcanic activity in the large magma bodies located beneath the nearby Valles caldera."

Marisol looked at her husband and, with a shaky voice, said, "How far do you think Soledad lives from the lab site?"

He looked away and answered softly. "It's a small town...less than a mile and a half." He squeezed her tightly and whispered. "Lo siento mucho, Querida."—I'm so sorry, Sweetheart.

On the TV, the news anchor was saying, "Professor, what about radioactivity? What's the likely scenario there?"

Morneau didn't respond immediately. She closed her eyes for a few moments, as if trying to banish the horrific scenes playing out in her mind. "Nuclear fallout only adds to this tragedy. It can be expected that the prevailing winds will spread it over an area of many, many miles. It could be uninhabitable for years." She paused again before adding, "The situation is greatly compounded by the fact that ground zero of the explosion was the facility where thousands of pounds of plutonium was stored. It's probably going to be another Chernobyl. Or worse."

The news anchor looked down at his laptop monitor briefly then back at the live camera. "I've just googled information on winds in the Los Alamos area." He glanced back at the laptop. "Typically, this time of year is the windiest. The prevailing direction of the winds is toward the northeast."

Carolina again became aware of the acrid smell. She recognized it and raced into the kitchen. The family's Mr. Coffee machine was still on, but what little liquid had been in it had evaporated, leaving a rapidly hardening residue in the bottom of the pot. She quickly unplugged the machine, then ran back to the living room. Her dad had helped her mother to her feet and was holding Marisol with both arms around her. One hand gently rubbed her back. Marisol had her fists clenched under her chin. Her face was buried in Al's chest.

"Mom," Carolina said. "Don't worry. I'll drive over to Los Alamos and try to find Aunt Soledad."

Al's head snapped around in her direction. "The hell you will! Use your head, Carolina. Most of the roads are impassable because of the blast damage and the earthquakes. Any that might be still be usable will have been sealed off by the military. The winds are spreading radioactivity. The newscaster just said all the towns north and east of Los Alamos are being evacuated all the way to Taos. Hell, a change in wind direction and they could start evacuating Santa Fe."

Carolina's mouth opened and closed a few times before words came out. "But I feel so helpless. What if Aunt Soledad or Uncle Ernesto need us? Somebody has to do something." Her frustration and anxiety made her voice sound almost like a wail, and she started to cry.

Marisol straightened and smiled weakly at Al as she gently pushed him away. "I will find out about Soledad."

"What do you mean?" Al said.

She began walking toward their bedroom in the back of the house. Over her shoulder she said, "I am going to get dressed and go to work."

"No," Al said. "You're in no shape emotionally to go anywhere. What if we're ordered to evacuate?"

"Then I should be at work where I can help. That's what law-enforcement people do."

CHAPTER 30
WASHINGTON, D.C.

MITCH CHRISTIE WOKE up a happy man, the happiest he could remember being. The sex with the woman lying in bed next to him was the best he'd ever experienced and it seemed to be getting even better. This euphoria had come as a total surprise. When his first wife Debbie had left him, he was a broken man; broken in heart, body, and spirit. At the time, he couldn't imagine ever being involved with another woman. His main concern had been surviving the debilitating digestive issues that had him eating Rolaids like a senior citizen at an all-you-can-eat-buffet. And then there was the demotion at work and the unwanted transfer from FBI headquarters in Washington to the relative boondocks of Albuquerque. But, oddly, that's where his life had taken a turn for the better. That's where he'd met Camila Ramirez.

He rolled on his side and stared at her sleeping gently next to him. His eyes soaked in the vision—the tousled mass of dark hair, the flawless olive skin that gave her a naturally tanned look, the impossibly long eyelashes, and those full red lips. He felt his desire beginning to swell and glanced at the alarm clock. They had made love passionately for a long time last night. Maybe, if he woke her up now, they would have time for a quickie before heading out to work.

He thought back to the night before and smiled. Earlier, before they had drained each other with their lovemaking, he had taken Camila to dinner at their favorite candlelight restaurant. They had ordered a bottle of their favorite wine, and, sipping it while waiting for dinner, he had proposed. He would never forget her response. She had placed one long, immaculately manicured finger to the side of her chin and looked pensively into the distance, as if debating her answer. His heart had frozen. Then she had shrieked in delight and thrown her arms around his neck, screaming, "Yes, yes, yes, yes, *yes*!"

They had planned the wedding over the second glass of wine. It would be in New Mexico, where they had met. Because it would be the second marriage for each of them, they wanted it to be a small affair attended by only a few mutual friends and members of Camila's immediate family. When they went into work today, they planned to put in for vacation time with their respective employers. With any luck, they'd be on their way to New Mexico in just a few days.

Christie leaned over and brushed his lips across Camila's cheek. Her eyelids fluttered open and she smiled and stretched seductively. He pulled her close.

Camila glanced at the clock. "We'll have to hurry. No marathon session this morning." She sounded disappointed.

A cell phone rang. From the particular ringtone, they knew it was Christie's office calling.

"Aw, shit, what timing," he said in frustration, as he reached over and grabbed the device from the nightstand. He shot Camila a look of deep disappointment.

He thumbed the green icon. "Yeah, Christie."

It was his boss, the assistant director of the Bureau's Counterterrorism Division (CTD). "Mitch, there's been an incident at the Los Alamos National Lab. A nuclear explosion. Might be terrorism involved. I need you to head out there immediately. Don't even come into the office, just go directly to Andrews. There will be a plane waiting. You'll be briefed enroute."

Christie sat bolt upright. "Christ! A nuclear explosion? Isn't that more in the jurisdiction of CDRG than ours, especially given that terrorism hasn't been confirmed?" He was referring to the Catastrophic Disaster Response Group.

"It's enough of a possibility that I already have a Fly Team in the air. But we suspect there may be an international element to this too—Islamic, of course. That's why I want you out there. You have the right background—Middle East liaison with the International Operations Division and before that ASAC in the Albuquerque field office. You're the perfect choice to be onsite heading up the Joint Terrorism Task Force."

"I'm on it," Christie said resignedly. "I'll call you as soon as I'm onsite." He disconnected the call and turned to Camila. "Nothing ruins a mood more than a call from the boss. I've been assigned to an incident in New Mexico. I'm sorry."

She reached out and stroked his arm gently. She looked pensive for a few moments, then smiled. "You know, there may be a silver lining here after all. I mean, you'll already be in New Mexico. I'll still put in for vacation time and fly out there. As soon as you have some spare time, we'll get married."

He stared at her for a moment while her words sunk in. Then he grinned and said, "If we really hurry, I think we can still have an ultra-quickie."

CHAPTER 31

SANTA FE

ONE OF THE two Gulfstream V aircraft available to the FBI had been waiting for Christie at Andrews Air Force Base. As soon as he scrambled up the plane's steps, the steward closed and secured the door and the plane began taxiing. The aircraft had three distinct areas in its passenger cabin. In each of them, the upper and lower sidewalls were covered in light beige Ultrasuede, while the carpet throughout was beige with bordeaux inserts. The furniture was a burnished walnut. The aircraft had a full-size galley that included a microwave oven, high-temperature oven, and coffee maker. Christie shook his head as he walked by. *Was it really necessary to spend taxpayers' money to such a lavish extent simply for transportation?*

As he walked through the plane, he was surprised to see that most of the seats were occupied by suits poring over data on laptops or conferring with other suits.

From behind him, he heard the steward say, "They're waiting for you in the aft cabin, Agent Christie."

The aft cabin had a four-place berthable conference table on the left and an opposing credenza on the right side. A large flat-screen

TV, tuned to a news channel, was bolted atop the credenza. Its sound had been muted. Christie settled into the single vacant over-stuffed bucket seat at the table and introduced himself to the other three people already seated there. The steward brought him a laptop that was already opened to the salient documents and reports on the disaster in Los Alamos. More intel was being received on a continuous basis.

The steward kept up a steady supply of coffee and pastries, as most of the passengers hadn't had an opportunity to eat breakfast before dashing to Andrews to catch the flight.

Christie was so engrossed in the reports and discussions with the others seated at his table that he hardly noticed the passage of time. The Gulfstream V's twin Rolls-Royce BR710A1-10 engines pushed the aircraft along at better than five hundred miles per hour at a cruising altitude of 40,500 feet. The plane arrived at its destination, Kirtland Air Force Base in Albuquerque, in less than four hours. It would have been more expedient to have landed at Santa Fe Municipal Airport, but its longest runway was only 8,366 feet and the Gulfstream needed over 9,000 feet in order to takeoff again. Kirtland's runway 8/23 offered over 13,000 feet.

A command post and processing center had been established at the headquarters of the New Mexico State Police on the southern outskirts of Santa Fe. The distance from Kirtland AFB to The NMSP headquarters was about sixty miles north of Albuquerque by motor vehicle, but Interstate 25 was so clogged with people fleeing south from the general area of Santa Fe that one of the two northbound lanes was being utilized to accommodate them. Fortunately, the Air Force had several Bell UH-1N twin-engine, medium-size utility helicopters at Kirtland and pressed them into service to transport incoming personnel to locations in Santa Fe. Christie boarded one as soon as he deplaned and was at NMSP headquarters less than thirty minutes later.

Equipment and personnel had been shifted around to create space for a JTTF command post. As a ranking Bureau agent on the task force, Christie was introduced to the state police officer in charge of the CP. Major Fermin "Frank" Cuellar was in charge of the NMSP Special Operations Bureau. The two men recognized each other immediately.

"Mitch Christie!" Cuellar said as they shook hands firmly. "What's it been? Three years or so?"

"Every bit of that, probably more. Seems like that week at the Gunsite Academy was a lifetime ago."

"A lifetime's not long enough to forget that friggin' wasteland." Cuellar grinned and slapped Christie on the shoulder.

"True, but it was a valuable weapons course, made bearable by your company."

The grin vanished from Cuellar's face. "How much do you know about the situation at LANL?"

Christie shrugged. "I read all the available reports on the flight out, but that still leaves a gap for the last hour or so. Anything new?"

Cuellar took Christie by the arm and led him down a hallway to his own office. "You need anything? Coffee? Food?"

"No, I'm good. I probably gained five pounds on the flight out."

Cuellar pointed to a chair in front of his desk. Instead of going around to his chair behind the desk, he sat in the other client chair next to Christie.

"Mitch, we got a bad situation on our hands." He paused and winced. "Preliminarily, it seems the explosion was caused by at least a ten-kiloton device."

"How the hell can that be? We're talking about one of this country's top-secret installations. Security was supposed to be so tight you couldn't take a shit without a full-scale butt exam first."

"That's just it, Mitch. Like I said, evidence is still preliminary and a lot of things haven't been confirmed yet. But we do know this. Some of the security force members were...how shall I say this?" An angry look flashed across his face. "Fuck this multicultural, politically correct bullshit. They were Muslims."

"And the thinking is they may have smuggled the device in and detonated it?"

Cuellar nodded his head. "Yeah, soldiers of Allah, now enjoying the proverbial seventy-two virgins." Cuellar's sarcasm was unmistakable.

"But this is strictly conjecture?"

"Not anymore. Just before you arrived, HAC, the Holy Army of the Caliphate, claimed responsibility for the blast and praised the two missing sentries as martyrs."

CHAPTER 32

SANTA FE

CAROLINA and her father were glued to the television, switching from channel to channel in an effort to find the latest news on the LANL disaster. They each had their cellphones in hand in case Marisol called with advance word of a forced evacuation of the area. They had gathered important documents, jewelry, and personal items just in case. There still were occasional tremors.

The anchorperson on the channel they currently were watching was an attractive blonde woman. She reported in a calm, matter-of-fact manner, unlike many of the breathless twits on some of the other channels. She said, "The effects of the earthquakes, which scientists call 'rifting,' has affected the course of the Rio Grande, causing flooding in some areas. In addition, nuclear fallout over the area is contaminating the river's waters, and that will raise serious issues as the waters flow downstream through New Mexico, Texas, and our neighbor to the south, Mexico. More importantly, it's going to affect the Buckman Well Field, a major source of water supply for Santa Fe."

Al stood up and walked toward the master suite. "Carolina, go fill the tub in your bathroom. We'd better build a reserve. As the local water supply is drawn down, it could be replaced by contaminated water."

She slowly stood up and trudged down the hall toward her bathroom. She was terrified and confused, but wanted to be strong for her parents—not a burden. She was seventeen, and an adult. Almost. She couldn't get thoughts of the terrible destruction of Los Alamos out of her mind. And her aunt and uncle. Almost certainly both were dead. She wondered how Tomás was reacting to the situation. He and his brother were new to the area. Would they know what to do if things got worse?

Then she gasped and stopped dead in her tracks. It all came tumbling into her consciousness at once. How Tomás had been upset when she had taken his picture. How he'd bolted from the house after the news report about a border patrol agent having survived a massacre, presumably at the hands of drug smugglers. And his accent. It was unlike any Hispanic accent she'd ever heard. He claimed he was from Argentina, but Spanish was Spanish. Each version had its own idiomatic expressions, but the distinctiveness of his speech was the result of much more than idioms. She felt a cold wave of fear and revulsion sweep over her as she remembered the two men she'd encountered at Tomás's house. They had the facial features of Asians, and didn't seem to grasp Spanish or English. Something was very wrong.

She spun around and ran to the master bedroom. "Dad, Dad, where are you?"

Al Avila was filling the tub in the master bath and stuck his head out the door. "Right here, Cari. What's the matter?"

"Something's not right about Tomás, Dad. It's more than just him. It's the people he lives with, too."

Al turned off the spigot then took her by the hand and led her into the kitchen. They sat at a four-place wooden table covered with a bright yellow tablecloth. "Now, what's this about Tomás?"

She told her dad all the things that she'd noticed that didn't seem to add up, including her encounter with the two strange men at Tomás's house.

When she was finished, her father nodded solemnly and sat back in his chair. Several moments went by before he spoke. "Your mother and I always thought there was something strange about his accented English and Spanish, too. And I remember the fuss he caused when you took his picture. And how he literally jumped off the sofa and ran out of the house when that news story came on." He paused and his eyes narrowed as he stared at her. "Did you tell your mother about those two…perverts at his house and the things they did?"

Sheepishly, Carolina looked down at the tabletop. "No. I… didn't want to get Tomás in trouble. I was afraid Mom would tell you and you'd go down there and speak to his brother…and maybe refuse to let me see him again."

Her father reached over and took Carolina's hand. Softly, he said, "Cari, you are everything to your mother and me. We will do anything to protect you. So, yes, I would have gone to their house and had a discussion with them. And, yes, we would have stopped you from having anything more to do with Tomás."

She nodded slowly and looked up. "I'm so sorry, Daddy." There were tears in the corners of her large brown eyes.

Al smiled. "That's all right, Cari. It's water over the dam. I share your concerns that something's wrong with this whole picture. Do you still have that photo of Tomás on your phone?"

She nodded again.

"Text it to your mother and tell her what you've told me. She'll know who to share this with at her office. It may be nothing, sweet-heart, but we're constantly told, 'if you see something suspicious, report it.'"

CHAPTER 33

ON THE NEW MEXICAN BORDER

THE SMALL KITCHEN in the ranch house was a mess. There was an inch or more of water on the linoleum floor. A sheen of blood floated on top of it. All of the walls, appliances, cabinets, and countertops were splattered with blood, spit, and pieces of teeth. What was left of the jihadists' camp commandant sagged limply against the ropes that tied his body to the chair. It had taken less than an hour to break him.

Marc Kirkland placed two fingers against the inside of the prisoner's right wrist. After several moments, he looked up at Whelan and shook his head.

"You want us to get him out of here?" Larsen said.

"No, that'll just spread the mess. Leave him where he is. Levell will send a cleanup crew once we're gone."

"The famous 'Janitors,'" Almeida said. "The butchering is the fun part, but the mopping up would suck." He went to the blood-spattered refrigerator and took out a six-pack.

"You read my bloody mind, mate," Stone said, as he helped himself to one of the cans. "It may seem like a fair suck of the sav, but a bloke needs a pint of piss after water boarding a bloody wog for an hour."

With his bright red pupils, skull-like features, and face drenched in blood, Nick Stensen looked like Satan himself. "All in all," he said with a demonic grin, "I'd say it was a productive session. Levell should be pleased."

Grinning, Whelan shook his. "Sometimes the thought of you guys being loose in society really troubles me."

Whelan fished a sat phone from a cargo pocket of his tactical response uniform pants and stepped out into the cold night air. The first traces of dawn were beginning to paint pastel colors on the eastern horizon. He could feel the dried sweat caked on his body from the evening's earlier exertions. The thought of a long, hot shower made him smile, as he punched in a sequence of numbers. Moments later Levell picked up at the other end.

"Yeah, whatcha got for me?"

"The commandant turned out to be very talkative. Verbose, even."

"Good. What's his status?"

"Deceased."

"Even better, the terrorist bastard. What about the intel?"

"The ambush of the CBP agents and deputies was done by two groups, as we thought. HAC soldiers who were already in country did the wet work. The second group was coming up from the border and acted as bait for the kill team."

"What about the nuke?"

"It's real. The commandant said he helped smuggle it across the border. He said he was told there were five more, but he didn't know where."

"And you're sure he was telling the truth?"

"Considering what we did to him, he told us absolutely everything he knew."

"Given what you've been doing, you wouldn't have heard the news. That particular nuke has been detonated."

"Holy shit! Where?"

"Los Alamos National Laboratory. A couple of hours ago. It's bad, really bad. Thousands of casualties, total destruction of the facility and most of the town, and exposure of the onsite stockpile of plutonium. The full extent of the fucking nuclear fallout won't be known for a while. To compound the disaster, the explosion set off earthquakes along the fault lines that run beneath the facility. Makes you wonder what moron selected that site for a nuclear facility."

"Sounds like something the political class would do."

"Well, they're paying for it now, in spades."

"So, we brought too little too late."

"Bullshit! We're not fucking miracle workers. We're moving as fast as we can, given what we have to work with." Levell paused momentarily then said, "Speaking of which, did you get anything else of value out of the sonofabitch, like names and locations of HAC's leaders embedded in the U.S., or where the hell the other nukes are?"

"No. He gave up everything he had, namely that thousands of HAC combatants have been infiltrated in-country. They include specialists in areas such as biological warfare, sabotaging electrical and communication grids, and running suicide missions to destroy the White House and the Capitol Building. He believed some of the nukes would be used for those purposes."

"But no information on how to identify or locate those bastards?"

"No. The cells purposely aren't linked with each other and none of their members will fraternize with local Muslims or attend Mosques. They disguise their Middle Eastern names and backgrounds and try to blend in as Hispanics, Italians, or other Mediterranean peoples."

"That helps to explain why the National Joint Terrorism Task Force's Operation Tripwire hasn't been able to identify any of these bastards' sleeper cells. It's frustrating the hell out of the Bureau. I'll pass this along to Christie. He's in charge of the JTTF being formed in Santa Fe."

"Cliff, if we're at a standstill, at least temporarily, I need to go back to Ireland and see my family."

"I understand. Give me a couple of hours to get up to speed on the latest developments, then I'll get back to you. In the meantime, I'm sending in the Janitors."

"They better bring Mr. Clean with them this time. It's a real mess in there." Whelan heard Levell turn away for the phone for a moment and speak to Nando.

When Levell came back on, he said, "I just arranged for a chopper to exfil you and the boys to Lordsburg."

"Lordsburg? In the past couple of days, we've been in two fire-fights, picked up assorted wounds and injuries, gone without any appreciable sleep, and conducted a beyond-classification interrogation. And you want to send us to fucking Lordsburg? I've got more than enough to deal with as it is, and now you want me to play den mother to six horny, dangerous, sociopathic bastards in fucking Hicksville! Are you a fucking sadist?"

"Do you realize how upset the Lordsburg chamber of commerce would be if they hear that?" Levell said dryly. "What's your suggestion?"

"Someplace where a man can get a hot shower, a clean, comfortable bed, and a damn near gourmet meal. And, for those so inclined, the companionship of several smoking-hot women."

"You don't think all of that is available in Lordsburg?"

"Dammit, Cliff, we're not talking about a mom-and-pop motel and a Burger King. Send us back to that place outside of Tucson. It has a number of places to eat, several watering holes, a fitness center, a spa, a pool, and a bunch of scantily clad nines and tens prancing around. Something for everyone."

"All right, dammit, the Casino Del Sol." There was a long pause at Levell's end before he said, "Sometimes you bastards are a real pain in the ass."

"And while the boys are getting their R and R, I'm going home to see my family."

"And you especially, Whelan, are a *royal* pain in the ass."

CHAPTER 34

SANTA FE

"Carolina Maria Graciela Avila!" Marisol shouted into her cell phone. "Why didn't you tell me about those disgusting creeps at Tomás's house? You could have been hurt, raped...maybe worse. Mother of God, what were you thinking?"

"I'm sorry, Mama, but I didn't think you'd let me see Tomás again if I told you."

"Of course, I forbid you to see Tomás again. If that's even his real name. Based on the things we've just discussed, I don't know if anything about him is real."

"What are you going to do now?"

"I'm going to bring this up with Frank...Major Cuellar, and show him the picture. The FBI JTTF is working out of our offices, and the major is our ranking member on the task force."

"What do you want me to do, Mama?"

"Stay home. Inside. Tell your father I said he's not to take his eyes off of you until those people have been dealt with." Marisol disconnected the call. As she started walking toward Major Cuellar's office, she tapped the "Messages" icon with her thumb. It brought up the text she'd just received from Carolina prior to the call. There, on her screen, was the selfie Carolina had taken of her and the young man who called himself Tomás.

Cuellar and Christie were in the large room down the hall from his office, gathered around a table with several other men, some in suits and some in a variety of uniforms. They were looking at infrared satellite pictures of the LANL site.

"Major Cuellar," Marisol said from the doorway. "I'm sorry for interrupting, but I have something you might want to take a look at."

"Sure," he said as he stepped away from the table. He paused for a moment and put a hand on Christie's elbow. "Let's take a look at this together."

The two men gathered on either side of Marisol in the hallway as she showed them the picture on her cellphone.

"The girl is my daughter Carolina."

"Wow," Cuellar said. "She clearly takes after her mother."

Marisol smiled indulgently. "The boy is her friend from down the street. He says his name is Tomás."

"Latino?" Christie said. "He looks Middle Eastern."

"That's the problem. He said he was from Argentina, but his accented English is not Hispanic. Curiously, his Spanish also is accented and has nothing to do with any Argentinian idiomatic differences. Plus, my husband and I have noticed strange behavior." She told the two men about Tomás's reaction to having his picture taken, and how he had been spooked by the TV news story about the border shootout.

Cuellar shrugged. "You said this boy is seventeen. That's an awkward age for males. They're not yet adults, but don't feel like kids either."

"There's more. Tomás hasn't been around since those incidents, so my daughter went over to his house the other day to see if he was all right." She described the encounter Carolina had had with the two strange men who were at Tomás's house.

"Sounds like she's lucky nothing worse happened to her," Cuellar said, shaking his head.

"Something definitely doesn't add up here," Christie said. "Frank, can you get your lab to isolate the kid's face. We can run it through the usual channels and see what, if anything, pops up. Also, send a copy to the authorities in El Paso and ask them to run it by that CBP agent, David Hidalgo."

"The guy who survived the massacre on the border?"

Christie nodded.

An hour later Christie got a call from an analyst named MacArthur at the National Joint Terrorism Task Force headquarters in McLean, Virginia.

"Agent Christie," MacArthur said, "we got a hit from one of our sources. The kid was picked up on CCTV coming through Aeroporto Internacional de Foz in the Tri-Border Area of South America."

"The hotbed of organized crime and terrorism," Christie said.

"Right, and it seems he arrived in a group of young men about his age, and they all departed together three months later."

"Do we know where he went from there?"

"The flight they were on was destined for Caracas. Our intel isn't so good in Venezuela these days, so we're not sure what actually happened there. But we do know that Caracas is part of a long-established route for Muslim terrorists. They train for a while in the TBA, polish their Spanish and English, then move on to Venezuela to pick up fraudulent passports and visas. Then it's on to Mexico."

"We got anything on him in Mexico?"

"Yeah, it seems he and several others in his group were picked up on CCTV at General Roberto Fierro Villalobos International Airport in Chihuahua about three months ago. Nothing after that."

Christie thanked the analyst and hung up. He found Cuellar in the hallway speaking with two high-ranking military officers. "Can I speak with you for a minute, Major?"

He and Cuellar went back to the Major's office and closed the door.

"You turn something up on the kid?"

"Yeah, he's definitely a POI," Christie said, referring to Tomás as a person of interest. He told Cuellar about Tomás's journey from the TBA to Chihuahua and the route's relevance as a pathway for Islamic terrorists.

"Whew, we owe Marisol one," Cuellar said.

"And her daughter for taking the picture," Christie said, as he followed the major out of the office.

"Does your gut tell you this Tomás kid is involved in the Los Alamos incident?"

"He's involved in something. If not directly in this, then he may have a connection with someone who is," Christie said. "Any word from the wounded CBP agent, Hidalgo?"

"Yeah, a positive ID. Reason enough to arrest him."

Less than thirty minutes later the two men had assembled a SWAT team that included members of Cuellar's Special Operations Bureau as well as the FBI Fly Team, a small, highly trained cadre of counterterrorism investigators. Members of local, state, and federal agencies assigned to the JTTF rounded out the SWAT team.

CHRISTIE AND CUELLAR briefed the other members of the team on the situation. The exact number of suspects was unknown, but thought to be four males. They were suspected of being Islamic terrorists who may have been involved in the disaster at the LANL. The numbers and types of weapons also weren't known, but, if the suspects were involved at LANL, there was a possibility they might possess additional nuclear devices. The presence of hostages was unknown, but considered doubtful. The layout of the area, a densely packed residential neighborhood, was examined in close detail and various approaches were studied and discussed. The houses were small and wedged in close together on small lots. One of the first tasks for the authorities was to clear the neighborhood, get the residents out of the line of fire.

While the briefing was taking place, dozens of local and state police officers, working with Marisol Avila, secured the perimeter and quietly evacuated approximately sixty-five homes in the neighborhood. School buses were used to move the children from an elementary school a block away to another school about one and a half miles east of the area. Some residents refused to evacuate. Marisol, who knew some of them as neighbors, was able to persuade some to change their minds, but a few stubbornly refused to move.

The NMSP's Special Operations Bureau had a large motor home that served as a mobile command post. It had been specially modified, including the addition of armor plating. Accompanied by several black Chevrolet Suburbans, it traveled the five miles from NMSP headquarters to the now-vacated elementary school and parked in the drop-off lane ordinarily used by parents. The targeted residence was less than four hundred feet away.

Usually, while SWAT team members secured positions to close off any escape routes, negotiators would begin trying to talk the suspects into surrendering peacefully. Not this time. Christie and Cuellar didn't want to alert them of the police presence. The fear was that they might have additional explosives, including nuclear devices, and Christie didn't want to give them an opportunity to detonate them.

"We're flying blind here," Christie said, as he paced the narrow confines of the mobile command post. "Are your men in position yet with the radar?"

"Should be anytime now."

Christie gazed out a window at the houses lining the street across from the school. They backed up to the row of houses where the target home was. "We got a court order for the use of the radar. What are you using? The Range-R?"

"Yeah, just hold the device against a wall, push a couple of buttons and radar pulses through the wall. It should detect whether there's any motion inside. Under ideal conditions it can even detect someone breathing."

"What's the effective range?"

"Up to fifty feet with a conical view of 160 degrees," Cuellar said.

"These are small houses, but they have adobe walls. What are they, maybe a foot thick?"

"About that, yeah. We've used the Range-R before on similar barriers. The only problem is detecting breathing, but it'll pick up motion."

Moments later, word came over the comm system that the radar hadn't detected any signs of habitation.

"That doesn't necessarily mean the dwelling's unoccupied," Christie said. "You said the walls prevent the radar from detecting breathing. If they suspected we were on to them and knew about the use of Range-R, they could be purposely remaining very still, armed and waiting for us to break in."

Cuellar nodded. "Technology only gets you so far. At some point, you just have to do things the old-fashioned way."

Christie stepped out of the mobile command post. It was a classic Santa Fe day—cool temperatures of the high desert and a cloudless sky of brilliant blue. It was quiet, too quiet. Christie knew there should have been normal neighborhood noises: kids on the school's playground, neighbors greeting each other on the street, traffic, the occasional intrusive sound of yard equipment in use. He feared the unnatural silence would alert the occupants of the target house that something was amiss.

The target was one of the more run-down residences. A search of the public records revealed that the owner listed an address in Albuquerque. When contacted by agents from the Bureau's Field Office in that city, the owner claimed to have moved to Albuquerque five years earlier for job purposes. He told the agents that he kept the house as a rental property and he used the services of a rental agent in Santa Fe.

The rental agent's records indicated that someone named Aquilino Cruz, claiming to be from Chiapas, Mexico, had rented it two months earlier. The agent didn't remember ever meeting Cruz. A relative of Cruz's had arranged the rental. The documentation had been handled by mail. She said a security deposit and first month's rent had been paid in advance, and that rent for the second month had arrived on time.

There was no vehicle parked on the cracked and stained concrete driveway. Marisol Avila had said Tomás's brother drove an older sedan—a Ford, she thought. Like most of the other houses in the neighborhood, its windows were barred with decorative wrought iron. Behind an uneven low wall of chipped adobe bricks was a weed-strewn yard peppered with small white rocks. A bushy Green Giant Arborvitae occupied one corner of the front yard. Such trees can reach sixty feet in height, but this one's top had been lopped off at about the twenty-foot mark. There were two other bare, long dead trees in the front yard, a twenty-foot tall birch and a sycamore that was closer to forty feet. The front of the house was plain and drab, like a dowager whose beauty had long ago dissipated. Its drabness was broken only by a faded brown front door atop a low stoop and a similarly colored wooden garage door. A six-foot wooden fence ran along the back of the property. It appeared to have been stained red a long time ago. Around the corner of the garage, a green plastic garbage can sat against the side wall, its color fading slowly in the eternally sunny Land of Enchantment.

Christie reentered the MCP and communicated with the leaders of the four teams that had closed in on the target residence. One team was concealed behind the fence that ran along the rear of the property. Another was hunkered down in the backyard of the house immediately south of the target, using a privacy fence for cover. A third team was in a similar position behind the house immediately to the north. They had come over a rear fence and were immediately confronted by the owner's dog, a large Rottweiler who had been left behind chained to a tree. Fearful of arousing the suspicions of the suspects next door, one of the men had silenced the animal with a single round from a suppressed Heckler & Koch USP9 Tactical 9 mm. The final team was pressed against the front wall of that same house. All teams reported that they were in position and awaiting Christie's signal.

"Hold your positions. Major Cuellar and I are on our way."

Christie had his Glock 17 holstered on his belt and grabbed an H&K416 A5. It had a Knight Master Key S mounted on it in an under-barrel configuration, with a three-round internal magazine and a fourth round in the chamber. The H&K gave him the fire-power of an assault rifle, while the Knight provided the benefits of a shotgun for guaranteed stopping power at close range, as well as the ability to fire quickly without taking careful aim. If needed, it could also open doors, and shots that were bounced off of hard surfaces could flush suspects from hiding places.

He and Cuellar strapped on their Kevlar combat helmets and ballistic SWAT vests and left the MCP, heading for the house where the boy who called himself Tomás lived. The four SWAT squads that were in position consisted of eight members each. They were armed with the usual SWAT arsenal of 9mm Sigs, Glocks, Berettas, and H&K USP series handguns. Most men also carried an assault rifle with a single-shot 40mm under-barrel grenade launcher. Some were armed with 12-gauge shotguns by Remington, Benelli, or Mossberg. They all carried flash-bang grenades. All wore fire-retardant camo uniforms and balaclavas, Kevlar helmets, and ballistic vests labeled with "POLICE" or "FBI." Additional protective tactical gear included knee-pads, flight gloves, and goggles.

Snipers were positioned in houses across the street and on the roofs of sheds in yards backing up to the target house. The distance to target ranged from twenty to forty yards, considered point-blank by members of the sniper fraternity. Christie had considered, then discarded, the idea of using choppers with additional snipers, fearing the noise could alert the suspects. The snipers were armed with the Remington M-24, a specially designed sniper rifle based on the legendary 700 model and its well-earned reputation for accuracy and ease of use. Their weapons utilized Leupold Mark IV M3 scopes. Ordinarily it would fire the 220-grain Sierra MatchKing Hollow Point Boat Tail very-low-drag bullet with a nominal muzzle velocity of 2,850 feet per second. But law enforcement was concerned that there could be a problem of over-penetration with these rounds. As a result, the SWAT team snipers used rounds made by Hornady or Black Hills, with ballistic tips for less penetration, while offering ballistic performance similar to that of the MatchKing.

Christie took charge of the team positioned at the front of a house immediately south of Tomás's house. Cuellar led the team hunkered down in the backyard of the home on the north side of Tomás's. Ordinarily, protocol would require that any suspects be given an opportunity to surrender peacefully. Given the fear that these suspects may have explosive devices, including nuclear ones, circumstances negated the need to follow that protocol.

When a SWAT team initiates a raid, it forms a single-file line known as the snake. Although the formation maximizes the risk to the point man, it minimizes the risk of the other team members. It was the point man's responsibility to enter the premises first and neutralize hostiles. He was the one who most often had to make split-second decisions. Christie assumed the role of point man. His team would breach the front of the home. Cuellar's team would breach the rear. The other two teams' responsibilities were to cover all potential exits and neutralize any suspects who might use them.

"All right," Christie said into his comm gear. "Launch the flash-bangs."

A DESIGNATED member of each team, using an H&K416 A5 with an under-barrel M203 grenade launcher sent the grenades crashing through windows on all sides of the house. Moments after the explosion Christie and Cuellar's teams rushed their respective doors. Utilizing a battering ram on the spot just above the door handle, the entryways were easily breached. Taking the lead of the snake, Christie burst inside followed closely by the members of his team. In order to avoid getting in each other's way during the operation, each man swiftly began to cover his preassigned area of responsibility.

Christie could hear Cuellar's team near the rear of the house. As the smoke from the flash-bangs began to clear, he could see they were inside a small living room. It was sparsely furnished, and filthy. One of the few pieces in the room was an old soiled and tattered sofa against the wall to their left. There was a slightly Asian-looking man slumped in one corner of it. His butt was on the edge of the sagging seat, his arms splayed out to his sides. His head was tilted slightly upward, as if resting on the back of the sofa. His eyes stared sightlessly toward the ceiling. There was a slightly bloody hole in the middle of his forehead. Behind him, the wall was stained a reddish brown. There were pieces of skull and brain matter stuck to it.

Christie looked at the second and third members of his team and motioned toward a hallway leading toward the part of the dwelling where the bedrooms were. He sent the fourth and fifth members toward the kitchen. The sixth member moved to the dead body and began to carefully examine it and the area around it without touching anything. The seventh man continued to cover the room, while the eighth secured the entryway.

Cuellar's team entered the kitchen from the other direction, having breached an entryway off the laundry room near the rear of the house.

Cuellar saw the body on the sofa. He took a closer look. "That's not the kid."

"No. Maybe he's in the back," Christie said, nodding in the direction of the hallway.

A moment later one of the two men Christie had sent down the hall emerged shaking his head. "There's another one like him back there," he said nodding in the direction of the body on the sofa.

"Same M. O.?" Christie said.

"Yeah. Looks like it could have been the same weapon. He doesn't look like the kid in the picture. Too old. And kinda Asian-looking."

Christie looked around. "If there's no one else here then let's get forensics on task. Maybe we can get a lead on the boy."

"If not," Cuellar said, "we got nothing."

"Yeah," Christie said with a look of disgust that matched Cuellar's. "Terrorists on the loose, maybe with more nukes, and we still have nothing."

CHAPTER 35

ALBUQUERQUE

BY THE THIRD MANHATTAN, the bourbon had lost its burn. Christie sipped at it, watching the top of the maraschino cherry emerge among the ice cubes. It would soon join the first two in his stomach. He hoped they wouldn't end up being his dinner. After hours of debriefing at NMSP headquarters in Santa Fe, he and Major Frank Cuellar had driven down to Albuquerque. Then they'd gone through more hours of it for the benefit of a gathering of state and federal law enforcement officials at the FBI field office in Albuquerque.

From his perch on a padded leather barstool, he glanced at himself in the mirror behind the bar. He hadn't slept in almost twenty-four tension-packed hours and it showed. He was overdue for a shave and dark circles were beginning to form beneath his eyes. His dark gray suit was rumpled. He'd loosened his tie and unfastened the top button of his white dress shirt. All told, he looked like he'd been on a three-day bender.

On the stool next to him, Cuellar signaled the barkeep for another round. "You know what I hate about this fucking work we do, Mitch?"

"What's that?"

"Often times you work for months, maybe even years on something and, in the end, it just slips away from you. It's frustrating."

"At least we haven't been working on today's clusterfuck for months or years."

"Yeah, there's that, but the end result is the same. We end up with two stiffs and the guy or guys we wanted to question have vanished. We still had to go through hours of debriefing and all the interagency finger-pointing, but bottom line—we don't have any more than we had this morning."

"Except bad news. Forensics couldn't find anything that might give us a lead for finding the UNSUBS," Christie said, using the Bureau acronym for Unknown Subjects. "But the hell of it is they did confirm that there were traces of radioactive material onsite. At least that's compelling evidence that the LANL nuke was probably there."

The bartender set a fresh round in front of the two men. Cuellar picked up the heavy tumbler that held his vodka martini and, for a moment, gazed over the top of it at his reflection in the mirror behind the bar. "How can we be this clueless? I mean, these perps fucking blew up a top-secret government installation with a nuke."

Christie shook his head vigorously. "We're not clueless. We have prints and DNA from the house that don't match the dead guys', so it's probably the UNSUBs'. We've got an APB out with the kid's photo and a description of him and the older brother. Maybe we get lucky and some cop somewhere stops them for a broken taillight."

"And maybe they blow up another place…or places. We need a break and we need it quick. You got any ideas?"

"I may. I know people who have assets we're forbidden to use. And they have access to places that we'd not only get fired if we went there, but prosecuted, too."

Cuellar turned and stared at Christie for several moments. "So, this is strictly outside the Bureau?"

"Way outside."

"Care to elaborate?"

"That wouldn't be a good idea."

Cuellar thought about that for a while then said, "You said something about assets. What kind of assets?"

With as serious an expression as Cuellar had ever seen, Christie said, "Motherfuckers deadlier than you could imagine. Smarter, faster, stronger than anyone you've ever known or heard of. They're the deadliest sonsofbitches on the planet, and they can go anywhere and kill anyone."

"Jesus! They sound like a bunch of super ninjas. Not somebody you'd want to have a beer with."

Christie smiled. "If you did, you'd like them; think they were the nicest guys around. But when you looked in their eyes, you'd know that they're not like you and me, or anyone else you've ever known." He paused. "They're genetic freaks."

"How come I never heard of these guys," Cuellar said with a puzzled look.

"You're not supposed to."

"But you know them. How?"

"Let's just say through a mutual friend."

"You must have some interesting friends."

Christie just smiled and plucked the cherry out of his drink, separating it from the stem with his teeth.

"You gonna talk to these genetic-freak guys about the situation?"

Christie shook his head. "I'll talk to the mutual friend. He's already had them gathering intel from people in places we couldn't touch."

Cuellar glanced at his watch. "When you planning on having that conversation?"

"Tonight, when I get to my hotel room. Under the circumstances, privacy is in order."

"I thought you said earlier that your fiancée was flying in to meet you?"

"She is. In fact, she's probably at the hotel now."

"Given the current holding pattern we're in, I understand you managed to get a day or two of personal time. What are you and she planning to do in our fair state?"

"Camila's a native. Her family lives in Ruidoso. We're going to drive down and visit with them."

CUELLAR DROPPED Christie off at the Hyatt Regency Tamaya Resort in Bernalillo on his way back to Santa Fe. Christie and Camila had chosen the hotel on purpose. It was in close proximity to where they'd had their first date, the Prairie Star Restaurant. The date had been a disaster, and it had taken a while for Christie to atone for his behavior. And now they were engaged to be married.

Camila had arrived at the resort only minutes before Christie. She had booked what was supposed to have been a six-hour flight including a forty-five-minute stopover in Dallas-Fort Worth. The stopover had turned out to be a seven-hour delay. She arrived travel-weary and frustrated. It was too late to have dinner at the Prairie Star. Their getaway was off to a bad start. All she wanted to do at this point was shower off the grime of air travel.

This worked out for Christie. It gave him an opportunity to call Levell. He ordered a bottle of wine from room service and listened sympathetically while she vented her frustration brought on by the journey. After sipping some of the wine, Camila headed for the shower. When he heard the water running, Christie dug out the sat phone Levell had provided.

When he heard Nando on the other end, he said, "Tell Cliff I'm sorry about the lateness of the hour, but I need to speak with him. It's important." While he waited for Levell to come on the line, he thought about the time difference between Virginia and New Mexico. It was two hours later in the Eastern U.S. That partially explained why he and Camila felt so exhausted. It was eleven o'clock in Albuquerque, but to their as yet unadjusted bodies it felt like it was 1 a.m.

Levell came on the other end of the line. "Yeah, Mitch, what you got for me?"

"First, I am sorry for the late hour."

"No sweat, I'm an old fart and old people don't sleep worth a shit anyway. But enough whining." Shifting verbal gears, Levell said, "I received word from an SAS member high up in the SECDEF's office and another in DHS that it definitely was a terrorist nuke. Apparently, the perps are unknown and on the loose. You're running JTTF out there. What's the status on the ground?"

Christie took a deep breath and let out a long sigh.

"That's not the response I was hoping for," Levell said. "You sound tired and maybe more than a little frustrated."

"Hell, Cliff, it's the same old, same old. Endless numbers of agencies involved, ancient turf wars and petty jealousies, bureaucrats more interested in looking good than working effectively. Even inside the Bureau it's layers of egos trying to polish their own résumés. Out of all the assholes out here elbowing each other for the limelight, there's only one guy that's cooperative, a major who runs NMSP's Special Ops Bureau."

"Nothing new there. You got any real leads that SAS can help you with?"

"Maybe. There's a kid who's been calling himself Tomás, but

that's probably not his real name. We're pretty sure he's not even Hispanic; probably Arab or Pashtun."

"Is that all you've got?" Levell's gravelly voice sounded even raspier tonight.

"No, we have a photo of the kid and a description of another UNSUB that the kid told neighbors was his older brother. We had a description of their vehicle from neighbors, but it was found abandoned at the Santa Fe Place Mall on Cerrillos Road south of town."

"I assume a blanket search of the area was performed, and the vehicle was searched for prints, DNA, and the like?"

"Yeah. Nothing turned up. An APB was issued with the descriptions and the kid's picture, but I suspect these guys are long gone."

"Does your veteran cop instinct tell you where they might be headed?"

"If I was in their shoes, the safest place to be is back across the border. The Mexican cops are useless and their feds are on the take. Worse, the gangs and cartels probably would protect them. If HAC has been willing to pay up to fifty grand a head to the gangs to smuggle jihadists across the border, it would pay a fortune to protect these perps. They're fucking gods in the Islamist' world after what they did at Los Alamos."

"My gut instinct also tells me they're going to head for Mexico," Levell said. "I'd bet they had a clean vehicle waiting for them at that mall in Santa Fe. Maybe even acquired some added muscle too. How much of a head start do they have?"

"Hard to say. The nuke was detonated at about four a.m. Mountain Time; almost twenty-four hours ago. They could have been gone before then or maybe stuck around for the fireworks. You know, kind of like pride of authorship; make sure it went off as planned."

"I understand roadblocks have been set up."

"Yeah, around Santa Fe and along the border-crossing points."

"Shit," Levell said. "They're long gone from Santa Fe, and they won't cross the damn border at any usual location."

"That's why I'm calling you, Cliff. As shocking as this catastrophe is, everyone's playing by the book. These perps never read that book. Special measures are needed. It needs to involve someone who isn't bound by fucking rules of engagement. Someone who couldn't care less about jurisdiction, sovereignty, or the glacial pace of American justice."

"I'll make a call," Levell said and disconnected.

Christie could almost see the nasty smile on the old man's face.

CHAPTER 36

DINGLE. IRELAND

WHELAN'S BROTHER-IN-LAW Padraig Murphy wheeled his car into the motor court of the Fianna House and stopped it by the front door. Whelan climbed out of the passenger side then leaned back in the open side window. "Thanks for picking me up in Cork, Paddy," he said in Irish Gaelic. "That was a three-hour trip for you each way. I appreciate you saving Caitlin the drive."

The other man smiled. "Anything for my sister's husband. But you do owe me a pint or two."

"I always pay my debts, especially when it's to the town's top cop. I'll call you later this evening, after I've spent some time with Caitlin and the boys." He waved Paddy off and turned toward the inn, a three-story, brick-and-mortar structure that he and Caitlin had built on the foundations of a centuries-old farmhouse.

The first thing that Whelan noticed when he approached the front door was the aroma of fresh-baked Irish brown bread. Using her mother's recipe, Caitlin made the best Whelan had ever tasted.

Suddenly the door burst open and, with a girlish shriek of

delight, Caitlin threw herself into his arms. He swept her up in a tight but gentle bear hug and spun her around several times. The aroma of the bread was forgotten as he breathed in the warm sweet scent of her smooth skin and thick, dark hair. Their lips met in a long, passionate kiss. When their mouths parted, they were both a little breathless.

The intoxication of her beauty and the sensation of her firm, gently rounded body against his immediately aroused him. He glanced at his watch. "When are the boys due home from school?"

"Any minute," she said with a beguiling smile, as she slipped her hand into his. "But save that thought for later tonight."

AMONG THE PART-TIME HELP, Whelan and Caitlin employed at the Fianna was the redoubtable Dearbháil. Not quite five feet tall and nearly as wide, she was an ancient woman of indeterminate age, who seemed to welcome any opportunity to supplement her social insurance payments. She had worked at the Fianna for several years and was considered family. The Whelans had no reservations about leaving her in charge of the inn and its guests' needs while they went out to dinner.

It was a pleasant evening, cool and surprisingly dry. The restaurant was a mere three hundred and fifty meters down the street from the inn. Dingle was a port town with a small commercial fishing fleet. Naturally, the restaurant specialized in seafood. It was located in the southwestern quadrangle formed by the roundabout where Mail Road intersected *An Meal* and *Sráid an Droichid*. The local *Garda* station, where Caitlin's brother Padraig Murphy was the sergeant in charge, was diagonally across the roundabout.

The restaurant patrons were the usual mix of locals and tourists.

The Dingle natives recognized the Whelans and waved or called out greetings. Every one of them knew of Whelan's genetic gifts. They appreciated the fact that his presence did more to ensure peace in the community than even that of the *Garda*. It was no secret that Padraig Murphy didn't hesitate to call on his brother-in-law when the occasion required it.

The restaurant's manager came over and greeted the Whelans, bringing with him a pint each for Caitlin and Brendan. After the server took their dinner orders, Sean, who was the oldest and had just turned seventeen, said, "Da, did Mum tell you about our football team?"

"American football?"

"Yes, I'm the starting running back for the Dingle Junior Football program," Sean said with obvious pride.

"I'm the youngest player on the club and the starting wideout," Declan said, not to be outdone by his older brother.

"I thought you had to be sixteen to play," Whelan said.

"I'm almost sixteen, close enough to be allowed to play. Besides, I'm their best player."

"Second best," Sean said indulgently.

"Are you going to be here for my birthday, Da?" Declan said in an anxious tone.

"Coach Saban and the whole Crimson Tide team couldn't stop me."

"You were a running back when you played in America, weren't you?"

"I was. And strongside-linebacker on defense."

Sean looked puzzled. "I thought American football used a platoon system?"

"It usually does, but a few athletes play both ways—offense and defense. I also played on special teams."

Sean's eyes opened wide. "You played all forty-eight minutes?"

Whelan chuckled. "Yeah, sometimes that's the price you pay for being good."

"How good were you, Da?" Declan, said.

Whelan glanced quickly at Caitlin. She winked at him and said, "No sense being too modest, Bren." She looked at the two boys and said, "Several months ago five of your Da's closest friends from America came to visit for a while. Do you remember them?"

Both boys' heads bobbed up and down vigorously. "Who could ever forget blokes like that?" Sean said. "The only person I've ever seen who's like them is Da."

"Well," Caitlin said, leaning in toward the center of the table and lowering her voice to a conspiratorial whisper, "those men shared some things with me about your Da before I knew him."

The boys leaned in closer also. Whelan smiled and just shook his head, wondering where the love of his life was going with this.

"It seems that every college football program in America offered him a scholarship to play at their universities. But your da never wavered in his decision. He had settled on the University of Miami when he was younger even than you boys are now. When he committed to "the U," as it's known in college football, two of those men we were just talking about joined him. And they both had as many scholarship offers as your da did, but they had played against each other in high school and didn't want to ever do that again." She smiled at her three boys and sat back in her chair. Sean and Declan continued to lean in, staring at their father.

"Tell us what it was like at the U," Sean said.

"The three of us graduated early from our respective high schools and enrolled at the U for the spring term. By the end of spring practice, we were all starters on offense and defense."

"What positions did you play?" Sean said.

"On offense, I was a running back, Mr. Larsen was a fullback, and Mr. Thomas was a wideout."

"What about on defense?" Declan said.

"Mr. Larsen was our middle linebacker or Mike, as it's called. I played the strong side linebacker, called Sam. Mr. Thomas was a lockdown cornerback. It's called an 'island.'"

"Did the U ever lose when you and your friends were there?" Declan said.

"Actually, we never played a down in regular season."

Both boys looked shocked. "How can that be?" Sean said. "After the way the three of you were recruited, I don't understand."

Whelan glanced at Caitlin again, as if seeking rescue. She just smiled prettily with a twinkle in her eyes that seemed to say, "You can handle this one. It was bound to come up some day, and today's the day."

"Well…it's complicated. Some people came along and recruited us to do something else." He looked up and was relieved to see the server headed their way with dinner on a large tray.

AFTER DINNER, Caitlin walked the two boys back to the inn to tackle their homework assignments. Whelan strolled across the roundabout to the *Garda* station. Passing locals honked their horns at him and waved. *The joys of living in a small town—everyone's a neighbor. I wonder if there are parts of America where that's still true.*

Paddy looked relieved to see Whelan, as if he was more than ready to call it a day in favor of a cold one at Darragh's Pub. The two men walked the two hundred and forty meters to the pub along Slea Head Drive, the short looping street that paralleled the quay. The familiar drizzle had begun again.

Paddy raised his head and squinted at the drops falling from the dark sky above. "Irish gold. It's what keeps this lovely isle so green."

"I grew up in Florida," Whelan said. "It was called liquid sunshine there."

Paddy chuckled. "A phrase no doubt coined by a chamber of commerce."

Reaching the pub, the two men ducked inside. Paddy led the way to an empty table in the rear.

They were barely seated when the proprietor, Brody Darragh, slipped a pint in front of each of them. "Nice to see you again, Brendan. Hope you'll be in town a while. The folks miss you." He nodded at the other man. "Always a pleasure, Paddy." He started to turn away, but said, "Just so you know, your money's no good tonight."

The two men raised their glasses in gratitude, then each took a sip.

Paddy smacked his lips and wiped the foam from his mouth with the cuff of his sleeve. He placed the glass in front of him and stared at it.

After several moments, Whelan said, "Out with it, Paddy. What's bothering you?"

The other man grinned briefly. "I'm that transparent, am I?"

Whelan said nothing, just watched his brother-in-law's face.

"I didn't want to say anything to you on the way over from the airport earlier. Didn't want to spoil your first few hours with your family."

Whelan said nothing.

"There was a man in town about week ago, a stranger. Big guy, had the look of ex-military about him. Maybe Special Ops."

"And you're telling me this, why?"

Paddy took a long pull on his beer. "There was something about him that made me uneasy."

"Did he seem to be a threat to my family?"

Paddy shrugged. "That's the thing. He actually stayed at the Fianna, but didn't seem to cause any trouble."

"What is it then?"

"He gave Caitlin the creeps, and you know for certain my sister's as tough as anyone can be. She doesn't scare easily." Paddy paused then said, "Had the same effect on the boys, too. Caitie asked me to keep a close eye on him."

Whelan knew why Caitlin hadn't mentioned this. She didn't want to worry him, distract him from the dangerous work he was doing for Levell. Ever since Maksym had sent five men to kill all of them, she and the boys had been guarded night and day by well-armed locals. But this new development made him feel as if his blood had turned to ice water. It was a feeling he got when things went to shit all around him and everyone else was in a panic. It was as if time slowed down; everything seemed to move in slow motion except his own thoughts and actions. It was when he was his deadliest.

"How long was he here?"

"Coupla' days."

"Where was he from? Where did he go? What did he look like? Did he associate with anyone locally?"

"His passport and accent pegged him as a Russian, maybe ex-Spetsnaz. Didn't really spend much time with anyone, but told some locals in a pub that he was heading for Spain. I told you he was a big guy, about my size. Dirty blond hair, some facial scars, a rough-looking guy. "And he could handle himself, too. A couple of young Brits on holiday made fun of his accent. When he told them to fuck off, one of the fools threw a punch at him. It wasn't very pretty after that."

"What did you do about that?"

"I used it as an excuse to chase his ass out of town."

Whelan thought about what Paddy had told him. He wasn't sure why, but something about the situation smelled of Maksym. "Did this guy have a name?"

"Yeah, it was on his passport. Andrei Ulyanin."

CHAPTER 37

DINGLE, IRELAND

WHEN WHELAN GOT BACK to the inn after his meeting with Paddy, he found Caitlin freshly bathed and wearing lace baby doll pajamas. Things moved very swiftly from that point; much too swiftly to initiate a discussion about Andrei Ulyanin.

He awoke the next morning in their large goose-down bed. Caitlin was nestled against him, his right arm around her shoulders. Her mass of fragrant dark hair was tickling his cheek as she breathed softly, still asleep. He lay there quietly, unwilling to disturb a moment that, because of his absences, had become rare in recent months. After several minutes her eyelids fluttered open. Her eyes were an incredible iridescent green with tiny pinpoints of light like pinfire opals, shaded by long thick lashes. As her eyes focused on his face, she smiled seductively and stretched her body against his. He'd been aroused since he woke up, but this was almost more than he could resist. *If only the boys could get themselves off to school on their own.*

He rolled out of bed and smiled mischievously at her. "Got any plans after the boys are off to school?"

She feigned a pout. "Unfortunately, I made plans with my mum to go shopping in Tralee."

Whelan didn't have to feign disappointment. "Just don't wear yourself out shopping."

"Why," she said, faking innocence. "Did you have something in mind?"

"What I'm thinking about won't involve our minds."

AFTER CAITLIN HAD LEFT to pick up her mother for the drive to Tralee, Whelan sat in the B&B's tiny office just off the kitchen, poring over bills and bank statements. He felt he should try to help Caitlin as much as possible while he was home. There was always a mountain of grunt work to be done. He'd been at it for about an hour, working on a second cup of coffee, when a phone rang. It was the special satellite phone; the one Levell had provided. He knew what the call meant—things were heating up at Levell's end. Family time was over.

He was tempted to ignore the call, spend more time with Caitlin and the boys, go to one or more of their football practices, create quality time together. But he knew that the Old Man wouldn't be calling him under these circumstances unless it was critically important. He put down the coffee cup and activated the call. "Whelan."

Levell's familiar raspy voice said, "I hate like hell to bother you, Brendan. I know you only just got there."

If he's using my first name, he needs something pretty badly, Whelan thought. "It seems to go with the territory. What's up?"

"It's about that nuke at Los Alamos. The authorities, thanks to Mitch Christie and a buddy of his who runs New Mexico State

Police Special Ops, got a lead on some people they suspect may be the perps."

A red flag went up in Whelan's mind. He anticipated where Levell was going. "Mitch knows his shit. I'm sure he'll handle it competently."

"Yeah, Mitch would, but that's not what's happening."

That confirmed Whelan's suspicions. He didn't really care about the answer to the next question, but asked it anyway. "Why isn't it?"

"The White House is afraid the perps may be Latinos. They were living in a predominantly Latino neighborhood, spoke Spanish, and claimed to be from Argentina. With election day almost here, the administration is overly sensitive to the Latino community and the voting block they think it represents."

"That's bullshit. Latinos living in America love their adopted country. They want murderers and terrorists dealt with just as much as anyone else does. Besides, this has Islamists' fingerprints all over, not Latinos."

"You and I and the rest of the country know that, but the current administration is all caught up in concerns over its legacy, as well it should be. Remember, part of this fool president's legacy is the attempt at rapprochement with the Arab world. Los Alamos has just been handed over to DHS; they're calling the shots now. And you know who's running DHS."

"Yeah, another political hack appointed by the president."

"Precisely, and he knows to do exactly what the administration wants."

"In other words, the pursuit and apprehension of these suspects isn't likely to happen."

"Not through the usually appropriate channels. What's so damning is the intel you and your colleagues obtained."

"The presence of additional nukes in the United States, and in the possession of the terrorists?"

"That's it."

Whelan shook his head. "And that brings us to the purpose of your call."

"Don't sound so sarcastic. You and the others were born for this kind of work, and you know it."

"Maybe what you label as sarcasm is really anger; anger at being asked to leave my family again. Not only did I just get home, but the threat of Maksym is still very much a reality."

"I know, I know." There was a certain tone of resignation in Levell's voice. "I promised catching and killing that sonofabitch would be priority number one, but you can't deny that jihadists with nukes in America trumps everything."

Whelan sighed in resignation. "I'll grant you that."

"Good. I've arranged for a private jet to pick you up in two hours."

"Two hours?" Whelan glanced at the clock on the wall in the kitchen. "Where?"

"At the airport in Kerry."

"Farranfore?"

"What?"

"There's more than one airfield in County Kerry. The official regional one is at Farranfore. It's about fifty-five klicks from here."

"Or thirty miles in American. That's the place."

"What kind of plane is it?"

"Worried about the length of the runway needed for takeoff?"

"Among other things."

"All things considered, it requires fifty-nine hundred feet for takeoff and about twenty-eight hundred for landing."

"The takeoff's going to be a little tight. Farranfore's sole runway is about sixty-five hundred feet."

"What are you complaining about? You're the most risk-loving bastard I know. Just make sure you eat lightly and take a healthy dump before departure." Levell chuckled.

"What's my destination?"

"Tucson International. In case you're wondering why not Ryan Field, it goes back to the runway length. Ryan's longest is only fifty-five hundred feet. Tucson International's are all over seven thousand."

"Then what?"

"The rest of the unit will be waiting for you in Tucson. I'll give you the details of the mission once you've landed."

There were a few moments of silence, then Whelan said, "There's a new wrinkle. A guy, Russian apparently, was in Dingle very recently. He actually stayed at the Fianna. Spooked Caitlin and the boys. Paddy, my brother-in-law, is as tough as an Irishman can be, but even he was unsettled by this guy."

"What did he want?"

"Didn't say."

"Maybe he was just an oddball tourist. You know, a guy who's weird in his ways and upsets regular folks."

"I didn't get that impression."

"So, what are you saying?"

"I think he was getting the lay of the land, casing the area."

"For what purpose?"

"I think it had something to do with Maksym."

"What do you want me to do about it?"

"Use your contacts, like Christie, to find out who this Andrei Ulyanin is." A second later, Whelan added, "And where I can find him." He paused for effect, then said, "After that, we can talk about my returning to the States."

"You son of a bitch," Levell said as Whelan disconnected the call.

CHAPTER 38

SAN ANTONIO, NEW MEXICO

SOUTH VALLEY WAS an unincorporated bedroom community southwest of Albuquerque and bisected by the muddy Rio Grande. Its population was more than eighty percent Hispanic. Interstate 25 paralleled the area's eastern edge. In the northwestern quadrant of the area's central core, was an older neighborhood in transition. Some newer, larger homes had been built in the past few years, but most of the houses were dated, humble dwellings that looked oddly out of place on the old subdivision's large lots. Although many lots were graced with large, mature trees, the eyesore factor was multiplied by a number of features. A majority of the home sites were enclosed with cheap-looking chain-link fencing. While all were painted in the typical neutral colors of the desert Southwest, many were in need of repainting. Few had garages, and their yards and driveways were cluttered with older small cars and pickups. In many ways, the area reminded Turan of the neighborhood he'd just left in Santa Fe. But, he admitted, on its worst day, the area was a paradise compared to his hometown of Wana.

For the past few days, Turan and Bazir had been staying in a safe house located in the 1800 block of Del Norte Drive SW, one of the east-west streets in Del Rio Acres. The house was small—two bedrooms, one bath—and they shared it with the two members of the infamous MS-13 gang. Óscar Amaya and Angel Bautista were Salvadorans who, as small children, had immigrated illegally to Los Angeles with their parents. Under the circumstances, the most natural path had led them to join MS-13.

Bazir had killed the two Uzbeks shortly before the nuclear device was scheduled to be detonated in Los Alamos. Then he and Turan had driven their car to the Santa Fe Place Mall, wiped it down, and abandoned it. That's where they had met up with Óscar and Angel. The two gangbangers had picked them up in a rusting 2005 Pontiac G6 and driven them to the tiny safe house on Del Norte Drive.

For Turan, being cooped up in the tightly confined space with the Salvadorans was far worse than living in the small house in Santa Fe with the Uzbeks. The Salvadorans wouldn't allow him or Bazir to leave the house. They even had to stay away from windows and doors to the outside. Óscar and Angel took turns sleeping and watching the two jihadis. They clearly didn't like being assigned as muscle for what they regarded as two ragheads from the Middle East, and it showed in almost everything they said and did. Even Bazir seemed oddly meek around them. At the moment, Angel was the Salvadoran on duty. Óscar had left the house earlier to walk to a Taco Bell a few blocks away. The car remained enclosed in the ramshackle garage behind the house.

Turan heard his stomach growling and unconsciously rubbed his abdomen. "When are we going to get some real food?" he said quietly to Bazir in Pashto. "I'm tired of the take-out food they bring us from that phony Mexican place."

They were sitting on a torn and filthy sofa in the small living room watching Spanish-language TV. The gangbangers continuously switched back and forth between Univision's KLUZ for sports and KTVQ for movies. The only time Turan or Bazir were permitted to leave the sofa was to go to the bathroom or to bed.

"There will be plenty of food when we finish our journey home," Bazir said expressionlessly. "There we will be honored as heroes."

"Shut the fuck up," Angel screamed. He was short and wiry, and covered in gang tattoos. He waved his revolver at them, a double-action Ruger Redhawk in stainless steel with a seven-and-a-half-inch barrel and western handle. It looked like a prop from a TV western, but the .44 caliber magnum bullets it fired weren't from any prop department.

"Mexican cowboy," Bazir muttered.

"What? What the fuck did you say?"

"I told my young friend that your weapon is a thing of beauty."

"And fucking deadly, too," the other man said with a snarl, pointing the gun at Bazir for several long seconds.

"Excuse me, sir," Turan said in an effort to redirect the conversation. "But how much longer are we going to stay here?"

"Until we fuckin' move you! Don't ask me that again you little *chavala.*"

Turan had a puzzled look on his face. "What is a *chavala?*"

"It means 'punk,' asshole."

The two jihadis looked at each other resignedly then settled back against the dirty upholstery to watch another grainy rerun of *Chato's Land* in Spanish with English subtitles.

A FEW HOURS later Óscar entered through the front door. He had a couple of large bags in his hands.

Turan groaned when he saw the Taco Bell logo on them.

Óscar set the bags on the small, battered kitchen table, reached into one of the bags, and pulled out two objects. He sat at a chair and unwrapped what turned out to be a triple steak burrito and a side of cheesy fiesta potatoes. He grunted and motioned with his head for the others to help themselves. Bazir and Turan knew that meant that Angel went before they did.

After several minutes of eating in silence, Bazir said to Óscar, "Have you been able to determine what our next move is and when it will be?"

Óscar was a hulking man with a shaved head and a nasty-looking scar that ran across one cheek and over the bridge of his nose. He belched loud and long and wiped his fingers on his shirt then tapped the cell phone in his pocket. "*Sí*, I spoke to your friends, the ones who are paying us. This is your lucky day, *amigo*. We are leaving tomorrow."

Bazir hesitated before asking, "Can you tell us where we're going?"

"You're going home, *señor*. Or at least back to where your people are." Óscar paused to pick his teeth then said, "Our job is to get you over the border into Mexico; others will take it from there."

"What time are we leaving tomorrow?" Turan asked softly.

Óscar shrugged. "I dunno, probably around ten o'clock. That way we blend in with the usual midday traffic. Getting caught with you muchachos in the car wouldn't be so good for me and Angel. All of Gringo Nation is looking for you."

"We need disguises," Bazir said.

"*Sí*, I'm already ahead of you. I got some clothes when I was out. Tomorrow, all four of us will be dressed like campesinos. If we get asked, we're going to Las Cruces to look for farm work."

"I can't wait to be done babysitting these *hijos de putas*," Angel said.

THE NEXT MORNING Angel went to the nearby Taco Bell and brought back a dozen grande scrambler combos and coffee. Turan choked down half of one of the scramblers. He didn't expect Pashto cuisine, but the steady diet of ersatz Mexican food was making him a little green around the gills. Bazir silently ate two of the scramblers. Angel and Óscar finished off the rest.

"You gonna finish that thing, chico?" Óscar said pointing at the uneaten half of Turan's breakfast. Turan shook his head and Óscar gobbled it up.

Bazir looked at Óscar. "Last night you said we would leave this morning. Is that still the plan?"

"Hell, yes. The sooner we're rid of you motherfuckers, the better," Angel said.

"So, when exactly will we leave?"

"When Óscar and I are good and fucking ready. Don't ask again." Angel pulled the Ruger Redhawk from the waistband of his jeans and waved it in Bazir's face.

"Easy, *amigo*," Óscar said. "We don't get paid for delivering damaged goods. Maybe you should go take care of that business next door."

Angel stared at Bazir for several seconds then shoved the revolver into the back of his waistband and walked to the front door. He paused before closing it behind him and said over his shoulder, "Time to shut up those noisy fucking neighbor dogs."

"What's he going to do next door?" Bazir said.

Óscar paused a moment before answering. "He's gonna change cars with the people that live there."

"What do their dogs have to do with that?"

"You and the *muchacho* there," he pointed at Turan, "have only been here a couple of nights. Maybe you sleep like a *bebé*, and don't hear nothin'. But me and Angel, we been stuck in this shithole listening to them fuckin' dogs yappin' for the past ten nights, waiting to meet up with you and haul your asses to Mexico."

"You're being well paid for that."

"Yeah," Óscar said with an icy smile. "Lucky for you."

"So, Angel's going to kill the neighbor's dogs?"

"Yeah."

"Don't you think that's pretty fucking stupid for people who are on the run?"

"Nah, we needed their car anyway."

Bazir looked puzzled. "I don't understand. What's the purpose of that?"

"Just being careful. Somebody could'a spotted us picking you and the *muchacho* up at the mall in Santa Fe. We need a different car; can't be too careful."

"Then you're just going to kill the neighbors and take their car," Turan said.

"And those fucking dogs."

"You kill people and steal their car. How smart is that for someone who doesn't want to arouse suspicions?" Bazir said.

"Way ahead of you, *amigo*. We'll be long gone and across the border before the people next door begin to stink enough for others to come looking. Then the stupid fuckin' cops will take a while to find our old car in the garage behind this house and put out an APB. Shit, by then you and your *amigo* will be back in your own country eatin' camel shit and fuckin' belly dancers."

IT WAS after 10:00 a.m. when the four men left the safe house and drove away in an older-model Kia Sorrento. The gangbangers were in the front, their two wards in the back. All were dressed like farm laborers. They rode in silence as Angel navigated Rio Bravo Boulevard to the intersection with Interstate 25. Bazir used the time to field strip and clean his weapon, a CZ 75 SP-01.

They had traveled several miles on the freeway and were well south of Los Padillas when Bazir spoke. "How long will this trip take?"

"What's a matter, *hombre*? You eager to be rid of us?" Angel said over his shoulder.

"I think that works both ways. So how much longer?"

Óscar said, "About four hours, give or take, to reach the border at Columbus. From there it's maybe a hundred and fifteen or twenty miles to Nuevo Casas Grandes. Just sit back and relax."

"What's at Nuevo Casas Grandes?"

"Your people said they'll be waiting with a private plane to fly you to Chihuahua. From there it's a hop to Mexico City on Aeroméxico."

"Why aren't we going back to the encampment at San Luis?"

"Ain't no encampment anymore."

"What? How can that be?"

"I heard some badass gringos, maybe Special Forces, wiped the place out the other night."

Bazir digested this information then said, "Do you know where we're going after Mexico City?"

"I don't fuckin' know, and I don't fuckin' care."

The four men traveled in silence for the better part of an hour and were ascending a small rise when Angel put on his right turn signal.

Immediately alarmed, Bazir said, "What are you doing? Why are you turning off the Interstate?"

"Shut the fuck up. I want shit outta you, I'll beat it out," Angel said with a growl.

"Relax, *amigo*, we're just stopping for lunch," Óscar said. "If we was gonna kill you, we'd a done it back at that fucking shack. Wouldn't be no need to drive anywhere."

Bazir and Turan hastily glanced around. All they saw was rolling barren desert and scrubby, stunted bushes. "Lunch? Where?" Bazir said.

Óscar pointed up ahead. "See that sign." Near the top of the rise was a green interstate sign announcing the intersection with U.S. Highway 380 East. "We goin' to stop at San Antonio."

"Texas?"

"No, you dumb shit," Angel said. "It ain't fuckin' Texas."

"What he's tryin' to say is there's a restaurant here that has some of the best food this side of L.A.," Óscar said.

Angel bore to the right on the exit ramp then made a wide curve to the left that brought them out onto a straight stretch of Highway 380 headed east. A half mile on, Angel turned into a small parking lot in front of a tired-looking building. A yellow sign with a red border announced it as The Loco Lobo: A Mexican Family Restaurant.

Turan groaned.

"What's so special about this place?" Bazir said. "It hasn't been that long since breakfast and there are other little towns farther down the road."

"You want to stay in the fuckin' car, you stay in the fuckin' car," Angel said. "But we ain't stoppin' before we cross the border at Columbus." He slammed the driver's door and went into the restaurant.

Bazir turned to Turan and shrugged. "Well, Óscar did say it was pretty good food."

"But it's Mexican again. I'd settle for a Big Mac—anything but more Mexican."

"You didn't seem to have a problem with Southwestern food when you were eating at Carolina's house in Santa Fe," Bazir said with a crooked grin. "Come on, maybe they have something else on the menu."

―――――――――

THE RESTAURANT HAD A SCREENED outdoor seating area with a smaller dining room inside. There were a number of ristras, or strung pods of dried red chiles, hanging from the ceiling. It was only a little after eleven, but the place was beginning to fill up. Angel was sitting at a cast-concrete Palladio table in the screened section looking at a menu. He didn't look up as Bazir and Turan joined him and Óscar.

The aroma coming from the kitchen was definitely better than that of the fast food from Taco Bell. Even so, Turan grimaced and rose to his feet. "I think I'll wait outside," he said, and quickly left the restaurant.

The blue sky was cloudless and the sun was directly overhead. Turan saw a small tree in the narrow space between the parking lot and the building that cast partial shade over a bench below it. He headed for it, sat down, and pulled out his cell phone. He hadn't been able to stop thinking about Carolina. Would he ever see her again? Bazir's comment about him dining at her house had brought back a lot of memories.

He hit the speed dial for Carolina. It rang several times. Just when he was afraid his call was about to go into voicemail, he heard it being picked up on the other end. There was a long, uncomfortable period of silence; no greeting. Finally, he hesitantly said, "Carolina?"

Another few seconds of silence passed, then she said, "You're unbelievable! How dare you call me after what you've done!"

Turan gamely offered, "I don't understand. What is it I've done?"

Without hesitation, Carolina screamed, "You killed my aunt and uncle…and thousands of other people, you…you murderer!"

Turan suddenly began sweating. His hands shook. His breathing was shallow and rapid. "But you don't understand. I had no idea anything like that was going to happen."

"But it did happen, didn't it! And you and your 'friends' killed those Border Patrol people too, didn't you!"

"I…I never thought any of this would happen."

"Really? You smuggled a nuclear weapon into our country, and you didn't think anything bad would happen? You must think I'm an idiot!"

"Carolina, wait. I can explain." Fearing she would disconnect at any second, the words tumbled out of him like water spilling over the top of a weir. "I admit that I've made mistakes. I wish I had never gotten involved with these people. I don't know what I was thinking. I guess I wasn't thinking. But I swear I never meant to harm your aunt and uncle. I had no idea who they were or that they were in Los Alamos."

"It doesn't matter whether you knew about them or not, Tomás, or whatever your real name is." Carolina's voice had suddenly become calm and measured. "What does matter is that you came to our country to kill as many of us as you could. And you did." She paused for a moment. "I hate you for what you've done. I will hate you for the rest of my life; and I hope they catch you, and the others like you, and make you pay for what you've done." She disconnected.

"No, Carolina! Please! Wait!" He moved the phone from his ear and stared at it, tears forming in his eyes. An area in his chest tightened and ached worse than anything he could remember. The realization dawned on him just how much he cared for the girl, her playfulness, her beauty, her companionship. And the realization also dawned on him that she was gone. Forever. *How could I have been so stupid as to believe that Allah wants us to kill those who aren't like us? Why did I listen to Bazir and the others?*

Turan sat on the bench in the partial shade of the scraggly tree, staring at the ground in front of him and slowly rocking back and forth in his grief. When he finally looked up, he saw an SUV pulling into the parking lot. A tall, lean man wearing a suit got out and came around to the passenger's side. He opened the door and a strikingly beautiful woman, a Latina, exited. She reminded him of an older Carolina. The way the two of them were smiling at each other and holding hands, Turan assumed they were involved in a new romantic relationship. Something he would never have with Carolina.

As the couple began moving in the direction of the restaurant, the man glanced at Turan, then did a double take. He stopped walking toward the eatery, and whispered something in the woman's ear, pulling her back towards their SUV. All the while, he continued to stare at Turan.

A cold wave of fear replaced Turan's heartache. He stood and quickly returned to the restaurant.

CHAPTER 39

SAN ANTONIO, NEW MEXICO

MITCH CHRISTIE FINISHED PLACING the suitcases in the back of the rented SUV and shut the tailgate. He climbed into the driver's seat next to Camila. They were barely thirty miles north of the humble dwelling in South Valley that had sheltered Turan and Bazir until this morning.

Camila Ramirez looked at the Tamaya Resort as they pulled away. "It would have been nice to have been able to stay longer," she said wistfully. "In a way, it was a part of our first date."

"As I recall, that didn't go so well. I'm glad we had last night to make up for it." He shot her a sly grin.

She returned a coy one of her own and said, "And you'll continue to make up for it, over and over again."

"Like last night?"

"Just like last night."

"But we'll be at your parent's home in Ruidoso tonight. How's that going to work out?"

"It's only for two nights. You can behave yourself that long."

"But we're getting married tomorrow. Are you telling me we can't...what's the word...consummate our marriage?"

She giggled girlishly. "Oh, you'll get a chance to consummate it, like I said, over and over again. I plan to wear you out."

"Why can't we start tomorrow, on our wedding night?"

"I told you, my parents are old-fashioned. Even though we'll be married, they still think of me as their little girl. I doubt seriously that my father wants to think about me having sex, particularly under his own roof."

"Even married?"

"Yes, even married."

"But you were married once before. What about then?"

"It was the same thing."

Christie mulled the situation over for a while. "What if we stayed in a motel nearby? They do have motels in Ruidoso, don't they?"

"Mitch," she sighed, "we've been through this before. My parents would be deeply insulted if we didn't stay with them. It's customary."

Grinning, Christie said, "Maybe when they're asleep, if you promise to be quiet, we can settle for a quickie."

"Not a chance. Papa's a light sleeper."

He mulled some more. "What if we stopped at a motel before we got to their house? A quickie is a quickie."

She giggled again and slapped his shoulder playfully. "Oh, stop it. It's only two nights."

Christie turned right off Highway 550 onto the on ramp for Interstate 25 South. "So, tell me about this home town of yours, Ruidoso. Is there anything going on there?"

"Absolutely. There's Ski Apache, owned by the Mescalero Apache Tribe, and Ruidoso Downs racetrack, and a casino, and lots of things. It's a rapidly growing resort community, not a hick town."

"Hey, I wasn't implying that it was. I mean, it has to be a special place. It's your hometown."

Recognizing the need to change the subject, and quickly, Christie said, "I'm getting kind of hungry. What with no breakfast...and all that energy I used up last night." He grinned.

She ran her hands along the top of her jeans as if to smooth them. It was an unconscious habit she had. "Well, Mitchell, this is your lucky day."

"How so? Have you rethought my suggestion for a quickie?"

Camila smiled flirtatiously. "Not that lucky."

Christie pretended to pout. "Then anything else is downhill from there."

She laughed. "You are so much fun when you're being playful, you really are."

"So, if I have to settle for a distant second best, what exactly is it?"

"A really good lunch experience."

"Lunch?"

"Yes, it's a really funky place with the best Mexican food in the state."

"Where?"

"In a couple of miles, we'll come to the intersection with Route 380. That's where we turn off to go to Ruidoso. There's a little town there, San Antonio. It has a wonderful little restaurant, the Loco Lobo."

Christie chuckled.

"What's so funny?"

"I was remembering what life was like before I met you. A lot of things—my job, the breakup of my marriage—it had me so stressed I was literally living off Rolaids. Mexican food would have killed me, for sure."

This time she favored him with a seductive look. "This food will restore that 'energy' you used up last night."

"Hmm, sounding better all the time. But if it's such a great dining spot, why is it in the middle of nowhere?"

"San Antonio isn't such a sleepy little town. It's a bedroom community for people who work in the county seat, Socorro, and the White Sands Missile Range. And it's the birthplace of Conrad Hilton."

"*The* Conrad Hilton, founder of the hotel chain?"

"The very same."

"Impressive."

THEY HAD ONLY TAKEN a couple of steps when Christie noticed a teenager sitting on a bench and holding a cell phone. From his facial expression and body English, he seemed crestfallen, as if his girlfriend had just dumped him. *The trials of young love.*

The kid looked up at them as they approached. Completely absorbed in his grief, he gave them a blank stare.

Christie glanced at him, then did a double take and stopped in his tracks. He knew that face. Quickly, he pulled Camila back towards their SUV.

"You saw something," she said, instantly shifting gears from flirtatious to serious. "What is it? That boy?"

Christie pulled the door open, nudged her in, then leaned closer. "I'm pretty sure that's the kid from Santa Fe, the one we're looking for."

"What are you going to do? He's almost certainly not here by himself. We need backup."

"It's not 'we,' Camila. I want you to stay in the vehicle and keep a low profile." He opened the glove compartment and pulled out a

Galco Cop Ankle Band holster. It held his backup gun, a Glock G43 with a six-round magazine and a seventh 9mm round in the chamber. He handed it to her.

"We're going to do this by the book and wait for backup, but if the shit hits the fan before it gets here, you keep your head down and let me deal with this. I don't want anything to happen to you." He pulled out his cell phone and speed dialed Frank Cuellar. The state police major answered on the second ring, and Christie explained the situation.

"I'll contact the nearest units and have them there as fast as we can. In the meantime, take care of yourself, Mitch," Cuellar said.

Christie clicked off and went around to the driver's side of the SUV. As he did, he glanced at the young man again. The kid was no longer sitting on the bench. He was moving quickly toward the door to the restaurant, glancing back fearfully at Christie.

"Dammit!"

"What is it, Mitch?" Camila said.

"The little shit is on to us. He just went back inside where there most likely are others. We know he was traveling with at least one other jihadi."

There was genuine concern in Camila's voice. "What are you going to do?"

With a snort of frustration, he said, "I'm not going in there alone, there are too many unknowns at this point. But if they start to leave before Cuellar's people get here, I'm not sure what I'll do. We'll just have to see how it shakes out." He slid onto the seat, drew his Bureau-issued Glock 23 from its hip holster, and watched the door to the restaurant.

A COUPLE OF MINUTES LATER, a late-model Ford Interceptor with New Mexico State Police markings came to a stop on the wide gravel shoulder across from the restaurant. Two uniformed officers emerged. Christie got out of his car, walked over, and showed them his cred pack, including his badge and ID card. The NMSP cops introduced themselves as Sergeant Phil Reynolds and Officer Anibal Esparza. To Christie's practiced eye, Reynolds looked to be in his early thirties. He was a little over six feet, and chubby with a florid complexion. Esparza, a rookie just completing training, was a good four inches shorter and wiry. Reynolds explained that they had been only a few miles away patrolling I-25, when Cuellar had reached them.

Christie gave them the read on the situation then said, "There's probably a back door. One of you needs to cover it. The other one and I will cover the front."

Reynolds nodded to Esparza, indicating he should go around behind the restaurant.

"We'll wait here for additional backup. Hopefully Major Cuellar is sending SWAT too. There are a lot of civilians in there right now, so it could turn into an active shooter or hostage situation," Christie said.

"Collateral damage lookin' for a place to happen," Reynolds said, referring to the other patrons in the diner.

Christie looked at the NMSP cop and said, "You're wearing body armor, right?"

"Yeah, level II-A. You?"

"No. I'm supposed to be on vacation. I'm getting married tomorrow." He looked over at Camila in the SUV and motioned for her to stay there.

A COUPLE of minutes passed during which a few patrons exited the diner. The boy in the photo wasn't among them. And, to Christie's practiced eye, none of the departees looked Middle Eastern.

Suddenly, the door flew open and Angel Bautista burst through it, the Ruger Redhawk in his right hand. He saw Reynolds's uniform and fired three full metal jacketed 220 grain magnum rounds while on a dead run toward him. The first round was wide to the sergeant's left, boring deep into the concrete block wall of an establishment one hundred feet from the restaurant. The second shot hit dead center in Reynolds's bullet-resistant vest, easily ripping through it and his chest cavity and exiting through his back. The third slug hit the officer just above the top of his vest, obliterating the seventh cervical vertebra and nearly decapitating him.

As soon as the door had flown open, Christie had dropped into a kneeling position, to present a smaller target. He aimed at Bautista's center mass and put three 9mm rounds in it. The gangbanger's forward motion carried him two additional steps before his corpse did a face-plant in the gravel of the parking lot.

Christie immediately raised his sights to the restaurant's doorway. Nothing was moving in the darkness behind it. He heard a noise off to his left and swung the muzzle of the automatic in that direction. It was the opening of a narrow alleyway that ran between the restaurant and an auxiliary building. Officer Esparza appeared in the opening, gun drawn and a panicked look on his face.

"I heard shots," he said. Then he saw Reynolds' body and turned toward it. Rookie mistake. It put his back to the restaurant's doorway. Óscar Amaya suddenly filled the space, a Beretta M9 in his right hand. He fired two shots at Esparza's back. The rear panel of the officer's BRV prevented the first 9mm+P FMJ slug that hit it from penetrating his body. But the gun's recoil raised the muzzle slightly and the second slug smashed into the back of the young cop's skull killing him instantly.

As Esparza's body collapsed, Amaya saw Christie in a shooter's kneeling position slightly to his left. The two men fired simultaneously. Christie was the better shot and put three slugs in Amaya's center body mass. Even so, the mortally wounded gangbanger managed to put a single round through the FBI agent's left upper chest.

Christie fell backwards and to his left, landing on his stomach. His only concern was for Camila's safety. Two of the bad guys were down, but how many were there? And what about the boy in the photo and the other suspected terrorist?

He heard a noise behind him and rolled painfully onto his back. A Middle Eastern-looking man was running from the restaurant, a CZ 75 in his right hand. The boy in the photo was right behind him.

Christie tried to aim the Glock at the man, but his hand shook as the result of the wound and shock setting in. He was reluctant to squeeze off a round for fear he would hit an innocent bystander inside the Loco Lobo.

Bazir saw the wounded man on the ground off to his left and shot him. The full metal jacketed 9mm parabellum slug shattered the seventh rib on Christie's left side and burrowed through his chest, including his left lung, before emerging from his back. The force of the bullet knocked him backwards and he sprawled in a rapidly spreading pool of his own blood.

Bazir paused for a moment and looked around to see if there were more law enforcement officers. Seeing none, he grabbed Turan and shoved him toward their Kia Sorrento.

Just before he reached it, Camila stepped from the SUV and placed her right foot on the ground. She glanced ashen-faced at her fiancé's prostrate form, then turned and aimed Christie's backup gun between the door post and the open car door. She took a deep breath, but her hands were shaking as she tried to draw on the many hours of practice she'd had on various gun ranges. Camila squeezed off three shots. Because of her shaking hands, only one of the 9mm slugs found its intended target. And just barely.

It tore into Bazir's back on the lower right side, passing through a portion of his right kidney and his colon. He sprawled against the right front fender of the Kia. Reaching backwards, and without turning around, he blindly sprayed the remaining bullets from the CZ 75's eighteen-round magazine. A couple of them struck bystanders who had been inside the restaurant when the shooting started. None of the slugs hit Camila as she crouched over Christie's body desperately dialing 911 on her cell phone.

Bazir pulled the passenger door of the Kia open, then shoved Turan toward the driver's side. "The keys are in the ignition. You drive. Hurry, get moving," he grunted between teeth clenched in pain.

The younger man started the car and whipped out of the gravel parking lot so quickly that he sideswiped another vehicle and almost lost control as he exited the lot. "Where...where are we going?" he stammered in Pashto.

Bazir pulled his hand away from his side and saw that it was covered in blood. "The highway, the interstate. Don't know how far Mexico is, but we have to get there. Go fast, don't stop for anything."

CHAPTER 40

DINGLE, IRELAND

IT WAS early evening and Brendon Whelan was in the tiny office just off the kitchen of the Fianna House, once again paying bills and reviewing menus for the coming week. It was off-season for the B&B, but an arts and crafts festival in nearby Tralee had filled half its rooms for the next several days. He had initialed the menu plans for the cook and slipped them into the rack on the kitchen wall just outside the office door when he heard the unique sound of an incoming call. It could only be Levell calling on the sat phone. He hesitated for a second or two, knowing the reason for the call, yet not wanting to hear it.

He picked up the sat phone and pressed the green button. "Yeah, Cliff, what's up this time?"

"I wish I could tell you something good, but I can't."

"What, no pillow talk first? The honeymoon must be over." Whelan's voice had a mocking tone.

"No time for that. Shit's moving too fast. I have to get you and the others back in play immediately, if not sooner." Whelan recognized it as one of Levell's favorite expressions.

"And this isn't something your new BFF, Christie, can handle?"

"Mitch is fighting for his life in a critical care unit."

Whelan sat bolt upright. "What the hell happened? He was good a couple of days ago."

"Bad luck on his part. He was on his way to get married and inadvertently stumbled upon the perps that did Los Alamos. There was a firefight. Two New Mexico state cops were killed, along with two MS-13 gangbangers. Some bystanders were wounded, a couple of them critically. The gangbangers each had lengthy criminal records and probably were providing muscle to get the perps across the border. Ballistics show that it was Mitch's gun that got 'em."

Sobered by the news, Whelan said, "When did this happen?"

"Literally minutes ago."

"What's Mitch's situation?"

"Initially, the medicos are saying he's in critical condition with massive blood loss, pneumothorax—a collapsed lung—shattered ribs, and internal bleeding. They're struggling to stabilize his vital signs."

Whelan whistled softly and sat down on a kitchen stool. "So, what's his prognosis?"

"Hell, what do you think I am, a fucking surgeon?"

"I think you have access to any information you want."

Levell's voice softened slightly. "Yeah, I do. But it won't get much better for a while. He's in shock, on a ventilator, blood pressure plunging. The docs are going to do exploratory surgery to try to stop the internal bleeding and re-inflate the lung."

"And this happened while he was on his way to his wedding? Anyone else with him?"

"Yeah, his bride-to-be."

"No shit! Is she all right?"

"Camila Ramirez, the fiancée, is a seasoned cop—Bernalillo County SO, now a member of the Capitol Police. Mitch had the presence of mind to give her his backup gun. It appears she may have winged one of the perps."

"How many perps?"

"Two. The young kid in the photo that the New Mexico cops turned up and a guy who was a few years older. He was the shooter. The one Camila may have plugged."

"What's their status?"

"Dammit, that's why I'm calling you. They're currently at large. Ms. Ramirez had the presence of mind to get a description of their vehicle and its license number. It was a beat-up blue Kia Sorrento with New Mexico tags. There's an APB out on it now."

"I'm at least ten hours from there by fast jet. I hope you're going to tell me that various U.S. authorities have this under control."

Levell snorted. "There's a full-blown turf war in progress. The State Police want revenge for their two dead officers. The Bureau wants to take charge because Christie was...is one of theirs. DHS wants all the glory for their boss in the Oval Office before his term is up in a few weeks. It's a fucking Chinese fire drill."

"And you're calling me because...?"

"Because I want your ass back here as fast as humanly possible. No way do I want to rely on any of these agencies getting the job done. Besides, Camila told me that Mitch, just before he lost consciousness, said he wanted her to call me. He doesn't want those camel jockeys to get away. He wants us to get revenge for his injuries and vengeance for the massacre at Los Alamos."

"Ten hours or more, remember?"

"I'm old, but I'm not fucking senile. There are two things I need you to do. One is to get your ass up to the County Kerry airport."

"Farranfore."

"What?"

"Maybe you are getting senile. I told you before, the airport is called Farranfore. It's fifty-five klicks from here, about an hour away."

"I don't give a shit what it's called or where the fuck it is. Just get your ass up there now!"

Whelan was amused by Levell's near-permanent crotchety state. "You arrange for a private jet? Otherwise it'll take the better part of two days to get to New Mexico by commercial."

"Yes, the Muellers have provided a corporate Gulfstream 550. It should be landing as we speak."

"You said two things; what's the other one?" Whelan slid off the stool and walked back into the office, settling into the desk chair.

"The second is to call whoever you left in charge at the resort in Tucson and get them in pursuit immediately."

"In charge? Are you shitting me, Cliff? You're talking about the most individualistic, asocial group of people on the planet."

"So? They consider you to be their leader."

"Yeah, because I show them respect and try to find ways for them to have fun during down time. Unlike some people I know."

"Wise-ass," Levell said dryly. "Do whatever you have to do. There's a chopper landing in minutes in the Casino's parking lot just east of the Anselmo Valencia Tori Amphitheater. It will take them to San Antonio, New Mexico, where the shootings occurred."

"Hold on a minute," Whelan said as he punched up Google Earth on his computer. After a few moments, he said, "As the crow flies, the distance from the casino in Tucson to San Antonio is about two hundred eighty miles. The bad guys already have a head start."

Levell again snorted impatiently. "You and your men are the best hunter-killers on the planet. If anyone can find them, you can."

"Do you know which direction they took."

There was hesitation at Levell's end. "No. The authorities scrambled aircraft and set up road blocks, but nothing definite yet."

Whelan went back to Google Earth and scanned the area around

San Antonio. "I can't conceive of them doing anything other than trying to get to Mexico, especially with HAC willing to pay hefty bribes to get its heroes safely home. Other than the interstate, there are no routes, even backroads, that can get them there. Plus, they're desperate. They'll be looking for the quickest, most direct way possible, and that means by air."

He focused in more closely on the terrain and said, "About fifty-five to sixty miles down the interstate there's a small airport in a place called Truth or Consequences, New Mexico. At a high rate of speed, they can be there in well less than an hour. That's where they're going."

Whelan zoomed out and scrolled down past the Mexican border. Using the software's ruler, he drew a line from Truth or Consequences to a point on the border. "It's about a hundred miles to the border over mostly desolate, uninhabited countryside. If they fly low and pour the coals to it, they'll get away."

"Shit!" Levell said. "We'll have to go after them in Mexico. I'll divert the chopper. Where do you think they'll cross?"

"Doesn't matter. They have too much of a head start."

Whelan scrolled beneath the border and into Mexico. "The closest airport to the border that would fit their needs is in a place called Nuevo Casa Grandes. It's maybe another hundred miles south of the border."

"That's where I want you to send the unit."

"Not gonna happen, Cliff."

"Why the hell not?" Levell wasn't used to being told 'no,' and it showed in his tone of voice.

"Simple. The plane will have enough of a head start that it will get to Nuevo Casa Grandes first. Plus, I can't imagine the Muellers agreeing to one of their aircraft violating the airspace of a sovereign nation. One in which they have a lot of capital invested."

"I wasn't planning to tell them. Besides, they were okay with using one of their corporate choppers when you nabbed that Zeta kingpin."

"That was right on the border and in the middle of nowhere. Going a hundred miles into Mexico and risking a firefight in a city of sixty thousand people is a different matter."

Levell sighed heavily. "You're right, dammit. But we can't let these murdering motherfuckers get away. Think of the lives lost at Los Alamos, the heartache of the survivors, the message their deed sent to the other Islamic extremists around the world."

"I didn't say they were going to get away, Cliff. Like you said, we are the best hunter-killers on this planet. There will be vengeance, and the message it sends to those who would harm us will make it clear that none of them are ever safe. Anywhere."

CHAPTER 41

TRUTH OR CONSEQUENCES, NEW MEXICO

THE ADRENAL RUSH of the shootout and the shock of the gunshot wound were wearing off. Bazir Haqqani felt the pain intensifying in the path the slug had chewed through his body. He slowly and painfully twisted around to peer out the rear window of the Sorrento. The effort caused him to gasp.

White-knuckling the Kia's steering wheel with both hands, Turan shot a worried glance at his mentor. "Are you all right?" he said in Pashto.

"I've been fucking shot! How all right is that?" Bazir slumped back in his seat.

"What can I do to help you?"

Bazir gritted his teeth and looked at a map in his bloody lap. "Just make this car go faster."

With a quick peek at the speedometer, Turan said, "We're going one hundred and ten miles per hour. I don't think it can go any faster. I'm having a hard time controlling it." He could hear the fear in his own voice.

"Just a few miles ahead we'll come to Exit 89. Take it."

"Then what? Those were policemen that were shot back there. They'll have everyone looking for us, and Mexico is still a long way off."

Bazir grunted. "Not driving to Mexico. Gonna fly."

"Fly?"

"The infidels will have an all-points bulletin—APB—out for us. The interstate will be swarming soon."

Turan gave him a questioning look. But Bazir had the CZ 75 in his right hand and had put a fresh magazine in it. *Maybe this isn't a good time to challenge Bazir's judgment.*

In less than two minutes, Turan saw the green highway sign announcing the exit. He slowed and Bazir told him to turn right. In about two hundred yards, he came to a t-intersection and was directed to take a left. Four quick miles later Bazir ordered him to turn right at a small signpost that said Airport Road. The speed sign said 25 mph. Turan ignored it.

The road was a short, narrow lane that ran ruler-straight for less than a quarter of a mile and ended at a parking area in front of a few nondescript metal buildings. A sign on one of them said "Truth or Consequences Municipal Airport." Behind the buildings were several unpaved runways and one paved one. There were a half-dozen small single-engine aircraft parked on a large area of tarmac near the metal buildings.

A group of four people—two men and two women—were standing next to one of the planes. One of the men was loading suitcases through a small hatch in the fuselage. Bazir pointed at them. "Go there."

Turan skidded to a halt about five feet from the group. One of the women gasped when she saw the bloody Bazir climbing painfully from the front passenger door, gun in hand. The gasp was short-lived. She caught the first bullet mid-thorax and staggered backward a step before collapsing. The man next to her started to scream, but it was abruptly cut off as the first round burrowed through his solar plexus and the second one destroyed his throat. He fell next to the woman who had been shot.

The second woman was beginning to turn to her right, as if to run away from the scene of horror exploding around her. The first slug tore through her arm and into her chest cavity. The second round missed completely and struck the plane's fuselage narrowly missing the man who had been loading the suitcase. The third bullet struck her in the side of the head.

The last man instinctively backed against the fuselage and held his hands in front of him as though hoping to ward off a rain of slugs.

Bazir waved the barrel of the CZ 75 at the man, motioning toward the plane. "Get in," he ordered in accented English.

The man stared at him and then at the woman lying dead at his feet. "But…but my wife…."

"Fuck her, she's dead. And you will be also if you don't get in the plane."

The man continued to hesitate and Bazir squeezed off a shot that caromed off the tarmac at his feet. That did the trick. He quickly hopped into the plane's pilot seat.

Bazir climbed painfully into the rear seat. He motioned for Turan to take the copilot's seat.

"I…I don't know how to fly." Turan's voice came out high-pitched and squeaky.

"You won't have to, unless this man does something foolish and I have to kill him." He prodded the back of the pilot's head with the muzzle of the gun. "Fly! Now!"

The man, ghostly pale and sweating heavily, started the plane's engine and began taxiing toward the runway. With a badly shaking hand, he picked up the headset and put it on.

"Take that off. Just fly."

"It's just to let other pilots who might be in the area know what we're doing, so we don't have a collision with someone who might be landing while we're taking off."

"No! Get this plane in the air immediately or I will kill you now." He smacked the back of the pilot's head with the muzzle.

"Ow! Hey, I'm doing the best I can." The whine of fear in his voice was clear.

In moments, the plane was gathering speed along runway 13, meaning it was on a heading of one hundred thirty degrees. It was the only paved runway. The nose began to lift and the plane quickly rose into the cloudless sky of azure blue.

"Whe…where am I going?" the pilot stammered.

Teeth gritted against the pain burning through his abdomen, Bazir said, "South. Go south. On the straightest line to Mexico. And stay low. If I think you're deceiving us, I'll kill you here and now, and take my chances getting this plane down."

WITH A MODEST TAILWIND, the Cessna 172 crossed the Mexican border less than forty-five minutes later at a point about eighteen miles east of the border crossing between Columbus, New Mexico and Puerto Palomas, Chihuahua. It was desolate, forbidding territory—like a talented set designer's concept of a dystopian world.

The pilot pulled out a chart of this general area of northern Mexico and unfolded it. "Where do you want me to land?" His hands were shaking, making it difficult to open the chart.

"Nuevo Casas Grandes."

The pilot studied the chart for several moments.

Turan wiggled uncomfortably in his seat. "Hey, shouldn't you be looking out the window?"

The pilot looked up at him. "Windscreen."

"What?"

"In a plane, it's not a window, it's a windscreen."

"Okay, but you're not looking out it."

"These planes all but fly themselves. I only need to control it for takeoffs and landings."

The pilot consulted a small notebook computer for several moments then said to Bazir, "According to the Notams, this airport is closed."

"Notams? What's that?"

"Notice to Airmen. The FAA publishes them to assist pilots. They say this airport is closed."

"Closed? What are you saying? We can't land there?"

"It means there is no active traffic control, no operating FBO."

Bazir snarled. "Stop speaking gibberish. What the fuck is FBO?"

"Fixed-base operator. It's a place to refuel, get repairs and refreshments."

"We don't need that shit. So, I'll ask you one more time." He again jammed the CZ 75 into the back of the pilot's skull for emphasis. "Can we land there?"

"There's no air traffic control. If other planes are using it, there could be a collision. The runway isn't being maintained. It could have debris or potholes that could cause us to wreck." The words came out in choppy sentences, and he was breathing rapidly.

Bazir ground the muzzle into the pilot's scalp. "You're not answering my question."

The airman grunted in pain. "All right, all right, we'll be on the ground there in about forty minutes." He paused before adding, "If the Mexicans don't shoot us down first." He reached for the headset again.

"No," Bazir grunted.

"If you're planning to kill me when we land, you should know that there's an infantry battalion of the Mexican army headquartered at the airport."

"If you do exactly what I tell you to do, I won't have a reason to kill you. Besides, someone has to make the funeral arrangements for your wife and friends."

The pilot's expression was a mixture of hope and doubt.

Minutes later, the plane neared the defunct Nuevo Casas Grandes airport. The badly faded number 13 could be seen as they approached the single paved runway. To the left of the runway they could see another plane on the ground. It was larger than the Cessna but, like it, was a single engine aircraft.

The pilot seemed surprised that the runway was still in decent condition. When they were on the ground, Bazir ordered him to taxi over to the other plane, a Piper M350.

Two large, Semitic-looking men with neatly trimmed beards got out of the Piper, a luxury six-seater. They walked over to the Cessna and assisted Bazir out. The men escorted him gently to their plane. He whispered something in the ear of one of the men. When Bazir and Turan were safely seated in the Piper, the man Bazir had spoken to walked back to the Cessna. He leaned in and shot the pilot in the head.

Watching from a window in the other plane, Turan was shocked. He turned to Bazir, being attended to by the second man. "You told him he wouldn't be killed."

"In the situation we're in, it's not wise to leave any loose ends."

CHAPTER 42

TUCSON, ARIZONA

JUST AS LEVELL HAD PROMISED, a Mueller enterprises Gulfstream G550 had been waiting for Whelan at Farranfore. And just as Whelan had feared, the takeoff had been a little tight because of the runway length and the full load of fuel the plane carried for the transatlantic flight. The aircraft had bucked a moderate headwind crossing the Atlantic, causing its fuel to burn off at a faster rate. As a result, the two-man crew had landed the plane at Gander International Airport in Newfoundland, a transatlantic refueling stop, before continuing on to Tucson.

Including the stop at Gander, the flight took a little more than ten hours, traveling through seven time zones. Whelan had left Farranfore at noon. His body clock told him it was almost midnight, but it was only 3:00 p.m. in Arizona. He emerged into the bright mid-afternoon sunlight and stretched muscles that had been tightened by the long flight in the cramped cabin. The desert heat immediately slapped him like an angry woman. *We're not in Kansas anymore, Dorothy.*

He paused at the bottom of the plane's fold-out steps, and,

squinting against the glare of the sun in a cloudless sky, saw a man walking rapidly toward him. He was wearing a civilian airman's uniform similar to the ones worn by the crew that had flown Whelan from Ireland. In the distance, a helicopter sat on the tarmac, its rotors slowly turning.

The man stopped a few feet from the Irishman and said, "Mr. Whelan, follow me please." He turned and began walking back toward the chopper.

Whelan could see a second man, similarly uniformed, sitting at the craft's controls. "Where are we going?"

"Mr. Levell wants us to take you to the Casino Del Sol. It's a resort a few miles from here."

"I know the place. Is Levell going to be there?"

"He didn't share that with us, sir. He just said there were people there that you know, and he wanted you to meet with them."

The chopper ride was a short one, covering the nine miles to the resort in a matter of a few minutes. There was no further conversation with the crew. At the Casino Del Sol, a young woman wearing a name tag with the resort's logo greeted him as he hopped down from the bird. The name tag said "Sheryl."

She led him into a building and to a small conference room. Five of the other Dogs were seated around a table in the room. The only one missing was Rafe Almeida. *Surprise, surprise.*

Larsen, Kirkland, Stensen, Thomas, and Stone nodded as Whelan entered the room.

"Almeida's missing. Anyone know where he is?"

The other five men grinned in unison.

"Wherever it is," Stensen said, "there's at least one female with him."

"That's it," Thomas said. "Just go where females are congregating and you'll find Rafe."

Kirkland said, "Nick's reference was more specific than that. He meant *in flagrante delicto*."

"The bloke is havin' a naughty with a sheila or two," Stone said. "Maybe more."

Everyone laughed except Whelan and Larsen.

"I don't have time for this shit," Larsen said. "The longer it takes to finish this job, the longer Maksym gets to live." He stood up. "I'll find Rafe and drag his worthless ass back here, pants or no pants."

Twenty minutes later Larsen returned with Almeida slung over one of his massive shoulders.

"Dammit, Larsen, put me down!" Almeida said as they entered the room.

Larsen obliged him, dumping the other man on the floor.

He landed on his butt and snarled. "I can kick your ass, Larsen. Anytime I want, your ass is mine."

Larsen ignored him and took a seat.

"Anybody want to put money on Rafe?" Stensen said. "No? Well, how about on how many seconds it will take Sven to rip off Rafe's head and shit down his throat?"

"Enough," Whelan said. He turned toward Larsen, "That didn't take long. Where did you find him?"

"He was in his room."

"How many chicks?" Kirkland said.

"Two."

"Blondes?"

"Yeah. Twins, I think. They looked underage."

"Bullshit," Almeida said. "They're eighteen and they *are* twins."

Stone shook his head. "Where do you find these sheilas, mate?"

"At the tennis courts."

"Tennis?" Thomas said. "You don't know anything about tennis."

"Fuck tennis, it's where you go to pick up hot chicks. Of all ages. I told the twins I was a tennis instructor and said I'd show them some new tricks back in my room. They looked at each other, giggled, and the rest, as they say, is history." Almeida grinned smugly.

"All right," Whelan said, "today's lesson on how to get laid is over. We've got serious business to address.

He briefed the others on what he knew about the San Antonio shootings and where he thought the two perps who'd escaped might have gone.

"So," Kirkland said, "are we going to Nuevo Casas Grandes?"

"I hope so," Almeida said. "Mexican tail is pretty fine. Remember the three chiquitas at Chacón's?"

Stone was sitting next to him. He leaned over and punched him on the shoulder. "You're a bloody root rat, mate. Just got out of the sack with two sheilas, and you're ready to shag the first prawn that comes along."

Almeida looked puzzled. "What hell did he say?"

"He says you do all your thinking with your tackle. That's the little head, since you don't speak Strine," Whelan said. "Now, if we can table the discussion of Rafe's imagined sexual prowess, I want to get Cliff on the phone for an update."

He pulled the satphone from a pocket in his cargo pants, dialed Levell's secure line, and put it in speaker mode. In two rings, Levell answered. "About fucking time you called," he said irritably.

"Can the sarcasm. I just got in and I'm tired."

"Everybody there?"

"Yes. Before we get into the business at hand, how's Mitch doing?"

"It's mostly positive. The surgery was successful in stopping the

internal bleeding. Percutaneous chest tube drainage has the lung re-
inflating, and they'll begin to wean him off the ventilator in a
couple of days. At that point, they'll probably move him from ICU
to PCU."

"What's PCU?"

"Progressive Care Unit. It's an intermediate step between ICU
and the medical/surgical unit."

"Keep us in the loop on his progress."

"You'll do more to hasten his recovery by catching and killing
the bastards who shot him."

"Speaking of which," Whelan said, "what's the latest on them?"

"Dammit, it seems you hit the nail on the head. They did go to
the airport in Truth or Consequences, commandeered a plane, and
forced the pilot to fly them to Nuevo Casas Grandes."

"And killed him."

"Yeah. And they shot and killed the pilot's wife and another
couple at the airport when they grabbed the plane. The sooner you
kill these guys the sooner the body count stops rising."

"Do you have any additional information on these scumbags?"

"Yeah. Their vehicle, a Kia, belonged to a neighbor of the place
the gangbangers were renting south of Albuquerque."

"Is he involved too?"

"No, he's dead. The cops traced the tag to his house and found
him and his dogs dead. Neighbors didn't know much, but none of
them liked the two gangbangers. Said they moved in a week or so
earlier. There was bad blood between them and the dead guy
because of the dogs."

"Did the cops find anything that could help us track down the
killers?"

"Place was empty, but they found the gangbangers' prints all
over it, along with those of two other individuals."

"Have they been ID'ed?"

"Can't find anything. Even INTERPOL drew a blank."

Whelan thought about that for a few moments. "You said they actually did show up in Nuevo Casas Grandes. Any leads there besides the dead pilot?"

"Forensics got prints from the Mexican authorities—they were willing to help because an Americano was killed on their turf."

"But I'll bet they made no effort to try to apprehend the killers."

Levell snorted. "Of course not. Given the graft and corruption south of the border, plus the very real fear of the gangs and cartels that are in bed with HAC, they won't lift a finger."

"Were the prints helpful?"

"Yes. Besides the dead pilot's, there were prints that matched the two unknowns from the house in Albuquerque and the getaway car they left at the airport in Truth or Consequences."

Whelan exhaled in frustration. "It looks like we're at a dead-end, at least for the moment."

Levell's voice seemed to brighten. "Not necessarily."

"Meaning what?"

"A CIA informant in Qatar told his handler that an HVI—a High-Value-Individual—was exfiltrated from Mexico to Doha in bad shape. He's under heavy protective guard in a hospital there."

Whelan's eyes narrowed as a faint, cold smile played at the corners of his lips. He looked around the table. The other Dogs had similar expressions.

"Brush up on your Arabic, men. We're going in-country."

CHAPTER 43

TEHRAN, IRAN

NADIR SHAH, self-proclaimed Caliph and leader of the Holy Army of the Caliphate, was in a typically sour mood. The Ayvān Hotel in Tehran was not his idea of the kind of luxury the Caliph deserved. Located in the Central Business District near the government offices, it *was* the hotel of choice for business people having to deal with Iranian officials. It also was chosen by his hosts, the Islamic Republic of Iran. If they had extended him the courtesy of choosing his own hotel, he would have picked one on the north side of the city, where he could enjoy the magnificent views of the mountains surrounding Tehran. Worse, the toilet in his suite was malfunctioning and hotel staff had refused to relocate him to another room, even though it was the low season because of December's extremely cold weather. In addition, the heater was centrally controlled, so the temperature wasn't adjustable. He'd had to open the windows as it became too warm. *Effete Persian bastards. Soon enough they'll become part of the Caliphate. I'll deal with them then.*

But his greatest concern was that there wouldn't be a "then".

That was his reason for being in the Iranian capital. He was meeting with the global power brokers who had the most to gain from the success of HAC's struggles against the West and their Middle Eastern puppet regimes, mostly in the Gulf states.

As he entered the meeting room on the top floor of the Ayvān, he stared poker-faced at the other occupants in the room, giving each the barest of nods. His host, Ali Sayad Kazemzadeh, the top general in Iran's Quds force, a special unit of their Revolutionary Guards, returned a broad grin as if amused by Shah's ever-present petulance. The general sat at the head of a long rectangular table. The other three attendees were seated next to him on either side. Shah purposely took the chair at the other end of the table. *I am the Caliph. I sit in the position of power.*

"All right," Shah said in Arabic. "I am commanding a great army in the midst of the final war this world will ever see. Don't waste my time."

"You are the one who requested this meeting," Kazemzadeh said, still grinning.

The caliph shifted uncomfortably in his seat. "Yes, of course I am. Do you think I have forgotten?"

The Quds general smiled knowingly at the man seated to his right, Zheng Bao Xun, the minister of finance for the People's Republic of China. Across from Zheng, Harland Fairchilde, the chief executive of the Alliance for Global Unity, stared at his shoes and tapped his carefully manicured fingernails slowly, rhythmically against the highly-polished tabletop.

The fourth man in the room was seated next to Fairchilde. Shah didn't recognize him. His massive physicality seemed to fill the room, and the aura of unspoken malevolence surrounding him all but sucked the oxygen from it. The giant fixed Shah with a baleful stare. Despite the coolness of the facility, in moments large beads of sweat began popping out along the caliph's forehead. He wiped self-consciously at them with the sleeve of his black battle fatigues.

"Who is this man?" Shah said.

Kazemzadeh translated the statement into English for Fairchilde.

"This gentleman is the head of my personal security force."

"He is a stranger. He doesn't belong here. I want him out."

Zheng smiled benignly and said, "I too can vouch for him. In as much as he carries out important intelligence operations for AGU, he should be present."

Shah looked at Kazemzadeh.

The Iranian shrugged. "I will accommodate Minister Zheng's and Mr. Fairchilde's wishes. He stays."

The caliph silently sulked for a few moments, then, in English, said, "I don't care about him. What I do care about is the future of our operations in America. We have thousands of well-trained, loyal followers in place across your country." He nodded at Fairchilde. "There are five remaining nuclear weapons available for distribution to the agreed upon target areas."

"I sense you may have some concerns about the employment of these weapons," Fairchilde said.

"I do. The presidential election in your country was very troubling to me. You assured us that the other candidate was certain to win the election. She did not. Instead, the winner is an unpredictable, thin-skinned, hothead."

Fairchilde shrugged and continued to examine his shoes. "So, your point is?"

"Why do I feel as though I'm talking to children?" Shah said with exasperation. "It should be clear to all that this egomaniac's political favor depends on his carrying through on his campaign promises, not the least of which is to destroy the Holy Army of the

Caliphate. The speed and vigor with which he is acting on those promises is more than troublesome to me."

Zheng said, "You are concerned that he will effectively damage or eliminate HAC before you can utilize these nuclear weapons in America."

Nodding vigorously, Shah said, "Yes. The Caliphate's best hope for survival is to accelerate the detonation before this new cowboy in the White House can assemble a force against us."

"You're hoping the effects of such terrorism will sway American public opinion and force their new president to seek peace with HAC?" Kazemzadeh said.

"Yes."

"And if you are wrong, and your actions have the opposite effect?" Zheng said.

Shah looked at Fairchilde. "They are your people. What do you think their reaction will be?"

The AGU chief thought about his answer for several moments. At last he said, "This will come as a shock to all of you, but we… AGU…are the ones who have been stoking the anger in the American electorate. We saw it as the inevitable result of our ongoing destruction of American freedoms and liberties. It wasn't difficult to foresee the alarm that the 'progressive' agenda was causing. Initially, we prepared for it by getting behind the obnoxious senator, but quickly saw how the political winds were blowing. We paid lip service and made modest financial contributions to the left's candidate, but basically she self-destructed on her own."

Shah stared at him in disbelief. "But AGU has controlled her party for years, decades. Through it you have been able to weaken your country. I don't understand?"

Fairchilde smiled down his long, thin, patrician nose at the self-appointed caliph. "There is an old adage, 'When your enemy is self-destructing, get out of his way.' In this case, our longtime adversaries, the conservative element, had the momentum. It turned out to be serendipitous, because their candidate and eventual winner, the businessman from New York, suffers from such colossal incompetence, ignorance, and egomania that his actions can only accelerate the destruction of the American government's apparatus and effectiveness."

"You haven't answered my original question," Shah said impatiently.

"I suspect your assessment is correct. Nuclear strikes in the heartland will terrify Americans, bringing down their new leader with it." Fairchilde turned to the huge man on his left and said, "What's your take, Maksym?"

"I don't give a fuck what Americans think. Kill them all."

Kazemzadeh snorted. "My kind of man. Americans are cowards. They're brave and tough as long as they think they are totally in charge. When they find out they're not, they run screaming for the nearest safe space."

"There is one thing," Fairchilde said. "Our adversaries, the Society of Adam Smith, and their paramilitary arm represent the only potential complication to the successful use of these nuclear weapons."

"The Sleeping Dogs," Zheng said.

Fairchilde nodded and turned toward Maksym. "I trust you can neutralize this situation?"

Beneath his shaggy mop of dark, oily hair, the huge man's scarred face slowly formed into a frightening smile. "Yes."

"Care to share your plans with us?"

"You're the one who likes bromides. How about 'cutting the head off the snake?'"

Kazemzadeh said, "The military application of that idiom means to take out the enemy's leader and the followers are ineffective."

Maksym's smile became even darker, even colder.

CHAPTER 44

DOHA, QATAR

ALL SEVEN OF the Dogs were gathered in the tiny living room of a rundown ranch house in New Mexico, close to the southern border. It was the same place where they had interrogated the late *commandante* of the HAC encampment at San Luis. "I don't get it," Rafe Almeida said. "When these rug merchants had Kirkland in their slammer, I said we should just raid it, kill everybody in sight, and burn the fucker to the ground. But Levell said it was a suicide mission. Now, you want us to go to the same damn place, raid a heavily guarded hospital, grab some sonofabitch, and waltz out of there?"

"What do you know," Stensen said. "For once the little shit has a grasp on a mission."

Almeida snarled. "You watch your fuckin' mouth, Stensen!"

"Or?"

"You don't want to know, you psychotic prick."

"Put a cork in it, both of you," Whelan said with a growl. He looked around at each of the other Dogs. "Rafe, you're the only one who doesn't speak passable Arabic. So, once we're in-country, you stay close to someone who does."

"As long as it ain't that fuckin' Stensen."

"I don't give a rat's ass who it is," Whelan said. "You're the one who was too lazy to learn foreign languages twenty years ago when the rest of us did. Don't be the one to fuck up this mission, or by God, I'll kill you myself."

"Geez, what's with the attitude? Have I ever screwed a mission up before?"

Kirkland laughed. "Hey, don't get us started or we'll be here all night."

"This isn't just any mission. It's critically important," Whelan said. "We need to accomplish two objectives. One is to obtain intel that will help us to locate five nuclear weapons HAC crazies are distributing in the U.S."

"Yeah," Stensen said. "I agree that one's important. That's self-evident. But the other is the one I like." The tiny red dots in the center of his pupils grew suddenly, like flames fanned by a sudden draft.

"That's the one where we drive the point home that there's no sanctuary anywhere for those who harm America or its citizens," Thomas said.

"I like to think it's more than just the U.S.," Stone said. "I see it as a statement on behalf of Western culture and civilization."

———

EARLIER, the Dogs had undergone accelerated training in the New Mexican desert near the old ranch house. It included running endless scenarios in anticipation of the mission to Qatar. The Mueller brothers even provided an AgustaWestland AW139 heli-copter complete with Saudi Aramco logo, colors, and markers, a duplicate of the one they would use in the operation. The training was crammed nonstop into a short period to reinforce their ability to perform under exhausting, high-stress conditions. None of them had a problem sleeping for much of the eleven-hour flight from Tucson to Madrid.

The refueling in Spain took almost an hour due to paperwork and other typical delays, including a long wait in a queue for service. It took another six hours for the Gulfstream 550 to cover the twenty-eight hundred miles from Madrid to Dammam, Saudi Arabia. After deplaning at the King Abdulaziz Air Base, the Dogs were quickly loaded into a van and driven to a waiting helicopter in a different part of the base. It was an AgustaWestland AW139, identical to the one they'd used in training in New Mexico. This one actually was owned by the Saudi Arabian Oil Company, also known as Aramco, the Saudi Arabian national petroleum and natural gas company based in nearby Dhahran.

Other than the pilot and copilot, there was only one other occupant in the chopper. Whelan immediately recognized the man in the desert camouflage uniform and visored cap sitting in a jump seat. Prince Bandar bin Nayif al Saud was president of the Saudi General Intelligence Presidency, or GIP, and a close friend of Cliff Levell. Some months earlier, he had helped Whelan and several of the Dogs escape a beheading in Dubai. Very recently, he'd played intermediary in the Dogs bid to liberate Kirkland from a maximum-security prison in exchange for the kidnapped Qatari royals.

The prince rose and extended his hand and a warm smile to Whelan. "We meet again, my friend. Welcome back to the Kingdom," he said in impeccable, British-accented English.

Whelan took the hand. The prince's grip was firm. "We appreciate your assistance with this operation, Your Royal Highness." Whelan reintroduced the five original Dogs who had been involved in the Dubai operation, and introduced the newest Dog, Liam Stone. "We're hoping things turn out better than they did in Dubai."

The prince stepped up and closely examined the left side of Whelan's face. "That was a nasty looking injury, but it seems to have healed with only the slightest of scars."

"Give credit to your surgeons in Riyadh."

"They are indeed among the finest in the world, but I suspect the healing had more to do with your unique genetic make-up."

Whelan shrugged. "I'm sure Cliff fully read you into the operation. My question is, what's the extent of your participation?"

"I will accompany you to the drilling site in Nebak, where everything is in place as Cliff requested."

"And after that?"

The smile left the prince's face. "After that, you are entirely on your own. I, of course, have informed the king and the crown prince, who, as you know, is our defense minister. They were very clear that under no circumstances is Saudi involvement to be revealed."

"Understood," Whelan said with a nod. "The Kingdom has various economic and mutual defense pacts with the Al-Thanis."

"Yes, but even so, relations have been strained for years."

"Because of Qatar's cozy relationship with Iran, your country's chief rival in the Middle East?" Whelan said.

"For me, personally, it's more than that. The Al-Thani regime clearly supports my religion's extremist elements. Muslim terrorists are a scourge on Islam. I'm happy to covertly support an effort to strike back at them."

Thomas said, "That may be true on a personal level, Prince, but many of your countrymen have supported Islamic extremists for decades."

Bandar sighed heavily. "Yes, that is true. Unfortunately, the House of Saud made a deal with the devil many, many years ago."

"The founder of the House of Saud agreed with the Wahhabis that theirs would be the official religion of the kingdom," Thomas said grimly. "And in exchange…"

"In exchange," Bandar said, "the Wahhabis proclaim the Kingdom of Saudi Arabia to be the sole rightful defender of Islam. It became the long-term strategy for the survival of the monarchy."

"So," Kirkland said, "you're helping us strike a blow against the would-be caliphate because you object to the Qataris' support of Islamic extremism, even though your country is the biggest exporter of Islamic extremism on the planet?"

Sadness clouded the prince's eyes. "A change is coming to the Kingdom. I don't know when or how, but I expect it will be sooner rather than later. And it will be cataclysmic."

THE CHOPPER FERRIED WHELAN, his men, and the prince one hundred and fifteen nautical miles to the small, grimy, oil production site of Nebak. It was a mere sixty-five nautical miles from Doha, the capital of Qatar. Once in Nebak, the Dogs began the final preparations for their infiltration effort in Doha.

"Why do I have to be the one who plays the injured guy?" Almeida said.

"Once again, because you're the asshole who wouldn't learn Arabic," Stensen said. "What better way to keep anyone from trying to speak with you than passing you off as critically injured and unconscious."

"Yeah, but I'm gonna be strapped to a cot and covered with some shit that looks a lot like blood."

"It's a gurney, not a cot," Kirkland said. "And it's real blood."

"Bullshit! It's not real…is it?" Almeida looked at Whelan.

The Irishman shrugged. "Ask Prince Bandar. His people are supplying it."

"Hey, Prince, what is that shit? Really?"

Bandar, who had been watching with amusement as the scene unfolded, said, "Yes, it is very real. Several of my men contributed some of their own blood for this mission."

With a look of concern on his face, Almeida said, "There's no fuckin' way you're gonna put somebody else's blood on me. I could get AIDS."

"HIV is the virus, you dumbass. AIDS refers to the symptoms," Stensen said. "Given where your pecker's been, if you were going to become HIV-positive, it would have happened decades ago."

Almeida's concern was reaching panic stage. "Whelan, do I have to do this?"

"Either that, or I personally will slice you open and use your own blood."

"You bastards always give me the shit jobs."

The usually taciturn Larsen said, "Why shouldn't we? You've worked hard for it all your life." He smiled his good smile—the one that only caused women and children to faint; his other smile caused macho men to lose complete sphincter control. "After all, who are we to deny you what you've earned?"

SHORTLY AFTER NIGHTFALL, Nick Stensen and Quentin Thomas left Nebak in a small four-wheel drive vehicle. They took Route 7075 in an easterly direction then turned north at the intersection with Route 95. Near Salwa City, they looped back south and followed the coast of the Salwa Sea. Using visas that identified them as Canadian journalists, they crossed the Saudi border with Qatar and passed through mostly empty desert. Once in Doha, the two men made their way along the Ring Road to the general hospital at Hamad Medical City, parked their vehicle, and waited for Whelan's signal.

BACK IN NEBAK, Whelan and the remaining Dogs finished having makeup applied by the people Prince Bandar had brought in to create their disguises. The Dogs' skin and hair were darkened, facial hair applied, and brown contact lenses placed over their glacier-blue irises. Special care was taken with Almeida to create the appearance of a victim critically injured in a fiery explosion. For anything less than a close examination, his skin appeared to be charred, and his blood loss significant. Simultaneously, the prince's explosive experts, working in tandem with petroleum engineers, rigged charges to an abandoned oil derrick and detonated them on Bandar's signal.

Moments later, Kirkland, in a medic's white lab coat, with Whelan and Larsen posing as the injured man's coworkers, loaded Almeida onto a chopper. Stone, in the role of the victim's supervisor, also climbed aboard. The three of them wore clothes that bore evidence of them having escaped a fiery experience. Soot and ashes dusted their skin and hair. The AgustaWestland AW139 was piloted by two members of Saudi Arabia's Special Security Forces. More importantly, to insure against treachery, they also were members of Prince Bandar's immediate family.

The AW139 was a 15-seat medium-sized twin-engined helicopter powered by two FADEC Pratt & Whitney Canada PT6C turboshaft engines. The rotary-wing aircraft was capable of reaching speeds in excess of three hundred kilometers per hour with a service ceiling of more than five thousand meters. It was a duplicate of several choppers in the Aramco fleet—white cabins and booms that transitioned from blue to green. It also displayed the company's logo on the nose—a stylized white star overlaying a split blue and green background.

The craft rose into a night sky illuminated by the furiously burning oil rig. As the pilot swung the nose toward the northeast on a bearing for Doha, the Qatari capital, the copilot raised air traffic control at Al Udeid Air Base. With approximately ten thousand U.S. military and civilians on site, it was the forward headquarters of the United States Central Command, headquarters of U. S. Air Force Central Command and 379th Air Expeditionary Wing, and the Royal Air Force's 83 Expeditionary Air Group. As such, the base monitored air traffic over much of the Middle East.

The copilot explained to the controller that the chopper was on a medevac flight taking a critically injured oilfield worker from Nebak to Hamad General Hospital in Doha. It was the closest triage facility equipped to handle major trauma, as a similar facility in Riyadh was three and one-half times farther. He said the medical technician accompanying the victim had diagnosed the injury as being greater than 15 on the ISS (Injury Severity Score). That meant it definitely was a major traumatic injury. Air traffic control acknowledged they were watching the fiery scene on satellite relay, and cleared the flight to the hospital.

Next, the copilot communicated with Hamad General Hospital, a 603-bed facility located in Doha. The copilot was given instructions for landing on the dual rooftop helipad atop the new dedicated units for trauma intensive care and surgical intensive care.

The chopper covered the one hundred twenty kilometers from Nebak in less than thirty minutes. One of the helipads was occupied by a lime-green hospital LifeFlight helicopter. This one was an AgustaWestland AW119Ke. As the landing gear of the Dogs' inbound chopper settled on the pad, Whelan used his comm gear to alert Stensen and Thomas that they'd landed.

A hospital trauma team dressed in scrubs emerged quickly from a doorway to the elevator that accessed the roof. They were hauling another wheeled gurney, but Kirkland waved them off as Whelan, Larsen, and Stone unloaded Almeida's gurney. The three men began rolling it down a ramp toward the elevator.

The trauma team was accompanied by a member of the hospital's security staff. He was fat and sweating heavily. There was a service revolver holstered on his right hip. The guard pushed his way forward and blocked the gurney's path. "What is wrong with that man?" He pointed at Almeida's inert body.

In perfect Arabic, Kirkland said, "He's been critically injured in an explosion at the Nebak oil field."

"And who are you?"

"I am Doctor Ahmed Al-Habib. This man…" he looked down at Almeida then made a sweeping gesture with his right hand. "All these men are under my medical jurisdiction at the Nebak oil field."

"And why are they here? They don't look like doctors."

"I'm this poor man's supervisor," Stone said. "It's my job to accompany him and speak for him, given the circumstances."

"These other men are coworkers," Kirkland said. "They assisted in the medical evacuation. They also have been injured and should be treated here at the hospital."

"Let me see what is under the blanket," the guard said.

"We don't have time for this foolishness!"

"It is my job to examine all incoming persons." He pulled aside the cover and gasped at the sight of the large volume of blood and what appeared to be Almeida's entrails.

Stone said, "Look here, our friend is in very bad shape. His survival depends on seconds, not minutes."

The guard continued to stare at Almeida's inert and gory form.

"Get out of my way," Kirkland said. "We must get this man to surgery immediately." He gave the guard an authoritative shove.

The man begrudgingly stumbled aside.

The trauma team stepped forward, but Kirkland waved them away impatiently. "We don't have time to transfer him to another gurney. Just lead us to the surgical unit."

Everyone took off at a quick trot heading for the elevator. They descended two floors and exited into a long hallway that smelled strongly of disinfectant. They resumed the fast pace toward the other end of the hallway.

"Wait!" Stone said. "There's something wrong with the gurney." He kneeled down and peered under the sheets that were hanging from it. When he stood up, each hand held a suppressed Heckler & Koch USP9 Tactical semi-automatic 9mm pistol with threaded barrels. Each weapon held fifteen rounds in the magazine and another in the chamber.

"Stay very quiet and you have my assurance that we won't harm you."

The guard was slow on the uptake. After a moment, he grabbed for the revolver holstered at his waist. Larsen, standing three feet away, moved so quickly that the motion went unregistered in the brains of the Norms. His right fist crushed the guard's jawbone and snapped his neck backwards violently, killing him instantly. With his left hand, the Man-With-No-Neck grasped the back of the guard's uniform shirt and swiftly dragged his body into an empty room.

Kirkland waved the terrified members of the hospital's trauma team into the same room. "Naptime is over, Rafe. Get up and start helping out," he said with a growl.

Almeida slid off the blood-soaked gurney and pulled it into the room, closing the door behind him. Whelan handed him a SIG MCX SBR assault rifle from the cache of weapons attached to the underside of the gurney. In addition to the two H&K pistols that Stone had pulled from their hidden stock of weaponry, there was a suppressed MCX and five polymer magazines loaded with thirty

7.62mm subsonic hollow-point rounds for each man. The combination of suppressor and subsonic ammunition would produce minimal noise if using the rifles became necessary. The weapons had single-shot, three-round burst, and full-auto capability. Each also had a TANGO6 4-24X50MM scope mounted on the pitcatinny rail. Whelan had chosen this particular rifle for its tactical advantage in close quarters combat.

Whelan looked around at the frightened hospital workers. Each was wide-eyed with fear. One of the female members was sobbing softly.

A man standing behind her said, "It isn't necessary to kill us. Please just tell us what you want." He had a stethoscope around his neck.

Whelan thought he might be a physician, perhaps a trauma surgeon. He had no interest in killing any of them unless it proved necessary. He said, "A man was brought here within the past few days. He's being provided round-the-clock armed protection. Where is he?"

The hospital staff looked at one another, but no one spoke. Stone stepped up to one of the young women wearing a hijab, presumably a nurse, and placed the muzzle of the H&K's suppressor against her forehead. "I'm going to count. When I get to three, the back of your head is going to come flying off and your brains with it."

The woman's eyes rolled back in her head and she fainted. Stone easily caught her before she could fall.

The man with the stethoscope motioned with his hand, pointing toward the ceiling.

"He's on the next floor up?" Whelan said.

The man nodded solemnly.

"Which room?"

"The one with the soldiers standing in front of it."

"More inside?"

The man nodded again.

"How many?"

The man said nothing, just stared expressionlessly at Whelan.

Stone pushed the suppressor of one of his 9mm pistols between the man's eyes and thumbed the hammer back. In a room silenced by fear and desperation, the click seemed ominously loud.

The man quickly said, "There are two in the hallway. I'm not sure how many, if any, may be in the room. It changes from time to time."

"Are there other soldiers or police stationed in this wing?"

"There are armed men patrolling the grounds."

STENSEN AND THOMAS exited their vehicle when they got Whelan's signal that the chopper had landed. The two men began walking toward the hospital's emergency entrance, Thomas supporting Stensen as if he was ill or injured.

As they neared the driveway that looped around the front of the building, Thomas softly said, "Hold up."

A Qatari military vehicle was coming slowly around the loop, as if patrolling. It was a KrAZ Spartan armored vehicle. Produced in the Ukraine under license from the Streit Group in Canada, it was used for carrying personnel in highly dangerous areas. Like the Middle East. Qatar, trapped in the crosshairs between the Saudi and Iranian regional powers, recently had purchased several.

It appeared to contain only the driver and another soldier in the front passenger seat. As Stensen sagged heavily in his grip, Thomas hollered out in Arabic. "Hey, help me brothers, my friend is in bad shape. I need your help."

The driver leaned out the window and said, "What is it you expect us to do? We are on patrol."

"I can see that. I just want you to wait with him while I run into the hospital and get help."

The driver stopped the vehicle and began an animated exchange with his passenger.

"Please," Thomas said. "I don't think he has much time."

Finally, the driver turned his head back toward Thomas and said, "All right, Corporal Yusuf will assist, but you better be quick about it." The passenger climbed out of the other side of the vehicle and came around to where the two Americans were standing.

Thomas lowered Stensen to the ground and said, "Thank you. I'll be back in a moment with help."

"What's wrong with him?"

Calling back over his shoulder, Thomas said, "I don't know. I think it's diabetic shock." Quickly, he ran to the driver and handed him a cell phone, pointing to a button on its keypad. "This is my friend's phone. If anything happens before I get back, push this button. It speed dials my phone."

The driver looked at the phone then at Thomas. "Why are you giving this to me? Shouldn't you have given it to Yusuf?"

Thomas leaned toward the driver and said in a conspiratorial whisper, "You look like the more responsible one." With that, he quickly walked around to the back of the vehicle, as if headed for the emergency entrance. When Thomas was behind the KrAZ Spartan, he pressed a button on his cell phone. The signal detonated a small tube in the phone in the driver's hand and released a cloud of gas. The driver gagged and grabbed at his throat. In less than three seconds, he was unconscious.

Simultaneously, Stensen drove a device that resembled a long, skinny icepick through the soft tissue under Yusuf's chin. Such was the force, driven by the power of a Sleeping Dog, that it pierced the victim's brain and emerged through the top of his skull.

Stensen dragged the corpse to the rear of the vehicle. Thomas swung the barn doors open and Stensen shoved the body inside then went around to the driver's side. Thomas climbed into the back of the KrAZ and closed the doors. He quickly changed into Yusuf's uniform. Not surprisingly, it was a couple of sizes too small.

Stensen opened the driver's door and threw the unconscious man over the seat into the back, then climbed in, stripped him, and changed into his uniform. It also was a tight fit. He reached down and pinched off the driver's trachea, effectively strangling him.

"Aw, man, do you have to kill everybody?" Thomas had a pained expression on his face.

"Only the bad ones."

"Problem is, they're all bad to you."

Stensen grinned. The red spots in his eyes were huge. Thomas opted to move to the driver's seat and used his comm gear to advise Whelan that transportation for the first portion of the planned exfil had been secured.

WHELAN, dressed in the Qatari trauma surgeon's scrubs, with the physician's stethoscope hanging around his neck, strolled down the hospital's top floor hallway. Kirkland, still wearing the lab coat, accompanied him. They appeared to be engaged in an amiable discussion of the Qatari national football team's recent performance.

When they reached the room with two guards posted beside the door, they were stopped. "Who are you?" one of the guards said as he blocked their entrance.

The two Dogs looked at each other as if in disbelief. "I am Dr.

Hassan, Chief of Surgery, and this man is Dr. Habib," Whelan said indignantly, as Kirkland stepped in front of the second guard.

The two guards appeared fit and well trained, and looked the Dogs up and down. Whelan assumed they were Qatari Special Forces.

"I don't recall seeing you before," the first guard said. "Are you authorized to treat the man in this room?"

Whelan rolled his eyes, as if in frustration then suddenly head-butted him with such violence it cracked the man's skull. Whelan ripped the guard's weapon free and tossed it to Kirkland, who had used an *empi*, or elbow, technique to shatter the second guard's left mandible and dislocate his jaw.

Whelan pulled one of the suppressed H&K USP9s from beneath the top to his scrubs. Using the body of the first guard as a shield, he kicked the door open and burst into the room. There were two additional soldiers in the room. One was just inside the door. The other was standing beside the patient's bed. Whelan snapped off two shots, putting one hollow point slug in the head of each man. Ordinarily, he would have double tapped both of them with second shots to the center mass of the chest, but he needed clean uniforms for the other Dogs to use.

Kirkland slid in behind him, dragging the inert form of the second guard. Whelan turned to him and said, "Once they've been stripped, no survivors."

Kirkland nodded. He swiftly removed his outer garments and put on one of the Qatari uniforms. Whelan gave the signal for Stone, Larsen, and Almeida to join them as soon as they finished securing the members of the trauma team. They were civilians who performed needed services to their fellow citizens. In his mind, that merited sparing them. He hoped he wouldn't regret the decision.

Moments later, the other three Dogs crowded into the room dressed in scrubs taken from the trauma team.

"Anyone see you on the way up?" Whelan said.

Stone said, "Yeah, a couple of sheilas, nurses I think, but they didn't seem to pay us any attention."

"Remember, if we get caught, the locals will immediately recognize Marc as the guy who sliced and diced the Taliban Five on Qatari soil. A half-second later, they'll figure out we're the ones who snatched their princess and crown prince in Monaco and ransomed them back in exchange for Marc."

"And then," Stone said, "they'll chuck a wobbly like a rat up a drainpipe, and off go our bloomin' heads."

Almeida scrunched up his face. "What the hell did he just say?"

"Get caught and they'll behead us on the spot," Whelan said. "You and Sven put on those uniforms. Stoney, we're short one, so keep the scrubs on and dangle that stethoscope from your neck."

Larsen pointed to the figure in the bed. "Is Sleeping Beauty over there our guy?"

"Yeah. I'm going to wake him up. Marc, get the camera ready. Remember, we only get one take. Make it count. The rest of you be sure to stay out of the camera's range."

Kirkland pulled out a smartphone from his discarded lab coat and set it for video.

Whelan walked over to the bedside and stared down at the sleeping Bazir Haqqani. He assumed that one of the tubes plugged into the terrorist's body supplied him with a mild sedative. Leaning over the bed on Haqqani's right side, he slapped the terrorist's face hard.

Startled, Bazir's eyes popped open and darted around the room. He seemed to relax when he saw men in Qatari military uniforms and a hospital worker in scrubs. He looked at Whelan. "Why did you strike me?"

Whelan nodded toward Kirkland who was standing off to Whelan's right filming the scene from an angle that caught a full-frontal shot of the terrorist, but only Whelan's back. "Things are not always as they seem, Bazir Haqqani."

"What do you mean? Who are you?"

Whelan smiled. It was a cold, hard mask of malevolence. "We are *Shaitan's djinn* and have come for your soul."

Bazir's eyes opened wide and he seemed to shrink back into his pillows, as though suddenly aware of the size and musculature of the men in the room. "But...but I have always served Allah. I've tried always to carry out His will to destroy infidels and apostates."

"Allah is a God of peace. Why would He desire bloodshed and torture in His name? Only evil men who lust for power and wealth use Allah and the Prophet to persuade fools like you to help them carry out their sins."

Bazir seemed to realize that his end was at hand. He stared into Whelan's eyes and said, "You are too late. The Holy Army of the Caliphate is prepared to strike at the heart of the infidels, America."

"When?"

A cruel smirk twisted the corners of the terrorist's mouth. "Very soon."

"Men such as you and your colleagues are heartless, and an abomination in the sight of Allah." With his left hand, Whelan effortlessly lifted Bazir out of his bed. His open right hand, palm up and fingers rigid, shot forward, piercing the terrorist's flesh, muscle, cartilage, and ribcage, plunging into his chest cavity. It grasped the wildly beating heart and ripped it out, holding it up for the camera to film amidst the thick spray of blood.

"You see, Bazir Haqqani, you too are heartless."

CHAPTER 45

SALWA SEA

"Did you get all of it?" Whelan said to Kirkland.

"Yeah, maybe too much."

"The comment about HAC and the coming strike against America?"

"Yeah, but we'll edit it out before sending it into the Ethernet."

Stone chuckled. "It's about bloody time Islamic terrorists got a taste of their own medicine."

Whelan quickly stripped off the bloody scrubs and donned a Qatari military uniform. He waved the others toward the door. "Exfil time."

In the hallway, the men turned left and headed toward the exit sign that hung above the doorway to the stairwell.

"Stairs all the way to the bottom?" Kirkland said.

"Yeah," Whelan said. "Quentin and Nick have procured a Qatari armored vehicle. It's maybe five klicks from here to the Palm and Pearl Hotel."

"And there's a helipad there, right? And a chopper ready to haul us the hell out of here?" Almeida said.

"That's the plan," Whelan said.

As they reached the landing on the next floor down, they heard noises coming up the stairwell from lower floors.

"What's that?" Larsen said.

"Sounds like a shitload of people running up these stairs as fast as they can," Almeida said.

Whelan agreed. "Back upstairs. Now!"

They scrambled back up to the top floor. At the landing, Kirkland looked through the glass plate set in the top middle of the heavy steel door. "We have company. Looks like Qatari Special Forces." He opened the door a few inches, stuck the short barrel of his SIG MCX through it, and squeezed off several three-round bursts. The full metal jacket bullets proved their ability to take out more than one target per slug, particularly when those targets were lined up one behind the other in a narrow hallway.

"Hope the rounds don't take out patients or staff," Kirkland said.

"You know what they say, hospitals are places where people come to die," Larsen said with gallows humor, as a hail of slugs bit into the other side of the metal door.

"Looks like someone reported Stoney, Sven, and Marc after all," Whelan said.

"Or we didn't do a good a job of trussing up the trauma team," Larsen said. "Should have killed them."

Thomas came through on their comm gear. "Things are totally FUBAR down here. Troops everywhere. What's your situation?"

"We may be trapped. Looking for a way out."

"What do you want us to do?"

"Get the fuck out of Dodge any way you can. You're on your own at this point."

Turning to the other men in the stairwell, Whelan said, "Our exfil plan just went south. Any ideas?"

"I may have a Plan B," Stone said. "We need to get to the roof." He took off, sprinting up the stairs to the next level with the other four Dogs right on his heels.

The door that opened onto the roof was locked. Stone put a slug from his H&K into it, then gave it a mighty kick. It flew open.

"Now what?" Whelan said to the Australian. "Choppers will pick us off like fish in a barrel up here."

Stone pointed to the LifeFlight AgustaWestland AW119Ke still sitting on its helipad. The rotors were beginning to rev up as if the pilot had been told what was happening and ordered to evacuate the chopper.

Stone slapped Almeida on the shoulder and said, "Come with me, mate."

Whelan, Larsen, and Thomas laid down a heavy cover fire. Stone and Almeida raced up the ramp toward the bird at a pace faster than a Norm could have run. Even so, the chopper was beginning to ascend as the pilot manipulated the collective, the device that enables the helicopter to climb and descend by altering the pitch of the rotor blades.

The speedier of the two, Stone, flung himself at the landing skid on the pilot's side and grabbed hold. A step or so behind him, Almeida had to leap higher to grab the other skid. Surprisingly, of all the Dogs, he had always had the highest vertical leap. Even so, he barely got his hands around the skid.

The two men hauled themselves up on their respective skids, as the pilot began to use the cyclic control to try to dislodge them. Stone was able to grab the handle on the cabin door behind the cockpit. He turned it, slid the door open, and scrambled inside. In an instant, he had grabbed the pilot, who hadn't had time to strap himself in, yanked him out of his seat, and slung him to the deck.

Stone jumped into the pilot's seat and stabilized the aircraft.

As Almeida climbed in through the other cabin door, he said,

"Like the tiger said to the kid who grabbed his tail, 'What you gonna do now?'"

"Land this bird and get our guys the hell out of here."

"You know how to fly this thing?" Almeida said incredulously.

"I flew choppers with Tag West."

"What do you want me to do?"

"Take the trash out."

Without hesitation, Almeida grabbed the pilot and tossed him through the still-open cabin door. The man's body hit the edge of the hospital's roof, caromed off, and free fell to the ground far below. He screamed all the way down.

The elevator doors opened, and a half-dozen Qatari soldiers poured out. More soldiers burst through the door to the stairwell that the Dogs had used. Slugs tore through the air like deadly wasps. Whelan, Larsen, and Kirkland had sprinted up the ramp to the heli-pad. Each had dropped to one knee to reduce their target area, and was firing three round bursts from the SIG MCXs. The men who had exited the elevator had all been downed by their fire, but others continued to emerge from the stairwell. It wouldn't be long before the elevator disgorged the next load of fighters. Qatari gunships would soon be circling the rooftop, raining down a deadly blanket of lead.

Whelan heard Larsen grunt and knew he'd taken a round. He saw Stone landing the chopper and yelled at the other two men to get to it. As all three ran toward the bird, Almeida crouched in a doorway, laying down a covering fire for them. Just ahead of Whelan, Larsen was staggering, a bloodstain rapidly spreading across the back of his left shoulder. To his own left, Whelan saw Kirkland grab his right leg and fall to the deck. Whelan scooped him up and threw him across one shoulder. A moment later, Whelan felt as though a fist had slammed into his left triceps muscle. The arm suddenly felt weaker.

Just as the three men reached the chopper, Almeida took a round in his right side and fell back away from the door. Whelan tossed Kirkland into the cabin and leaped in simultaneously with Larsen.

The copter bucked wildly with the suddenly added weight and the turbulent wind caused by the backwash of the rotors coming off the landing pad. Stone worked the collective and cyclic to get the bird moving away from the roof top as more and more lead tore into the fuselage. A moment later, he flicked the tail up and dove down the side of the building before leveling out and flying low and fast on a due west heading. He donned the headphones and began monitoring various frequencies.

"Stoney," Whelan hollered above the noise of the engine and rotors, "use the frequency Bandar gave us in case of emergency."

The Aussie punched it in and began broadcasting.

Whelan checked his men's wounds. There was a lot of blood on the chopper's deck. Some of it was his own. Larsen had caught a round through his massive left shoulder, but the slug had left clean entrance and exit wounds. The mark of a full metal jacket round. It didn't appear to Whelan that anything vital had been hit.

He turned to Kirkland, who, as it turned out, had been wounded twice. One was in his right thigh, and the exit wound seemed to be clean. From the rate of blood flow, it looked as though no major blood vessels had been affected. The other wound was to his left buttock. It probably would make sitting a painful challenge for a while, but otherwise didn't seem to be serious.

Almeida was curled up in a ball, clutching his right side with both hands. His face was screwed up in a grimace so tight his teeth were bared. Whelan crawled to him and began examining the wound. Blood was flowing freely from it. Whelan tried to rip the left sleeve off of his own shirt, but was weakened from loss of blood. Larsen saw him struggling and reached over with his right hand, the good one. Together they managed to rip it off. Whelan balled it up and stuffed it against the wound in Almeida's side. "Press it as tight as you can, Rafe, and keep it there."

Through clenched teeth, Almeida grunted so softly Whelan almost couldn't hear him above the roar of the Pratt & Whitney PT6B-37A turboshaft engine and four-bladed fully articulated main rotor. "Are the fuckin' ragheads gonna get us?"

"Not if Stoney can fly this bird as well as I think he can." He looked at Larsen and mouthed the words, "Watch him."

The neckless head sitting atop Larsen's massive shoulders nodded.

Whelan crawled back across the deck slick with blood to a position behind Stone. "What's our situation?"

"No worries, mate. Qatar's a narrow peninsula. We'll be across it in another couple of minutes. It's a dark night, and I'm flying lights-out just above the bloody surface. Even if their flyboys can scramble in time, I doubt they have a Buckley's of locating us in time."

"In time for what?"

Stone chuckled, obviously enjoying himself. "Before we're out over the Salwa Sea and into Saudi territorial waters."

"Salwa Sea?" Larsen said.

"Yeah, mate. It's a long, skinny sound extending south-southeast from the Gulf of Bahrain."

"Did Bandar say the Saudis are going to intervene on our behalf?" Whelan said.

"No. Bandar's people told me their official line is that the Qataris are their allies."

"Are you saying they're going to turn us over to the Qataris?" Larsen said.

Stone shook his head. "That's not Bandar's style. His people just instructed me to ditch this bird in the sea. Saudis have a naval vessel, a spy ship, disguised as a fishing boat that gathers

SIGINT"—signal intelligence—"from Qatar, Bahrain, and the Emirates."

"Because of Iran's designs on the entire Middle East," Whelan said.

"Right."

"So, where is this ship?"

Stone pointed to a screen on the control panel. A light was blinking in the middle of it. "The ship's broadcasting on that frequency. We're on a dead heading for it."

Whelan, still on his knees, looked past Stone out the windscreen. "Where are we now?"

"Just passing over the coastline. Ship's about five nautical miles ahead."

"How long before we reach it?"

Stone glanced at his instruments and did some fast calculations in his head. He turned to look at Whelan and grinned. "Two minutes."

"I've gotta ask you something, Stoney."

"Shoot, mate."

"Back there on the rooftop, why did you pick Rafe to help you?"

Stone smiled. "The poor bloke catches a lot of shit from his mates, but at the end of the day he's still one of us. I just wanted to give him a shot at showing it."

"And if he'd fucked it up?"

"Never gave it a thought. I knew he'd come through."

His remark was punctuated by an enormous whooshing sound and the chopper went funky, bouncing and bucking like an angry rodeo bronc.

The grin instantly vanished from Stone's face, as he fought the controls. "Shit! We've got company."

Whelan twisted his head and looked up through the cockpit

windscreen. A Qatari Dassault Rafale fighter jet was climbing and banking. "He's going to make a second run. This time he'll come in hot."

"I see the ship dead ahead," Stone said. "If I can get close enough, I'll put her down, and we'll have to swim for it." He motioned with his head. "Can the boys in the back do that?"

"Larsen, maybe. Kirkland and Almeida, no."

Large caliber slugs were whipping around the chopper. Pieces of the rotors snapped off. The craft began wobbling crazily despite Stone's strength and skill. "Fuck, mate, I've got to put her in the soup while I still have some control. Tell the others to brace; we'll be comin' in hard."

A few seconds later, the bird smacked into the surface of the Salwa Sea, tilted slightly to one side, and began rapidly taking on water. Larsen wrestled one of the cabin doors open with sheer muscle, grabbed the back of Kirkland's collar with his good hand and dragged him out into waters that felt as warm and viscous as spit.

Whelan grasped the collar of Almeida's shirt, but Stone brushed him away. "You got a damaged wing, mate. I'll look after Rafe." He quickly pulled Almeida through the door and began swimming away from the sinking chopper. Whelan was right behind him.

They were still only a few yards from the downed craft when they heard the fighter jet approaching on another run. "Shit!" Stone said. "We're like fuckin' ducks on a pond."

Just as the jet reached the point where its cannons would begin spitting death, it suddenly veered away and began heading back toward Qatar.

Whelan craned his neck and saw four Saudi Royal Air Force F-15 fighters roaring in from the west.

"Here comes the cavalry," Larsen said.

"And like any good oater, just in the nick of time," Whelan said. "I think we owe Bandar big time."

"His people said they wouldn't get involved officially," Stone said.

"I guess that changes when it comes to invading Saudi airspace," Whelan said.

CHAPTER 46

WANA, FEDERALLY ADMINISTERED TRIBAL AREAS, PAKISTAN

TURAN SALAM FELT STRANGELY ISOLATED. For the first time in more than a year, he was back in his home town of Wana, close to the border with Afghanistan. Yet, the landscape seemed alien to him. In the year since he'd last seen Wana, he'd trained in the rugged mountains in North Waziristan, travelled to the Tri-Border Area of South America, then to Venezuela and Mexico, and ultimately to the United States.

Why does home seem so different now, so foreign? He strolled through a neighborhood he had known since birth. The ancient marketplace was unchanged. The throngs of people still crowded closely together as they moved slowly from stall to stall. Men's clothing was still a mixture of western styles and the *shawal*, loose pajama-like trousers wide at the top and narrow at the ankle and worn with the long shirt or tunic known as *kameez*. In the FATA, many of the women still wore the full head-to-toe black *burqa*. A few wore the *duppatta*, a long scarf that matched the wearer's garments. But among the younger generation of women, even the *ḥijāb* and the *duppatta* were becoming unpopular.

Motor scooters buzzed through the crowd, mixing their fumes with the ever-present body odors and market smells. The familiar curtain of smog still embraced the valley. The temperature was typically chilly for this time of year. Yet, Turan definitely felt like a stranger in a strange land.

He had been a boy when he left. But now he was a man, seasoned by combat and skilled in the war of terrorism against the infidels of the West. He had lost many of his friends along the way, martyred for the jihad. He had even seen his mentor, Bazir Haqqani, gravely wounded in a gunfight in America. *How had Bazir survived the long and difficult journey from New Mexico to Qatar?* He liked the man, even if he was beginning to harbor doubts about HAC and jihad in general. Turan was still relieved to know that Bazir was expected to make a full recovery. But he hadn't enjoyed being confined to the hospital where Bazir was being treated, especially in a foreign land.

Then, just yesterday, he had unexpectedly been driven to the airport in Doha and placed aboard a Qatar Airways nonstop commercial flight to Islamabad. From there, he'd been flown to Wana and driven to a small guesthouse that bore the scars of the incessant fighting in the area. The accommodations were primitive and dirty. That didn't bother Turan—he'd seen worse. What did disturb him was the mystery surrounding the journey. All he had been told was that someone extremely important wanted to speak with him.

But the question that disturbed Turan the most was whether he wanted to rejoin the fight. He had experienced the standard of living in the West. *How could having enough food to eat, or a comfortable home, or a good education, or a well-paying job be sinful?* He had met people in Santa Fe, good people. *Why would Allah care whether they were followers so long as they were good at heart? Why would He want them dead? Could it be that the Islamists were wrong? That they were driven by a sickness, a hatred that defiled the words of the Prophet?*

At that moment, a girl about his age passed in front of him. She wasn't wearing a *duppatta* or *ḥijāb*. Her thick, dark hair reminded him of someone he'd met in Santa Fe. Someone named Carolina. In an instant, it was as if his innards had dissolved, leaving a vast empty space inside him. And a painful ache.

Who was this "important man" that had arranged this journey? And why does he want to meet with me? Is it the same man who arranged for Bazir and me to escape from the West? The one who had arranged for Bazir's treatment at the hospital in Doha? Until yesterday, Turan had assumed that he would be expected to continue to follow Bazir's lead in waging jihad against the infidels. After all, there were five more nukes to use against the Americans. But now Turan wasn't certain he wanted to continue the fight against the West. He was very sure he didn't want to return to the poverty and hopelessness of his former life in Wana.

Forty meters ahead, he saw a sign for a combination video game arcade and Wi-Fi hotspot. Next to it was a hookah parlor. His destination, a small, narrow coffee shop, was next to the parlor. There were a few tables made from battered plywood cable spools in front of the place. They were occupied by a half dozen beefy, openly armed men who looked like Arabs. They obviously were out of place in the wilds of Pakistan's Pashtun country, although their weapons weren't. It was one of the most lawless areas on earth, populated by smugglers, escaped convicts, and jihadis of every stripe. Most men were armed at all times.

Turan edged his way past the men, who never took their eyes off him. And never took their fingers off the trigger guards of their AK-47s. He paused in the doorway and peered into the darkened interior. Another dozen well-armed Arabs were scattered around the confines in twos and threes. Two tables of three men each flanked a narrow hallway in the back of the shop. All of the Arabs were wearing comm gear.

One of the men was holding a photo. He looked at it, then back at Turan. The man stood and motioned Turan forward. When he reached the table, the man said in Arabic, "Stand still and raise your hands above your head."

When he finished thoroughly frisking Turan, he spoke into his comm gear. He motioned toward the hallway with his head and said, "There is a door at the end. Knock on it, and wait for it to be opened."

Turan did as he was told, wondering who was the man who traveled with so many bodyguards. He knew there had to be more of them strategically placed in and around the building. When he got to the door, he knocked then waited. In a few moments, it opened and Turan found himself staring into the muzzle of another AK-47. After a moment or two that seemed more like hours, the gun was moved to the side. The man holding it said, "Enter," and nodded his head toward a small wooden table in a corner of the cramped room, indicating that Turan should approach it.

When the guard stepped aside, Turan saw that there were two wooden chairs at the table. One of them was occupied by a thick-bodied man whose acne-scarred face was one of the cruelest Turan had ever seen. He was clean-shaven, and his skin was very dark, but his features were more Middle Eastern than African. He was wearing a black, HAC battle-dress uniform. There was something familiar about the man, but Turan couldn't quite identify it.

The man stared at Turan for several moments with cold, hard eyes, then pointed at the other chair with a pencil he was holding in his right hand. Turan, heart pounding and more than a little frightened, quickly took it.

"You are Turan Salam," the man said, more as a statement than a question.

"Yes."

A tiny trace of a smile played at the corners of the man's lips. "The hero of Los Alamos."

Turan shifted uneasily in the hard, uncomfortable chair, but said nothing, merely nodding.

"Do you know who I am, Turan?"

Turan shook his head back and forth, as he struggled to try to identify the man.

"I am Nadir Shah."

Turan's eyes shot open wide. "The Caliph!" Now he knew why the man had seemed familiar to him. And so many armed guards in the vicinity. He was sitting across the table from a man who was at once the most wanted man on the planet and the hero of radical Islamists around the world.

An empty smile flickered briefly across Shah's pock-marked face. "Do you know why I have called you here, Turan?"

The younger man, now sitting painfully, but oblivious to it, on the sharp edge of his chair, shook his head again.

"You have proven yourself as a true warrior of Allah. Because of your exploits in America, you are a hero of our people, our cause. I believe you are ready for a greater role in our efforts to destroy the infidels and apostates." Shah paused for a few beats before continuing. "I want you to go back to America and help the Holy Army of the Caliphate in the use of the remaining nuclear weapons. You will be replacing Bazir Haqqani. It is because he thought so highly of you that I am assigning you such an important task."

Turan was stunned. "But the doctors assured me that Bazir will make a full recovery. Shouldn't I be assisting him?"

Shah growled suddenly and snapped the pencil he'd been holding. After a few moments, he seemed to regain control. "That's right, you were traveling yesterday and probably haven't heard the news. Haqqani is dead."

"Dead!" Turan half rose out of his seat.

The guard at the door raised the barrel of the AK-47 and pointed it at him, but Shah waved him off.

"I saw him yesterday morning at the hospital in Doha. He seemed to be improving. How could he be dead?"

The muscles around Shah's jaw tightened visibly. Through clenched teeth he said, "Someone...somehow...breached the hospital's security...and butchered Bazir."

"Were they captured or killed?"

Shah shrugged. "Some people died, but only Allah knows if they were the true killers."

"I don't understand," Turan said. "The hospital was well guarded by Qatari Special Forces. I saw them myself. They were everywhere. Who could have done this?"

"Djinn...demons. I don't know. But it was done. I saw the videotape of it myself. It's all over the internet. His killer ripped Bazir's heart out. With his bare hands!" From the look in Shah's eyes, it was as if he was possessed by a djinni.

Speechless, mouth agape, Turan could only stare at Shah.

"What is even worse than the loss of Haqqani is the message it sends...that our warriors are not safe even in the most heavily guarded situations."

Turan took a deep breath. "How many djinn were there?"

"It appears that there were five," Shah said.

"And they are the ones who died?"

Shah shrugged. "They supposedly died in the crash of a helicopter they commandeered."

"Supposedly? What does that mean?"

"It crashed into the Salwa Sea off the coast of Saudi Arabia. The Saudis claimed all died and showed the badly mangled bodies of men who were supposed to have been aboard it."

"It sounds as if you don't believe the Saudis."

Shah's upper lip curled back in a snarl. "The fucking Saudis lie about everything. They had as much to gain from Bazir's death and the message in the videotape as anyone." He paused and looked at Turan, his eyes narrowing. "This has the effect of disheartening our people while encouraging the enemy. We must employ our remaining nuclear weapons against America as quickly as possible."

HARLAND FAIRCHILDE LOOKED across his huge and ornate desk, the size of a conference table, at his chief of security, Maksym Kozak.

The massive brute stared back at him impassively.

Fairchilde often wondered what went on inside the killer's head. On the other hand, he thought, it probably was better not to know. He knew Maksym was extremely intelligent despite his menacing appearance, but Fairchilde sometimes wondered about his loyalty.

He glanced at his watch, a Grand Complication timepiece, unveiled at the twenty-third Salon International de la Haute Horlogerie in 2013. It was made by A. Lange & Sohne, a German watchmaker who was considered by many to be the best in the business. Fairchilde had paid $2,497,000 for it.

Looking over at Maksym, he said, "Zheng should be calling any moment now." A minute later, the phone he had placed in the middle of his desk buzzed. Originally made by a small firm in Israel, its operating system had been hardened even more by the Chinese to increase its protection from attacks. There were no applications on it that didn't relate to communications, all of which were encrypted end-to-end. The process encrypted information through all phases of a communication, assuring that it would be encrypted all the way to the party on the other end of the call. Without the robust password, the device was nothing more than an expensive doorstop.

Fairchilde bent forward and pressed the speaker button. "We're on."

"Excellent," Zheng said. "I also have our friend Nadir Shah on the line."

"Oh," Fairchilde said "I was not aware he was to be part of our discussion today." There was a note of peevishness in his voice. He didn't like surprises and telegraphed his concern in a narrow-eyed glance at Maksym.

"Yes, I understand your surprise, and I do apologize for this sudden development. I'm afraid it was unavoidable."

"And why, if I may ask, is that?"

"I'll let the Caliph tell you in his own words."

"First," Maksym interrupted, "is he using the same encrypted device?"

"Nice to hear your voice, Maksym," Zheng said with mock sincerity. "Of course, the Caliph's device is the same as ours."

"Enough! I do not have time for a lovefest," Shah said. "Let's get to the point. I have become concerned about the chances for success of our remaining nuclear devices."

"Why is that?" Fairchilde said. "I distinctly remember you assuring us that everything was in place."

"This is not my fault! The fools in your country elected an outsider as president. He has vowed to eliminate the Caliphate and has already increased the war effort against us. Our best strategy is to move these nuclear devices into place and use them as soon as possible."

"Attacking the American homeland won't deter their troops already in the Middle East," Zheng said.

"Perhaps not, but, as I said in Tehran, the magnitude of the terrorism and its effect on public opinion will force this new president to seek peace with the Caliphate."

Fairchilde chuckled.

"What is so humorous, *kafir*?" Shah said, angrily using a racial slur.

"You have a short memory. I told you in Tehran that AGU was instrumental in getting him elected."

"It didn't make sense to me then, and it doesn't now."

"Let me try explaining it one more time. At first, we didn't want to; we were happy with the leftist candidate from the other party. She, like her predecessor, was deeply indebted to us and subordinate to our will. But as we began to see the depth of the anger building in the American electorate, we realized we needed to make a change of plans."

Now it was Zheng who chuckled. "Yes, but that anger was a foreseeable result of AGU's ongoing destruction of American freedoms and liberties."

"Yes, well, it's not like it caught us napping," Fairchilde said. "When we realized the anger was as pervasive as it is, and that this nation of sheep was becoming restive, we began quietly supporting a pliable candidate in the opposition party. Unfortunately, he lost his bid for the nomination. On the other hand, we're quite pleased that the current president won."

"Again, I don't understand you. How can his victory be a positive for AGU and its agenda?" Shah said.

"It's quite simple really. The new president's immense ego, thin skin, and narcissism, coupled with his complete lack of experience and the opposition within his own party will undermine his effectiveness. This can only accelerate the destruction of the American

408 JOHN WAYNE FALBEY

governmental apparatus. That, after all, is what we are seeking. In a worst-case scenario, he will so damage his own party that our candidates will sweep into power in the next election."

"We don't have time to wait for the next election," Shah shouted angrily. "America and its Western and Middle Eastern allies are steadily winning back lands from the Caliphate. If this keeps up, we will soon control no territory."

Zheng spoke. There was a clear note of irritation in his voice. "Are you blaming us? China and AGU have been very generous in providing financing, training, and weapons to the Caliphate."

"I am not disputing that." There was no tone of contrition in Shah's voice.

"Are you trying to tell us that you're about to lose your war with the West? Because from here, it sounds like you're beginning to panic," Maksym said.

"Not at all. Those are tactical, not strategic, losses. And that is exactly the thinking that will bring about the defeat of the West. As expected, they wasted time and frustrated themselves attempting to create a force consisting of so-called 'moderate' Muslims. When that failed, they came at us militarily. But we are people of the desert; their soldiers are not. We will not fight a superior force face-to-face. We will revert to our guerrilla tactics. The fight will drag on. The enemy will tire of its continuing attrition and lack of decisive military success. They always do. Eventually they will slink away with their tails between their legs, like the Russians did in Afghanistan. Like the Americans in Vietnam, Somalia, and Iraq. And while they are chasing us around *our* desert, our operatives should be delivering terror to them firsthand in their homelands," Shah said.

"And the end game?" Maksym said.

"Phase Two depends on us taking the fight to the enemies' homelands. We have built cells in most of the nations in the West, especially America, the Great Satan. Through terrorism and cyber-attacks at the local level, we will disrupt their ability to function. Then it will become a global war, and we will win."

Fairchilde said, "I must admit, I'm a bit confused. First you complain that despite our aid, you're on the retreat. Then you claim that's all part of your master plan. What is it you want from us?"

"Indeed," Zheng said.

"There has been an unexpected development. The Great Satan seems to have a...a force or unit of some kind capable of assassinating my most important commanders regardless how well protected they may be."

"Yes, now I understand," Zheng said. "I have seen the video of the assassination in Qatar. Gruesome. You have grounds to be concerned."

"I am sympathetic, of course," Fairchilde said. "But you might be overreacting to a single incident. In any event, I don't understand how we can be of assistance."

"Perhaps we can," Maksym said, leaning forward in his chair.

Fairchilde gave him a questioning look. "Please explain."

"I, too, have seen the video. Several times. Although the image and the voice of the assassin have been disguised, I believe I know who did this." Traces of a cynical smile played across Maksym's mouth.

"As one who has witnessed firsthand your extraordinary skills, I assumed you were the only one capable of such a thing," Zheng said.

"There is no one else like me. But there are a few others who have similar, but lesser skills."

"Levell's special operatives," Fairchilde said.

"Yes, the so-called Sleeping Dogs," Maksym said derisively.

Shah said, "I thought you told us when we met in Tehran that you know who these people are, and that you would eliminate them? Why has this not been done?"

"I can eliminate anything. But the question is who will pay for it?"

"AGU is already paying you quite handsomely," Fairchilde said.

"This would be above and beyond my ordinary duties. These men are almost as dangerous as I am. In addition to the obvious risks, I will want to employ an assistant."

"I assume you're speaking of Andrei Ulyanin," Fairchild said.

Maksym nodded.

"All right," Fairchilde said resignedly. "What is your plan?"

The trace of a cynical smile blossomed across Maksym's scarred face. "A simple one. They are disparate individuals with little in common. They don't particularly like each other."

"Then how is it that they're so effective?" Zheng said.

"They have a single unifying element."

"Levell," Fairchilde said.

"Are you fucking kidding me? On some plane, each of them might have a measure of regard for that old man, but they don't follow his directions."

"Who, then?" Zheng said.

"One of their own kind, my brother, Brendan."

Shah said, "You would kill your own brother?"

"With pleasure."

"I like you," Shah said. "A man after my own heart."

"A bit more detail would be welcome," Fairchilde said.

"It's simple. I know where he lives. I know who his family members are. I'll track him down, kill him in front of his wife and children, then kill them. The others in his 'dog pack' will drift off in their separate ways and cease to be problems."

Shah said, "How soon can you do this?"

"Immediately."

CHAPTER 48

SALWA CITY, SAUDI ARABIA

A LAUNCH from the Saudi spy ship had plucked the Dogs from waters of the Salwa Sea and brought them to the mothership. It took the vessel two hours to reach Salwa City, where they received preliminary medical treatment at the bare-bones Salwa General Hospital. It's also where Prince Bandar bin Nayif al Saud met them. Accompanied by aides, he swept into the small treatment room where a physician and two medical assistants were attempting to stop the flow of blood from Almeida's wound. The other Dogs already had been patched up temporarily.

"What is it you Americans call the unexpected? Murphy's Law? If something can go wrong it will?"

"Yeah," Whelan said. "In this part of the world, you would say it's *insha'Allah*, the Will of God."

Bandar looked around at the wounded Dogs. "It *must* be the Will of God. All of you are alive, if injured, and you accomplished your objective. The Internet is abuzz with reports of your exploits."

"What's the political blowback like?" Whelan said.

Bandar sighed deeply. "As to be expected, there are incriminations that the Kingdom was complicit in the raid. The American air base at Al Udeid tracked your chopper from Nebak to Hamad hospital. Apparently, witnesses saw you and your men at the time the terrorist was killed."

Whelan nodded. "Will you be able to put a positive spin on it?"

A broad smile spread across Bandar's face. "We already have. We've released a video that shows one of the Aramco AW 139s being commandeered by hostile forces at Nebak. It is identical in all ways to the one you flew to Doha. The video shows our brave soldiers apparently being wounded in a failed effort to stop it.

"Nice," Whelan said.

"No one is more devious or better at distorting reality than an Arab." There was an element of pride in the prince's voice. "Apparently, the Qatari's are convinced that you and your men actually were Arabs."

"Doesn't that raise an implication that we may have been Saudis?"

"Indeed, but the Kingdom maintains a prison for dissidents in the desert near Nebak. Two days ago, in preparation for your raid, we announced that several militant right-wing anarchists had escaped. Today, we announced that they were responsible for the destruction of the oil well, the theft of the Aramco helicopter, and the raid on Hamad Hospital."

"Why would right-wing dissidents raid the hospital and kill Haqqani?" Whelan said.

Bandar smiled. "As you know, Wahhabism is the official state-sponsored form of Sunni Islam in the Kingdom. Because it is austere, even puritanical, many in the Kingdom despise it, and consider it a deviant and vile sect, that it is a corruption of Islam."

"So, your sham dissidents would have wanted to make a statement against perverted forms of Islam, including the worst of them —HAC."

"Exactly."

"And out of curiosity, what is supposed to have happened to these dissidents after their chopper crashed into the Salwa Sea?"

"Tragically, there were no survivors," the prince said with mock sorrow.

"The Qataris would expect there to be bodies."

"And indeed, there were."

Whelan looked at him quizzically.

Bandar's smile broadened. "Several dead Houthi fighters killed in an ongoing engagement in Yemen 'volunteered' for the job. Unfortunately, they were too badly injured in the crash to be identifiable by witnesses from the hospital in Doha."

Now, a smile slowly etched itself into the corners of Whelan's mouth. "You do good work, Your Royal Highness. Once again, we owe you."

The prince made a dismissive gesture with his right hand. "Over the years, Cliff Levell and I have done many favors for each other."

They heard a vehicle approaching and turned toward the sound. It was a KrAZ Spartan armored vehicle bearing Qatari military symbols. The prince's guards quickly surrounded it, weapons at the ready.

"It's all right," Whelan said. "I know these guys." Bandar waved his men away.

Nick Stensen and Quentin Thomas climbed out of either side of the cab with big grins.

"Nice of you to drop by," Whelan said.

The four men began walking toward a pair of Eurocopter X3s bearing the Aramco colors and logo. Whelan knew they were among the fastest choppers in the world. They would transport the Dogs from Salwa City to Prince Sultan Military Medical City in Riyadh in less than an hour. There the special medical services needed to treat their wounds would be administered. A single bird wouldn't hold all of the Dogs plus crew and medical technicians. He motioned the two newcomers to the second chopper, where Stone was waiting.

As Whelan was preparing to join the other three wounded Dogs aboard the first craft, Bandar said, "Cliff asked me to have you call him as soon as you're on the ground in Riyadh. He said it's very important...and that it involves your friend Larsen, too."

Something in the statement made Whelan pause. "Yeah?"

Sensing Whelan's alarm, Bandar said, "I'm sure it's just Cliff being his usual cryptic self. Something about a Russian man and a visit to your bed and breakfast in Ireland."

CHAPTER 49

DINGLE, IRELAND

THE FLIGHT from Riyadh Air Base to County Kerry Airport was scheduled for a little over six hours, but it felt like the longest single period in Whelan's life. After being patched up at the nearby military hospital, he and Larsen had left the other Dogs behind. Kirkland and Almeida had more serious wounds that required hospital stays. Stone, Thomas, and Stensen had asked to go with them to Ireland, even expected to go, but this trip was personal.

When the choppers transporting the Dogs had arrived in Riyadh from Salwa City, Whelan had immediately called Levell. The news wasn't good. Throughout the flight to Kerry, he replayed the conversation in his mind.

Levell hadn't wasted any time with pleasantries or congratulations on the success of the mission in Doha. "There's a Gulfstream 550 waiting for you at the air base where you just landed. Prince Bandar will direct you and Larsen to it."

Whelan instantly knew something was wrong on a personal level. The fact that only he and Larsen were to be involved screamed one word: Maksym.

"The plane's going to Dingle," he said, feeling an icy dread beginning to spread through his body.

"Close enough. The airport in Kerry. Or, as you locals insist on calling it, Farranfore."

"We'll need local transportation."

"A car is waiting for the two of you at the airport. I thought about arranging to have the *Garda* escort you, but decided that could get complicated."

"What's the status of my family? Are they all right?"

There had been a long pause at Levell's end of the call. Finally, he'd said, "I don't know."

"Goddammit, Cliff, what *do* you know?"

"I know that we located that Russian guy you were worried about, Ulyanin, and put a tail on him. Then, suddenly he flies back to Ireland. I alerted your brother-in-law Paddy, the Irish cop in Dingle."

"What has he reported? Does he have a location on this guy?"

Another pause. "We lost contact. He stopped responding."

"What the hell are you saying?"

"Well, this is a part of it you're not going to like. Our contacts in the *Garda* reported Paddy's body was found early this morning. Along with those of three of the townspeople who had volunteered to guard your family."

Whelan had remained silent for a long time. Paddy was Caitlin's brother and the Sergeant in Charge of the *An Garda Síochána* station in Dingle, Ireland. He was someone Whelan genuinely liked and respected. And that was a short list. He'd thought of Paddy's wife and two boys and felt rage surging inside him. And a thirst for retribution.

"What about Caitlin? And Sean and Declan?" To him, his own voice had sounded hollow and monotonic, like it was coming from someone else, someone he didn't know.

"I honestly don't know, Brendan. I wish I could offer you something."

"You spoke to Tom Murphy about this?"

"Sure, Caitlin's and Paddy's father and the *Garda's* District Superintendent for County Kerry. I spoke to him briefly, right after I heard about Paddy."

"Did he…mention Caitlin and the boys?"

Again, hesitation at Levell's end. "He said they were…he said he was searching for them."

"Then they're not at the Fianna?"

"No." From there, the news had gotten worse. Levell had gone on to say that the *Garda* had searched the bed and breakfast thoroughly. They found no sign of Caitlin and the boys, but they had found the bodies of Paddy and the three men who'd been helping to guard the place. And there clearly had been a struggle, as if the members of Whelan's family had not gone willingly.

Since leaving Riyadh, there had been little conversation between Larsen and him. Whelan assumed the Man-With-No-Neck was beset by demons of his own, replaying the memory of the murder of his own wife and sons and lusting for Maksym's blood.

Whelan stood and went forward to the cockpit.

The copilot looked up from his screen. "Yes sir, can I help you?"

"Can't you get more speed out of this crate?"

The pilot responded. "We're bucking a bit of a headwind, but we'll try."

As it was, the G550 touched down in Farranfore almost twenty minutes sooner than originally estimated. Whelan and Larsen emerged from the jet to find a pleasant-looking young woman in a dark business suit waiting for them. She handed a set of car keys to Whelan and pointed to where their vehicle was parked. The two men bolted across the tarmac and jumped into the Range Rover Evoque.

Ordinarily, the driving time between Farranfore and Dingle was about an hour. Whelan drove it in barely more than half that, sliding to a halt on the gravel of the motor court at his bed and breakfast, the Fianna. There were a number of official-looking cars parked nearby. Some had the *Garda's* logo on them. A uniformed member of the force was standing by the front entrance. Whelan didn't recognize him. *Must be from district HQ.*

As the dust was settling, the man advanced toward them with an officious air. "Gentlemen, this establishment is temporarily closed. You can't park there."

In Irish Gaelic, Whelan growled, "I own this place. If you don't move your ass out of my way, I'll snap your neck like a pencil."

The man stared at him and Larsen for a brief moment. "I believe the Superintendent wants to speak with you. Please follow me."

Whelan and Larsen brushed the man aside and strode through the entrance to the Inn. Inside, forensics techs were carefully searching for prints, hair, and other potential evidence. A large, sturdily built man with iron-grey hair was talking to two other men. He looked up and saw Whelan, and immediately walked toward him and Larsen.

"Tom," Whelan said and embraced his father-in-law.

After a moment, the two men separated, and Whelan said, "I heard about Paddy. I don't know what to say."

Tom Murphy shook his head, but didn't say anything at first. Whelan could see he was struggling to contain his emotions. After a couple of moments, Tom said, "He was a fine lad. Made his da proud. But all of us in law enforcement know the risks. Each morning when you kiss your family goodbye, it could be for the last time."

Whelan put a hand gently on Murphy's shoulder. "He will be deeply missed by everyone who knew him." He paused for a moment. "How is Ciara taking this?" he said, referring to Paddy and Caitlin's mother.

"Like you would expect, she's a basket case."

"Is someone with her?"

"Her sisters, Grainne and Múireann."

Then Whelan asked the question that was foremost on his mind. "Any word on Caitlin or the boys?"

The moisture vanished from Tom's eyes, replaced by a steely look of anger. "There is a note."

"Note? What are you talking about? What does it say? Who's it from?"

Tom motioned for Whelan to follow and led him and Larsen into the kitchen. He pointed to an open file folder on the countertop and motioned for Whelan to read it. "Don't touch it," he said. "Forensics is going to be testing it."

Whelan stared at the folder in front of him and examined what was written on the 4 x 6 piece of notepaper inside.

Little brother, you knew this day would come ever since you and your associates spoiled our efforts to assassinate the American president.

And now it has come. I hope you brought your posse of mange-ridden hounds with you. It will save me the trouble of hunting them down individually.

As for my sister-in-law and nephews, you can save their lives by forfeiting your own. But only you and your colleagues can be involved. If any cops or others show up, I'll kill your brats in front of their mother. Then I'll take my time killing her in ways beyond your ability to imagine.

I left a burner phone in your office. I'll call you and tell you when and where to meet. You'll have thirty minutes before I start to kill them.

WHELAN WENT IMMEDIATELY to the cramped office that opened off the kitchen, followed by Larsen and Tom Murphy. There in the middle of his small desk and sealed in shrink-wrap, was a Samsung Galaxy J3. Whelan had to admit it was a clever move on Maksym's part. It was a prepaid, unlocked Android phone that worked on any GSM network in the world. All that was needed was a prepaid SIM card, and he was sure Maksym had added it. The phone was virtually untraceable.

He picked the phone up and tore off the shrink-wrap without regard to forensics. Maksym was too clever to have left prints or DNA evidence anywhere. He quickly strode back through the inn and out the front entrance, sliding behind the wheel of the Evoque. He started the engine, as Larsen wordlessly climbed in on the other side.

Tom Murphy leaned down and looked in the driver's side window. "What's your plan?"

"Maksym said we'd have thirty minutes once he called. Depending on where he wants us to go, seconds could be precious."

"I'll go with you."

"You've got your hands full here and with Ciara. And Maksym said no cops. Sven and I can handle this."

To Whelan's surprise, the usually reticent Larsen said, "We've waited a long time to kill this bastard. Today's the day." He punctuated it with his bad smile.

Even Tom Murphy, who was a tough Irish cop and former

member of Great Britain's version of the Navy SEALs, the Special Boat Services, felt his knees go a little weak. "At least let me provide you with weapons."

"Not necessary," Whelan said. "We've been packing since we left Riyadh." He pulled his windbreaker aside and showed Murphy the butt of the Sig 226 sticking out of his waistband.

As he did, the burner phone beeped, signaling an incoming call. Whelan plucked it from the tray in the center console and pressed the answer icon.

"You were only two years old," Maksym said, "but do you remember our parents picnicking with us at a place called Mare's Castle?"

"Yes."

"Be there in ten minutes."

"Ten? The note said thirty." But the line had gone dead. He slipped the transmission into gear, stomped the gas pedal, and spun a tight one-eighty before charging out of the motor court and onto the N86 heading south out of town.

"Where is he?" Larsen said between clenched teeth.

"At a place the locals call Mare's Castle."

"How far?"

"Thirteen klicks, give or take."

"Roughly eight miles." Larsen was silent for a moment, then said, "Can you make this thing go any faster?" If speeding along on the left side of the road bothered him, it didn't show.

THE N86 WAS A PAVED, two-lane road from Dingle to the tiny village of Banogue Beg. Mostly straight, it enabled Whelan to hit speeds close to one hundred and sixty kilometers an hour and cover the distance in six and a half minutes. But when he turned off for the final three kilometers on Kilmurry Lane, the narrow, twisting, potholed passage was barely wide enough for a single vehicle. The farms along the road raised the possibility of traffic, but Whelan kept a heavy foot on the accelerator. They flew past farmhouses and fields where snow white sheep grazed peacefully in striking contrast to the emerald green that surrounded them.

Cresting a small rise, the two men could see the waters of the Irish Sea ahead of them. They made a sharp turn to the right and saw the crumbling, but still majestic ruins of the castle ahead. The road twisted to the left and abruptly intersected another one, forming a tee. Whelan cranked the wheel hard to the left and skidded into a ninety-degree turn. The vehicle fishtailed briefly as they slid to a stop at the base of a small hillock below the ancient fortification. The journey had taken nine minutes.

The structure was known to local's as Mare's Castle because a local farmer let his mare and her annual foal run free near the fenced-in property. It was part of a hallowed plot that contained the ruins of the Church of St. Mary, St. John's Holy Well, and an Iron Age ring fort. The castle had been built in the sixteen hundreds by the Knight of Kerry, one of three Anglo-Irish hereditary knighthoods of the FitzGerald dynasty. One of them had built the castle as a stronghold, but it had suffered a cruel fate. An Irish rebel named Walter Hussey and his followers had holed up there after plundering nearby British estates. They were pursued by Oliver Cromwell, whose forces detonated explosives at the castles' four corners. While the fortification didn't crumble, the blown-out four corners of the structure made it appear to be precariously balanced on the crest of the hillock. The explosions killed Hussey and most of his followers. The survivors were immediately put to the sword by the British. Built as a four-story rectangular-shaped tower, the explosives and the passage of time had reduced it to a three-story pile of sandstone blocks and crumbling mortar.

Whelan was familiar with the tragic story and wondered whose blood would be added to the castle's already blood-soaked ground tonight.

THE TWO MEN scrambled up the steep hillside, easily leaping a barbed-wire fence and then a narrow metal gate set into a low, stone wall intended to keep tourists from venturing too close to the dangerous ruins. Whelan had brought his sons, Sean and Declan, here as a part of their instruction in Irish history. There were a few very narrow, slit-like openings at ground level. But Whelan knew that Cromwell's cannoneers had blown out much of the east wall. It would provide the best point of entry for avoiding an ambush.

As they rounded the remnants of the north wall of the castle, the two men saw a small seaplane moored close to the rocky storm beach below.

"That would be Maksym's plan for exfil," Whelan said.

"He won't need it. He's not going to survive," Larsen said.

"Don't underestimate this bastard, Sven. As far as I know he's healthy, but we're not because of our wounds from Qatar."

With weapons in hand, they scaled a large pile of rubble that was overgrown with moss and weeds. The debris had been caused centuries earlier by the effects of Cromwell's cannons. They dropped down into the interior of the crumbling structure.

Although the eastern side was open and the roof long missing, it seemed dark and sinister in the bowels of the castle. The ancient gray walls were dank and covered with moss and lichen. The stench of decay in the air suggested an undertone of death. It was quiet, very quiet.

The two men, standing back to back, craned their necks, examining the recesses and crannies on the upper levels. Other than themselves, no one seemed to be present.

Then a voice rang out. "Whelan, you're late!"

Both men turned, trying to determine where it had come from. In the stony chamber, sounds echoed and bounced off the walls, making it hard to trace their origins.

"You said ten minutes. It was pretty damn close."

"This isn't horseshoes. Close doesn't get it."

A moment later, Maksym emerged from a deep recess on what would have been the third floor of the old redoubt. His huge right hand was wrapped tightly around Caitlin's throat. She was struggling with both hands on his wrist trying to free herself, but it was hopeless.

Maksym stepped to the edge of the recess and dangled Caitlin in space. Her legs and feet kicked wildly. "There's a price to pay for not being punctual." He let her go.

Whelan dropped the Sig and did something no Norm could have done. He leaped across the rough, debris-strewn open area, and managed to catch Caitlin just before she would have slammed onto the hard, rocky floor. While she survived the fall, it wasn't without injury. At fifty-five kilograms—(120 pounds)—and falling twelve and one half meters—(40 feet), Caitlin was moving at thirty-five miles per hour at impact, the equivalent of being hit by an automobile at that speed. Given Whelan's muscle density, it wasn't a soft landing. It would later be determined that she'd suffered a compound fracture of the femur in her right leg, three broken ribs, and a whiplash injury to her neck. The impact caused her to lose consciousness.

Whelan gently laid her on the flattest area he could find and began to assess her injuries. He glanced up to where Maksym had been when he dropped her. He wasn't there. Whelan quickly twisted his head to look at Larsen, but the Man-With-No-Neck had also taken his eyes off Maksym when Caitlin fell. Now he too looked back at the spot where the brutish killer had been.

Maksym had leaped from the edge of the recess to a lower outcropping then to the ground at a point fifteen feet behind Larsen. The massively built Dog heard the thud-like sound made when Maksym landed, and swung the muzzle of the Sig to point at Maksym's center mass.

"Are you going to shoot an unarmed man?" Maksym said.

"My family was unarmed and sleeping when you blew them up." The words came from somewhere deep inside Larsen, dull, flat, and heavily laced with hatred.

"But think of the satisfaction that would come from beating me to death with your bare hands." A grin that could only have been matched by Lucifer lit up Maksym's face.

"Dammit, Sven, shoot him!" Whelan said.

A voice came from behind the two Dogs. "That wouldn't be advisable." It had a slight accent, to Whelan's ear. *Eastern European? Possibly Russian?*

They turned and saw a man standing in the mouth of a tunnel-like opening. He was tall and broad-shouldered with dirty blond hair. And held an AK-47 fitted with a forty-round magazine. On the ground in front of him, trussed hand and foot and gagged, were Whelan's sons, Sean and Declan.

Whelan was torn between tending to Caitlin and rushing to his sons' aid. He stared at the stranger, taking in his appearance and trying to place his accent. "You're the one who was here a while back, stayed at the Fianna. What was the name on your passport...Ulyanov?"

The man's lips pulled into a tight little smile. "Ulyanin. And tell your comrade to lose the Sig."

Whelan looked at Larsen and nodded. Sven laid the weapon on the ground in front of him.

"Now, step away from it," Ulyanin said.

Larsen backed up two steps, about five feet.

Maksym walked over and picked it up. He ejected the magazine and the cartridge in the chamber, then threw the gun and magazine on a weed-covered outcropping that once had been part of the second floor of the ancient stone keep. He looked at Larsen, "Now, let's see how badly you want revenge."

Larsen uttered a low growl and took a step toward him.

Maksym held up a hand. "But first, let's try to make this as fair as possible." He pointed at Whelan. "I want you in the fray too, 'brother'." He spoke the word derisively.

Whelan looked at his unconscious wife, then at his two boys sprawled helplessly at Ulyanin's feet. Rage overwhelmed him. His adrenal medullas began dumping large amounts of epinephrine into his system. His heart rate increased and blood rushed to his brain and muscles. He stood and glanced over at Ulyanin. "What's your role after we've killed this bastard?"

Ulyanin shrugged noncommittally. "Excuse the pun, but I don't have a dog in this fight. You win, and everyone's free to go."

"If we don't win?"

Again, Ulyanin shrugged. "That's up to the big man," he said in reference to Maksym.

Maksym laughed. It sounded like a voice from the tomb. "If you lose, everyone dies."

The three combatants looked at one another for a moment, then Maksym stepped forward. Larsen, in a blind rage, charged him. For Whelan, it was like watching two bull elephants in a fight to the death.

Larsen, at six one and two hundred sixty-five fat-free pounds, was the strongest of all the Dogs. But they had never experienced Maksym. At six five and three hundred equally fat-free pounds, he presented a challenge they had never encountered.

Whelan was shocked when Larsen's headlong charge only knocked Maksym back half a step. Shock turned to alarm when he saw Maksym pick up his best friend and effortlessly sling him against a moss-covered stone wall ten feet away. The alarm morphed into apprehension when Larsen's body slid down the wall and lay motionless as Maksym turned his attention to Whelan.

Larsen had always used his incredible power with little regard for finesse. With his strength, he didn't need it. Whelan, on the other hand, sometimes had beaten Larsen in training matches by relying on skill and perfect form to counter the stronger, heavier opponent's bull rushes. He would use that strategy against Maksym.

The two men circled each other—Whelan warily, Maksym with full confidence.

Whelan knew he had to make the bigger man commit to an aggressive action, one that would briefly put Maksym off-balance, so Whelan could counter with a defensive move intended to disable the opponent. Theoretically, that would leave Maksym open to a finishing technique designed to kill him.

He realized he would have to draw Maksym into making a move. He feinted a kick a, *mae geri*, or front snap kick. But he misjudged the big man's quickness. Maksym's hand shot out and grabbed a part of Whelan's foot before he could pull it back. When he tried to yank it free, Maksym suddenly released it. The maneuver left Whelan off-balance. He stumbled backward and Maksym was on him. The giant snatched him, swung him high above his head, and slammed Whelan into the rocky ground.

Whelan landed hard on his right shoulder, and the side of his head bounced off a small rock. Fire shot through his shoulder. His right arm was unresponsive. Lights flashed through his head.

Instead of finishing him right away, Maksym walked over and picked up the Sig Whelan had dropped when he'd run to catch Caitlin. He ejected the magazine, inspected it, then reinserted it.

Maksym yanked the slide back and inspected the chamber. After shoving the weapon in the waistband of his trousers, he strode over to where Ulyanin was standing and grabbed the two boys by the back of their necks. He took them over where Caitlin lay and dropped them. Next, he went over to Larsen and dragged his unconscious form back to the same spot. Finally, he walked slowly, with a triumphant smirk on his face, over to Whelan and yanked him to his feet. Whelan nearly passed out from the pain that shot through his injured shoulder.

"Well, 'brother'," he said, "looks like the gang's all here. Time to party." He picked Whelan up and casually tossed him ten feet to a spot beside Caitlin.

Whelan turned in the air to avoid coming down on his damaged shoulder, but landing on his left arm that had been wounded in Qatar was still painful. He rolled over and looked at his wife. Her eyelids fluttered, then opened. He suspected from her extremely large pupils that she was concussed. She tried to speak, but all she could muster was unintelligible gibberish.

"Easy, sweetheart, don't try to speak. Just close your eyes. Everything's going to be fine." He felt warm tears of frustration and sorrow begin to run down his cheeks. With his genetic gifts, he'd never before experienced helplessness. It was a horrible feeling. For a few seconds, whole sections of his life spun through his mind. Childhood, his parents, school, but mostly Caitlin. There had been girlfriends before her, but never anyone like his Irish rose. From the moment he'd met her, she was his perfectly crafted match. The term 'soul mate' was nauseatingly overused, but Caitlin was so much more than that. A partner, a playmate, a companion, a coconspirator, a consummate lover, and the perfect feminine foil for his hardcore masculinity.

Now, the love of his life and the two sons they cherished were moments from death. What was most painful was the knowledge that he bore full responsibility for it. He'd underestimated Maksym and overestimated his and Larsen's prowess, and not sufficiently factored in the wounds they'd suffered in Qatar. He'd left his loved one's in the protection of lesser beings, Norms, who had given their lives in the effort. Their deaths weighed on him too.

When he looked back at Maksym, the big man was standing about ten feet away. The Sig was back in his hand.

"I've waited a long time for this moment, little brother, and I want to enjoy it."

"I'm the one you have a problem with. Caitlin and the lads have nothing to do with it."

Maksym's eyes turned to ice. "Wrong. They're a part of you. I want more than *your* blood. I want everyone's." He looked at each of his victims. "I'm going to start with the youngest kid, then his brother." He turned and looked at Larsen's inert body. "I'll kill him next. Then your precious bitch. And finally, you, little brother. You'll have these final seconds of life to torment yourself for bringing death upon the ones you love most."

Maksym slowly brought the muzzle of the Sig around and pointed it at Declan.

Whelan wanted desperately to close his eyes, to blind himself to what was about to happen, but he couldn't. He stared in horrid fascination at his youngest son. Both boys, their eyes open as wide as possible, were struggling against their bonds. They stared at Whelan, silently begging for help from the father they'd always believed was invincible.

Whelan heard the loud report of the gunshot and the sharp, momentary whine as the full metal jacketed slug exited the body and caromed off stone. Nothing about Declan seemed to change. Whelan whipped his head around and looked at Maksym. The big man had a puzzled look on his face. He held the SIG in front of his face and looked at it. A red stain on the front of his shirt began to expand slowly.

Maksym brought the weapon around and again aimed it at Declan. There were two more gunshots, their noise magnified as it echoed off the tall surrounding stone walls. Maksym stumbled forward a step, regained his balance, and then turned slowly to look behind him.

As his brother turned, Whelan could see Ulyanin. He had the stock of the AK firmly against his shoulder, sighting along the top of the barrel.

Maksym struggled to bring the Sig up, but Ulyanin sent three more rounds slicing through the center mass of the big man's body. Maksym staggered a half step backward before his knees surrendered to gravity and buckled. He crashed face-first into the rocky ground.

For a few brief moments, there were only echoes as the sound of the final three shots faded away.

Finally, Whelan said, "I don't understand. Why did you do that?"

"That was for my friend Kirill Federov. I owed him that."

PAART THREE

DAYS OF RECKONING

"To sensible men, every day is a day of reckoning."
—John W. Gardner

CHAPTER 50

DINGLE, IRELAND

LEVELL AND WHELAN sat at the table in the kitchen of the Fianna House. Sean and Declan were outside practicing basic capoeira techniques with Nando. Caitlin, still recovering from her injuries had gone with her father to visit Megan, Paddy's widow, in hopes of helping her adjust to the unadjustable.

Whelan's right arm was still in a sling following his recent surgery to repair a grade-five separation of the AC joint. In his left hand, he held a heavy glass tumbler. It had three-fingers of Redbreast Single Pot Still 21-Year Irish Whiskey. He slowly swirled it between sips.

"How are Caitlin and the boys?" Levell said.

"Recovering."

"And what about you and Caitlin?"

"Rocky."

Levell was silent for several moments. "Is it going to smooth out?"

"I hope so. Time will tell."

"That was a rough experience for her."

"Rough? Are you kidding me? She was abducted by a madman, saw her brother shot to death trying to help, suffered serious injuries herself, and came within a second or so of watching her sons being killed." Whelan took a deep breath. "Yeah, I'd say it was a bit more than rough."

"Does she blame you for all that happened?"

Whelan looked off into the distance, and silence closed around them for a while. "She did at first. Needless to say, Sean and Declan thought it was odd that their da was sleeping in a guest room."

"And now?"

"Things are better. I have her parents, Tom and Ciara, to thank for that. They've helped her see that I did the best I could to provide for her safety while I was away." He looked down at the glass. "And, seeing how easily Maksym handled Sven and me made her realize she wouldn't have been all that safe if we had remained here full time."

"Does she understand why you had to go away?"

"I told her you were blackmailing me."

Levell sputtered. "What the hell?"

The stern expression on Whelan's face relaxed into a grin. "Gotcha."

"Smart ass. Does Caitlin understand why the situation today requires the unique services only you and the other Dogs can provide?"

Whelan seemed irritated by the question. "She's very intelligent; understands full well what's happening in the world. Obviously, more than most, she understands why the Dogs had to be involved." He looked at his glass again and said, "Dingle's a long way from D.C., Cliff. Although I think I know why you're here, why don't you tell me anyway."

"As you said, you already know."

"You want me to keep the Dogs together."

"Precisely."

Whelan was silent again for several moments, as he continued to swirl the pricey whiskey in his glass. Finally, he said, "The world is totally FUBAR. Third World nations are in the throes of revolution and sectarian violence. The industrialized nations, including the U.S., are fractured into myriads of political sects loosely aligned around two poles, left and right. It's unlikely there will be any improvement in the foreseeable future."

Levell took a sip and held his glass up, looking at it admiringly. "Never took you for a pessimist."

"I'm not. I'm a pragmatist."

"You've got a pretty dim view of the world at large."

"Just look around you. What part of that isn't true?"

"I'm not disagreeing. But I think change may be at hand."

"How so?"

"There's a new order of things emerging."

"You mean your new president?"

"That's one factor, but there are more."

"I'd reserve judgment, if I were you, Cliff. The new guy is charging forward with the promises he made as a candidate, and he definitely represents a change from the same old, same old. But, at times, he can come across as a wackjob."

Levell nodded thoughtfully. "Part of that is because of the way the media portrays him, and part of it is him being him."

"I think what America needs, if it's going to escape the quagmire it's sinking into, boils down to two things. A unique leader, like another Reagan, plus a set of dire circumstances."

"Like?"

"Total economic collapse and the threat of annihilation. That might wake the citizens up."

"That's definitely pretty damn dire."

Both men were silent for a while as Whelan refilled their

glasses. Then Levell said, "In case you're interested, Mitch Christie is recovering nicely. Should be able to return to the good fight in a few more weeks."

Whelan nodded. "I'm happy for him. He's one of the good guys. What about his wedding plans?"

"They had to be postponed, obviously, but he and Camila are planning on tying the knot in February, on Valentine's Day."

"Smart move. He'll never have to worry about forgetting his anniversary. Hallmark will start reminding him many weeks in advance. Speaking of recovering, what's the status of Rafe and Marc?"

"Hell, you guys are too fucking mean and nasty to be laid up for long. They're both recovering nicely."

The men each took a sip, then Whelan said, "So, Cliff, what do *you* see going forward?"

Levell set his glass down on the table and shifted in his wheelchair. "In the U.S.?"

"Yeah."

"I see the rise of ineffective, constantly squabbling splinter groups ala Western Europe. Rampant socialism that weakens the country financially and spiritually—everyone wants free shit, but they don't want to go to war to defend basic liberties."

"My, my, aren't we the unhappy camper. And you called me a pessimist. I thought you expressed some measure of confidence in your new president."

"I do, and I expect things may be a little different, but it's really too early to tell."

"Getting back to the reason for your visit, if this new guy is what he says he is, it looks like they'll be no need for SAS to operate in secret." He paused for a sip. "And no need for the Dogs to be involved anymore."

"I don't think it's that simple. We'll see. Remember, the Dogs were formed at a time when the political climate was very similar to today's. The new guy has asked me to meet with him. To discuss 'matters of strategic national importance,' as he put it."

"Oval Office?"

Levell shook his head, a sour expression on his face. "Are you kidding? If the left-wing bastards in the media started digging and got a line on SAS's membership and past activities, it could wreck his presidency."

"Let's cut to the chase, Cliff. Out of the closet or otherwise, what is it you have in mind for the Dogs?"

Levell tossed back the last swallow of his drink and held his glass out for another refill. "The election is only a beginning. AGU, HAC, the Chicoms, Putin, North Korea, and a host of other global ills remain. Today, a president can only dream about dealing effectively with them. There's a limit to what can be done openly on the world stage.

"China is the real threat—it's using Islamic terrorists to help destroy America by force. This way, the Chinese won't sully their reputation in the eyes of the world, or waste their men and materiel in a war with the United States and other Western powers. They can simply step in when America is on her knees, or worse, and take over. They'll kill off their jihadist lackeys afterwards. That's a far more attractive prospect for them than confronting America while its military is still a viable force.

"And there's the matter of those other missing nukes. Los Alamos proved the terrorists are intent on using them."

Whelan looked at Levell over the top of his glass, as he took a sip of the Irish whiskey he only brought out on special occasions. "So, the bottom line is you believe our unique services are still needed?"

"As much as ever. Probably more."

CHAPTER 51
ZÜRICH

To Zheng Bao Xun, the minister of finance for the People's Republic of China, the Dolder Grand Hotel looked like the offspring of a liaison between Neuschwanstein Castle and the Hotel del Coronado in San Diego. The five-star palace was his favorite resort in all the world. To him, it was the quintessence of decadence. It was what he loved most about the West. Perched atop Adlisberg hill at the edge of a forest, its view was impressive. It stretched from the distant snow-bound grandeur of the Alps to the glistening waters of Lake Zürich. And, best of all, it was less than twenty minutes driving time from the Zürich airport.

The minister was seated at a small corner table in his favorite spot in the hotel, the Bar. Its cozy confines were made more intimate by the myriads of small lights shaped like candles that dangled at different levels from the soaring ceiling. Zheng had thought about sitting at the bar itself, a thick slab of lustrous granite that served a mere eight stools. But he needed privacy for the discussion he planned to have with the man who would soon be joining him. Two bodyguards sat at the bar, sipping sodas and warily scanning the room.

Zheng had chosen a seat where he could watch the Bar's entrance. It was at the bottom of an elegant staircase. From his table, the minister could watch his guest's entire descent. A great deal of Zheng's success in life was attributable to observing people in the course of ordinary events. For example, would the man lope down the stairs with ease and confidence? Or would he appear to be more timid, perhaps even anxious? Would his air be one of superiority? Desperation? Curiosity?

Zheng glanced at his watch. It was two o'clock in the afternoon, Zürich time, the precise moment when the meeting was to begin. He looked at the staircase. It was empty. Perhaps this man suffered from the Eastern European disregard for punctuality. That would not be a good sign.

The Chinese minister suddenly jumped, startled when a man slid into the chair across the table from him. The man was tall and powerful-looking with dirty blond hair and a three-day growth on his face. The muscle at the bar stood and reached inside their jackets. Zheng raised a hand and they sat back down, but the scowls remained glued to their faces.

"Ah, Mr. Ulyanin, I didn't see you come in."

For several moments, Ulyanin, wearing black jeans, expensive running shoes, and a black leather bomber jacket over a black Greek fisherman's shirt, regarded Zheng impassively. Finally, he said, "I try never to do the expected. It can get you killed."

"Quite so, but how did you get in here? I didn't see you use the staircase."

"There's a service elevator behind the backdrop of the bar." He pointedly looked at his watch.

The motion wasn't lost on Zheng. "How clever of you to use the service elevator. And, yes, I realize your time is important, as is my own. Shall we discuss business?"

Ulyanin gave a barely perceptible nod, his eyes stayed focused on the two large Chinese bodyguards at the bar.

"You are aware that the late Maksym Kozak was in my employ."

Another nod.

"And you also know he is dead."

"I killed him."

Zheng seemed surprised. "I knew he was killed in Ireland. I thought it was by the men he'd gone there to kill."

"Actually, he beat the shit out of them. I offed him because he'd killed a friend of mine. It was payback time." Ulyanin's voice was cold, dispassionate, almost bored-sounding.

For a moment, Zheng seemed thoughtful. "Well, I'm not surprised that Maksym met a violent end. It seemed inevitable. I suppose I have mixed emotions about it. He had very unique skills, but could be difficult to deal with." *And I no longer have to tolerate his insistence on a "partnership."*

Another nod and glance at the watch.

"I'll get right to the point, Mr. Ulyanin…or may I call you Andrei?"

Ulyanin shrugged.

"Yes, well…, Andrei, I need a replacement for Maksym, and you seem the perfect candidate."

"How so?"

"You already are employed by Harland Fairchilde, and are familiar with the workings of the Alliance for Global Unity. You would continue in that role, except you actually would be working for me, reporting everything Fairchilde says and does, who he meets with, that sort of thing."

"Because?"

"It is China's destiny to rule the world, and we are using AGU to help pave the way."

"How so?"

"AGU has strong relationships with America's enemies—the various jihadi organizations, North Korea, and others. Their actions serve to weaken America and other Western powers, making our path easier."

"What about my 'homies', the Russians?" The irony in his tone was clear.

Zheng sighed. "That's become a bit more confusing with the new American president in the mix. We're working on a strategy to drive a wedge between the Russian and American presidents."

"Yeah, good luck with that." Ulyanin stared calmly at Zheng. "How much does this job pay?"

Zheng told him.

"And I'll still get paid by Fairchilde too?"

Zheng smiled and nodded. "Of course."

Ulyanin thought about it briefly, then said, "When do I start?"

CHAPTER 52

SANTA FE

Chapter 52—Santa Fe

IT WAS A TYPICALLY CLOUDLESS, blue sky-day, the kind of January day the local Chamber of Commerce prays for. Even better, it was unseasonably warm with the high around seventy. The wind created a chill, particularly in shady areas. But if one could get into both the lee of the wind and the open sunlight, it was a perfect day.

Carolina Avila had found such a place in the backyard of her parents' home on Santa Inéz Road. She was lounging in a deck chair and reading a homework assignment for a class at Santa Fe Community College. At eighteen, she still lived at home in the same house her parents had owned since before she was born. One reason, of course, was financial. Another was the absence of on-campus student housing. But the primary reason was fear.

Ever since Islamic terrorists had detonated a nuclear weapon, destroying Los Alamos, Santa Fe had been a city paralyzed by anxiety. Would it happen again? When? Where? In Santa Fe itself? Her aunt and uncle had been vaporized in the explosion, and her parents were reluctant to let Carolina stray too far from the nest.

She and some of her friends at school had watched a hideous video of the ringleader of the Los Alamos attack having his heart ripped out by a man using only his bare hand. It had quickly been removed from YouTube, but it reappeared immediately on the Dark Web, that part of the Deep Web accessible by networks such as Freenet, 12P, and Tor. Some of her friends had been horrified, but Carolina, still grieving the loss of her aunt and uncle, thought the punishment was justified. She wished all of the terrorists involved in the act would suffer the same fate.

Sometimes, she thought of the young man who had called himself Tomás. She had no idea what his real name was, but he wasn't Latino. *Probably Mohammed or Abdul or Yusuf.* He had been a part of the terrorist cell that had smuggled the nuke into the United States and participated in its use. She admitted to herself that, at first, she'd been attracted to him, believing he was what he said he was, a boy from Argentina. He was cute, funny, and kind of sexy. They'd hit it off from the beginning.

Then, despite the warmth of the bright sunlight, she felt a chill and shivered. Tomás…whoever…was a coldblooded killer. She remembered the last time she'd heard from him. It was a few days after the explosion. He'd called her cellphone and tried to convince her that he hadn't known what his people had been planning, claiming he would never have participated if he had known. *He was a killer* and *a liar.*

She put down the textbook she'd been reading for Biology 202, a three-credit hour required course in genetics for the school's associate's degree in Biological Sciences. It was a precursor for a premed curriculum in a four-year university, a step toward her goal, medical school. The air seemed chillier now. She wondered if her thin, brightly colored tights and sky-blue cable-knit sweater were enough.

Her cellphone rang, and Carolina reached down to pluck it from the ground beside the deck chair. She looked at the number and didn't recognize it. But she'd exchanged numbers with most of the people in her classes. *Maybe one of them is calling about a homework assignment or class project.*

"Hello," she said pleasantly.

"Hello, Carolina."

She recognized the voice instantly, and an icy fear swept through her. She was unable to speak.

"I'm back," Tomás said.

DEAR READER,

IF YOU ENJOYED READING *The Dogs of War*, please leave a favorable review on Amazon.com, Apple Books, Barnes&Noble/Nook, Goodreads, Kobo or Google Play. Reviews not only help writers succeed at their craft but also provide valuable information for prospective readers. Thank you.

John Wayne Falbey

PREVIEW OF A DEADLIER BREED, A
SLEEPING DOGS THRILLER

The Day of Jihad is at hand and America's new administration is still learning the ropes. Hundreds, perhaps thousands, of Islamic terrorists are now entrenched in cities and towns throughout the United States. In addition, there's the increasingly aggressive Chinese, Putin's Russia, the crazed hermit king in North Korea, and a host of other global ills. Today, a president can only dream about dealing effectively with them. There's a limit to what can be done openly on the world stage. But this new president might call on the shadow government known as the Society of Adam Smith, or SAS, to deal with these threats covertly. And SAS desperately needs the skills possessed only by that unique species of hunter-killers, the Sleeping Dogs and their newest member, the Aussie, Liam Stone.

But, are the members of the Sleeping Dogs the only humans of their kind? What if there were others? What if they weren't friendly towards the U.S.? And what if they could be organized into a force that opposed Western culture and civilization?

OTHER BOOKS BY JOHN WAYNE FALBEY

THE SLEEPING DOGS SERIES: The Far Left has succeeded in undermining the America of freedom and opportunity as we knew it. Their goal is to destroy our democratic, capitalist system by eradicating the middle class. In its place, they are establishing a New World Order based on radical socialism that consists of them as the elite and absolute rulers over an enormous mass of poor and struggling souls who have no freedom of speech, expression, even thought. But a small group of patriots well-placed in politics, industry, and the military fight back. They bring back a forgotten band of exceptional warriors who purposely have been in hiding for almost twenty years—the Sleeping Dogs special operations unit. The Far Left is about to find out why, as Chaucer noted so long ago, it's a bad idea to wake a sleeping dog.

Sleeping Dogs: The Awakening, a Sleeping Dogs Thriller
Endangered Species, a Sleeping Dogs Thriller
The Year of the Dog, a Sleeping Dogs Thriller
A Deadlier Breed, a Sleeping Dogs Thriller
The Devil's Litter, a Sleeping Dogs Thriller

The People's Republic of America, a Sleeping Dogs Thriller

The Quixotics: Three disillusioned special ops veterans of the Vietnam War run guns to anti-Castro forces in Cuba. And find more than they bargained for.

The Taxman Cometh: A rogue IRS agent leads a raid on the wrong house and destroys Finn O'Casey's world. A sympathetic neighbor who is also the leader of organized crime is not who he seems. He and the IRS agent thought O'Casey was a mild-mannered accountant. They thought wrong. O'Casey, a former member of an elite special operations unit, goes dark and joins his warrior comrades to wreak vengeance. The moral: *Be careful who you choose as a victim.*

ALL BOOKS ARE AVAILABLE in digital versions at Amazon/Kindle, Apple Books, Barnes & Noble/Nook, Google Play, Smashwords, and all online booksellers. Available in print versions at Amazon, Barnes & Noble, and can be ordered at bookstores everywhere.

ACKNOWLEDGMENTS

No one writes a novel, let alone several of them, without a lot of help from many other people. I'm especially grateful to you, my readers. I write for you. Your support and enthusiasm continually inspire me. Thank you for buying my books, recommending them to other readers, posting reviews, and helping to spread the word.

I also appreciate the input and encouragement I've received from other writers, including Lee Child, Steve Berry, Doug Lyle, and many others I've met through International Thriller Writers–ITW.

My thanks also to the past and present members of law enforcement and the United States military. Your efforts, bravery and sacrifices keep all of us safe and free. Thank you.

Many individuals have contributed significantly to this novel. It's blessed with another great cover from the amazing Tatiana Villa at Vila Design. Tatiana has designed the cover on every novel I've written.

No novel is ready for the editors until it's been reviewed by qualified beta readers. In my case, I'm fortunate to have the finest group of thriller readers to rely on for their input on what works, what doesn't. I'm deeply grateful to my volunteer Beta Readers for their time and suggestions. Their incisive critiques made *The Dogs of War* a far better book.

Finally, I am most appreciative of all for the support of my family, especially the warm and wonderful girl I married, "Annie." Thank you, sweetheart, for your ever-positive, unwavering support and faith in my efforts. I believe if we "keep the faith," we will see the success we're working so hard to achieve.

A NOTE FROM THE AUTHOR

As is true of all my novels, this thriller is a work of fiction. It's just a tale intended to meet a writer's foremost responsibility—to entertain the reader. The story is told from the diverse perspectives of various fictional players and any resemblance to persons living or dead is purely coincidental.

What is not fictional are some of the underlying storylines. American and Western culture and society have been badly eroded over the past several decades, and the pace seems to be accelerating. The elected governments have weakened the military and intelligence communities.

Many citizens seem to be unaware, are misinformed, or don't care. But make no mistake—human beings are the deadliest and most dangerous species ever to have inhabited this planet. Few other animals kill, torture, and imprison solely in a lust for power, wealth, glory, and dominion. Think about the history of civilization—a kaleidoscope of empires built upon war, conquest, torture, murder, and subjugation.

Nothing's changed: today there are Russia, China, North Korea,

454 A NOTE FROM THE AUTHOR

Iran, and other nations ruled by ruthless tyrants and would-be conquerors. Greed and the lust for power are still in mankind's DNA. And always will be. It's who and what we are. As Pearl Buck wisely noted, *"When good people in any country cease their vigilance and struggle, then evil men prevail."* Many want to believe that the pen is mightier than the sword. You bring your pen; I'll bring my sword. Care to wager on the outcome?

What also is not entirely fictional, is the theory of genetics explored in the books in this series. It's based on considerable research, but necessarily includes a certain amount of speculation. It is a fact that scientists have determined that persons with Western European bloodlines contain Neanderthal DNA. The European Early Modern Humans, or EEMH, interbred with the Neanderthal. These early Homo sapiens ancestors were as large as humans today and were more powerful and physically robust. Intriguingly, their brains were one-eighth larger than modern man's. Sound like Whelan and his colleagues?

My personal philosophy as a writer of fiction, a teller of tales, is that my first obligation to my readers is do my best to entertain them. A second important duty is to be authentic. In fantasy or science fiction, the author has free rein to shoot from the hip, making it up as he or she goes. But with fiction based on the world we live in today, places, objects, and global situations should be accurately described and depicted. This is why I exercise a ratio of 4:1—research to writing. If I describe a weapon, vehicle, or any other object, I want readers familiar with them to be satisfied that I nailed the description and know what I'm talking about. Likewise, with locations, I want readers who have visited those locales to think "that's exactly how I remember it."

The fiction writer also has an opportunity to educate the reader. Not to proselytize them politically or glaze their eyes over with an "info dump," but present them with facts and information that help broaden their knowledge, all within the context of the storylines. One of my undergraduate majors was History. Most people seem to loathe taking those courses because of all the names, dates, and places that must be memorized for exam purposes. But to me it was a fascinating panorama playing out chronologically on a global stage. I could see the "players" and places in my imagination. That thirst for knowledge about the "world out there" remains as strong as ever. Consequently, when I write, I research to learn about the people and the places that are woven into the storylines. When I read other writers' works, I like to be educated as well as entertained. I try to do the same in my books.

ABOUT THE AUTHOR

With Lee Child at ITW—ThrillerFest

John Wayne Falbey writes thrillers set in the contemporary world of international espionage and geopolitical intrigue. His debut novel, *Sleeping Dogs: The Awakening*, became an international best-seller.

He followed it with *Endangered Species, Year of the Dog, Dogs of War, A Deadlier Breed, The Devil's Litter,* and *The People's Republic of America.* All are thrillers in the Sleeping Dogs series.

He's also the author of *The Quixotics,* an action/adventure Vietnam-era tale of gunrunning, guerrilla warfare, and suspense in the Caribbean. His most recent non-Sleeping Dogs novel is *The Taxman Cometh,* a mystery/thriller in which a CPA accused of murder must dodge local, state, and federal law enforcement agencies until he can find the real killer.

Wayne is a native Floridian, transactional attorney, real estate investor and developer, and reformed academic. His wife likes to say, "Wayne has more degrees than a thermometer (four)," including a law degree and a doctorate in business. In addition to practicing law and developing real estate, he spent five years in academia, creating and chairing a Master of Science program in real estate development at a graduate school of business in Florida. But writing has always been his first choice.

CONNECT WITH ME ONLINE:

I hope you enjoyed reading *The Dogs of War* as much as I enjoyed writing it. I invite you to connect with me at:

www.falbeybooks.com

where you can sign up for my occasional newsletter announcing publication dates, signings, and appearances, previews of my next novel, and other matters relating to my Sleeping Dogs thrillers and other novels. I also invite you to connect with me through any of the social media below and look forward to hearing from you.

https://www.facebook.com/wayne.falbey
instagram.com/falbeybooks/
falbey@sleepingdogs.biz

www.ingramcontent.com/pod-product-compliance
Lightning Source LLC
Chambersburg PA
CBHW030544020726
47494CB00005B/1481